PAPERS IN
THE WIND

ALSO BY EDUARDO SACHERI

The Secret in Their Eyes

PAPERS IN THE WIND

Eduardo Sacheri

Translated from the Spanish by Mara Faye Lethem

 Other Press | New York

This work has been published within the framework of the "Sur" Translation Support Program of the Ministry of Foreign Affairs and Worship of the Argentine Republic. *Obra editada en el marco del Programa "Sur" de Apoyo a las Traducciones del Ministerio de Relaciones Exteriores y Culto de la República Argentina.*

Production Editor: Yvonne E. Cárdenas
Text Designer: Chris Welch
This book was set in 10.25 pt. Mercury Text by Alpha Design & Composition of Pittsfield, NH.

10 9 8 7 6 5 4 3 2 1

LIBRARY OF CONGRESS CATALOGING-IN-PUBLICATION DATA
Sacheri, Eduardo A. (Eduardo Alfredo), 1967-
  [Papeles en el viento. English]
  Papers in the wind / Eduardo Sacheri ; Translated from the Spanish by Mara Faye Lethem.
    pages cm
  Originally published in Argentina as Papeles en el viento by Alfaguara in 2011.
    ISBN 978-1-59051-642-3 (pbk.)—ISBN 978-1-59051-643-0 (e-book) 1. Family life—Fiction. 2. Sports stories. I. Lethem, Mara, translator. II. Title.
  PQ7798.29.A314P3613   2014
  863'.64—dc23
  2013031989

To all my friends,

who always keep life moving.

1.

When they leave the cemetery they stop and just stand on the sidewalk for a while, as if trying to get their bearings, as if trying to decide what to do from then on. Fernando glances at the other two. Mauricio looks down. But Ruso holds his gaze, his eyes flooding with tears.

This is it. This is Mono's death. It's happening. It looks like the images Fernando constructed in his head during eight months of insomnia. It looks like them, but it's not them. Reality is simpler, more basic. This is it. This winter sun coming down over Castelar, the cemetery's high wall, the long sidewalk to the street, the trucks, the three of them there, not knowing what to do.

Ruso lifts his chin, toward Yrigoyen Avenue.

"Want to get some coffee?"

Mauricio nods and the two of them begin walking toward the corner. Fernando is slow to follow. He doesn't feel like having coffee. But he doesn't feel like just standing around either, or going back into the cemetery. He doesn't feel like doing anything.

He starts to walk with his hands in his pockets and catches up with them. Crossing the avenue, they find a miserable dive that advertises hamburgers and hot dogs but also sells coffee. Ruso approaches the bar to order and the others take a table by the window. Mauricio looks around the place. One of the refrigerators filled with drinks is leaking badly. The windowsill is filthy. On the wall they've painted a hamburger overflowing with toppings. BURGER WITH THE WORKS $8 is written in enormous orange letters.

"What a crappy place," he comments.

Fernando nods with a halfhearted smile. "Mono would love it. He always did love this kind of ramshackle spot."

Now it is Mauricio with the sketchy smile, and Fernando realizes that it's the first time he's talked about Mono in the past tense. Ruso comes over with the coffees. The table is unsteady, making the plastic cups wobble, and Mauricio's spills out a fair amount. Ruso goes back to the counter to ask the employee for a rag.

"This guy, when it hits him . . ." says Mauricio in a whisper, watching as he heads away. "Because it hasn't hit him yet."

"No. It hasn't hit him," agrees Fernando, as he recalls the images of the wake and the burial.

Yesterday and today Ruso had cried several times, but he didn't keep still for more than five minutes. He also took the precaution—Fernando was positive—not to go near the coffin at any point. Did that make it hurt less? Was there any point in denying things?

"We can stick a wad of paper under the short leg, if you want," offers Ruso, when he comes back with the kitchen rag.

"Don't bother. We won't lean on it, that's all."

Fernando wonders if there's some way to assess pain. Weigh it, measure it, compare it. Which of the three is suffering more? He is seized by another doubt: does kinship affect the depth of suffering? Because if so, he would have to be the saddest. The other two are Mono's friends. Were. But he's his brother. Was. Damn verb tenses.

On the other hand, Ruso was Mono's best friend since fifth

grade. What weighs more, in grief? A lifetime being brothers or thirty years being the best of friends? A difficult question. Useless, too, but difficult.

"What's wrong with you, why are you just staring at the table with that blank face?"

Mauricio pulls him from his reflections, or shifts their course. Because now Fernando, as he shakes his head, stops to think that it must be Mauricio—of the three—who's feeling the least pain. He's too self-centered to grieve over anything for very long. Fernando thinks that and then he feels bad. As if what he'd just thought was too cruel, at a time like this.

"Nothing, just spacing out."

He takes a long sip of coffee. It tastes bitter, like it had been kept warming over too many hours. He makes a disgusted face. The others concur. Along the avenue a truck loaded with cows passes, giving off a deafening racket. They look out the window, at the swarm of cars, buses, and trucks that cover the asphalt.

"I think if they held a contest for ugliest avenue in the world, Yrigoyen would win," says Mauricio.

"It could," says Fernando, and he finishes his coffee in one last sip.

Mono

The nickname "Mono"—"Ape"—never had anything to do with his appearance, because he was always blond and pale and almost hairless, and even though he wasn't very tall he always stood up straight. It wasn't like with Daniel, whom they called "El Ruso"—"The Jew"—because, well, he was a Jew. Mono was never very hairy or bowlegged or hunchbacked, all traits easily associated with monkeys. Actually, it was Mauricio who gave him the nickname, an early example of Mauricio's precociously elegant and merciless imagination. He came up with it the day Alejandro—the last day he was ever called that, when he'd just turned ten—almost killed himself.

The four of them were out on the street, wiling away the hours after lunch on a February afternoon, in the shadow of an enormous weeping willow, when Alejandro pointed to its top and claimed that he was the only one of the four who could climb all the way up. It was an old, lush tree, and its roots, which had broken through the sidewalk years earlier, had caused problems for the National Gas workers sent to dig the trench to lay pipeline cable.

The others said no, he couldn't get all the way up there, but more as devil's advocates than because they really thought he couldn't. Besides, it wasn't even four and the boys had nothing to do until the neighbor ladies got up from their naps and they could play soccer again.

Alejandro stood up, shook the dirt from his palms, and leaped up to one of the low branches. As soon as he started his ascent, the others started making fun of him, trying to scare him, criticizing his climbing technique and threatening to tell his mother. But Alejandro kept going from branch to branch, higher and higher, and the others, at the foot of the willow, squinted to keep the falling leaves and bark out of their eyes as he got farther up. Despite shouting themselves hoarse, the other three could tell that Alejandro was getting closer and closer to the ring of light that opened above the crown. The last stretch he climbed clinging to the trunk with his arms and legs, like a koala, partly because of the fragility of the upper branches and partly because, at that point, he got vertigo if he looked down.

Finally he got to the top and turned around to see them, with the utmost care, very slowly shifting his feet. When he felt secure he released his hands, grabbed his genitals, and dedicated a few obscenities to those on the sidewalk. Then, satisfied, he looked around to capture the details of an unexplored panorama, because the neighborhood houses were all low, and no one had ever seen their roofs from such a height. Being the first, and supposing that he was seeing something the other three would never see, felt like the prelude to unlimited status.

His chest puffed out with pride, he closed his fists, opened his arms, and let out a guttural shout filled with deep notes and falsettos that he'd learned watching Johnny Weissmuller and Ron Ely on television, and he started beating his chest as he shouted, "I am Tarzan, king of the apes!"

Carried away by his enthusiasm, he started jumping a little on the branch that held him. They were prudent, timid jumps, but jumps nonetheless. Until all of a sudden the branch broke with a crunch that froze all the little hairs on the backs of the necks of the boys below. The climber went down fast, in a screwball journey bouncing from branch to branch in the most unlikely positions amid shrieks of terror.

Luckily, Abelardo Colacci was still alive in those years. He had a Ford Falcon that he pampered like a devoted lover. Since old Colacci claimed that the January sun would burn its paint job, he parked the Falcon beneath the enormous willow from December to March, and that allowed Alejandro, instead of falling onto the sidewalk, the ground, or the pavement, to land on the roof of the car with a dreadful thud. In the weeks following, the four of them would go over to Colacci's car and let their fascinated gazes run over the sinuous curves of the crater Alejandro left when he fell on the tinted rear window. "Here's where I hit with my butt," Alejandro would say, like someone exploring the vertebrae of a dinosaur exhibited in a museum. "Here, with my head."

Ruso would add, "Everything you see dented is where the Falcon gave under your weight. That's what saved you. The sidewalk and the asphalt wouldn't have dented. And you would be dead." He'd first said it when they entered Alejandro's room at the Modelo Hospital, and found the boy lying in bed with casts on. And since it seemed like an enormously sensible and pertinent comment, he kept repeating it every time they went back to the willow.

The day of the fall, after the clatter of metal and glass, and as the neighbors began to peek their heads out to see what they imagined was a car crash on the corner, and one of the more lucid neighbors started to call an ambulance, the other three boys approached the car on which Alejandro lay, dirty, scratched, moaning, but undoubtedly alive. And that was when Mauricio, as soon as the fright and the fear that his littlest friend was dead had passed, made a face, smiling sideways, and labeled him with the nickname that would stick for the rest of his life.

"Yeah. Not exactly the king of the apes. You? You're just an ape."

And that's the story.

2.

Mauricio opens his briefcase, pulls out a notepad, chooses a page filled with headings and scribbled numbers, and starts to explain.

"I have it all more or less clear. Some details are missing, because I don't have all the bank statements. Your mother," he says, addressing Fernando, "said she would look for them today or tomorrow. But I don't think she has much of an idea where they are. Maybe you could give her a hand . . ."

"I haven't lived with her in seventeen years, Mauricio. I haven't the slightest idea about her papers."

"Yeah, but your mom is old. You see how she is . . ."

"Yeah, but it was Mono who took care of that stuff."

Fernando's eyes meet Mauricio's and he shuffles in his seat. It doesn't take a genius to make out the accusation weighing down that gaze. Mauricio is thinking that Fernando should have taken over the reins a couple of months ago, when it was clear that Mono was dying. It was precisely for that reason that Fernando didn't do it. Because Mono was dying and, for Fernando, taking over and making those decisions, getting the papers in order, resolving gray areas, clarifying doubts, would have seemed like rushing him to the conclusion. Ruso gets up and goes over to the bar, so he doesn't have to wait for the guy to come over and take their order. But also, thinks Fernando, to avoid being there when Mauricio starts with the bad news.

"I'm listening," says Fernando.

"Things are worse than we imagined. There's practically nothing in the bank. Nickels and dimes. I made sure with your mother that there wasn't any safe-deposit box, or bonds . . ."

"Bonds, Mono, bonds?" Fernando isn't trying to be hurtful, but sometimes Mauricio and his calculations drive him nuts. He is in his lawyer role. Notepad, silver fountain pen, brand-new briefcase. A friend of the family, a concerned friend, but always a lawyer in the end. So no bonds or safe-deposit box.

"I asked your mother and she confirmed it for me," responds Mauricio, not catching his sarcasm.

"Ay, Mauricio. The only bonds Mono ever knew about were the ones the Morón Volunteer Firemen sold, my friend."

"Okay. But I had to check."

"All right. So then what?"

"Then nothing. There isn't a cent. There's nothing left of that money he got when they laid him off. And that was a load of pesos. Twenty-six thousand, four hundred and seventy-five dollars, to be exact," clarifies Mauricio, consulting another page of his pad. "Don't forget that I was the one who handled his dismissal with the company."

Yes. And you were the one who charged him a fee, even though you'd been friends since you were both ten years old, Fernando thinks, but says nothing.

"And so?"

"That's it, Fernando. I don't know. The whole bundle they paid him as severance, Mono used it to buy a player. And this . . ."

"Pittilanga. Mario Juan Bautista Pittilanga," specifies Fernando, in a tone that could easily be implying *you should know that*. Since they've already started in with the admonishments, they might as well be mutual.

Just then Ruso comes back, juggling the three cups to keep from burning himself.

"Wouldn't it be easier to let the waiter bring them?" asks Mauricio.

Of course it'd be easier, thinks Fernando. But Ruso has never been one for simple procedures. He distributes the little cups before sitting down.

"And? How's it going?"

"It sucks," says Fernando, in the worst way possible, as if his tangential, stale anger was somehow useful.

Simple Conditional

When Mono finished high school he had his future crystal clear. The next year they would offer him his first professional contract to play for Vélez. In three or four seasons he would become the best number four in Argentina. At twenty-three—twenty-four, at the most—he would be traded for millions to an Italian team. Then he'd play about twelve seasons in Europe. Finally, he'd return to his country to finish his career with Independiente and retire on a high note. But the verbs Mono was conjugating in a self-assured conditional tense didn't stop there.

Once he retired, and in order to continue his association with the world of soccer, he would become a coach. He'd start running a minor league club and after a few seasons of gaining experience he'd make the leap to the first division. At some point, before or after, as a player or as a coach—or better yet before and after, as a player and as a coach—he would take Argentina to another world title, after defeating England or Germany in the semifinals and Brazil in the final game.

He had dreamed of it so many times, and he had talked about it so many times—because Mono was convinced that you shouldn't keep your great joys quiet, not the past ones and not the impending ones—that his friends could repeat his future biography to the smallest detail. Fernando and Mauricio both saw it as a waste of their time, but Ruso would get really excited about it, taking on the roles of agent, masseur, assistant coach, or image consultant, depending on his mood.

Sadly for both of them, when Mono turned twenty he was called in to see the secretary of Vélez Sarsfield, who used the only conditional verb he wasn't prepared for: he would be released, because the club had decided they had no further need for his services.

They gave him a free transfer so he could continue his bright career with another team, then they wished him luck and asked him to send in the next guy because there were seven other kids outside waiting to hear the same news.

3.

They pass through the entrance gate, where they get a lackluster patdown from a sleepy policeman. They go up to the top row, wipe some of the dust off the cement, and sit down. Fernando estimates that in that single stand, which runs along the sideline from one end of the field to the other, they could fit fifteen hundred or two thousand people, at most. But that Saturday it had rained all morning, the sky was threatening more, and there were only about two hundred fans scattered here and there, in small groups like theirs.

The local team comes out, wearing green jerseys and white shorts.

"Heh," says Ruso sardonically as soon as he sees them. "Just like I told you, the most common jersey color in Argentina is green."

"There you go again," Mauricio cuts him off. "When are you going to accept you're wrong, Ruso?"

He ignores him, raises a hand, and starts listing: "Ferro, green jersey. San Miguel, green jersey. Ituzaingó, Deportivo Merlo, Sarmiento in Junín, and today"—Ruso pauses for suspense—"San Martín in Nueve de Julio."

"Don't you guys think that after we've come three hundred kilometers to watch this game you could leave this competition for another day?" attempts Fernando.

But Mauricio is already preparing his attack.

"No, sir. There are a lot more red-and-white ones than green." Now it is his turn to raise a hand and count on his fingers. "Independiente, River, Argentinos Juniors, Estudiantes de La Plata, Huracán, Los Andes, San Martín in Tucumán, Huracán in Tres Arroyos . . ."

"You're counting clubs from the heartland," maintains Ruso.

"And you're counting a ton of clubs that aren't first division. I can go on, if you want: Unión, Deportivo Morón, Instituto de Córdoba. You want me to go on?"

Fernando listens to the string of names that Mauricio lists; his confidence, his cold determination, his smugness. When his friends face off in these debates Mauricio seems to have all the weapons and Ruso comes off looking way too naive.

"What are you laughing at?" asks Mauricio.

"I'm not laughing. I'm smiling." Fernando enjoys being enigmatic.

"And what are you smiling at?" His attack is heating up. It's amazing how easily he loses his patience.

"Wait! Mandiyú in Corrientes!" Ruso is beaming again, as if he'd just tied up the stats in a single stroke.

"Here come the Santiagueños." Fernando is pleased to be able to distract them, as if ending the competition there might save Ruso from another defeat.

"Which one's Pittilanga?"

"That one against the side, warming up."

"Which one? The skinny one who looks light on his feet?"

"No. The big one that looks like a refrigerator."

"Ah . . ."

When the game starts, Ruso comments that he feels like one of those undercover people sent by coaches to spy on rival teams a day or two before they have to face them. But the other guys ignore him. Fernando because he's jotting down everything that seems important in a Centinela notebook, and Mauricio because he adopts that superfocused attitude he always has when watching soccer games: serious, silent, arms crossed.

At the end of the first half—tied scoreless, thwarted and boring—Ruso goes to the bathroom and comes back a little while later with hamburgers and cups of soda.

"Can you believe I spent thirty pesos on this junk?"

The other two dig in their pockets and each hands him a ten-peso bill. When the teams come back on the field, they realize with relief that Pittilanga is still among the eleven players starting the second half. The local team plays better and scores two goals in a row. Presidente Mitre, on the other hand, looks lost on the field. Pittilanga is replaced with fifteen minutes left in the game. When he passes the coach, he gets a distracted pat on the shoulder.

"So Mono paid three hundred thousand dollars for this son of a bitch." Mauricio's voice sounds dismal, and it's not a question but a statement, definitive proof of something obvious.

"Three hundred and ten thousand," stipulates Ruso.

"But wasn't he on an Under-Seventeen national team?"

"Yup. He was."

"And what the hell happened to him?"

The conversation stops there and they watch the rest of the game in silence. When the referee blows the final whistle the local fans stand up to applaud their players, who wave from midfield with their arms aloft.

The three of them stand up and, following the others, go down the dirty white concrete steps. With an occasional "excuse me," they make their way to the visitors' locker room. Ruso knocks on the door and a short man opens it, dressed in a sweat suit and a visor cap that reads EL TANITO WINERY—MENDOZA.

"We need to talk to Mr. Bermúdez. We've come from Buenos Aires. We're Pittilanga's owners."

Fernando listens to Ruso's introduction and wonders if that's the right way to present themselves. Are they the owners of the player or of his transfer? Actually, they're neither of those things. When Mono knew he was dying, he had some contracts drawn up, assigning the transfer to his mother's name. That makes Fernando the son of the figurehead. Everything is so complicated . . .

"Let me see . . . one second."

Through the partly open door they can see the comings and goings in the locker room. Half-dressed players, steam from the showers, clothes on the floor, somber faces. What you'd expect after losing 2–0. A tall man emerges, dressed in the same sweat suit and cap as the previous one. Fernando finds it hard to believe they couldn't find a single business in Santiago del Estero to sponsor their hats, that it seems they had to go all the way to Mendoza.

"Yes," he says, and looks at them alternately, as if he didn't know which one to address.

"We own Pittilanga's transfer. We've come from Buenos Aires," stammers Ruso. "I wonder if you have a moment."

Bermúdez furrows his brow into a puzzled expression.

"I thought the transfer belonged to that guy . . . Raguzzi, who came to see me a while back."

Ruso blinks, but doesn't know how to answer.

"That's true," intervenes Fernando.

He again feels that they are making fools of themselves, that they are playing a part, and playing it badly. That when the three of them are alone, even as bad as they sometimes fight, things can work. But the minute they take their panto-mime out into the light of day, into contact with others, it's only too clear that they're improvising, that they don't have a clue, that they're utterly pathetic.

"So? Is it yours or is it his?" Bermúdez sounds more bored than impatient.

"Raguzzi died a few weeks ago," says Mauricio. "He was very sick. He transferred the rights to us. Now we're the owners."

The coach gives a slight, barely noticeable start. Fernando sees it because he was expecting it. Everyone, when they find out about Mono's death, gives that start. The error, very human it seems, of thinking that youth and death never go hand in hand.

"I'm—I'm sorry," he stutters, and extends his hand in an im-provised, belated show of condolence.

"Do you have a moment? We don't want to bother you, but we've come from Buenos Aires . . ." begins Ruso, "and we need to get an idea of where we stand."

Bermúdez leans against the wall, his arms behind his back and his legs crossed. He clears his throat as if bothered by the sun, which, at this time in the afternoon, is already low.

"With Pittilanga?"

Of course, thinks Fernando, but he doesn't show his impa-tience because it's clear that Bermúdez is making time so he can decide how to begin, to find his path.

"That guyyyyy . . . It's a tough situation," he finally says, looking down. "The team's no help neither. Really, we're useless." He gestures to a door made of sheet metal that leads to the locker room where his players are showering. "And the kid tries, he really does try."

Fernando appreciates the effort Bermúdez is making to rummage around in the reality to find a bit of good news to give them.

"He's here for a year on loan . . ." interjects Mauricio.

"Yes. He just got here. Last month."

"A yearlong loan with an option to buy, right?" asks Fernando.

"Well, yeah. But I don't really have any say in that. I mean, I work with the players I have, for the season, you know? If they buy them later, that's not my business. That's up to the managers."

"Sure. It's probably too early to know if they're going to buy him, right?" says Ruso.

"I honestly don't know. I guess so. He's just getting started."

The four men stand there for a little while without speaking, until Bermúdez seems to make up his mind.

"One question. I mean, I don't want to be nosy . . . this Pittilanga guy . . . how much you pay for him?"

They hesitate. Fernando doesn't know if the other two hesitate for the same reason he does. Is he bringing that up to try to get a commission out of them? He's heard it a thousand times. Coaches who ask for cash to make a player first-string, so he's worth more. But then he looks around at the place where they're having this conversation. The cracked concrete floor. The sheet-metal door. The caps advertising the winery. That can't be Bermúdez's intent.

"Three hundred thousand dollars," responds Mauricio.

"Holy smokes!" Bermúdez's choice of words, which could have sounded flattering in a different context, there, on that flat expanse darkened by the August twilight, barely reaches compassionate.

"He was coming out of the U-17 selection, he was doing well, he showed promise," asserts Fernando, as if he had to defend his brother and his brother's impulses somehow.

"Sure. Of course," nods Bermúdez before concluding, "And yeah, these things happen."

"Well, okay. Thanks anyway for seeing us." Fernando sticks out his right hand in a somewhat abrupt gesture because he wants to get this over with and get out of there.

"One more thing," interjects Mauricio. "Do you think he'll keep playing first team?"

Bermúdez scratches an unshaved cheek.

"Well, sure . . . I guess so."

"It's important to us. For his value assessment," continues Mauricio.

Ruso sounds excited when he adds, "That's awesome. That he plays first-string, I mean. That he feels secure in his spot. For his confidence, and all that."

Bermúdez looks at him as if he's not sure he should respond.

"The thing is, kid, you have no idea just how awful his replacement is."

He gives them a vague wave and heads into the locker room.

Vocational Guidance

Fernando and Mauricio were sincerely upset about the abrupt conclusion of Mono's soccer career, because they loved him. Ruso, on the other hand, reacted just like his best friend did: he denied the facts. And then he signed on for all the useless ploys Mono resorted to in trying to resuscitate it. Because Mono just wasn't ready to see his future demolished like that.

He wandered around for a year to every practice he could, and he ended up convincing a coach for the Excursionistas, who was less impressed by his talent than by his mulelike persistence, to let him join the team. Mono and Ruso celebrated his signing as an act of justice and a prelude to greatness. Everything was as it should be. He'd just have to postpone his projects for a couple of years.

But a few months later, when he had just turned twenty-one, the coach thanked him and repeated the blood-curdling ceremony of sending him to the club secretary for his free transfer. Mono thanked them, went home, and drank for three days. Our star player ended up locked in the bathroom with Ruso, hugging the toilet and puking up bile as Ruso patted him on the back and held him up to keep him from falling.

When Mono was able to get out of the bathroom, dragging his puffy eyes and greenish face, he sat at the dining room table and started to turn the pages of that day's newspaper, which his mother had left half-read. Beside him, standing, like an aide-de-camp or a guardian angel, was Ruso.

"What are you looking for, Mono?" was the only question he allowed himself.

"I'm looking to see what jobs are on offer. I have to figure out what to study."

"Ah . . ."

"Help me decide. Not medicine, because I don't have the stomach for it. Law, no friggin' way. You turn over a rock and out crawl two thousand lawyers. Same with accountants."

"It's true," agreed Ruso, abandoning his post in the rearguard and sitting down with him.

"Maybe something with computers. That field's growing like a motherfucker, you know?"

"Computers, but with what?" Ruso was treading on such slippery territory that he didn't even know how to ask.

"I dunno. Systems analyst. Systems engineer. Electronic engineer . . ."

"But is that all the same thing?"

"I have no idea, Ruso. I'll have to find out. You coming with me?"

And that was how Mono's entire career decision took four minutes, from when he grabbed the classifieds until they left the house and headed to Castelar station.

4.

Mauricio looks in the rearview mirror and asks Ruso, once again, to move away from the middle of the seat because he's blocking the view. Ruso moves, again, but he immediately, unconsciously, returns again to the middle. When Mauricio is just about to repeat his request—less diplomatically this time—he is distracted by Fernando, who sticks a hand in the glove compartment, pulls out his notebook, and reads aloud.

"'He touched the ball fourteen times. Five in the first half and nine in the second, when he had a higher work rate because they were losing and on the offensive.' We have to see them play on their home field. Maybe he'll get more playing time. But there's no way in hell we're going out to Santiago del Estero. Right?"

Mauricio makes a gesture that unmistakably reads *no*. He had only reluctantly gone to Nueve de Julio, which is in the province of Buenos Aires, so Santiago del Estero was out of the question. Not even in Fernando's dreams.

"'Of the fourteen times he had the ball, two he was trying to return a wall pass, but his aim was off.'"

"You know what you sound like?" interrupts Ruso, who seems amused. "A basketball commentator, the kind that makes statistics out of every tiny little thing that happens in the game. They do it in tennis too, but more in basketball."

"Go on," says Mauricio, ignoring Ruso's comments.

"'Of the other twelve plays, five were well-returned passes, but way out of the goal area. Worthless passes.'"

"I heard there's a company here in Argentina," Ruso insists, "that compiles all that info on every player. Every single thing, even the tiniest crap. To sell to the clubs outside the country, when they come scouting. To the clubs and to the owners, same thing."

"'That leaves seven. Two out of the seven he lost the ball trying to dodge and weave his marker.'"

"Those guys come over from Europe and they say: 'Let's see, I want someone to tell me how this dude did this year and last year.' Let's say Mauricio Guzmán. They push a button and *beeeep*"—Ruso imitates paper coming out of a printer. Mauricio sees it because he is sitting, once again, in the middle, blocking the view in the rearview mirror. *"Here you go, they tell him. Go to the register. That'll be such-and-such dollars for the service."*

"'Two high headers. An off-mark shot to the goal. And two balls stopped by the goalkeeper.'" Fernando closes the notebook and looks at Mauricio. "That's all."

"I'm not sure if it's much of a business. I think it could be . . . What do you guys think?"

The others are silent for a while, until Mauricio can't take it anymore.

"So basically he sucked, big time."

Fernando looks out onto the yellowish pasture beside the road.

"He's bad," he finally confirms. "Train-wreck bad."

Ruso seems about to make some comment, but he ends up keeping his mouth shut.

UTN

The train Mono and Ruso boarded in Castelar, en route to register the ex–soccer player at the Engineering Department of the University of Buenos Aires, left them stranded in Liniers. They ran toward the avenue as the station's loudspeakers announced "delays due to a fatal accident in the Floresta Station." Ruso suggested they go back to Castelar, but Mono needed to end that day with some certainties. So he inquired at a newspaper stand and they ended up climbing onto a packed 88, toward Plaza Miserer, with the idea of then switching to the subway to get to the Engineering Department. But when the bus passed Primera Junta and took Calle Rosario, Mono made another sharp turn on the rudder of his professional future. Amid pushes and *pardon me*s he made his way to the door and got off before the light turned green, with Ruso on his heels.

"What's gotten into you, man?" asked Ruso, smoothing his clothes.

"I'm gonna study here, Ruso. In the Rosario annex of the UTN, the Tecnológica."

"But weren't we headed to UBA to sign up?"

"Yeah, but it's the same difference. I'm sure they have systems engineering here, too, Ruso."

"How do you know, man?"

"Because it's called the National Technological University." Mono pointed to the sign on the building's face. "What do you think they teach? Cooking?"

Ruso had no choice but to accept this flawless logic. With Ruso at his side, Mono registered in the Department of Systems Analysis. Until that point, as Fernando was quick to point out when they filled him in on the news that night, his contact with computers was limited to playing tons of tokens in the video games at the Sacoa in Mar del Plata. But to the surprise of friends and strangers alike, Mono became a computer systems engineer at the age of twenty-eight.

5.

T hat's him," points out Ruso from the backseat, when about thirty yards ahead a skinny, rather short, blond guy with big teeth comes around the corner, heading toward where they are parked. He is carrying a bag of groceries in each hand. It is hard to reconcile this image of "Polaco" Salvatierra with the one a few years earlier, those dazzling years when he appeared in gossip magazines and on daytime talk shows. More than hard, it's impossible, even though he has the same irrepressible teeth, the same light eyes. It's his bearing that's changed. As if he'd shrunk and gotten tarnished. Ruso notices his surprise when they emerge in unison from Fernando's Fiat Duna and cut Polaco off.

They greet him with a curt "Good day, Polaco," because they have decided to show their displeasure from the very start. After all, Mono's failure at buying a player was based on this guy's recommendation. Salvatierra doesn't seem to grasp their hostility. Or his reflexes are bad, or the time he spent in jail has hardened him enough that he's lost interest in such subtleties. He nods toward his mother's house, on the next block, and suggests they accompany him there.

"We can look for a cafe near the station," says Fernando, and Ruso figures he prefers to talk someplace neutral.

Salvatierra looks at the bags he's carrying, particularly one filled with vegetables.

"My mom is waiting for the chard."

"We won't be long," says Mauricio, sharply.

They walk a few steps toward his house. Salvatierra stops and leaves the bags on the ground.

"I don't know, what I can tell you is that . . ."—he begins suddenly, perhaps knowing that everything said before was a useless prologue, like most prologues—"about . . . I don't know . . . three years ago, more or less, Mono came to see me with the idea of—"

"Yeah. We know that already," Mauricio interrupts again.

"Okay. At that point I was trying to get back into the market, I had a few juvenile players under consideration, we talked about it . . ." Polaco nods toward Ruso, as if naming him as an eyewitness to those encounters. ". . . And that was when I thought to offer him that kid Pittilanga. I guess you know—"

"Yes. Pittilanga and another one," Fernando said, rushing him.

"That's right. Pittilanga and Suárez. But Pittilanga was my boy. You see how Suárez has already quit soccer."

"Right. Pittilanga, on the other hand, hasn't quit soccer. Soccer quit him," Fernando cuts him off, bitterly.

"No, well. It's true that he isn't going through a good patch . . ."

"A good patch?" Mauricio is getting angry. "Do you think we're blind? He's playing on loan with Presidente Mitre in Santiago del Estero! You sold Mono a player who—"

"I didn't sell him to him. I recommended him."

"Don't even get me started! This Pittilanga is in a club that plays the Argentine A Tournament! It's not that he's not playing in First A. Or in National B. No, no. The guy is on a team out in the sticks . . ."

"But in terms of Santiago del Estero . . ."

Salvatierra sounds pacifying, and Ruso is tempted to agree with him about looking for the bright side of the whole situation, but Fernando intervenes, inflamed. "How in the hell are we going to recover the three hundred thousand dollars, will you tell me that? You made my brother spend three hundred grand on a hack who's not worth two pesos! And now my brother's dead and the cash is up in smoke, and the one who fucked up was you!"

"I didn't fuck up! Nobody forced him to buy Pittilanga!"

"Oh, no?"

"Of course not! He bought him because he wanted to!"

"Because you recommended him!"

"I recommended him because I thought he was going to be a good investment!"

"You don't say?"

"Yes, I do. The kid played in an Under-Seventeen selection."

"And what the hell does that have to do with it?"

"What do you think you look at when buying, Fernando? If it were that easy any idiot would get into this business and strike it rich."

"Okay. I'll let the evidence speak for itself," adds Mauricio, gesturing to Salvatierra, who pays no attention to the insult.

"It's not what it looks like. I didn't make anything off the deal."

"Why wouldn't you, if you were Pittilanga's agent?" Mauricio corners him.

"No! I didn't get a commission on it!" Salvatierra lifts his hands to chest height, as if to reinforce his protests of innocence.

"And why did you want him to do it? Out of the goodness of your heart?"

"No, but these things happen every day. What do you think? That putting your cash into this is like a fixed-term deposit? For every kid who's a gold mine another hundred are failures."

"Well, the one you happened to sell my brother is a failure!"

"I didn't sell him! The club sold him to your brother! Platense sold him the player! And I repeat, I didn't make a dime."

The conversation dies down, because they all knew it was going nowhere. In the end, the most important thing had been made clear as they watched Salvatierra walk those forty yards over to them on the sidewalk. He is no longer representing players. He's a beaten man, without work, without any better prospects than running errands for his mother and mowing her lawn once in a while. A question of bad luck. His and Pittilanga's. Polaco's for being an idiot, for losing control, for fooling himself, for choosing bad company. And Pittilanga's for growing two inches too tall. For scoring four goals less. For injuring his knee and being out for four months right when they changed head coaches and losing his spot. For gaining fifteen pounds and getting slow and heavy. Four or five key mistakes, right there in the final stretch where it counts. That's all it takes. Ruso understands that. He's felt that way many times, a close defeat, for not understanding in time which is the dangerous square he has to avoid landing on at all cost.

The three men turn their backs on Salvatierra and go back to their car without saying a word, or even waving, partly because of the foul moods they are in and partly because they feel the need to show their displeasure, although both things—their displeasure and showing it—are absolutely useless.

Manager

Polaco Salvatierra was the youngest of three siblings who grew up on the corner of Mono and Fernando's street and just a block away from them, to the despotic screams of his mother, a Spaniard as big as a mountain who ruled with an iron hand, there being no husband around to help her with that or other necessities. Despite his nickname, he wasn't Polish, nor descended from Poles; he couldn't even find Poland on a map. But he was totally blond, almost transparent blond, and had light eyes and very pale skin. The nickname was actually given to him by Mono, who at ten years old was convinced that Salvatierra looked just like the players in the Polish soccer team who came to play in the '78 World Cup. And since Salvatierra didn't object, the nickname stuck forever.

He grew up in the neighborhood and he made it into the Ferro farm system, even though as a soccer player he was no great shakes. In the fourth division they let him go, but that was when he had his stroke of luck: some of his friends from the minors did manage to become pros and Polaco, who perhaps was more intelligent without the ball than with it, figured out a way to help them out with their first contracts. With his blond hair and cherub's skin he knew how to assume an utterly imbecilic expression that confused the board of directors and threw off the treasurers. Closing three or four more or less advantageous contracts for his friends was enough to lead to the most significant step of his career: he became a players'

PAPERS IN THE WIND 31

representative. His rise was meteoric. He burst into the soccer pantheon with some stunning deals, and for six or seven years he went around the neighborhood in cars and motorcycles that the residents of South Castelar had seen before only in photos. He was usually accompanied by lovely, fleshy ladies, also of the kind seen only in photos, although in this case they were a different type of photos. Every once in a while Polaco's behavior was the subject of analysis in the four friends' conversation. Fernando was surprised that, with the dough he was making, he wasted so much of his leisure time in a neighborhood filled with squat homes and skittish housewives. Mauricio thought, and the others eventually agreed, that the only place in the world where Polaco could give his success epic proportions was the place he'd come from. Anywhere else Polaco was just a young man who spent a lot on luxury cars and expensive women. Nothing more. But on the four blocks that made up their neighborhood, which had seen him grow up over days and years, everybody remembered the small, bland house he had come out of, the thundering voice of his Spanish mother, the ramshackle bicycle he rode for years, without brakes or mudguards, that was too small for him and made him look like an overgrown kid. And the comparison made him legendary. Mauricio maintained that was why he came back. Because only there could he demonstrate the enormous distance that separated him from his past.

All of a sudden Salvatierra disappeared from the neighborhood. It was supposed that he was still managing soccer players, and every so often his name would appear linked to some transfer abroad, or the conflict between some player and his club. One morning the news channels announced that Polaco was in jail, as a member of a gang whose crimes ranged from drug trafficking to car theft, with a number of stops in between. As the months passed the story changed, doubling back to its start, before finally exhausting itself. Two years after that scandal Polaco was released. But without a doubt, he was a shadow of his own shadow. To pay the lawyers he'd had to sell his cars and motorcycles, all his girlfriends had left him, and almost all his old clients in the soccer world had replaced him without qualms.

Mono ran into him sometimes at the butcher's and they would say hi, with the discomfort of those who had shared the same world, but too long ago. They chatted as the butcher cut him thin rump cutlets for his mother, nicknamed "La Gallega" for her Spanish roots. Somehow or other they got on the subject of Polaco's profession. Delicately, Mono avoided talking about jails and trials, and Polaco thanked him by lavishing him with details of his most resounding successes, his thorniest negotiations, the juiciest gossip about famous players. They walked the two blocks from the butcher's shop to Polaco's mom's house together, shook hands, and made plans to see each other again sometime.

6.

"'How's it goin'," is Fernando's neutral greeting as he pulls back the free chair and sits down.

"Should we order some appetizers?" suggests Ruso.

"It's ten in the morning, Rusito," scolds Mauricio. "I haven't digested my breakfast."

"If you're hungry, order something, Ruso. Why not?" Fernando puts in, a bit too forcefully.

Bad sign, thinks Ruso. They've barely exchanged twenty words and his friends are already at each other's throats.

"I feel like the child of divorcing parents," comments Ruso, waiting for them to ask him why. When they don't, he continues, "Mauricio is always coming down hard on me like he was my mom, and you let me do whatever I want, like a dad who doesn't see me a lot and doesn't have the heart to say no."

"And what the hell would you know about divorcing parents?" challenges Mauricio, whose mood seems to get worse with each word said.

"I don't—I—I—" Ruso is completely flummoxed.

"It was a joke, Mauricio," injects Fernando. "Don't bust his balls."

"Go ahead, guys. Just keep ganging up on me," concludes Mauricio, glumly.

Ruso wishes he had just kept his mouth shut. Humor is always the master key, the road he knows by heart that takes him everywhere. But sometimes it backfires. It happens more with

Mónica than with anybody else. It's strange that here, with his friends, the same thing has happened. When it does he experiences it as a failure, a defeat. And he'd come to this meeting with the silly pretense of keeping the peace. He had even arrived on time, running against his most ingrained habits, precisely to avoid Mauricio and Fernando being alone together and starting to argue, or fight, or closing off all the paths between them.

"Well," says Fernando. "What do you guys think we should do?"

It's a good start. That plural in the question invites dialogue, and might keep the arguing at bay. But Ruso doesn't even consider answering, because the plural doesn't mean Fernando includes him. The other two count on his consent, on his collaboration, on his help. But never his voice or his opinion. The dialogue is between the other two, and he doesn't even bother, because being outside of the dialogue also means being outside of the fighting he can see coming, in a stampede, lifting dust as it makes its way toward them.

Mauricio keeps his eyes low. He plays with his cell phone, opening and closing the top again and again. The waiter brings the espressos with milk and Ruso attacks the small cornstarch *alfajores* that come with them. The silence lasts a long minute, until Mauricio finally stops fidgeting with the phone.

"I don't think there's much we can do, honestly."

Fernando looks at him with an expression that makes Ruso think that if looks could burn, he'd have reduced Mauricio to a small pile of embers.

"And why do you think there's not much we can do?" Fernando's tone quickly slides into sarcasm.

"Because Pittilanga is a lummox, and we aren't going to find any fool anywhere willing to shell out three hundred grand to buy him. Without even mentioning that we don't have the faintest fucking idea of how to handle ourselves in a business like this."

Fernando doesn't answer right away, but Ruso knows that it is just a superficial retreat.

"So?" he finally says.

"So nothing."

"Nothing? You know what losing that money means."

"Let's not start with that."

"Let's not start? That's the money for Guadalupe. Nothing more and nothing less. If we lose it we screw the girl over and we're all screwed, because we'll never see her again."

"Your mother will have visitation rights."

"Did you see what they are? Didn't you say it was an outrage what they did to us in court?"

"Forgive me, Fernando, because sometimes someone could hear you talking and think you live in a cloud. Whose idea was it to put all the severance money into buying a soccer player?"

"No, of course. It was the idea of one of your idiotic childhood friends."

"There's no need to get sarcastic. You think I like that things turned out like this?"

"I don't see you too worried."

"And what do you know? Do you have a thermometer that calculates how worried everybody else is? Are you a psychic?"

"No, but you make it easy: 'There's nothing we can do about it. Period. Go fuck yourselves.'"

"Well, if you're such an expert, you must already know the answer." Mauricio opens his arms wide, in invitation. "Come on, Fernando. Enlighten us. Tell us what the hell we can do."

"I don't know what we can do."

"But you know that we have to do something and we can't just sit around with 'our arms crossed.'"

"Who's the sarcastic one here?"

"Well, just listen to yourself! You have no idea what to do, yet you're sure there's something that can still be done! Doesn't that sound ridiculous?"

"It sounds more ridiculous to me that we cry uncle."

"'Cry uncle'? Why are you talking like the father in the Ingalls family? Is there a hidden camera recording your every heroic move?"

"Stop, Mauri." Ruso fears the conversation will veer too far off track, irretrievably.

"The hell I'll stop, Ruso! The hell I will!" Mauricio, about to lose it, points to Fernando. "This guy's dumb optimism, his moronic stubbornness, it's driving me nuts!"

"Stubbornness?"

"Yes, stubbornness! You want to hear more? Altruism. You're always playing the altruist, the supportive one, the—"

"I don't play—"

"Noooo!" Mauricio rises up in his seat. "You're right! You don't play the altruist! You're convinced you are one! If you don't go to bed at night knowing you did a good deed, you can't sleep a wink, isn't that right? Good, Fernandito, good job. Always helping little old ladies across the street, giving up your seat to cripples, letting pedestrians cross. I'm sick and tired of you and your boy scout complex."

They are shouting at each other with the table between them and Ruso wants to die. The people at the other tables are staring at them, and there is no sound in the bar other than the two of them yelling.

"Do you know what kind of person you are, Fernando? You want me to tell you? I thought of it the other day."

"So nice to know you were thinking of me . . ."

"Yes, I was talking about it with Mariel."

"Ah, your wife participated in the debate? Wonderful. Then it must have been practically a scientific symposium."

Now, thinks Ruso, it's Mauricio's turn to look at his rival as if he wanted to pulverize him, but he just picks up the thread of what he was saying.

"That your optimism has a lot to do with your obsessiveness, or the other way around, but it's the same thing."

"I don't understand."

"Of course. You're a textbook obsessive. How you correct your students' exams. How you clean your house. A thousand things, I can't remember them all. The closet in your bedroom, no need to look further. Everything in your life is like that. Organized, tidy, polite. You know why you're like that?"

"Tell me."

"Because somewhere in your head is the idea that if you organize everything, if you foresee everything, if you arrange everything, things are going to work out fine. Of course, you don't understand." Mauricio looks at Ruso, as if trying to force him to be involved. "As if having petty, stupid things in order could make sense of the big things! It's utterly ridiculous, but you act like it was a revelation. That's what's so unbearable about obsessives like you."

"And what are you?"

"Don't change the subject, I just had a brilliant idea." He looks alternately at Fernando and Ruso, with an enthusiasm that the latter finds unhealthy. "Don't you get it? Your obsessions are an act of faith. You think that the world has order,

rules, and if you look for them, if you can discover them and
respect them, life adjusts and turns just as clean and happy."

"I think you're going too far . . ."

"You're the one who went too far, a while ago, Fernando.
Not me. You've got us dancing the conga with this Pittilanga
business since Mono died, and you know better than me that
it's bullshit. That Mono fucked up. Fucked up bad. That he
threw away his money. That he was never able to hold on to
two pesos without them slipping through his fingers."

"Stop, Mauricio," Ruso tries to intervene.

"Like hell I will. And you, Ruso, you're the last person who
should be telling me to stop about the money, because you are
the same or worse. The difference is that you never had a dime
in your fucking life and dumb Mono was lucky enough to have
a good stretch and get some dough together, but since he was
always flighty and immature he threw it all away when he got
the silly idea of becoming a businessman. What the hell could
Mono know about buying and selling players, tell me that.
What the hell could he possibly know? And you, Ruso, you are
as guilty as him, because instead of stopping him you egged
him on, instead of putting his feet on the ground, you encour-
aged him because you loved the idea. And you, Fernando, you
didn't do shit either."

"I didn't know."

"You didn't know or you didn't want to know?"

"Are you calling me a liar?"

"I'm not calling you anything. But if you wanted to play
good Samaritan it would have been better for you to get him
to back out when there was still time. But of course, you never
said anything to Mono. Orders are orders."

"What orders?"

"Don't play dumb, Fernando. At your house all your little brother had to do was have an idea and your mother would bend over backward to indulge him. And there you are, always floating, always dispensible. Wanting to be in, for them to consider you in, but out, always out."

Ruso squints his eyes, as if he was about to witness a catastrophe.

"Why do you have to butt in with what happens or doesn't happen with my mom?" Fernando shouts in the middle of the bar. Out of the corner of his eye, Ruso realizes that the waiter, who knows them, is about to intervene.

Instead of answering with the same ferocity, Mauricio sighs. He is red with rage, but his voice comes out slow and deliberate.

"You're right, Fernando. Exactly. I shouldn't butt in. And the truth is that I've been helping you too long, with this whole mess."

Fernando turns toward Ruso.

"It looks like we've been abusing the kind sir's patience. If I were you I'd apologize, Ruso."

"Don't bring Ruso into this, because it's not about him."

"Ah, it's just about me."

"Of course it's about you. Ruso is going to follow you in every frigging thing you come up with. He's too good. And you take advantage of him."

"I take advantage? I can't believe what I'm hearing."

"Then don't believe it. But don't count on my help anymore."

"We've known that forever. That you can't count on the counselor."

Mauricio exhales loudly again.

"I've reached my limit, Fernando. If you want to keep pretending that reality is the way you want it to be instead of how it is, go right ahead. But don't try my patience. Because you're the one with the ideas, you're the eternal optimist, the one who always has to keep busting balls and trying, you're the one who doesn't accept when they say no and quit bugging us, you're the one who is too immature to understand that there are things that can't be fixed, Fernando. It's not Ruso and it's not me. It's you. If Ruso wants to follow you, he's welcome to. But don't fuck with me anymore, I'm asking you, please. I've had it up to here, Fernando. Because I *do* know when to say enough's enough."

"Sometimes I think it's the only thing you know how to say."

They look at each other for a long moment and Ruso, who sees them both, thinks that the damage they are doing is, perhaps, irreparable. Finally Mauricio gets up, drops a ten-peso note on the table, and leaves without saying goodbye.

Senior

The prediction Mono formulated immediately after finding out that he would never be a professional soccer player, still hungover and in Ruso's watchful custody, seated at the dining room table of his house with the classified ads—the whole "this computer stuff has a future"—turned out to be dead-on. In those years, computers were getting cheaper, faster, and more versatile, and Mono—even before graduating—threw himself into designing systems tailored to small clients. At a time when many engineers and students offered the same thing, Mono designed an enormously ingenious prefab system, which with slight modifications could be used in a video club, a service station, or a pharmacy. And, in the words of Ruso, "it sold like hotcakes." But his good reflexes didn't end there, because when, at the end of the nineties, that market began to give signs of waning, Mono came across a notice in the newspaper for a business with Swiss capital that was looking for the services of a senior analyst.

Mono and Ruso gathered with Fernando—who as older brother served as both adviser and guide, except when his opinions didn't coincide with what Mono wanted to do, in which case Mono figured out a way to ignore them—but none of them could shed any light on the meaning of the term "senior," because the only way they had heard the word used was to designate a world tournament that had been played years back, among veteran players.

Mono requested and received an interview, anyway. It turned out that the Swiss were expanding their medical administration branch. Mono described in full detail the prefab that he'd sold to everyone and their mother. They hired him, after settling on a salary considerably higher than Mono could have ever imagined in his most optimistic dreams. That night, as they were celebrating in a bar, Fernando rose above the drunkenness he was carefully cultivating to ask, "Hey, Monito, did you ever find out what they meant by 'senior analyst'?"

Mono looked up at him and blinked in puzzlement.

"No . . . I didn't ask."

"It's that world tournament from years back," declared Ruso, who had far exceeded his Fernet quota.

Mauricio furrowed his brow. He hadn't been a part of the conversation prior to the interview and he knew perfectly well what a senior analyst was.

"You guys don't know what 'senior analyst' means?" he asked.

There was a certain hint of superiority in his voice. But the others were so drunk that not only were they oblivious to his tone, but they started trying to remember all the teams that had participated in that old world championship of veteran players, and the results of the games.

7.

After the argument in the cafe, Fernando spent several days reflecting on how to proceed with the whole business. He wasn't surprised by what had happened with Mauricio. He was sorry about it, but he wasn't surprised. It was one of those things that you know is going to happen, sooner or later. It could definitely have been handled more elegantly, that's for sure. Mauricio could have made some excuse, claimed he had a lot of work, or marital problems with his birdbrained wife, or some other vague commitment. But no. He didn't even bother. Typical of Mauricio. And the way he did it, seeing Fernando's supposed purism where there is only his own egotism, the unyielding, ruthless egotism he's always had.

– Thank goodness Ruso is different. And not only because he was Fernando's dead brother's best friend. Because of that too, but it goes beyond that. Ruso might be a walking mess, but he is an upright and obliging guy. The kind that never leaves you in the lurch. That's just how Ruso is.

Fernando arrives at Ruso's car wash a little past ten in the morning. It's a splendid day, after three days of the endless drizzle that Buenos Aires punishes its inhabitants with every so often throughout the winter. He is somewhat surprised to find the place almost empty. A shiny gray Volkswagen rests in the area of finished jobs. And that's it. The machines are stopped and there are no cars waiting their turn. The two operators Ruso hired are sitting in a corner, drinking maté.

Fernando greets them from a distance and asks them in body language where the boss is. They make expressions indicating they don't know but indicate, also in gestures, that Cristo is in the office. Fernando heads over there.

"How's it goin', Fernando?" Cristo, the manager, greets him.

"Everything's fine, Cristo. And you?"

"Everything's cool. Coffee?"

Fernando nods and Cristo pulls a mug from the shelf and starts fiddling with the espresso machine. Fernando sits on one of the high benches on the other side of the counter. When Ruso told him about his plan to include a cafe in his car wash, Fernando had thought it was a good idea. But now that time has passed, he suspects that, like so many other times, Ruso erred in his diagnosis or methods, and that the only thing all that paraphernalia of metal, knobs, and blasts of steam is good for is a nice, hot cup of coffee for him and Cristo when they want one.

"The boss?"

Cristo looks at him over the machine, lifting an eyebrow. Then he points with his chin at the wall clock, which says it's ten-thirty.

"At this time? Forget about it. Ruso never shows up before eleven."

"Ah. I thought that with a day like this, maybe it'd be in his best interest to show up early."

Cristo scratches his thick black beard that, along with his long, tangled hair, is the main source of his nickname. He looks through the window. Outside everything is the same: the Volkswagen, the employees, and the maté.

"There's nothing going on anyway . . ." is all he says as he hands Fernando the cup of coffee.

Fernando thanks him and thinks, as always, that Ruso is a real case. Since they finished high school he has set up an infinite series of businesses. Fernando can't even list them all. All small businesses, all on his own, all preceded by fantastic predictions of "this is a surefire business" and "I'm going to wear out my shoes walking to the bank." And all of them buried, sooner or later, in debts and failure. Fernando and Mono talked about the issue, more than once. Because Ruso's surefire knack for missing the mark in his investments seemed forced, as if he were intentionally avoiding success. Mono claimed that Ruso's problem was a question of timing: all the businesses that he thought up were sound, but two years before Ruso got involved in them. By the time Ruso considered them, and put all his hopes and his shrinking pesos into them, they were on their way out. Fernando, for his part, didn't know whether to be sorry about the fact that Ruso, when he left high school, had been able to count on a modest fortune his father and grandfather had amassed in their leather workshop in Morón. On the one hand, that money had financed only failure after failure. On the other, it still allowed Ruso, his wife, and his daughters to eat every day.

Now Fernando and Cristo are standing in the physical epicenter of Ruso's latest venture. The car wash. It didn't take a soothsayer to calculate how this new scheme would end. If after three days of rain they'd had only one customer all morning . . .

But it's not just bad luck. In fact, it's almost eleven and the guy still hasn't shown up for work. What kind of owner is that disengaged from his own business?

"Hey, Cristo . . . if on a bright sunny day like this Ruso comes in at eleven . . . what time is he here on rainy days?"

"Huh? No. When it rains he comes in early. He brings in the PlayStation and the four of us play."

"You play PlayStation," repeats Fernando, trying to figure out if Cristo is joking.

"Uh huh. If we start early enough we can do a long tournament, round-robin."

No. He's not kidding. Cristo is telling the truth. Fernando guesses that if his grandfather Moisés could see his ingrate of a grandson playing video games on the ruins of his leather shop, he would rise from his grave to beat him to a pulp.

"And who wins the tournaments?" asks Fernando, although he thinks he can guess.

"Ruso. You should see how he plays."

Fernando can't help but notice the deep admiration with which Cristo talks about his boss. He doesn't seem worried about the uncertain future of the car wash, nor the fact that, sooner or later, he'll have to find another job. This is a point in Ruso's favor. The employees of his successive failures lavish him with unflagging affection. He brought Cristo with him from the hired-car agency—his penultimate venture. According to Ruso, he is integrity personified. It must be true. But his appearance—Nazarene on his last legs, hollow cheeks, cigarette always dangling from his lips, skinny as a fakir—doesn't really seem like the most appropriate image as the business's front man. Especially with that old white T-shirt, with all types of stains, that reads GRAB HOLD OF IT in huge red letters, with a red arrow pointing beneath his belly button. It seems hard to imagine the ladies of Castelar feeling particularly inclined to entrust their cars to such a manager.

Which is what Fernando is thinking when Ruso shows up. Simple, worn jeans, striped tee, sunglasses with metal frames

and green lenses—Fernando calculates that they went out of
style when they were still in high school—and the same face
as ever: tiny little eyes, huge nose, untamed curls. Kind of like
a version of "Pibe Valderrama" raised in a kibbutz, as Mono
used to joke. And the ironclad smile, of course. He hugs Fernando and Cristo, and he drops onto one of the empty stools.

"Where are you coming from at this hour, Ruso?"

"Make yourself a coffee, Cristo. From dropping off the twins
at school, Ferchu."

Fernando can't help looking at the clock.

"Thing is, on gorgeous days like this I stay in the square
reading the paper," clarifies Ruso, who has caught the insinu-
ation. "It's amazing out there. Did you see?"

The question is addressed to Cristo.

"Awesome," confirms his manager.

"Anything new?"

"Well . . . no, Ruso. We did that job." He points to the gray
Volkswagen. "Ah. Did you see that place they're renovating on
Bartolomé Mitre, at the end, near the square?"

"Yes. What about it?"

"You were right, Ruso. They are putting a car wash there."

"Ha! What did I tell you, Cristo? What did I tell you?" He
turns toward Fernando. "No, I should have been a fortune-
teller, look at that. About two weeks ago they put up the FOR
RENT sign on that place. And I came and said, 'I bet they're
putting in a car wash.' I totally called it. That is an amazing
spot for a car wash."

Fernando tries to understand the reason behind his friend's
carefree joy.

"But isn't it going to be a problem for you if they open up a
car wash seven blocks away?"

Ruso shrugs.

"Uh . . . if I worried about that . . . I'd go crazy. Do you know how many car washes there are in Castelar, baby?" He beckons to Cristo to conclude his thought.

"Seven."

"Seven," confirms Ruso. "And that's just counting down-town."

Fernando is dying to ask, or actually to scream, what to him is the obvious corollary to the statement: *And don't you realize, you pinhead, that if you keep just scratching your belly, reading the paper, and playing video games, the worms are going to eat you alive?* But he doesn't say it.

"And what brings you here? Don't you work today?"

"I have class this afternoon, Ruso. I have the morning off."

"What a life these teachers have, eh, Cristo? And then they ask for a raise."

"Don't start, I'm here because we have to talk about something."

Ruso's face clouds over. Suddenly, it's as if his tall bench is uncomfortable. Fernando is reminded of how much these things affect him. Ruso hates arguing, confrontation, tension.

"I was convinced it was going to happen, Ruso. That sooner or later Mauricio would leave us in the lurch."

Ruso furrows his brow.

"What do you mean 'in the lurch'?"

"That he was going to leave us hanging with this Pittilanga business."

Fernando pauses, to make sure that Russo understands him. But Ruso looks at him, blinking rapidly, as if somewhat perplexed.

"What's wrong with you, Ruso?"

"Me? Nothing, nothing."

"So why are you looking at me like that?"

"Like what?"

"What? Do you think it's right what Mauricio did?"

The rapid blinking is joined now by the drumming of his fingers on the counter and blowing up toward his forehead, as if to clear away the curls. Fernando is starting to get irritated.

"I asked you a question."

"Eh? No, it wasn't right, Fernando. But I don't know . . . what is 'right'?"

"Well, I guess being willing to help out friends would have been 'right.' And leaving them hanging is the same as 'wrong.' Am I confusing you?"

"No, no. But on the other hand what Mauricio says makes . . . I don't know, it also . . ."

"Also what, Ruso?"

"Everything is so complicated, Fernando. Everything. You say we have to keep trying, keep on trying. But how?"

"I don't know . . . Maybe you have some idea if you're so clever?"

"All right. Well, maybe that's what Mauricio was saying. That until we think of how to keep trying the best thing to do is wait."

"Wait for what?"

"Wait. I don't know, Fernando, wait. Wait to see what's the best . . ."

"But don't you realize that if we don't sell this guy they are going to release him, he's not going to be in a club, and Mono's money will be gone forever?"

"I know, Fer. Don't yell at me. I know."

"I'm not yelling at you, but in the end you're giving me the same dumb song and dance as your friend Mauricio."

"My friend? But he's your friend, too . . . And Mono's."

"Honestly, I can't believe this. I can't believe you. In the end it turns out I'm the one who's wrong."

"Not wrong, Fernando. I understand the urgency."

"So if you understand the urgency, how can you tell me we have to wait?"

"Because we have no idea how to do this."

"So, what? We stand here with our arms folded over our chests? Wait for the vultures to swoop in? Like you with . . ."

"Like me with what?"

Fernando stops short. He breathes several times through his nose, his nostrils dilated by anger and the effort to keep quiet.

"Forget it. Forget about it."

"Tell me." Ruso's tone makes it clear that offense is taken, no matter how tacitly.

Fernando turns toward the bar and takes the last sip of his coffee. It is bitter and freezing cold. He feels he's been tricked. He had imagined a solidarity with Ruso that doesn't exist. He is alone.

"Let's talk about something else. Let's not argue over nothing. How is Mónica?"

"Fine." From Ruso's expression, this subject of conversation doesn't seem much more promising than the previous one.

"Any problems?"

"Bah. No problems."

Just then a car stops on the street. Solicitous, Cristo goes out to talk to the driver.

"Thing is she's driving me nuts over the car wash. She says we're going to go out of business, like always."

Fernando thinks about the PlayStation soccer tournaments and finds it hard not to share Mónica's pessimism.

"Well. I guess the competition must be complicated . . ." ventures Fernando.

"Not really," Ruso is quick to say, scratching his aquiline nose as he always does when he's about to reveal a secret. "In fact . . ." He moves closer to Fernando's ear, for no real reason, since they're alone in the office. "Cristo and I have a theory."

Fernando doesn't dare ask. He opens his eyes wide, ready for anything.

"The more car washes they open, the better."

Fernando nods, in silence. Why ask anything, if Ruso's brain is impervious anyway?

"Aren't you going to ask me why?"

"Why?"

"Because the moment will come when there are so many that nobody's going to have enough work."

Ruso makes a smug face, as if his argument was now complete and irrefutable. He turns toward Fernando and perhaps detects some doubt, because he adds, "Of course, man. The moment will come when there are so many car washes that nobody's gonna be making a cent."

"And?"

"And when that happens, all the other owners will be wanting to kill each other. Because they're gonna be losing dough like Bedouins. Are you following me?"

Murkily, yes, Fernando begins to understand.

"And then they'll start closing, those guys. They don't know what a bad patch is. They don't know how to handle losses. Now you get me?"

Cristo waves off the driver, who backs up and disappears down the avenue. He stands there for a second with his hands on his hips and then returns to the office. Ruso finishes his idea.

"But we're used to bad patches. We're comfortable there, when things are fucked up. The others will nose-dive, one after the other, I don't know if you understand what I'm saying."

Fernando nods, as he thinks back to the matter that brought him there that morning. Maybe in the end it's not that important to have Ruso's help. Maybe Ruso is, in business terms, hopelessly inept.

"And what did that guy want, Cristo?" Ruso asks, about the driver who just left.

"Nothing, Ruso. A friend from my old job who I told about the PS2 tournaments and he wanted in."

"And what'd you tell him?"

"I told him no, that we have enough players." Suddenly he hesitates. "Bah, I don't know, Ruso. I told him that 'cause I thought . . ."

"You did good, Cristo. You did good. More than four is a hassle."

He turns toward Fernando.

"You want another coffee?"

Volovolatile

In March 2004, Mono was called to a meeting with the top brass of the Swiss company. By that point, he was already their systems manager. They offered him a coffee and they sat him in a pretty comfy armchair. That night, when he told his brother and his best friend about the meeting, Mono said that he went in there feeling on the edge of a cliff.

The Swiss guys started by congratulating him on his performance, praising themselves for having hired him, admiring the rapid chain of promotions that had brought him to managerial level.

Inside, Mono translated that flattering introduction into abrupt and concise terms. *They're going to fire my ass*, he said he was thinking. And he thought how ironic his fate was, that after having survived the torrent of firings in 2001, in the midst of the recession, his kick in the ass should come three years later.

"So did they fire you?" asked Ruso, who usually loved the way Mono told stories, but in this case the anxiety was eating away at him.

"Hold your horses, Ruso," said Mono, stopping him because he was convinced that things should be told slowly and in full detail. He took up his story again, telling them how the Swiss saw that Argentina was very unstable, very volatile. Actually his boss had said something like "volovolatile" (because he was Swiss and didn't speak Spanish well, but Mono

had understood him anyway), and he had gone on about the
need to adapt to a very changeable world. *Uh-oh, this is where
I get slam-dunked,* Mono had figured. Just then the Swiss guy
in charge of the meeting lowered his voice—something that
in Argentina, Switzerland, and everywhere means that the
speaker is about to say something confidential—to announce
that the company was merging with another, larger, Mexican
one.

Mono—according to the way he told it that night to his
brother and his best friend—deduced that he was down for the
count. All that introduction could only lead to the infamous
boot in the rear for the systems manager. But that was when
the third Swiss guy, who until that point had been as quiet as a
mouse, lifted a finger, pointed to Mono, and told him that he—
Mono, not the Swiss guy—was the best person to take over the
regional management for the new conglomerate.

"Shit," said Ruso when he heard that part of the story.

"Wait, Ruso. Wait, I'm not finished," said Mono, cutting
him off again. Because when the Swiss guy called for silence,
probably expecting to hear joyful exclamations from the local
manager turned regional manager, the candidate had only
scratched his chin, shuffled in his seat, and asked what other
options he had. The boss thought he hadn't understood and he
started to reiterate the extensive prologue about the volovolatile market, but Mono had stopped him, assuring him that he'd
understood the offer they'd made, but that he wanted to know
what other options he had if he didn't accept it. The Swiss
guys' small blue eyes exchanged fast, puzzled glances. Well, in
that case, and taking into consideration the inevitable down-
sizing of the staff, they would be forced to dispense with his
services. With all the compensation due, added the number

two Swiss guy, as if anticipating a demand that Mono wasn't formulating. Far from it. According to what he explained to Ruso and Fernando that night, the reluctant candidate for regional management was considering various matters simultaneously. He asked for a day to think about it. The Swiss guys, who had expected a much warmer reception for their offer, recovered from their surprise, extended a hand to him, and said goodbye until the next day.

8.

At the bus station they tell him how to get to the field. It isn't more than ten blocks, and Fernando decides to walk. A taxi is a splurge he can't afford, and besides the afternoon is cool and sunny, perfect for a stroll.

He stops in front of a pay phone and digs in the smallest pocket of his jeans. He drops the coins onto the shelf and counts them. Three pesos seventy-five has to be enough.

"Hi, Mom," he says when he gets through. "It's Fernando."

"Hello."

"How are you?"

"Same."

Fernando sighs. He hates that response from his mother. He knows her like the back of his hand and can anticipate what she'll say, because she always responds the same way. But he hates it. As if she were making him responsible for the pain and tediousness.

"Listen, Mom. I need you to look in the living room dresser, in the first drawer, to see if Mono's video camera's instructions are in there."

"Why?"

"I need to know how long the battery lasts. I came to Santiago del Estero to film Pittilanga, the player I told you about. Maybe this way we can sell him and get back the money for Guada."

On the other end, his mother is silent. Fernando continues.

"But I want to film him to show potential buyers. That's why I came. And I need to know how much battery life I have."

Fernando pauses. Deep down he hopes that his mother feels sorry for him. That she says how nice, poor Fernando, look what sacrifice he's making for his brother and his niece. But on the other end of the line he hears only silence.

"Hello, Mom? Are you there?"

"Yes, Fernando. I was just wondering why you keep calling him Mono when you know I don't like it. I never liked it. I always told you that."

Fernando sighs again. She doesn't care that he just traveled twelve hundred kilometers on a microbus to try to save Mono's dough and use it so that Guadalupe—who by the way is her only grandchild—can have a more solid, more secure future closer to them. No. From his mother's tone, this trip is just his obligation or his whim. The important thing is that he doesn't dare call Mono Mono. "Your father and I named him Alejandro for a reason. So you can call him Ale, or Alejandro."

"Okay, Mom. Sorry. But can you have a look at the instructions, and quickly, because I'm going to get cut off."

As he waits, he listens to the coins dropping through the telephone. *If she doesn't hurry up I'm going to get cut off*, he thinks.

"Hello."

"Yes, Ma. Did you find it?"

"Yes, but I don't know what you need me to tell you."

"How long the battery lasts, Ma. Look at the index."

"Ah, no. I can't. The type is really small."

Fernando lets out a third sigh and scratches his forehead with the telephone receiver.

"You don't have your glasses on hand, Ma?"

"No, Fernando. They're in the kitchen. Do you really need to know this now?"

A warning is heard on the line before it cuts off. Fernando hangs up. He hears a tinkling of coins inside the phone. He sticks his hand in the compartment where the change comes out and extracts a twenty-five-cent coin. Lately pay phones have been working better. They almost never have broken cords, or steal your money. As he starts off again he realizes why: everybody uses cell phones, and pay phones are an eccentricity that only dorks without cell phones, like him, use regularly. That's why they work now. What a pathetic country, he concludes bitterly: the only things that aren't broken are the things nobody wants.

He can only make out the field when he turns the last corner, because the sole grandstand is very small and could easily be mistaken for the wall of a factory or a school. The only distinctive sign is the four squalid light towers that emerge from the corners.

He pulls out his ticket and goes through a superfluous police frisking. He goes up the barely ten steps and sits down in the uppermost row. In the following months he'll get his fill of poorly tended fields inching back to a wild state, but since this is the first, he studies it with interest. The low fence, the midfield and goal areas without a blade of grass, the peeling ads on the wall that encloses the opposite side.

When he turns on the camera he remembers the conversation with his mother. "Alejandro." There's no point. He can't think of him as Alejandro. He is Mono. Always, since they were kids. He wonders if his mother would show the same ferocity about defending him from unflattering nicknames. He thinks not. And he suspects, punishing himself with gratuitous severity, that he never accepted a nickname precisely in order to comply with his mother's mandate. "Fernando" his mother called him, and still calls him. Never in a million years "Fer," so fond, so intimate. But "Ale," yes. There were a ton of Ales.

"Psst. Psst."

Fernando turns toward the sound. It is a fifty-year-old wearing a beret that's too small on him.

"Do you know how San Martín de Pico Truncado did?"

He hasn't the slightest idea. Confused, he shakes his head. The other thanks him with a nod, anyhow.

"I thought you were a journalist, because of that." The guy with the beret points to the camera.

"Ah . . ." Fernando understands. "No, no. I'm not a journalist."

They smile at each other perfunctorily as a way to end the conversation and they look back at the playing field. The teams come out and Fernando focuses the camera, but he leaves it paused to avoid shooting useless things. He is afraid of running out of battery halfway through the game. What if Pittilanga scores an incredible goal after the battery dies? Unlikely, he tells himself. Especially the incredible goal part.

He looks at the camera. The screen informs him that the battery level is at its highest. Maybe it'll last the whole game. He remembers the phone conversation with his mother again. She wasn't even surprised to learn that he had traveled to Santiago del Estero to shoot the game. It was as if he'd told her he was out in Ituzaingó teaching. Really, his words usually go in one of her ears and straight out the other. The next time he'll test her: "I'm on Mars, Mom. I came to see if I can do something to save Mono's money. That's why I came to Mars." He doubts it'll make a difference.

He starts taping and adjusts the focus, because they just made a deep pass to Pittilanga, who dribbles, dodging his defender. The ball goes out of bounds along the goal line. Fernando pushes pause. Now he can't remember at what point this expedition seemed like a good idea. It must have been after the fight with Mauricio and the wishy-washy response he got from Ruso when he went to the car wash. That must have been when he was overcome by his usual messiah complex.

He turns the camera on again when Presidente Mitre puts together an attack. The visiting team shoots the ball into the corner. Fernando focuses on Pittilanga, who is waiting for the cross near the penalty spot. He practices the slight turn of his wrist that would allow him to capture the goal as well, if Pittilanga heads it in there. The ball comes long and high, hitting the far post a few meters above Pittilanga's head. Fernando pauses again and lowers the camera.

Dollars

That night, when Mono called them together to tell them the details of his meeting with the Swiss bosses, Fernando and Ruso needed a couple of minutes to digest what Mono told them.

"Let me see if I understand," Fernando wanted to confirm. "They offered you regional manager."

"Yes."

"They are merging and getting bigger. And you would be in charge of the whole Southern region."

"Yes, that's the idea."

"The salary must be incredible. Even better than what you're making now. Right?"

"Well, yeah. I didn't ask for details, but yeah."

Fernando paused.

"And despite all that, you ask for time to think about it."

"Yes. Until tomorrow."

They were silent again, until Ruso had an idea and spoke.

"You're thinking about whether to keep the job you have now, or take the new one?"

"No, Ruso. That's not an option. Either I take this regional management job or I'm out."

"What do you mean 'out'?"

"I'm out, Ruso. They give me a severance package and I'm gone."

"But then you'd have no job . . ."

"I know, genius."

"The money, I'm wondering . . ." insisted Fernando. "How much are we talking about?"

"The severance package or the new salary?"

Fernando made a gesture indicating he could answer whichever he felt like.

"I didn't ask about the new salary. I already told you that. But listen, I'm going to have to be traveling and all that, because the region includes Chile and Uruguay. And maybe even Paraguay. I didn't ask. And remember, I have Guadalupe. That bitch Lourdes drives me crazy over the visits. She makes them as difficult as she can. If I start bouncing around, from one place to the other, it's going to get even more complicated. No doubt about that."

It was true. Neither Fernando nor Ruso wanted to go into it, but it was true.

"And the severance package?" asked Fernando.

"That's the thing. That's what I wanted to get at." Mono responded with such energy that Fernando suspected he had already made his decision. And all that was left was for them to give their blessing. That was it. "The personnel manager gave me an estimate. She didn't say any exact figure. She is a fantastic gal. And she's hot."

"Which one is she? Do I know her?" interjected Ruso, suddenly interested.

"Well, yeah . . . I think. Her name's Mariana. She must have been at that New Year's Eve party you went to with me. Tall, dark . . ."

"Is she a petite blonde, very pretty?" Ruso's hands convey what his words leave out.

"What was the estimate?" asked Fernando, trying to get back to the previous subject.

"No. The blonde that blew your mind was Gabriela, from Supplies. This one is dark, tall . . ."

"What was she wearing?"

"Monito, I asked you a question."

"I don't know, fool. That was like two years ago . . . I think a green dress. Like this, low-cut . . ."

"It wasn't red?"

"No, Ruso. The one in red was Gabriela, the blonde, but I tol—"

"Will you answer me already, you moron?"

When Fernando lost his patience he managed to get them to stop talking. But they looked at him, both of them, as if he were an extraterrestrial. For a second, Fernando thought about justifying his anger by pointing out the obvious: they were discussing Mono's professional future and not the physical attributes of the women who worked at his company. But years of experience being the brother of one and the friend of them both deterred him from even trying. For them, there was no way that the amount of the severance payment could be more important than reliably determining who was Gabriela and who was Mariana. So he just looked at Mono to try and force him to respond.

"Look: she told me that, like, more or less, give or take, I'd get two hundred thousand, two hundred and ten thousand, approximately."

"Pesos?" asked Ruso, with amazed eyes.

"No, Ruso. Dollars."

"Shit," was all that Ruso managed to articulate.

9.

The two knocks on the door were accompanied by a jingling. The jingling of the bracelets Soledad always wears on her left wrist.

"Come in," says Mauricio, and she sticks her head in.

"Mr. Williams says to come by his office when you can, he has to talk to you."

"According to Williams's urgency meter, which you are a pro at, . . . where does this land on the scale?"

The girl smiles. She is wearing black pleated pants and a white shirt with ruffles that show off her numerous curves.

"I'd say a . . . six."

"Six? Good. There's time for a coffee. That is if my kindly assistant is willing to prepare one. Or is there still some left over from this morning?"

"No and yes," the girl pauses. "No, there's none left from the morning, and yes, I'm willing to make you a cup. But . . ."

"But?"

"Six is a dangerous rating. It's tricky. Five is relax. Seven is alarm. Six is hard to classify."

"Suggestions?"

"Go see Williams while I make your coffee."

Silent glances. A smile met by another smile. The code is a bit saccharine for Mauricio's taste, but what can you do? Gotta just grin and bear it.

"On one condition. I am a magnanimous boss, and you were typing something up. If I am going to interrupt your sacred professionalism, at least have a coffee with me."

Long, silent looks.

"Seems fair."

Mauricio's smile widens. It is a crucial moment, one in which he has to make decisions. She is ripe for the picking.

The phone rings and Soledad goes back to answer it. As he waits, Mauricio does a quick list of pros and cons. Con: she is his personal assistant, and therefore the risk of problems arising multiplies dangerously. Sexual harassment charges, for one. He's heard some stories that made his hair stand on end. Another con: she's the best secretary he's ever had. When it all goes bad, as will happen sooner or later, he won't only be left without romance, but also without an assistant. Another con: she is a highly intelligent, competitive woman, the kind who doesn't do something for nothing. A minefield. He isn't up for challenges, he's just looking for a little tenderness. In short, a ton of cons. But, noblesse oblige, there is also a pro: the chick is incredibly hot, really and truly. Hot enough to overcome all the cons.

Soledad pokes her head in again.

"It's Ruso. Should I tell him you're here?"

Mauricio makes an expression that reads *of course*. Which firms up his image as a loyal friend. Every little bit helps. Soledad closes the door from outside while he picks up the receiver. These lists of pros and cons are pointless, because they never solve anything. Finally he'll have to act on impulse, as always. And he does pretty well with that. Usually.

"Hello, Ruso, what's up?"

"Hello, Mauri." The voice on the other end sounds agitated. "It's me, with a new problem. I got a letter in the mail."

"From who?"

"The owners of the place in Morón."

"Ah. What does it say? That you pay the back rent, blah blah blah blah, I'm guessing?"

"Yes . . ." Ruso stammers a few words as he locates the paragraph he's looking for. ". . . hereby warned of possible legal actions . . ."

"Yes, Ruso. I know. Pay them no mind."

"Really?"

"Don't worry. I'm already on it."

There is a pause. Then Ruso's voice is almost back to normal.

"What a relief, Mauri. I was shitting bricks when I got it. They left it at the house, too, and Mónica saw it. You wouldn't believe the scene she made."

"You know how chicks can be."

"I tried to explain! But—"

"Don't worry. They'll call me and we'll work it out then."

"You sure?"

"Yes, Rusito. Relax. How's the car wash going?"

"Eh . . . What do I know? It's going. To top it all off, it hasn't rained in a month. Business is down a little."

Mauricio weighs the phrase "down a little." If business was terrible before, he'd rather not imagine what "down a little" means.

"Anyway," continues Ruso. "Me and Cristo have a theory that if things keep up like this, a ton of car washes are going to have to close down."

Starting with yours, nutjob, thinks Mauricio, but he is careful not to say it.

"Another thing, man."

"What, Ruso?"

"The other day Fernando came to see me, about the Pittilanga business."

Mauricio snorts.

"And?"

"And nothing. Since you told him you didn't want to keep . . . To see what I thought . . ."

"And what did you tell him, Ruso?"

"I—that I don't know."

Mauricio relaxes. Thank goodness he's Ruso. Salt of the earth, with the willpower of flan and the self-discipline of an infant.

"You did good, Ruso. That's a waste of time. There's nothing to be done. And the longer it takes him to understand that, the worse off he'll be. And us."

"Thing is I think I kinda offended him, maybe . . ."

"Pay him no mind, Ruso. It's always the same with Fernando. You do what he says or we're all just a bunch of fools. Or traitors."

"That's what I thought! He looked at me like I was letting him down."

"Pay him no mind. Listen to me. Sooner or later he'll understand. But if you go along with him it'll be worse, because he's going to keep driving you crazy."

"That's what Mónica tells me, too."

Of course. The poor woman must be desperate. Married to a good-for-nothing unable to set up a coherent business, the last thing she must want, on top of it all, is for him to get distracted with other people's failures. They say goodbye promising they'll see each other soon. After hanging up, he dials Soledad's internal number.

"And the coffees, Miss Secretary?"

"Didn't you say you were going to go to Williams's office and then we'd have them, Counselor?"

Mauricio smiles.

"You know what? I need that coffee. Let Williams wait."

Inequalities

When Mono had to come clean about how much compensation he could get for leaving the Swiss laboratory, the night when he updated them on his plan, he said it timidly, almost embarrassed. Fernando knew why. Of the four, Mono was the one, by far, who earned the most. Mauricio wasn't doing too badly either, quite the contrary. Things were getting better and better for him, but only recently was he making good money. He had graduated from law school around the same time Mono graduated in engineering, but he hadn't had the same luck as his friend, and he hadn't been helped along by the same talent. He worked like crazy. Holidays and weekends. Now, he was settling into a big office, his bosses thought highly of him, and his future seemed to be opening out wide and happy. In any case Mono's qualms had nothing to do with Mauricio, who wasn't even there that night. They had to do with Ruso and Fernando. The poor ones in the group. And by a long shot. Fernando didn't know for sure how much his brother was earning, and he would never put him in a difficult position by asking. But comparing a systems manager's salary with a high school teacher's was almost ridiculous. And Ruso . . . well, his case was a serious one.

Sometimes Fernando was curious about how their friendship could continue when their lives had taken such different paths. As boys everything was more even, more predictable. They had grown up in the suburban middle class that filled Castelar in the seventies. And all of them, more or less, continued in that same undistinguished social position. Fathers who were office workers, shopkeepers, laborers, almost all the mothers housewives. That was their story and everybody else's. But now, thirty years later, their realities had nothing in common with each other. To take an easy example, the living room of the house Mono was renting but hadn't yet decided to buy, where they were sitting that night, was about the same size as the little condominium house that had belonged to their grandmother and where Fernando now lived. And yet you couldn't say that their friendship had suffered because of that. They still talked the same way. They shared the same way. They enjoyed the same things, and in the same way. Almost always. Except in moments like this, when Mono was embarrassed that his potential severance pay could be such a large chunk of change that it would set Ruso adrift in the wide ocean of incredulity and silence.

In any case, Ruso emerged easily from those turbulent waters. First he let out a brief "ha." Almost immediately he added a "ha-ha." And a volley of "ha-ha-ra-ha-ha." And that start of a guffaw was enough to tempt Mono to join in with Ruso's laughter. And it went on like that until they both ended up in a symphony of chortles that Fernando, from experience, knew he shouldn't try to interrupt, although anyone in their right mind would have considered it more useful to continue the conversation about what Mono was telling them and its consequences and repercussions. He also wouldn't interrupt because he knew it would only lead to them turning him into the butt of the joke, and the spiral of lunatic laughter would go on forever.

So he remained silent, watching them crack up. Because, anyway, he thought, much as he hated to admit it, those two laughing together was always a sight worth watching.

10.

Fernando goes into his house and tosses his backpack on the table. The muffled sound it makes reminds him that it holds two hundred written exams he should grade before Monday. Resigned, he heads to the kitchen and puts the kettle on. When he gets back he notices the light on his answering machine blinking. "Hello, Fernando. It's Nicolás, from Palm Tree Productions. Give me a call when you can." The final straw to ruin his weekend is that call.

He pulls the first pile of tests and a red pen out of his backpack. The bad news continues, because that stack is the fourth-year afternoon class, which is so big and so doltish correcting their papers will take his entire life. To complete the bleak picture, the one on top is Jonathan Vallejo's. Actually he's not sure if his last name is Vallejo or Vallejos, since Jonathan sometimes writes it with the *s* and sometimes without, depending on how his day is going or the mood he's in. Answer No. 1: "They think that it was them on the trak but it was'nt. Yesterday they found them and realissed that it was'nt them." First he circles the four spelling mistakes and adds the commas that Vallejo/Vallejos has left out. Then he underlines the theys and thems, to show the pupil that it is impossible to determine whom the theys and thems refer to.

Nicolás from Palm Tree Productions. Tangible proof that he, Fernando Raguzzi, is an imbecile. After filming ten of Presidente Mitre's games without Pittilanga scoring a single goal, he'd had the genius idea of faking the videos. Usually Pittilanga kicked the ball toward the goal two or three times in each game. So, if there were a way to turn those unimpressive shots—which usually ended up sailing over the crossbar or into the goalkeeper's hands—into shots into the corners of the goal or into surefire headers, maybe some unsuspecting investor would be willing to buy the forward's transfer. Fernando mentioned the idea to Ruso, who went into a fever pitch of enthusiasm and in turn told Cristo, who, infected with the same fervor, put him in touch with Palm Tree Productions. Now, as he advances with difficulty through the snarl of idiocies and errors that Vallejo/Vallejos committed on his exam, Fernando reproaches himself for having followed that chain of recommendations. But now it's too late. He's in it up to his neck.

The first time he talked with this Nicolás—owner, manager, secretary, and sole employee of the company—the guy assured him that the job could be done for twelve hundred pesos. Fernando had accepted the price. Three weeks later, when he saw the finished job, he wanted to kill himself, but not before finishing off the genius of computer animation. It was such a clumsy, obvious job that you could tell it was fake from a mile away. The ball made suspicious parabolas, the faces of the players didn't correspond at all to the ball's supposed trajectory, and—worst of all—when the ball went into the goal the net didn't show the slightest movement. When Fernando pointed this out to him, Nicolás reviewed the tape with some puzzlement and the best he could do was nod with an "oh, clearly." Fernando had thought, *No, it's not clear at all, you son of a bitch,* but he hadn't said a word.

In retrospect, that would have been the right moment to tell him off, slap the owner-manager-operator of Palm Tree Productions a few times to blow off steam, and take his business elsewhere. But he didn't. First of all, because he hadn't raised a hand to anyone since he was fifteen, and second, because his indecisiveness made him nip the angry impulse in the bud, as often happened to him.

He finishes marking Vallejo's/Vallejos's exam and gives him a two out of a possible ten. *Boy, is he thick.* He puts it to one side and immerses himself in the next one. He sucks his teeth. This one is Murúa's, but Murúa still hasn't learned to write his name with a capital *M* and an accent mark, so he presents himself to the world as "murua." So you can easily imagine what the rest of his exam looks like.

He opens up his phone book, stretches for the phone, and dials the number of Palm Tree Productions. Naturally, the call is answered by Nicolás himself.

"Hello, this is Fernando Raguzzi."

"Ah, hello, Fernando! I left you a message today!"

Fernando wonders whether the guy is actually an imbecile or just pretends to be one. Isn't it obvious he's returning his call?

"I'm listening."

"I was thinking, you know . . . about this business of the goal not looking completely natural."

"Not completely natural," repeats Fernando to himself. This clown is a true optimist.

"Yeah. And?"

"I was talking with some guys who have a production company, too. And I told them about it. And they thought of something that could save us."

"What?"

"Instead of faking Pittilanga's goals, use the team's real goals and fake the player. I mean, put Pittilanga in the place of the player who scores the goal. Are you following me?"

Something tells Fernando it would be better not to follow him. But he follows him anyway.

"And you're telling me that it's going to look good . . . ?"

"It's gonna look awesome. I swear."

"And how much is this going to cost?"

He finishes the question and regrets it. Because if the previous job was a disaster, but he paid him punctually anyway, this Nicolás should repair the disaster without charging him again. But in his recklessness he had left the door open and the guy slipped right through.

"The work would be done by those guys I told you about. The ones from the other production company . . . I think that with a grand, a grand and a half, we're cool."

"How much?!"

"I'm not charging you anything, eh . . . That money is what they're asking me for. I'm doing my part as a favor . . ."

Fernando swallows hard and sighs loudly. He thinks. What if this doesn't work? Desperation leads him to accept the offer. They say goodbye and hang up. Fernando picks up Murúa's exam—or murua's, according to him. Just reading the first two answers is enough to show him that, next to Murúa/murua, Vallejo/Vallejos is a brainiac.

To Be

"Do you know what I could do with a golden handshake of two hundred thousand dollars, Monito?" asked Ruso, bright-eyed and panting from laughing so hard.

"Yes, Ruso. You could screw up a lot of shit with money like that," Fernando answered for his brother.

They looked at each other. There wasn't the slightest hint of offense in Ruso's expression. He turned to focus on Mono again, who did the same. And they started laughing like lunatics again, stopping every once in a while to say, Yeah, Fer was right, Ruso could make two hundred thousand screwups with that kind of dough.

At long last, when they were breathless, Fernando decided it was the right moment to continue.

"It is a good chunk of change, but . . ."

"But?"

"But I don't see the advantage to getting let go, Monito. I don't know. It seems like a much better idea to take the promotion they're offering you."

Mono pursed his lips, rubbed his hands together, and kept his eyes low, as if his older brother's words were dead-on but incomplete. Fernando looked at Ruso, who added, in an identical tone, "It's true, Mono. No matter how much money it is. I mean, looks like you'll be raking it in working with the Mexicans. Right?"

"Yes. That's true." Mono nodded reluctantly. "But remember that I'll have to be traveling. Coming and going, here and there all the time. And it's going to make everything complicated, not just with Guadalupe."

"What is gonna get complicated? Besides your daughter, I mean . . ."

"Everything, Ruso. Everything is gonna get more complicated. Visiting my mom, seeing you guys, going to the games, everything. I'm good now. I don't want more headaches. You know what I mean?"

"Yeah, sure." Ruso never liked to contradict anyone, much less his best friend.

For a minute they remained in silence, each of them engrossed in his own thoughts.

"What do you think?"

Mono directed the question right at his brother like a whiplash, certain that Fernando was bothered by something and it was best he got it off his chest as soon as possible.

"Don't worry about Mom and the traveling. I'm always around."

"I know that, bud. But you look like something's on your mind. Is anything bugging you?"

"Yes, Mono. I can read you like a book. And I know you're playing dumb. There's something you're not saying, because otherwise it makes no sense."

"What doesn't make sense?"

"None of it, Monito. You went into a meeting thinking they were going to fire you. You come out of the meeting with a promotion and a raise. But here we are in your house and it's not like 'let's party!' We're here because you have something to tell us. Go ahead, fool. Tell us and be done with it. But stop beating around the bush."

The silence returned, until Ruso spoke again.

"This one should have been a psychologist, don't you think?"

"Uh-huh. He would be rolling in it. Or a priest. You ever thought about becoming a priest, Fernandito?"

Fernando smiled.

"I'm not that perceptive. It's just you guys are so damn stupid I can see right through you."

Ruso let out an exclamation of fake indignation and looked at Mono, expecting him to follow suit, but that wasn't the case. His friend was still highly focused, tense, as if making up his mind once and for all to start speaking.

"Look, Fernando. You've known me since the day I was born," he began.

"Exactly."

"Okay. If you had to say what I am, what would you say?"

Fernando turned toward Ruso.

"Don't look at Ruso. Just answer me. I mean . . . For example, I don't know . . . Mauricio is a lawyer. You ask: What's Mauricio? And you answer: lawyer. With you, same thing. Fernando is a teacher. And not because that's your job now. It's always been that way. I don't know if you know what I mean."

"No."

"Yes you do, don't act dumb. We were kids and you always knew everything. And we'd mess with you, asking you things and you always answered. Or you tried to. As if you were born to be a teacher. It was something you always had. Now do you understand me?"

"I guess so."

"Same with Mauricio. Always landing on his feet. Always with an argument, that guy."

"Always underhanded," added Ruso.

"Yeah, that too," conceded Mono. "Same thing."

"What about me?" Ruso asked with such enthusiasm, such naïveté, that Fernando thought, like so many other times, that the only thing to do with Ruso was give him a kiss on the forehead. "What am I?"

"You are . . . forget about it, Ruso." Mono didn't want to get off track, otherwise he never would have missed an opportunity like that to crack a joke. He continued talking to Fernando. "That's what I'm asking you. What am I?"

Fernando took a second. What did he want him to answer? He said the first thing he could think of.

"A systems engineer."

"Nooooooo! Not in a million years!" Mono stood up, as if he couldn't continue advancing his arguments without the help of movement. "You say that because you can't think of what to say. You know how I chose working in systems. I've told you a thousand times."

"Should I tell the story again?" asked Ruso excitedly.

"I don't know where you're going with this, Monito, I—"

"What am I? And don't say engineer. I look as much like an engineer as I do a geisha."

"Should I bring you your kimono?"

"Shut up, Ruso. Am I right or am I right?" Mono took Fernando's silence as agreement. "Okay. So I'm not an engineer. What am I?"

Fernando searched for support, even fleeting, from Ruso. But Ruso just looked at him, obviously desperate to avoid any accountability.

"You don't know!" concluded Mono. "Do you realize that? You can't answer me. Don't worry, it's not your fault. It's me. That's the point."

11.

Before knocking on the door, Mauricio stops in front of the mirror to check the knot in his tie and the fold of his handkerchief in the upper pocket of his suit coat. Mariel had been right when she suggested he buy that brown tie with the matching handkerchief. His wife had an infallible instinct for stuff like that. He congratulates himself on having taken her advice. Well, actually he always listens to her in such matters. If Mariel tells him that mint green goes well with navy blue, he goes for it. With blind faith. After all, she always listens to his advice, and in areas that Mauricio likes to consider less trivial than the sartorial. That kind of complementing each other is the secret to a happy marriage. Separate areas, ambits, realms: the key to avoiding useless fights.

He knocks on the door and listens, but the answer is slow in coming. Mauricio hesitates. Should he insist and risk looking anxious? Wait in silence like a pushover? It also occurs to him that Williams might not have heard him. Unlikely. Never mind that Williams is always going around his office with a distracted air and obscure gestures. Mauricio is convinced the absentmindedness is an act, and that nothing escapes his consideration and his reach.

"Come in," says Williams's voice, finally, and Mauricio congratulates himself for having waited.

"Good morning, Humberto. Soledad told me you needed to speak with me."

"Yes . . . come in, Mauricio." Williams motions toward a seat, but his gestures always have a trace of indolence, as if made with the least possible effort, with minimal energy, just barely enough to be perceived. "It's nothing urgent . . ."

Mauricio makes himself comfortable, lifts his pant cuff slightly to keep it from wrinkling, and crosses his legs, but being careful not to get too settled. In that office the only one with the right to make himself at home is Williams.

"The other day . . . You want a coffee?" he interrupts himself and leans a hand on the intercom. "Yes, Elena, two coffees, mine as usual, and for Mauricio . . ."

"A little milk, and sweetener."

"A little milk and sweetener, Elena."

Williams hangs up, while Mauricio makes a solemn promise to himself to, at some point, exercise that offhand command over beings and things. Williams smiles.

"Yesterday I was in court and ran into Coco Sanlúcar. He spoke wonders about you."

Mauricio smiles with an expression that strives for modesty. "The truth is that case was pretty complicated."

"Well, Coco told me you handled yourself perfectly. He told me . . ."

Williams pauses when the secretary comes in with the tray and the coffees. He isn't saying anything confidential, but Mauricio likes that silence. As if Sanlúcar's praise were more personal that way.

"He told me, 'Tito'—Coco is a friend from grade school, so I have to tolerate that dreadful nickname, but what can I do, we've known each other for so many years—'that guy representing the Las Tunas Shipping case is phenomenal.'"

"Well, Humberto, thank you very much."

Williams barely tastes his coffee and puts the cup down on its saucer. Mauricio has seen him do that a hundred times, and it still strikes him; his suburban middle-class complex doesn't allow him to leave things half drunk. Even that gesture of tiny waste is a subtle vehicle for Williams to exercise his authority. Or is it that Mauricio is dazzled like a little boy before abundance and power?

"Don't thank me, you more than deserve it. Tell me something." He looks at him. For the first time in the meeting Williams looks directly at him. "What do you think of that Sabino guy?"

Mauricio is slightly surprised and almost disappointed, because he would have liked the conversation to continue being about him, about the compliments Judge Sanlúcar had gushed onto his lucky personage. But he recovers.

"He's good. Very good. He's responsible, dedicated . . . I have no complaints."

"Wonderful, Mauricio. I want you to keep giving him more rope. Let him take on more."

Mauricio is dying to ask why, but he restrains himself. It's better to be satisfied with understanding what Williams is keeping quiet, in addition to what he's saying. It would be nice if he said, "Put Sabino to the test because before too long we're going to make you a partner and he'll have to take over your clients." And to be able to respond with a shout of joy, with an effusive handshake, or raising his arms in celebration like at a sporting match. But that kind of enthusiasm wasn't well looked upon in Williams's world. This is the way things are here. An elegance that doesn't require projecting your voice. These types don't feign superiority. They hold up their supremacy as a right, as a lifelong habit. That's why it's so natural, so offhand. It doesn't come naturally to Mauricio. He grew up in Castelar, his dad was a banker and his mom is a retired teacher. Doesn't matter. He'll learn.

Returning

The telephone rang, but none of the three guys went for it. The click of the answering machine was heard, but whoever was calling didn't leave a message. Fernando didn't know if he should speak or remain silent. What was wrong with being a systems engineer? He didn't fully understand his younger brother's identity crisis. But he remained quiet, going against his habit of filling uneasy silences with words, and waited for Mono to get where he needed to go.

"Don't look at me like that, Fernando. Understand me instead of making that face. I feel . . . I've been feeling for a while . . ." Mono moved his hands, groping around in the air in front of him without finding the words he was looking for there, either. "You know when you get lost? When you go somewhere and you get lost? You don't realize it at the time. It's not like you turn a corner and say, 'Here, right here, I'm getting lost.' Otherwise you wouldn't get lost. It doesn't work like that. You get lost but you don't realize you're getting lost. You keep going and going, thinking that you more or less know where you're headed, until you get to a point where you stop and say, 'I'm lost, I don't have the slightest fucking idea where I am.' Well. That's where I'm at."

Fernando nodded but didn't say a word. And not only because he didn't want to interrupt his brother, now that he seemed to have found an opening—although that was also true—but because he was surprised. He wasn't ready for such an introspective speech. Or, to be more specific, for that speech to come from Mono. If he'd heard the same thing from Mauricio's lips, he wouldn't have had a problem with it. Mauricio was enough of a brooder to come up with something like that. But Mono? Since when did he reach such heights of abstraction? Hearing him talk like that was like witnessing Ruso monologue on Sartrean existentialism. They were simple guys. A simplicity that both appealed to Fernando and amazed him. Fernando admired that about them. There was no affectation. No complication. They called a spade a spade. Fernando adored them, precisely for that simplicity, because they were the closest thing he knew to purity, even though it sounded trite to his ears every time he thought of it in those terms.

"And the fact that you can't tell me what the hell I am confirms what I'm thinking. You understand? And I wasn't always like this. Now I am. Or I have been for a few years. Fourteen, to be exact."

Fernando was beginning to understand. For years he hadn't stopped to think about it. He felt bad for Mono. Perhaps, if he had realized, he could have asked him, he could have listened to him.

"I *was*, you understand? When we were juniors in high school. As seniors. I—what was I?"

"A soccer player."

Fernando barely stammered out those words, but there was no need for him to repeat them because all three of them had thought the same thing. They grew silent again. Perhaps what had occurred to Fernando had also crossed Ruso's mind. That sudden sadness at finding, in the depths of a friend's soul, a pain so old and so vivid.

"There you have it. Did you see how easily you came up with it? I was a soccer player. I was number four. Right full-back. I played in the Vélez minors. I played in the sixth division. I played in fifth. I played in fourth. That's what I was, Fernando. A player. The thing is I stopped being that. Ever since those pricks released me from my contract, I never was a player again. The problem is that was the last thing I was. After that I haven't been anything."

"Stop. Stop for a second." Suddenly Fernando had lost his compassion and respect for his brother's grief. "You have a daughter who adores you."

"I'm not talking about that."

"And what are you talking about?"

"I'm talking about me as a person. About me and my things."

"Your things? Perfect: look at the house you have."

"I rent it."

"You could buy it if you wanted to, Mono. Look at the car you have. Give me a break."

"Don't come back pointing to the money. You've known me forever, Fernando. You know I don't give two shits about money."

"Now all of a sudden you're a philanthropist." Fernando hadn't even finished saying it when he already started regretting it. What had he just said? His comment was not only unfair, it was horrible. Mono had showed them a thousand times that he was far from obsessed with money. He liked having it. He enjoyed spending it, like anyone. But he had never been stingy or materialistic. Why had Fernando responded like that?

"I interrupted you. Go on," he finally said, backing down. For Fernando, it was the closest to an apology they could expect.

"That's it. For almost twenty years I've been stumbling around," Mono went on, staring at his brother. "And I couldn't care less if between one stumble and the next I made a ton of dough. I don't want to live like this for the rest of my life. I want to do something else. I want to be something again. Do you understand?"

There was no latitude for continuing the debate.

"Yes. I understand."

"Tell us the rest," urged Ruso, leaning forward in his armchair, as if he knew that the juiciest part was still to come.

Fernando realized that the whole meeting was designed just to convince him of whatever it was Mono had up his sleeve. Ruso, as always, was a loyal soldier to Mono's cause. It didn't matter what the cause was.

"Go on, Monito. Tell me the rest," conceded Fernando, resigned.

"I'm a little old to begin a new career. I'm not going to start inventing something now."

"Of course."

"And it's not like I need to go looking for a calling. I already have a calling. I always have."

"Aha. I guess you're going to try out as a fullback for Excursionistas . . . I mean, take up where you left off."

"No, dummy. Although I tell you, with the crappy soccer they play nowadays . . . There's all kinds of losers playing first-string . . . But no. I know that at thirty-seven I'm not gonna make it as a pro player."

"So?"

"Wait. I'm getting there. What I'm saying is that is what's mine. My world. That field."

"You're going to study to become a manager?"

"No! Or maybe, but not now. That would be something long-term. I want to make the change now."

"What change? What do you want to get into?"

Mono and Ruso exchanged a look that made Fernando understand the dramatic revelation was at hand. He prepared himself for the worst.

"Do you remember Polaco Salvatierra?"

"Oh, God," was all that Fernando could articulate when he heard that name. Because he had understood.

12.

Ruso knows he's got his work cut out for him. He's coming off of a 3–1 loss in the first game and Chamaco's set up a game plan with a lot of defenders, hard to break through. Behind him he hears someone banging on the counter for service and, still pressing joystick buttons and without taking his eyes off the screen, he shouts to Cristo to please deal with the customer. This is a key moment. His killer play, as he calls it. A run deep into the corner with his right winger, who cuts inside his defender and dribbles toward the box, then shoots to the far post. And what's more he'd better hurry, because a 1–0 score isn't enough. He darts a quick look at Chamaco. God damn him. He's blessed by the gods. He is a wizard at PlayStation. Ruso has to bust his balls to beat him. Sometimes, when he envies his skill, he tries to console himself with the idea that Chamaco is from a different generation, that those kids grew up around computers and he had to learn as an adult. Again he hears someone banging on the counter.

"Come on, Cristo! Are you deaf? Help the customer, I'm busy, you idiot!"

Just then Chamaco turns his head and freezes, looking toward the desk. Ruso doesn't see him, because he is at a crucial point in his game. He is so concentrated that he doesn't notice his opponent has stopped moving his joystick. Ruso's forward enters the penalty box, swerves past the two defenders, and scores. Ruso shouts out his goal and dedicates it to Chamaco.

Only then does he see that the other has disengaged from the game and is looking behind him, behind his back. He turns, too.

There, standing on the other side of the counter, is Mónica. Ruso's cheering stops abruptly, his thoughts freeze up. He stands and walks over to her.

"What's up, babe? What brings you here?"

His wife doesn't answer. She looks at him as sternly as she can muster and hands him a piece of paper. Ruso can see it's an official letter.

"Ah, Moni. Don't worry about that. It's from the owners of the place in Morón. I already saw Mauricio about that the other day. He told me there was no problem."

"No," responds his wife, and she keeps holding out the paper. "It's from the credit card."

Now Ruso takes the paper and reads it. It's true. The terms are similar. Hereby warned, payment required, blah blah blah.

"Yes, you're right. But it's the same . . ."

Mónica is tight-lipped. She looks over Ruso's shoulder at Chamaco who, realizing he's in the way, makes a quick exit toward the washing floor.

"How long are we going to keep up like this, Daniel, do you mind telling me?"

Ruso weighs a few possible answers.

"What do you mean 'like this'?" he finally murmurs, and the second it is out of his mouth he realizes it wasn't a wise choice.

"Are you pulling my leg? Don't you realize what's going on?"

"Don't I realize . . ."

"We're up to our eyeballs in debt! And you act as if nothing's wrong, Daniel!"

"Why do you say I act as if nothing's wrong?"

"Because you're playing video games with one of your employees, for fuck's sake!"

Ruso swallows hard as he thinks how Mónica, who never curses, must be at her wit's end to say such a thing.

"Just because I'm playing—"

"You're playing video games and the wolves are at the door! You have two daughters, Daniel! Two daughters! How long are you going to keep this up?"

Ruso shifts his weight from one leg to the other, uncomfortable. He extends one hand off to the side.

"Don't get like that, Moni. Sooner or later, this is going to change, you'll—"

"That's enough, Daniel! Enough lying! Sooner or later? Don't you realize you're going to run this business into the ground, too? Like all the others!"

"You'll see, I won't."

"You will! What do you think happens to a business where the owner spends all day playing video games with his employees?"

"And what do you want me to do while we wait for customers?"

"While you wait for customers we're going broke, Daniel! Or can't you see that?"

Ruso still has his hand extended, pointing to the washing area, but the words don't come out. Cristo is there, polishing a black Toyota. Chamaco and Molina are sitting on the wooden bench, waiting for another car to come in. Ruso doesn't see anything wrong with the business. It's not bringing in much, that's true, but he prefers to think it's getting off the ground slowly, and that things will get better. He starts to say that to Mónica, stammering, but she cuts him off.

"Enough. I can't take anymore. I put up with a lot. I put up with it all from you. But I've reached my limit. If you won't do it for me, do it for the girls."

His wife's eyes fill with tears and Ruso wants to die. There is nothing worse for him than seeing her cry. He feels like garbage. He lifts the wooden countertop so he can go from one side to the other but she stops him with a motion.

"No. Don't come near me. I'm begging you. Just one thing," she tilts her head sadly toward the car wash. "For our sake, do something."

And without giving him time to answer, she leaves with a slam of the door that makes the armored glass tremble. Ruso scratches his head and looks around. It's hard for him to understand such pessimism. It's true things are slow, but he doesn't think it's anything to get alarmed about. Sooner or later things have to pick up. There's the television, with the game paused. He wonders if it's wrong to shout over to Chamaco to come and finish the game. But then he remembers Mónica's tears and turns off the console, as he thinks that, lately, life has been foisting some dramatic lessons on him: his friends don't live forever and Mónica's patience has an end.

Entrepreneurs

Two days after the conversation that night when Mono explained his plans to his older brother, he showed up with Ruso to a meeting he had set up at Salvatierra's house.

Polaco received them in a white linen suit that was now a bit big for him, as if it missed the boom years and the dazzling girls, too. He offered them beer, sodas, iced tea. Mono accepted a soda. Ruso chose the tea: even though he hated tea, he had never been offered it cold and was curious.

The armchairs were large, covered in white leather. They weren't entirely comfortable, because they were very low and the cushions slid when you moved. Ruso took forever to find a more or less stable position. Then he realized that holding a glass of iced tea, which was beginning to sweat, made things even more complicated.

Mono cleared his throat and made a gesture with his hand that swept the room they were in.

"Nice decoration, Polaco. Did you do it?"

The host took a quick glance around, as if the visitor's comment made him notice, for the first time, the walls and their ornamentation. They were painted white. The ceiling was high, typical of older homes. On the largest wall was a gigantic poster of the Argentine national team at the Youth World Cup in Qatar. The selection of that photo wasn't arbitrary. Three of those players had been represented by Polaco, when he was blessed by luck and the future promised abundance and success. On the other walls were framed soccer jerseys, all original, some from Argentine clubs and others from European clubs. Written across them with wide black markers were autographs of the players who had worn them, who naturally had all also been Polaco's clients. Ruso sipped his tea, looking dumbstruck at that mural-sized résumé Salvatierra had designed to cater to his self-esteem and dazzle his occasional visitors.

"The other day," said Mono, cutting to the chase, "when we bumped into each other in the butcher shop, you told me you're still involved in the world of soccer . . ."

"Yes." Polaco settled into his armchair, as if talking about business required a more relaxed posture. "Really, I don't know what your idea was, what you guys know about the business, if what you are thinking about is investing . . ."

"Honestly, I haven't decided. Not yet. I want you to give me some advice about that, since you are an agent—"

"Entrepreneur," interrupted Polaco. "Just for the record, the term that best describes me is entrepreneur. An agent is limited to agenting, to representing players in exchange for a commission. An entrepreneur has other functions. Sometimes he agents. In fact, many of us started out that way. But an entrepreneur combines those functions of representation with others that are . . . shall we say . . . I'd call it proprietary. Buying, selling, lending players, mediating between clubs . . . Which is to say, managing the capital that is the players. Investing, in a word. I don't know if I'm making myself clear."

"Crystal clear," conceded Ruso, who was grossed out by the iced tea but kept drinking it so as not to offend his host.

"That's why I was asking you guys—"

"Ask him the questions," said Ruso, stopping him. "He's the one with three hundred thousand dollars. I'm broker than the ten commandments."

Salvatierra turned toward Mono with an admiring expression. Mono felt the need to clarify.

"I come to this with a severance package and some money I've been saving up."

"To start out, three hundred grand is nothing to sneer at, Mono. Not at all."

"You mean to start out with an investment . . ." said Mono.

"Because in the long term, that's what makes money. The other is a lot of work and a little cash, you know what I mean?"

"That's what I've been telling him," Ruso bragged, detaching the lemon wedge from the rim of his glass to suck on it.

"But that's not how you started out." Mono wanted to start small. Understand it.

"Because I didn't have a dime!" He laughed, condescendingly. "But I made the real dough buying and selling players."

"And you didn't do too bad," interrupted Ruso, excited, and underscoring his point by miming someone laying slabs or sections. "First you were an agent, then an entrepreneur . . . and so on."

Ruso stopped, somewhat startled, and the others joined him in an uncomfortable silence when they realized that what followed after "agent" and "entrepreneur" was "criminal," "convict," and "their host in his mother's house."

"It went good until it went bad." Salvatierra adopted the sincerely contrite tone of someone who can't sidestep his debacle. "Look: I never talk about that stuff, but the confidence you are showing me by coming here demands frankness." He paused, as if chewing on his imminent confessions. Finally, he seemed to make up his mind. "My business grew fast. Too fast. I guess . . . I guess I didn't choose my friends well. Or to put it better: I chose them terribly. By the time I realized it, I couldn't get out without it looking like I was stabbing them in the back. I had to man up when I drew the short straw."

He swiped his hand in front of his own face, as if to shoo away a fly or bad memories. Then he continued.

"Don't hesitate, Mono. As an agent you work like a dog and they use you like a doormat. The players, the managers, the families—everybody. As an entrepreneur, the ball is in your court. If you really have some capital, don't think twice."

Mono placed the glass of soda down on a paper napkin, so as not to dampen the coffee table.

"And . . . what should I do to get started?"

"We have two basic options," began Polaco, ignoring the saccharine admiration that grew, clearly, in his listeners. "Investing in a percentage participation in a more expensive player or buying a less expensive player outright. Remember," he raised a finger and looked at them alternately, "when I say less expensive I don't mean less valuable. Not at all."

He stood up, walked over to the wall with the giant poster, and ran his hand over it as if wiping off a stain or a spiderweb from the face of one of the players.

"I mean, if you come and say to me, 'Look, Polaco, I want to invest in Pocho Insúa' (just an example, because Pocho isn't mine, of course) . . . How much is Pocho worth these days? Three mill? Okay, do the math: supposing someone wants to sell you ten percent of Insúa, you can buy it. But forget about being in charge of what happens to him. I don't know if I'm making myself clear."

"And the other option?" Mono understands that it was the more advisable, but he wanted to hear all the details, to see if they matched his intuition.

"The other is buying a hundred percent of a kid on his way up. But not just any kid. A kid that you get starting out, before his first contract, and sell him to Europe two years later for a ton of dough. I don't know if you're following me: in that case, who do you think is the full owner of that ton of dough?"

He ran his hands through his hair, combing it back with his fingers. He was just as blond and toothy as he'd been at eight years old.

"In the end it's the old question of what's better for you, being a small fish in a big pond or . . . That's up to you."

"I guess I understand." Mono adopted an expression that he thought was the height of astuteness.

"I'll break it down for you," Salvatierra announced, with a dramatic pause that gave Ruso time to finish sucking the lemon rind and drop it into his empty glass. "You need to buy Mario Juan Bautista Pittilanga."

13.

For almost an entire year, Fernando has devoted all his efforts to selling Pittilanga. He has always been struck by the expression many journalists used when referring to the transfers of players. They often say that such and such a player has been "offered" to this club, "offered" to that investment group, "offered" to some coach over there. That "offering" sounded, to Fernando's ears, like humiliation, usury, exploitation. But after six months of failing with exquisite perfection, he is also offering Pittilanga as if he were a set of pots and pans or a raffle ticket for the Neighborhood Development Association.

At first he carefully selected the people he spoke with, seeking out the few he had heard of from sports journalists. The problem was that they wouldn't see him, not even their associates or assistants. He met with young guys whose suits were still too new, who warded off their panic with tanning beds, abundant hair gel, and cell phones with implausible functions. Apprentices whose weight in the organization they claimed to represent was equivalent to a rowboat in the Royal Navy. But on closer inspection, this turned out to be good news, especially in the beginning. Fernando was so inexperienced that it was better he suffer through his absurd stammering with those rookies, who were as cobbled together as he was. The situation had its comic side: a language arts teacher trying to sell a player he didn't believe in, for a price he wasn't worth, to a Johnny-come-lately who didn't want to buy him, but who wouldn't even have known how to go about it if he did.

Over time Fernando has improved. He shortens the introductions, adopts less frightened body language, limits his politeness so it won't be interpreted as a sign of weakness, and learns to attribute invented virtues to Pittilanga without his voice trembling. Yet by the time he learns it is already too late. He is so far down the list of potential buyers that all that's left are the impromptu, the wet behind the ears, and the shameless. The worst part of it all is that not even among that fauna is there any interest in Pittilanga. Not by a long shot. They often end up offering him players, putting their lies ahead of Fernando's, trying to dazzle him with their own little colored mirrors.

At first his faith, or his desperation, was so high, that he preferred to ask for unpaid leave from his school to have all day without distraction from classes or evaluations. But as the days and the weeks passed, his delusions dwindled along with his savings. After the first month he restarted his job on the morning shift, although he consoled himself by thinking that soccer entrepreneurs mostly attend to their business in the afternoons. Halfway through the third month he started teaching afternoon classes again, betting on making appointments after six or seven.

Sooner or later he is going to sell him. Success is near at hand, around the corner, behind the next armored glass door, hidden behind the crimson smile of the next secretary. And after success would come revenge. The sweet revenge of calling Mauricio and telling him, *Draw me up the papers. Pittilanga is sold*, and hanging up almost immediately, leaving him alone with his shock and shame. And when she grows up, and is able to understand and value it, telling Guadalupe. She'll think her uncle is a hero. These images, endlessly re-created, console him in his inertia until six months have passed, until it becomes clear that it's not true, that he'll never succeed. Not with selling Pittilanga, not with humiliating Mauricio. He won't ever have his triumphant victory, or his niece's admiring gaze.

He keeps trying, because he's never been good at admitting his defects and mistakes. Every time with less energy, with less realism, more aware of the conclusion, more sunken into the jungle of hustlers the soccer world tolerates as a side effect of its generous ups and downs.

He sees his friends every once in a while. On their birthdays, their wives' and Ruso's twins' birthdays, plus a dinner each month, just the three of them. The equivalent, for them, of not seeing each other at all. No one says anything about the argument they had in the cafe, or about the things that were said, the things that weren't said, the things they each thought later. No one says anything about Pittilanga and his hard luck in Santiago del Estero, either.

In all that time, Fernando manages to see his niece barely four times. Mono's ex is particularly testy, and does all she can to sabotage the meetings. On three of those occasions he brings Guadalupe to see her grandmother. The first time is a bit difficult. Fernando has to buttress his mother again and again so that she doesn't break down, so she doesn't start bawling in front of her granddaughter. The other meetings are more relaxed. It's a shame they are so few and far between, that the girl's mother makes everything so difficult.

The fourth time he manages to get Lourdes to allow him to take Guadalupe coincides with Ruso's girls' birthday. Fernando brings her over to Ruso's so the others can see her, so they can share some time, so the ties don't fade, if they haven't already faded, as Fernando fears as he drives Guadalupe back that night, sleeping on the backseat.

In one of those infrequent meetings of the three of them, Ruso suggests they all go to the stadium. Fernando hesitates, but Mauricio quickly says no, that with the way Independiente is playing there's no motivation to get the car out of the garage. Ruso, who gives up easily, agrees with him and Fernando feels ashamed for his initial hesitation, knowing deep down that if Mauricio had said yes he would have swallowed his pride, his protests, all that has been bugging him since their last argument, and he would have gone too.

During that fall and winter it barely rains. The playing fields of the Argentine A Tournament look like miserable pasturelands, with grass green only in the corners. Ruso, half joking and half serious, interprets the drought as a test that Yahweh has decided to subject him to. That April a car wash in Morón closed and in June two others in Castelar. He and Cristo are sure that they've reached the turning point of the trend. Imagining the two simpletons, PlayStation joysticks in hand, analyzing the macro- and microvariables of his business, Fernando is sometimes moved to laughter and other times to anxiety. Then he and Mauricio exchange a look, above the hand motions Ruso uses to spice up his analysis, and they wink in a complicity that, deep down, irks Fernando because he's convinced that, in his absence, Mauricio must exchange that same look and wink with Ruso to condemn his own foolhardy attempts.

Mauricio is doing the same as ever, which is to say, better and better. They gave him a raise with the understanding that his promotion to partner is imminent. Fernando and Ruso don't ask how big his raise is, but they get a pretty good idea when they see him arrive at the birthday party for Ruso's girls in a black Audi they'd only seen before at a dealership. In September Mauricio suggests bringing flowers to the cemetery, because the twelfth would have been Mono's birthday. Fernando is about to say no, out of pure spite. The guy is available for these useless posthumous tributes, but unable to roll up his sleeves for what would make a difference. Fernando supposes that it also pisses him off that it was Mauricio's idea and not his, since he is the deceased's older brother. Anyway, since Ruso thinks it's a brilliant idea Fernando has to shut his trap and say yes.

To top it all off, it starts raining on September 10 and doesn't let up until the night of the thirteenth, and the image of the cemetery like that, all gray and muddy, breaks his heart. And, even though he doesn't talk about it with the others, he's sure they feel the same disquiet.

Leap

"I don't think it's a good idea, Mono."

"What don't you think is a good idea?"

"Doing business with Salvatierra."

"Cut it out, I didn't say I'm gonna do business with him."

"Don't take me for a fool, Mono. You just said it."

"I asked you if you remembered him."

"Oh, yeah, you only asked to give my memory a workout. Please. Cut it out."

"Let's just say I considered it. What's the problem with Polaco?"

"Is that a serious question?"

"Absolutely."

"He was in jail, Mono."

"But not for fraud."

"No, that's true. For car theft, drugs, and I don't know what else."

"But he wasn't convicted."

"He was in there for two years, Mono. You can't be serious."

"Two years without a conviction, Fernando!"

"And how do you know that? He told you himself?"

"Yeah. And?"

"Don't be naive, Mono. What do you expect him to tell you?"

"And why couldn't he be telling me the truth?"

"Okay. Suppose he did tell you the truth. He was still in the can."

"And what does that have to do with it? Someone who's been in the can has no right to do anything once he gets out?"

"I didn't say that."

"What about when you taught in jail? Why were you teaching classes? Huh?"

Fernando was slow to answer, as if to halt the frenetic pace of a conversation that had lost all meaning.

"What are we arguing about, Mono?"

"That I want to get in touch with Polaco Salvatierra and you think it's a bad idea."

"Let's see, Mono. Listen to me. You are about to get a ton of cash. Instead of putting it in the bank you want to gamble it on buying a player, or something like that."

"Putting it in the bank? Are you screwing with me? You already forgot how they froze our accounts in the *corralito*? This guy lives in a bubble," he said, turning to Ruso, who was silently witnessing the discussion.

"Don't put it in the bank then," conceded Fernando. "But from there to throwing it down the drain . . ."

"And who told you that buying a player is throwing it down the drain?"

"Because you don't know anything about that world, Monito."

"That's a lie. I do. I lived for years in that world."

Fernando thought, no. His brother had lived on the outskirts, in the suburbs, in the waiting room of that world. And when it was time for him to take the step to enter it, they'd slammed the door in his face. And that was part of the problem. In Mono's enthusiasm, in his haste, in his vehemence, there was an element of revenge, of outstanding debt. But he didn't have the heart to say that to him.

"Let's say you do. Which is true, you do have some idea. Why don't you try another door? Or do you think that Salvatierra is the only guy who can hook you up?"

"Exactly!" said Mono, answering eagerly as if the discussion had gotten to just the point he wanted it to. "He is the perfect guy at the perfect time."

"I don't understand."

"Salvatierra spent two years in the can. But he still has a ton of contacts and players."

"Ay, Mono. You think that in two years behind bars all his contacts and players haven't gone up in smoke?"

"Not all of them. There are contracts. Deals still going on. Don't make that face, Fernando. It's true. I checked it out."

"You checked it out with who? With Polaco?"

"No, with other people."

"And why don't you do business with these other people?"

"Because the advantage of Polaco is exactly how far he's fallen." He turns toward Ruso. "Is it that hard to understand?"

Ruso didn't give his opinion. It was a family matter. Besides, he didn't need Mono to convince him. He was already convinced.

"It seems risky to me," said Fernando.

"I agree. It is a risk. But the bigger the risk, the bigger the profit. And besides, there's something else."

"What?"

"You think that if I multiply that cash, Lourdes the backstabber is still going to be able to give me problems about seeing Guadalupe?"

"Monito, you have money now. And you still have those problems."

"Yes. But if I have a lot more money—" Fernando raised a hand to stop him right there, but Mono raised his voice to keep from being interrupted. "If I have a lot more money maybe I could even get custody of my girl, you understand?"

Fernando looked at his brother. He was wrong. No matter how much money he got together, they weren't going to give him custody. Lourdes was an utter bitch, but she treated the girl well. As hard as it was for him to accept, because he couldn't stand her, he had to face the fact that she was a good mother. Or at least—because to be a good mother she had to be good to the girl's father, which is to say his brother, and she didn't do that, not by a long shot—she took care of Guadalupe. In a selfish way, in a way that sought to exclude Mono as much as possible. But no judge was going to pay attention to that. Or maybe he would, and Fernando was a skeptic and defeatist, and he was bursting his brother's bubble without any basis or any right to do so.

Mono sat back down in front of Fernando. He looked right into his eyes.

"And if I can make that leap? And if I make that leap with Polaco?"

14.

After ten months of useless attempts, Fernando opts for a dramatic move. He's through with going down the dismal, gory pyramid of entrepreneurs, intermediaries, and supposed investors. He's had enough. He's sick of meeting with poorly dressed, terribly groomed guys. Guys who just scream defeat, incapacity, and apathy. He doesn't need a self-help book (although in those months he has read a few, particularly an entire American collection aimed at small entrepreneurs) to notice the obvious: if he flies so low, it's natural that he only comes across these downtrodden birds.

No, sir. He should go back to the beginning. Now that he is experienced, now that he understands the pace of a meeting, its delicate strategies, its careful twists and turns, he has to go back and knock on the big door and make them open it for him. No more settling for fourth-rate courtesans. He has to aim for the bosses. The ones that call the shots. He has to do it with no qualms and no turning back. Fernando's not offering the rotten merchandise that others are trying to sell around him. Fernando has Mario Juan Bautista Pittilanga. A twenty-one-year-old kid in the prime of his youth. A forward with all kinds of goals in sixth and in fifth. Selected for the U-17 Youth World Cup in Indonesia. A kid who was an alternate in the first division of Platense for almost an entire season. Now he's playing badly, it's true. He's overweight, also true. He is suffering the ostracism of playing in a third-string division in the sticks. He's had some bad luck. But he's still a player with an enormous future. There's a reason why Mono bought him, paying what he paid. For the same reasons that Fernando is going to be able to sell him now.

So he starts again at the beginning. Straight to the most influential businessman of them all. Mastronardi, why the hell not? He manages to get an appointment on a Thursday at ten in the morning. He calls in sick at school and promises to bring in a doctor's note later. He dresses correctly. He brings his briefcase, a file with Pittilanga's information, a DVD with Pittilanga's best plays in Presidente Mitre, which includes the two goals he scored that season.

Mastronardi doesn't receive him alone, but with two of his assistants. Fernando congratulates himself secretly. This is serious. They are interested. Maybe they regret having rejected him almost a year earlier. Mastronardi extends a limp, unpleasant hand. Doesn't matter. The important thing is to be clear, direct, concise, and convincing. Fernando can do it. In fifteen minutes he gives them a summary of Pittilanga's biography, his virtues, his potential. He doesn't leave out his weak points, because he is convinced that, since they are interested enough to meet with him, they've done their own research. Better to confirm what they've found than refute it. Convince them frankly that he's a good opportunity, an excellent deal. The moment to talk numbers arrives. Fernando feels like a poker player with a good hand.

In a fit of inspiration he decides he's not going to ask for the three hundred thousand that Mono paid. "Four hundred thousand dollars," he says. "Or three hundred thousand for fifty percent." He says it holding Mastronardi's gaze. Then he looks at the other two, who are observing him attentively and seriously. Mastronardi taps his pen against the desk a couple of times. He sighs. He looks at his assistants, who give him an inscrutable look in return. He turns to face Fernando again. He says he has to think about it, that they should schedule another meeting in a few days. Fernando dares to think that yes, what's happening is what he's been preparing himself for over the last ten months. So he says no, unfortunately he can't wait because he has other offers, he needs an answer today.

Mastronardi opens his eyes wide and turns toward his employees. Again the inscrutable gaze. He asks for at least a few minutes to think it over amongst themselves. Fernando feels a mix of such tension and joy that he can barely keep from shouting. He stands up, nods, and bids them farewell.

He goes back to the waiting room and asks the secretary where he can find a bathroom. She tells him that Mastronardi has one in the office he just left, but Fernando prefers to let them deliberate without interruption. The woman suggests he use the one in the hallway, past the elevators, but to be careful because there's construction going on and various materials are piled up.

Fernando follows her directions, turning twice to the left at successive forks. It's true about the construction workers and their stuff. He makes his way to the urinals, cutting through a mess of boxes of tiles, dirty buckets, and bags of material. As he pees he thinks it's almost over, though it's hard to believe. He is startled by some voices, some strident laughter. He lifts his head. The back wall of the bathroom is gone. It has been provisionally replaced by a drywall panel that doesn't even reach the ceiling. He can hear the water running in a washroom. And the voices of several men, who are laughing like crazy.

"It's pretty amazing. We should have filmed it."

Fernando is speechless. That is Mastronardi's voice. Due to a combination of architectural quirks, his office bathroom is next to the one Fernando's in, allowing him to eavesdrop on their private deliberations. He's thrilled at the additional advantage he wasn't counting on. He starts to listen, not missing a single word.

"Becerra, who works with Leonetti, told me about him."

It is the voice of one of the assistants.

"I told you too, Luciano. You just don't remember."

That's the other one. Fernando keeps listening.

"Now, you have to give him one thing, he's enthusiastic," resumes Mastronardi.

"Faith! The guy's got blind faith."

"It can't be, Luciano. It's a pose."

"No way, boss!" interjects the first of the two. "I met with him months ago. That's why I called you guys. You had to see it."

Now Fernando understands why one of the assistants' faces had seemed familiar. But he doesn't have time or energy to think about that. If he gets on all fours he can keep listening.

"It was impressive. What was it he said?" Mastronardi imitates Fernando's voice: "'Four hundred thousand dollars. Or three hundred thousand for fifty percent.'"

They crack up again. Fernando leans against a wall. He feels so weak he has to sit down on a pile of cement bags.

"Don't we have a place in the company for him, boss?"

"Not in your dreams, kid."

"Think about it, the guy has gotten almost famous in the last few months! Any minute now we're gonna see him on the daytime talk shows."

More laughter. Mastronardi speaks in a lower voice, but he can still be perfectly heard.

"Man, lower your voice, he's going to hear you. You know they told me something about this guy. That he's a school-teacher, or something like that."

"And what's he doing selling a player?"

"What do I know? Obviously soccer's a whole wide world. Seems anybody thinks they can do anything. I don't know what's next."

"And what are you going to tell him, boss?"

New laughter, now restrained.

"Look. What do you want me to say? On one hand I feel a little sorry for him, but I don't want to miss his thrilled face when we tell him we're closing the deal. Can you imagine?"

"Oh my god!!"

"Should I call him in?"

"No, no. Wait a little more. The more we string him along the more nervous he's gonna get."

"We could tell him we're not sure yet . . . make him suffer a little."

"Ha! And what if we make like we're arguing amongst our-selves, to see what he does?"

"Maybe, maybe. Have some coffee, Hornos. We'll call him in in a couple of minutes."

Fernando gets up and walks to the door. It's a swinging door, but it doesn't close behind him because it gets stuck on some debris. He goes down the hallway, turns once to the right, and calls the elevator. On the ground floor he makes his way through those waiting to go up and he walks with absent steps toward the building's entrance. Someone stares at him, partly because of his sickly pale expression, and partly because he has an enor-mous pale white cement stain on the back of his suit pants.

Love

As with many other matters, the only one of Mono's friends who thought it was a good idea for him to move in with Lourdes was Ruso. Fernando did everything possible to dissuade him, and Mauricio, who at that time was going through the most demanding period of paying his dues at Williams and Associates (working Saturdays, Sundays, and holidays), barely intervened in the debates.

Mono had met her when he started working for the Swiss. Lourdes was a supervisor in the production department of the laboratory, and once in a while they had to meet to agree on criteria and fine-tune strategies. Mono took the plunge on their fourth or fifth meeting, and asked her out.

Unfortunately—maintained Fernando since then—Lourdes had said no. It was unfortunate because in those days Mono had some smooth moves and he wasn't at all used to being turned down. If she'd said yes—Fernando grew pointlessly bitter going over the events—the whole thing never would have gone as far as it did. In the best-case scenario, one or two dinners, sleeping together, and on to the next. After all, she was a pretty girl, but far from unforgettable. But the young lady's rejection spurred on Mono's pride and redoubled his expectations. And since the "no" was said with eyes that suggested her heart held some painful enigma, she became an obsession for Mono, partly because he got turned on by impossible projects and partly because, like most men, he really hated when someone turned him down.

He chatted her up, he courted her, he pestered her, he seduced her, he waited for her, he drew her in, he captivated her, he convinced her of the depth of his feelings and the seriousness of his intentions, until finally Lourdes agreed to have dinner with him.

Mono was overjoyed, and applied himself to preparing the date as if it were an assault on the fort at Curupaytí. He left no detail unplanned, from his shaving lotion and the restaurant to the wildflowers and sober elegance of his underwear, and he didn't include a serenade by mariachis only because he got their contact info too late and the musicians had already accepted a gig at a silver wedding anniversary celebration in Lomas del Mirador.

However, the romantic night Mono had planned down to the tiniest detail didn't get off to the best start. Because Lourdes, when her fragrant suitor invited her to open up, to tell him about herself, to unlock her heart in the candlelight (Mono secretly was convinced that playing it deep and understanding was his guarantee of being able to unlock other things in the future), launched into telling him the tragic love story she'd shared with Ianich Letoin, one of the Swiss engineers at the firm. Not only was this Letoin Swiss, chubby, soft, and rosy-cheeked—thought Mono as he listened to the young lady—but he was also married, as Lourdes informed him among desolate hiccups.

The next day, when Fernando heard the details of the date, he told Mono that a chick like that wasn't good for him, that she was trouble, that he should look for somebody else.

But Mono paid him no mind. He was crazy about her. And he was walking on air, because after suffering through the listening and softening up in the first part of the evening, he saw his efforts progress into tender exchanges in the second, so Mono felt it had more than paid off, and he was the happiest of men.

15.

Fernando arrives at his house, puts his backpack and jacket down any which way on the kitchen table, urinates with the door open, goes back to the kitchen, and puts on the kettle for maté. He searches in his phone book and dials a number. They answer quickly.

"Palm Tree Productions, good afternoon."

Fernando can imagine the scene. Nicolás—owner, manager, secretary, and sole employee of Palm Tree Productions—in shorts and a T-shirt, hunched over his computer, playing some game online with an indeterminate number of losers like himself, answers the telephone without taking his attention off what's happening to the monsters on his screen.

"Hello, Nicolás. It's Fernando, the one with the soccer games."

"Oh yeah, Fernando . . . What's up?"

In the background, distantly, he can hear Nicolás's frenetic typing. One of two things: he is programming a system at lightning speed while he talks to Fernando, or some oversized dragon is about to eat him in the virtual universe of his little game. Second option, definitely.

"I'm calling about the faking the goals thing. Remember?"

Pause, while the imbecile rewinds. He quickly starts typing again. It seems he does remember, and the dragon is still attacking.

"Yeah, cool. Perfect. Those guys I told you about are working on it. Must be almost done."

Fernando sighs. It's not Nicolás's fault. He is an imbecile, too. Two thousand four hundred pesos down the drain. Worse. Two thousand four hundred pesos so Nicolás the idiot can vegetate at his expense.

"Okay. Listen."

"I'm listening, dude."

"I'm sure you have the videos in VHS, I left you a copy of everything."

"Uhhh, yeah, I should have it all around here."

"Okay, well, I need you to get them together."

"Okeydokey."

"And you have the compact discs with the tricks you put in"—*the ones that look like a science fiction movie from the fifties,* thinks Fernando. "And some forms with information I brought over the last time."

"Yeah, cool. I got all that."

"Well, I need you to get that all together too."

"Done."

"And when those guys give you what they're working on—"

"Yeah, the other touch-ups, the final ones. That they're gonna send me all on DVD."

"Awesome, on DVD. Well, get it all together, the video cassettes, the forms, the DVDs, okay?"

"I'll get it together, no sweat."

"And when you've got it all together I need you to do me a favor."

"Sure, what's that?"

"Shove it all up your ass."

Advice

How do you know it's yours, Mono? asked Mauricio with that brutal honesty he had when dealing with other people's problems, as if it were taking time away from more important things. Mono, confused, looked at Fernando and Ruso, who suddenly had their eyes on the floor or out the window.

Actually, the question was pertinent. Cruel, but pertinent. Mono had gathered them for an emergency meeting, because he had news that couldn't wait. Lourdes was pregnant, two months to be precise, and she'd suggested they move in together. Fernando, repressing his desire to slap him, had asked him if he used protection. Mono first answered yes, then no, and then more or less, with an expression of shock and confusion similar to the one Fernando saw in his female students when he asked them the same question. But those girls were fifteen years old, not thirty like his moron of a younger brother.

And in the silence that followed, Mauricio asked that poisonous question that, deep, deep down, all three had been formulating, or all four, because Mono was slow to respond and when he did he said, "I think it is." And in that "I think" were all the doubts, his and everybody else's. That Lourdes was still seeing the Swiss guy, that she kept her relationship with Mono on the outskirts of legitimacy, that their meetings had enough chaos and secrecy and improvisation that he couldn't be sure of anything, that it wasn't clear in what sense they would be sharing a roof, that this Lourdes was the poster child for ambiguity and vagueness and the "I'm not sure of anything," and with things like that Mauricio, and much less Fernando, weren't in favor of Mono's going to live with her.

Ruso was the only one who said yes, he should go for it. And when Fernando asked him why, Ruso said because he loves her. And he said it without turning, without looking them in the face, not in Fernando's furious face and not in Mono's grateful one, because deep down Ruso wasn't sure either about its being the right thing for his best friend. He only knew what Mono wanted, which was to completely win over that woman, have her for himself, and he knew him so well that he knew that Mono was sure living together would eliminate Lourdes's vagueness and doubts and his friend would be happy.

16.

Whatever moronic Fernando says (in his stupidity mixed with messianic furor, he can't see past his own belly button and the problems that originate there), Mauricio is going through a very delicate moment.

Going against all rules of prudence and common sense, he had stored in his cell phone the messages from Soledad, his secretary turned occasional lover turned everyday lover turned I won't give you a moment's rest. At first he kept them because they made him proud, gave him the satisfaction of knowing he was an inveterate lady-killer. But as the weeks and months passed, when Soledad became a habit increasingly taken for granted, more predictable, more regular, Mauricio made the decision to end their sexual chapter as painlessly as possible. And that was when he was betrayed by his legal instincts. He suspects (Mauricio always suspects everything, and feels he is usually right in his suspicions) that Soledad might be less inclined to the breakup than he would hope. And if Soledad is reluctant, it could turn into a scandal. Along that line, it's not crazy to think she might report him for sexual harassment. After all, Mauricio is her boss. And that's when he thinks up the fateful idea of storing the messages to use them, if need be, as proof that nobody was forcing the young woman to go to bed with him.

Mauricio speaks to Soledad, and a couple of tears are shed. There is a tepid reproach, a feint at redefining frequency and intensity, some attempt at remorse, nothing serious, but in the

end there is a farewell on friendly terms. It never comes to any
real blows. But since you never know with women, he saves
the messages. Around that time he gets hit with a ton of expi-
rations in the Las Tunas Shipping Company lawsuit, which is
the most complicated one he has on his plate, and his life turns
into a muddle of hearings, interviews, lunches, dinners, and
late nights in the office. Soledad fades into a memory, but bad
luck leads Mariel—who has too much free time on her hands—
to start torturing herself with her husband's possible infidel-
ity. And she happens to go through his phone and there she
finds the forty-seven text messages from Soledad that don't
leave much room for doubt about the highly personal nature
their lawyer–assistant relationship had taken on.

Chaos ensues. Mauricio comes out of the shower and finds
Mariel, cell phone in hand, exhibiting proof of the crime. A
crime which, upon closer inspection, is no longer one (thinks
Mauricio as Mariel yells at him, her face out of joint), since
his behavior fits more precisely into the category of voluntary
desisting, because while it is true that Mauricio was sleeping with his secretary, he desisted from that behavior prior
to his wife's outburst. Mauricio is convinced that, if it were a
criminal offense, there would be no problem simply because
there is no crime. It's a shame that Mariel doesn't seem willing to take those arguments into consideration and, quite on
the contrary, hits her husband a few times with weak blows
that surprise more than hurt him, and then she starts shouting through the house to such an extent that Mauricio does
begin to grow alarmed, because sooner or later the neighbors
are going to hear. But Mariel won't listen. Worse, the more discretion Mauricio asks for, the more violent her screams and
insults become.

Mauricio sleeps that night and the ten following ones in the guest bedroom, which is really the bedroom for their firstborn—whom they have yet to conceive—but that's another problem, or the same one, because Mariel yells that she is going to stop the fertility treatments she's been taking for six months, because he's a son of a bitch and who does he think he is, that she's going to subject herself to all those tests and shots and humiliations to give him a child and all for what, so the son of a bitch can go around screwing the first female that crosses his path, and Mauricio just keeps quiet and waits for her to get over it. But two days pass and she doesn't say a word to him, and another three and she won't even look at him, and the only good thing is that she isn't throwing his things into a suitcase and kicking him out, and Mauricio has time to wonder what he wants to do about his marriage, because that is the pertinent question. For the first two or three days he questions his feelings for her, if he loves her or not, if he desires her or not, but these aren't questions he wants to answer, because in the end they're not useful. What's important is the concrete, what he does and not what he feels. And if there is one thing that Mauricio is convinced of—and those days sleeping in the other room and eating alone in the kitchen confirm it in spades—it's that he doesn't want to separate, he's not interested in going through the failure of a divorce. He will stay married to Mariel no matter what the cost, come hell or high water, because he likes the life he has and that life includes certain possessions and a certain stability, and his only example of a single guy is Fernando, who married and then got separated after a while, and was never again able to get involved in any remotely serious relationship. And if there is something or

more specifically someone Mauricio sees as an example it's
Fernando, a negative example, an example of what he doesn't
want, because Fernando's life is the last thing that Mauricio
wants to see or have or live through.

On the tenth day Mariel agrees to dine at the same table and
talk afterward, and Mauricio realizes that it's now or never,
that this is a match he should have lost but has a chance to
pull out, a penalty kick at the last minute, and if he sends it off
the bar he'll have no one else to blame, so he sits down with all
his prudence and all his levelheadedness willing to negotiate
a dignified way out of this crisis.

Mariel tells him that the only way she'll forgive him is if
he promises that he will never do it again as long as he lives
and he says yes, he promises, never again. And if he fires
that woman from the office right away and never sees her
again and he says wait a minute, it's not that simple. Mariel
blinks, somewhat perplexed, because she wasn't expecting
Mauricio to start objecting on the second clause, but her
husband says that she needs to think it out clearly, that she
shouldn't get carried away with her rage and spite, because
if the girl wants to she could accuse him of harassment, and
as he says those words all of Mariel's apparent calm goes
out the window and she starts shouting and cursing again,
but Mauricio manages to stop her by saying think, take a
second, and realize everything we have to lose. Because
they are in a moment of economic growth, progress, and
he is about to make partner, and a scandal like this could
ruin everything, and it is much more reasonable to talk with
some of the other lawyers and suggest switching assistants,
and he is about to say that it happens a lot but he stops himself in time and thank goodness, because otherwise Mariel

would get the idea that all the lawyers in the firm are a
bunch of womanizers that pass the secretaries around once
they've screwed them but thank goodness he doesn't say
it. And Mariel makes a doubtful face and Mauricio knows
that's enough, that that doubt will be sufficient, that he'll
have time to shift things around in the office with the least
possible headache. And the third condition, says Mariel, is
that they do couple therapy to get over this situation. And
Mauricio for a moment forgets the real balance of power
and says no, no way, he's not going to spend his money on
something stupid like that, but all it takes is Mariel starting
to sob and scream again for Mauricio to realize he has no
margin for maneuvering, that there is a time to sow and a
time to reap and this is the moment to sow, or to give in and
say yes, although the mere possibility of sharing his business with a strange guy, or worse a strange woman, horrifies
him, but Mauricio says yes, okay, all right, they are going to
do it, that he'll do anything so long as she forgives him and
things go back to the way they always were.

And the conversation ends there. Mariel clears the table
and is about to wash the dishes and Mauricio, out of habit, gets
up from the table and follows her, but she isn't up for anything
more that night, and she makes that clear when he approaches
to embrace her, sticking out her elbows with a furious look,
and Mauricio understands that there is still work to be done,
that he's been too optimistic, that he'll be sleeping in the guest
bedroom for a few more nights and there'll be more silent
meals and, although he doesn't want to even stop to consider
it, it is entirely possible that Mariel won't budge on the couple
therapy, that she will hold it up as a sine qua non condition
and there Mauricio is screwed. But he doesn't even want to

think about that, and it gets really late as he tosses and turns in that uncomfortable bed and he wakes up with his back stiff, and god damn the moment he decided to save those messages from dumb old Soledad, who wasn't even that hot after all, or she was, but there's no lay in the world that could be worth putting up with this mess.

Disappointment

The deepest affection is no guarantee of anything, not when forming a couple and not when giving sound advice. The first was proven to Mono two or three months into living with Lourdes, and the second was confirmed to Ruso around the same time, when he realized that he'd been wrong to support Mono's desire to move in with her.

There wasn't a week, in the fourteen months they shared a house, without an argument where they blew up and shouted horrible things at each other. There wasn't a week without several days buried in a gloomy silence where they avoided looking each other in the eye or speaking a single word. Of course they had some good days, some amazing reconciliations, but not enough to make up for the shouting and silence.

And meanwhile, the pregnancy continued and her belly grew. More than once Fernando was shocked by nature's tenacity. Lourdes and Mono hated each other almost all of the time. The few strings that linked them were getting snipped with no hope of being retied. But the child growing in Lourdes's womb was ripening toward the moment of birth with the arrogant perseverance of instinct, detached from the frenzied turmoil of those who would have to raise it.

17.

"**C**an I ask you something, Fer?"

They are leaning against the window from the outside, and Fernando is uneasy about them being there. He's no business owner—never has been—but he's heard a thousand times that if you had a business, you should never ever stand at the door doing nothing, because that leads people to believe that you have nothing to do because nobody ever comes in to buy anything. He doesn't know how to say it to Ruso without sounding offensive or pedantic. But on the other hand he can't get it out of his head. Which is why five minutes earlier he suggested going into the office to drink some maté—Ruso said thanks but no thanks—and he now suggests going in to watch how Cristo and Molina are playing PS, beneath Chamaco's watchful gaze. But Ruso refuses again. And that passivity, that indolence makes Fernando nervous. And its public display. Every car that passes, every pedestrian, sees them there, with nothing to do, on the sidewalk in front of that empty car wash. And on such a beautiful day.

"Don't you want to go inside?" insists Fernando. Maybe now Ruso will agree.

"No, we're fine out here," responds his friend, and Fernando swallows hard. In the end, Mauricio's right when he accuses him of being neurotic. But he can't get the idea that they have to move out of his head.

"Why don't we take a walk around the block?" he suggests.

"Eh . . . okay," accepts Ruso, somewhat perplexed.

Okay, now Ruso can ask him whatever he wants. He's all ears.

"What did you want to talk about?"

"When—when you got separated from Cristina . . ."

It's Fernando's turn to waver. Where is Ruso going with that subject?

"Yeah, what about it?" he responds cautiously.

"No . . . I was wondering," Ruso is having trouble getting to the point, ". . . I was thinking, you know? How . . . how you guys decided to do it, how you got there, I mean . . ."

Fernando, who is walking with his hands in his jeans pockets, scratches his thigh through the denim.

"Are things that bad with Mónica, Ruso?"

"No, we're not doing that bad," says Ruso, but his voice is so hesitant that it's obvious he's lying. "Or yeah, I don't know. She's not even talking to me, man. I don't know what to do."

They turn the corner. Fernando sees a rock on the sidewalk. Round, not very big. A bit farther on there is a telephone pole. He picks up the rock, takes a running start, and throws it at the pole, thinking that if he hits the pole, he wins. He doesn't know what he wins, but he wins. He misses by a small margin.

"But that doesn't mean you guys are going to separate, Ruso. Or do you want to?"

"Me? No way, Fer."

"Did she say something about separating?"

Ruso reflects.

"No, not about separating. But she says she's fed up, that we aren't going anywhere, that things are only getting worse . . ."

"What things are getting worse? Money or between you two?"

"I . . . I'd say it's the money. But there comes a point where you don't know. Always with the crabby face. Always angry . . ."

Fernando thinks over Ruso's description.

"Look, Ruso. I don't think I'm the best person to give you advice."

"Why?"

"Because when I got married I sucked at it, Ruso. That's why."

"But you and Cristina . . . I don't know, things didn't always suck between you."

Fernando takes a few yards to think. They turn at the next corner.

"That's true. Not always."

"I remember you guys loving each other a lot."

Fernando smiles reluctantly. It's true. They used to love each other a lot. They loved each other a lot and then? They loved each other a lot and what? He doesn't need to search to remember Cristina's words, at the end of argument number two thousand five hundred. "I was very happy with you, Fernando. I was. We were. We're not anymore. And if we keep going, if we don't face facts, we're going to destroy the memories." The woman was blunt. And wise. And brave, because Fernando knew that he never would have made up his mind.

They turn the third corner. They have walked almost the entire block in silence. Fernando wonders what to say. He doesn't want his friend to continue in such torment.

"It's different, Ruso. My story has nothing to do with yours."

"Why?"

"For a thousand reasons, what do I know. You guys are going through a bad patch. It'll pass."

Their eyes meet for a second and Fernando sees, in Ruso's eyes, how badly he wants to believe him.

"It's like those teams that have a shitty season. I don't know, some players replaced, a coach that doesn't hit the nail on the head. Then things change . . ."

"Like us after we won the 2002 championship."

"Exactly. Like us after winning that championship. Exactly. Over time, things shift."

"Are you sure?"

Ay, Ruso. If only I were sure of something in this fucking life, thinks Fernando.

"Of course. You'll see."

They arrive at the car wash again. To his surprise, there is a car beginning the wash cycle. Chamaco is covering it with suds. They go into the office. Cristo is embroiled in a fierce battle against Molina, Inter against Juventus, 2–2. Ruso joyfully celebrates the tight match, takes a seat in one of the spectator chairs and motions for Fernando to sit in the other.

Guadalupe

I t was a girl. They chose the name Guadalupe, and all the family members and close friends were surprised by their harmonious agreement over the name. It was, thought Fernando later, like being in the eye of a hurricane, that moment of deceptive calm in the middle of a massive storm. Seeing them in the hospital, Lourdes exhausted, Mono filled with joy, the strikingly beautiful little baby, one could think they just might have a chance of being happy together.

But it was a moment, an illusion, a pipe dream that barely lasted longer than any of those reconciliations they had fooled themselves with. Their life together went back to being a nightmare, until Guadalupe was seven months old.

More than once Mono talked about it with his friends. Mauricio, from the beginning, suggested they split up. Fernando hesitated a bit longer. He felt bad for the child, starting off her life without a father, growing up without him close by. Ruso was the one that most enjoined him to persevere. For them to talk it out, give it time. That sooner or later they would find the way. Mono took his advice for as long as he could, but in the end, one night—not right in the middle of a shouting match, but in the middle of one of the gloomy silences that followed them and that lasted days and days—he asked Fernando to come by and pick him up, gathered his things, stuffed them into the trunk of his car, and left.

18.

The two weeks after the visit to Mono's grave turned out to be the hardest ones for Ruso in the year since his best friend's death. The day of Mono's birthday, particularly, he feels horrible, the three in silence beneath the drizzle, the bouquets of flowers they don't know how to handle, how to place beside the tombstone. But the days after aren't much better. He calls Fernando three times and doesn't reach him. He talks to Mauricio just once, about the notification from the credit card: jovial, eloquent, Mauricio assures him he's in no danger and that everything is under control. And nothing more. Of course it's good that Mauricio reassures him like that, but when he hangs up Ruso feels empty, expectant, although he doesn't know of what. And when he tells Mónica the same thing happens. His wife's sigh of relief doesn't reach him. Surely it's good that Mónica takes it well. Just like it's good that she smiles, hopeful, every night when Ruso places the wads of money made that day on the dining room table and Mónica sees that it is growing. It's good that she notices and says so, and that he can answer, yes, the truth is business is getting better.

It's good but it's not enough, that's the problem. That's what's not good. It's not good that Mauricio doesn't ask him anything about Fernando. It's not good that he seems so content, so at peace with things, so comfortable with life just the way it is. And what about him? Is Ruso so different? Ruso

suspects he isn't. That's why one Wednesday morning in late
September, as he is walking along Mitre away from the station,
Ruso realizes that he can't allow his friendship with Fernando
to end up dying from neglect, and then he turns down Monte-
verde and takes the 238 to Morón and buys a ticket to Santiago
del Estero on the eight o'clock bus.

Early Days of Fatherhood

Before making a decision you have to take a DNA test. Mauricio told him that, one night when the four of them got together, weeks after Mono left Lourdes's apartment.

Independiente was playing a game ahead of schedule on a Friday night, and Fernando thought that it would be a good idea for the four of them to get together to watch it, talk, and drink. Mauricio took care of the drinks, and he brought enough Coca-Cola and Fernet for an army. And Ruso, who was in charge of snacks, claimed to be low on cash, and just brought a salami and two bags of peanuts.

To boot, Independiente played an atrocious game that ended tied and scoreless. And with empty stomachs, their team's terrible result, the anguish over Mono's family failure, they started knocking them back methodically, because what they lacked in happiness, they more than made up for in Fernet. At some point Ruso asked if he had seen her again and Mono said no, but that he had to see her soon, one way or another, to work out a couple of important issues. What? Fernando had asked with his eyes half-shut and the room spinning. Visitation rights and child support, said Mono, slurring his words out of drunkenness and sadness.

And it was in the silence that followed that Mauricio dropped that comment about the DNA. Mauricio was capable of reasoning with the precision of a surgeon even when quite sloshed.

Simple, like two and two are four: if you are going to chip in money on raising a baby, if you are going to use part of your assets to support it, make sure it's your kid, said Mauricio.

They all looked at Mono, because the question was out there, floating like a toxic ghost. Toxic and silent, because they hadn't touched the issue since that time Mono had called them together to ask for their opinion about moving in with Lourdes. Each of them, on their own, had scrutinized the baby's features, in a clumsy search for similarities. They hadn't even met the Swiss guy from the lab, so they had no way of comparing. Each of them, on their own, had hoped with all their might that yes, the girl was Mono's, because they loved him and they didn't want him to go through another terrible disappointment.

Besides, continued Mauricio, you are going to spend a fortune on the civil trial for the visits and the custody and all that.

Mono didn't look at them: he kept his eyes on the tiles of Fernando's patio, where the four of them sat enjoying the welcoming October evening. He extended a hand toward a bottle of Fernet that was half full and chugged on it like it was water. You're going to get sick, fool, said Fernando flatly, but he didn't stop him. Mono choked, coughed, and spit out some of what he had drunk. He gasped, regained his breath, closed his eyes, and tilted the bottle up again, until he'd emptied it completely. Then he tried to break it by throwing it against a wall, but it fell onto a laurel bush whose branches cushioned the impact and kept it from shattering.

Shit, said Mono, disappointed.

Mauricio pressed hard on the neck of a new bottle, turning the cap to open it. I mean it, he insisted, as if to say that his observation deserved some response beyond guzzling a half-liter of Fernet.

What do you think? Mono asked his brother.

Fernando sniffled. The tile floor was making him feel chilled. Maybe Mauricio is right, he finally said, and he felt he'd given in, as if they'd cornered him and he was tired of running.

I want to say something, announced Ruso, who had drunk the least because alcohol didn't sit well with him; it made him much more sad than merry. He cleared his throat, waiting.

Speak, said Mono.

Go on, seconded Mauricio.

I have something to say, Ruso insisted, but not because he was fuzzy from the alcohol, but because he was having trouble speaking his mind. He cleared his throat again. I think a lot about this kid stuff. Kids by blood, adopted kids, all that. Because of my brother, I think about it a lot. 'Cuz his wife couldn't have kids, and they had to adopt.

Your brother's kids are adopted? asked Mauricio, confused.

Of course, man, you didn't know that? Or are you just so wasted you didn't remember?

Mauricio blinked, as if he didn't know the answer to these questions, or couldn't even comprehend them.

Ruso continued: And you know what I thought?

No, what'd you think? asked Mono.

I was thinking about my own girls.

What? Your girls are adopted? asked Mauricio.

No, fool, how could they be adopted? Don't you remember Mónica pregnant?

Yeah, I remember.

So? asked Ruso.

Mauricio nodded, as if admitting he was right.

I'm saying that DNA can suck my balls, if you know what I mean. Imagine they come and tell me that Luli is adopted. Or Ana, my Anita, is adopted.

But are they adopted? insisted Mauricio.

I told you they're not, you fool! It's hypothetical! Imagine one day the cops come to my house and tell me there was a mistake, that they slipped up at the hospital, in the nursery, and they gave me another girl.

What do you mean another girl?

Like, they made a mistake with those little bracelets they put around the babies' feet. And they gave me some other girl, instead of mine.

Ruso opens his hands, as if his argument were definitive, but the other three were still waiting for him to explain. Do you get it? The three men nodded. Mauricio filled their glasses again.

I mean, continued Ruso, that if they come now to tell me, now that the twins are three years old, that they're not my daughters, that they are somebody else's daughters, I couldn't give two shits, you know what I mean? Because I changed their diapers, and I gave them their bottles, and I sang them to sleep. What do I care whose sperm they came from? That's not what makes them my daughters. They're my daughters because of all the rest.

There was silence. Mono got up, pushed aside one of the glasses, which fell over onto the tiles, crossed the patio on his hands and knees until he reached the facing wall, and hugged his best friend.

19.

The trip seems short because he sleeps all night like a baby. Thank goodness his credit card went through when it came time to pay for the ticket, because he could travel in the Sleep Suite Class, which has spectacular seats, includes dinner on board, and goes direct. Once he's in Santiago del Estero, Ruso asks around and easily gets directions to the Club Presidente Mitre. Nobody asks him for any explanation at the entrance gate, and he joins another dozen family members and curious onlookers who take their places in the only stand to watch the training.

The coach is still Bermúdez, whom they'd met the year before. He orders his team to run three laps around the field, hands out bibs, and moves to one side. Pittilanga gets a yellow bib. From that distance, it looks like he's gained weight. Not a lot, a couple of kilos. He is still tall as a door, but more ungainly, his shoulders more laden, with a bigger gut and less energy. He handles the ball just as he did the first time they saw him. He faces up to it bravely. He knows how to move his arms, stay vertical, defend the ball with his back to the opposing fence. But when he tries to lift his head, to find the goal, to pass effectively to a teammate, Pittilanga comes up short. Within the group, he doesn't seem out of place. Almost all of them are horrible, worse than him. There are two or three that are light on their feet and can try for a feint or run someone down, but nothing fancy or very subtle. Anyhow, nobody seems to be losing any sleep over it. For these guys, playing the Argentine A Tournament is the high point of their careers. And they know it. The problem is Pittilanga. Because he cost three hundred grand and no other player on Presidente Mitre is worth that. Actually—Ruso corrects himself—Pittilanga's not worth that either. That's what Mono paid for him. But that doesn't mean he's really worth that.

Ruso spends the first half hour watching the tedium of practice—every once in a while Bermúdez stops the training, gives some orders, points out weaknesses—and occasionally glancing over at an old man sitting a few yards to the right who's steeping some maté that's making Ruso's mouth water.

"Listen, mister," he says when he can't take it anymore, "how about we join forces. I'll buy some cakes and you serve me up some maté?"

The old man accepts and Ruso takes a trip to the concession.

"Should I open the sweet ones, or the savory?" he asks when he returns.

"Uhhh . . . let's start with the sweet, what do you say?"

Ruso nods, sits down beside the old man, and opens the package of cakes. By the fourth and fifth round of maté he already has a sketch of the old man's life story. He is from La Banda, a retired policeman, four kids, seven grandkids. The sixth is the one who plays for Mitre, lateral defender, left side.

"And what brings you here?" asks the old man in turn.

Ruso explains that he is one of the owners of Pittilanga's transfer. The old man nods, comments that Pittilanga is "a little less bad than most of them," and then asks, "Is it true he played in a U-20 selection?"

"In a U-17. The one in Indonesia," clarifies Ruso.

"And then what happened?" asks the old man.

Ruso smiles, but reluctantly, as he weighs the old man's politeness. He didn't ask him the entire unpleasant question directly. He didn't ask how it's possible for a kid chosen as one of the twenty best players under seventeen in all of Argentina to end up, four years later, playing with these deadbeats, and not standing out from the bunch.

"And . . . well, you know how soccer is . . ."

"I do," agrees the old man, as he bangs his maté against the edge of the grandstand step to detach the remains of the leaves so he can replace them.

When the sweet cakes are finished off, they start in on the savory ones. The old man brews good maté. Ruso tells him that and the old man smiles.

Bermúdez whistles the end of the game and wraps up the training. Ruso walks down the stands to greet Pittilanga.

The kid is surprised to see him and gives him one of his meager smiles. Ruso realizes that Pittilanga has his hopes up that he's come bearing important news, and he feels a little bad saying he hasn't, that he just came to see him, to see how things were going and if he needs anything. They chat for a while about trivial matters, shake hands, and Ruso promises to return soon.

Ruso goes back to the center of town and spends the afternoon strolling around the plaza, the pedestrian streets, visiting a couple of churches, grabbing a bite to eat. At ten that night he walks to the station and at eleven he gets on the bus that takes him back to Buenos Aires.

Bad News

When Fernando got to the cafe, he saw Mono waiting for him at one of the back tables.

"Am I late?" he asked with some surprise, as he greeted him with a kiss on the cheek.

"No, Fer, not at all. Why do you ask?"

"Getting here to find you waiting . . . I don't know, I'm not used to that."

Mono ignored his sarcasm with a crooked smile and searched for the waiter. That was only the second or third time Mono had ever arrived before his brother. Every time before that—thousands of times—Fernando's punctilious promptness had burst the freewheeling bubble of tardiness Mono dwelled in comfortably.

"How's it going?" asked Fernando, almost with his back to him as he turned toward the bar, also trying to locate the waiter.

"Fine," answered Mono. But it was just convention. A reflex that Fernando, anxious to order his coffee, didn't catch.

"To what do I owe the honor, Monito? The last time you expressly took me out for a coffee, if I remember correctly, was when you got laid off after you didn't take that job in Mexico. Remember?"

"No. Ah, yeah. No, but that time we were with Ruso."

"Speaking of Ruso, he'll be here any minute, right?"

"No. Ruso's not coming. I didn't tell him we were getting together."

That was a surprise for Fernando. The second, after his younger brother's sudden attack of punctuality.

"What? You didn't tell your bosom buddy?"

"No, I didn't. I called you because I want to talk to you, not to the others."

Fernando didn't insist, despite his surprise. Ruso and Mono had had an almost symbiotic friendship since they were eight. They went everywhere together, they laughed at the same jokes, chose the same ice cream flavors. Not only at the age of eight, but still when they were almost forty. That's why Alejandro's seeming naturalness when explaining the other's absence was the least natural thing in the world.

"Okay," accepted Fernando. "So you are going to tell me something you haven't told Ruso, or Mauricio, or Mom, or—"

"Nobody, Fernando. First I want to talk to you."

Mono shut down his speculations in a tone so severe, so unusual in him, that Fernando felt lost. What was all the mystery about? Fernando did what he always did to prepare himself against pain: he imagined something terrible. Something upsetting. Something that left him paralyzed with fear. That way, any news that his brother gave him would be less terrible. The player died, decided Fernando. He lost the player he bought and he's left with nothing. And now he doesn't have a pot to piss in. Or worse. Lourdes hooked up with some dumbass who lives in Asia and is taking Guadalupe there. He stared at his brother. From his face it could be anything. Fernando got really scared.

"What's going on, man?" asked Alejandro. "You're white as a sheet."

"Me? No. Me? Why do you say that?"

"Is something wrong?"

"Nothing, man!" and the dismissal sounded a bit more abrupt than he would have liked. He softened his tone. "Quit being mysterious and tell me."

"It's not that easy, Fer. I . . . I don't know how to begin."

"Begin at the beg—"

"I have cancer."

Mono's three words swept away all the others and installed themselves, awful and plain, taking up all the space around them. The waiter, now that they had stopped trying to get him to come over, was approaching docilely, ready to take their order. Mono asked for two coffees, but Fernando didn't even notice. The world had vanished from beneath his feet, all objects, all sounds.

"What?"

He let out the question just because, or to make things recover their throb and their movement, or to give the world a chance to settle on its foundations again.

"You heard me, man," said Mono in a whisper, and smiled, and Fernando wondered what the hell was so funny, why this fool was smiling.

"What kind?" Later, when he recalled that conversation, Fernando himself was surprised at his control, at his attempt at cold-bloodedness with that question, as if he were asking about the filling of an empanada or a cake.

"Pancreatic."

Again they were silent, because Fernando had used up all his composure in the previous question and because Mono didn't seem able to guide him in any other direction.

"Okay," began Fernando, finally. He didn't get far, but he started. "The pancreas is a gland, right? What the hell does it do? Have them take it out and that'll be that."

Mono scratched his head and smiled again.

"That's what I say."

"Of course," confirmed Fernando.

"Of course," Alejandro imitated him, still smiling. "But it seems they can't. I don't know why the hell not, but they can't."

The waiter brought the coffees.

"And what are you going to do?"

Fernando would remember that conversation a thousand times. He would recall what each of them said. What he was thinking. What he feared. But he wouldn't remember the superhuman effort he made not to cry. It was dumb, useless. But a large part of his attention and energy was devoted to not letting a tear escape from his eyes.

"What do I know, man? I don't know. I'll do what I can. What do you want me to do?"

Even though they never spoke about that conversation, Mono too was grappling with the same childish arm wrestle to keep back his tears. An unspoken faceoff typical of boys out on the street.

"Do you know the treatment yet?" asked Fernando.

"I'm working on it. Tomorrow I have to go to the doctor. I wanted to ask you if you'd come with me."

"Of course. I'll skip class and we'll go."

"No, not if you have to miss class. Forget about it."

"What's the problem? It's no big deal. I can get leave for a sick family member."

"I didn't know you had that."

"Ever since you became a soccer entrepreneur you sit around scratching your balls. But us simple mortals get leave for stuff like that."

They smiled unenthusiastically. Fernando was the first to speak.

"How long have you known?"

"Two weeks."

"Well, then they can try something. They say that with cancer, if you catch it in time . . ."

"Uh-huh. That's what they say."

"That's what they say."

Fernando lifts his head to locate the waiter and order more coffee.

"I need you to give me a hand, Fer."

"Tell me. With what?"

"I need your help."

"With what?"

"With a ton of things. To start with, because I haven't told Ruso anything. And I don't have the energy. Same with Mauricio."

Fernando, with mechanical movements, emptied a packet of sugar into his coffee. He spent a long time watching the rain of shiny little crystals sink into the liquid. He grabbed another packet and repeated the operation. He did the same with a third. He wasn't going to drink it anyway. It wasn't even a way to take up time. It wasn't anything.

"And you haven't told Mom?"

"Not yet." Mono drank the second coffee. "But I'll tell Mom myself."

Fernando weighed the possibility of emptying a fourth packet of sugar into his cup, but decided against it.

"Goddamned mother-fucking bull-fucking shit," he said finally.

"Finally you say something coherent, fool," answered Mono.

20.

Two weeks after their cease-fire conversation, Mauricio and his wife attend their first couple therapy session. In the interim things have evolved little, if at all. Mauricio has managed to return to the conjugal bedroom, and that is his only big victory. All the rest is terse remarks, the occasional tear and silences in the car, don't even think about touching me, and stuff like that.

Mauricio trusts that his docile acceptance of seeing the marriage shrink will smooth the way once and for all. The shrink turns out to be a lady, middle-aged, with eyeglasses, curls, and an aura of serenity that bugs Mauricio from the moment they shake hands, although he is careful not to show it.

In the first questions Mauricio takes the initiative. It makes him really nervous that the psychologist writes everything down, nods at everything they say, stares at them during every silence. He is dying to see what the hell that snake in the grass is writing down, but he restrains himself.

The good news is that Mariel isn't exactly confident either. Mauricio had feared she would hit it off with the woman, that they'd become allies, that they'd corner him with their questions and demands. But Mariel isn't comfortable at all. *Take that*, thinks Mauricio. *Suck on that. You wanted us to come. Now suffer.* The tension he perceives in his wife relaxes him, it calms him down gradually. Mauricio isn't having a good time (that's impossible with some lady sitting in front of you giving you the hairy eyeball about all the faults you've been lugging around since birth), but he is comforted knowing that Mariel is having an even worse time.

The best moment comes when the psychologist asks his wife to talk about the assets in their marriage. Mauricio laughs to himself at the words these people use. "Assets." Why can't they use a less pretentious, less earnest word? Do they think it's less serious to say, "What do you like about being married to this guy?" Are they afraid that people would try to negotiate their fees down if they talked like regular folk?

But okay, she asks Mariel about the damn "assets." And Mariel starts to go on about each person's sphere of action. That's what she often calls them. Mariel brags about the fact that they've always been a couple who complement each other well, with plenty of reciprocal compensations and bilateral retributions. Mauricio knows that, deep down, she considers him an imbecile who can't take responsibility for practically anything in everyday life. But he also knows that she respects him as a lawyer. She wasn't able to get past her second year of studying to be a public accountant. The fact that he graduated, that he works where he works, that things are going the way they are for him, evens things out in his wife's eyes.

And that's what she's talking about, the complementary spheres, when the therapist very politely interrupts her to ask her what they have in common. "You two," she clarifies, when Mariel stares at her with a confused expression. "Of course," continues the psychologist, "I understand what you are saying about each of you taking care of certain things, but I'm not clear on what aspects of your lives you do share, you do take on together, as a couple." Poor Mariel, thinks Mauricio: the lady had cut her off in the middle of her display of brilliance, and she doesn't know how to answer. She remains silent. Silent and confused. Mauricio doesn't make much of an effort to get her out of her fix, either. Her silence and her duped expression have the double advantage of making him look very respectful of what his better half has to say and, above all, is a wonderful payback that Mariel, who was oh-so-insistent on this special adventure of airing their problems in front of a perfect stranger, gets the unpleasant surprise of not knowing what to say or how to escape.

In the car, on the way back, Mauricio challenges Mariel's glum face, asking what she thought of the therapist, and his wife starts criticizing her with all her ferocity, which is quite considerable. Who does she think she is, with her tough guy act, with those little know-it-all eyeglasses, with that notebook where she jots down god knows what, and how dare she criticize the way I handle my relationship, and Mauricio just nods and agrees with everything. When he feels confident he dares to criticize the therapist himself, something sarcastic that strikes Mariel as funny, and they end up imitating the woman's gentle mannerisms and exaggeratedly serene countenance amid gales of laughter.

They arrive home euphoric, and Mauricio casually gets up the nerve to kiss her and Mariel doesn't push him away and they hug and they take off their clothes and they go to bed with an abandon and conviction that surprises and delights Mauricio, and all's well that end's well because the couple therapy was a one-time thing and in the file marked Soledad he could consider the case if not forgiven at least dismissed and it was a learning experience and never again in his whole damn life does he ever save a text message again.

Silence

He called Mauricio the next morning. Fernando said he needed to speak with him urgently about a personal matter, and Mauricio suggested five p.m., because he had no more client appointments after that. Fernando said okay, but at six, so he would have time to get there from school. It was always the same with Mauricio. Fernando had been teaching on Thursday afternoons for nine years, but his friend seemed incapable of retaining such a simple piece of information. Was it because deep down—or not so deep down—he thought little of Fernando's profession, or simply because, like everything that didn't personally and directly affect him, it slid off his back and was quickly forgotten? Neither of those two options spoke very well of Mauricio, but Fernando couldn't come up with a third.

The secretary smiled when she recognized him. She offered him coffee and sent him in. Fernando saw her as so beautiful, so smiling, and so elegant that he couldn't help wonder what he always wondered, which is to say, if his friend received more than professional services from this beauty. When he was left alone he felt bad, because a thought like that had nothing to do with the worry he had come to share with his friend. He was a shirker and a weakling, unable to bear his sadness without tiring and getting distracted.

Mauricio hugged him and sat him down in one of the low, soft armchairs. Fernando had another distraction. Suit versus jeans, shiny tie versus unbuttoned collar, cuff links versus rolled-up sleeves, lustrous leather versus canvas sneakers, hair shiny with gel versus shaved close.

"What's up, Fer? You were so mysterious this morning!"

"That's true. But it's not something to discuss over the phone."

"What's wrong?"

"Mono."

"What's wrong with your brother?"

"He has cancer and he's fucked."

The discreet charm of simplicity. No beating around the bush, no meandering. And Mauricio, a gentleman. No incredulousness, no indignation, no rebelliousness. Barely a succinct question.

"Where?"

"Pancreas."

And that had been all. Or almost, because it was still missing Mauricio's final, unmistakable stamp. He leaned back in the armchair, adjusted his tie two or three times with an absent gesture, sighed loudly, made that strange expression he had been doing since he was a kid that consisted of folding up his upper lip as if to smell it, all the rituals that helped him think. Then he stood up, opened the door, and told his secretary to call his house and tell Mariel that he had a meeting and not to wait for him for dinner. Meanwhile Fernando also stood up and approached him to say goodbye. The idea of suggesting they have a coffee together, or calling Mono, or staying awhile longer right there in the office trying to absorb the blow, didn't even occur to him. Fernando knew that the only thing Mauricio wanted was to shoot off, go far, get lost, disconnect. Burn all bridges with other people, as if pain were a plague that always arrived over those bridges. He knew he was going to the movies to see whatever film was showing, even if it was already halfway through the screening, and that he was going to arrive home well after midnight so he wouldn't have to speak to his wife, and that he wasn't going to call Mono the next day or the one after that, because Mauricio was convinced that in the face of pain, and much more in the face of possible death, the only conceivable response was silence, silence, and more silence.

21.

When he returns from Santiago del Estero, Ruso has several tempestuous days. Mónica treats him with palpable coldness. She isn't mad about his untimely trip. She had tried to get annoyed when she learned he was going, but Ruso found the right words: "Fernando has been taking care of all of this for the past year. I have to lend him a hand." Magic words. Because Mónica thinks Fernando is the bee's knees. According to her, Fernando is responsible, dedicated, serious, intelligent. He's educated, he has a steady job. Ruso can recite all of his friend's qualities by heart, Mónica has listed them that many times. An exasperating list, because Ruso isn't stupid and he knows that extolling Fernando's virtues is Mónica's way of telling him, Ruso, that she's sick of his being the opposite. But comparisons aside, when Ruso lets her know that "poor Fernando" is fed up and needs help, she shelves any potential complaints.

And everything is still the same. Not better or worse than before the trip. She still bristles with demands, with exasperation waiting to pounce. And Ruso is somewhere between conciliatory and angry. There are days when he promises himself he won't speak to her, won't ask anything of her, won't brush past her for anything in the world. But he always ends up seeking her out because he needs her for so many things.

In the car wash things continue to rise steadily. Cristo has shown himself to be a natural-born businessman: he began offering coffee to waiting customers and four months later he has a well-stocked stand set up. Ruso can't believe that, for once, he has hit upon the right employee. The right employees, actually. Because the car washers are also amazing, all really good guys. There is so much demand for washes that they hire a helper, one of Molina's nephews, a tall, skinny prettyboy who is immediately baptized as Feo—the "Ugly Kid." Since he doesn't like being called that, and he lets them know, the name sticks like superglue.

The only bad thing about this prosperity is that it makes it hard to get to their PlayStation tournaments. They do what they can, but in the peak hours all five of them are busy with the cars and there's just no way. Sometimes they stay on for a couple of hours after closing. And they play on rainy days. Chamaco comments that his wife gets pissed at him, because he's the only car washer she knows who goes to work on rainy days. Chamaco defends himself by saying that his boss is a tyrant, a ballbuster who doesn't pay them if they don't show up, no matter how much thunder and rain. Ruso goes along with it. He doesn't tell Mónica that when he comes home late it's because the video game session went on longer than expected. Besides, he likes the idea of having a reputation as an authoritarian and a despot.

Feo's arrival poses some difficulties for the electronic soccer tournaments. First because they have to turn rectangular tournaments into pentagonal ones. But mostly because Feo has a disconcerting playing style. He arms his team with eight defenders and only one striker. As always, they have a gentlemen's agreement: each opponent has the right to invent—"edit," in beginners' lexicon—a player for his team, and endow him with whatever virtues he wants. All of them—Cristo, Molina,

Ruso, Chamaco—create a perfect forward: light, fast, ambidextrous, and with a good kick. Not Feo. Feo builds a tall, heavy, thick defender. And with that Frankenstein mutant, the newcomer scatters the balls that come near the box and destroys their attacks. The others accuse him of being defensive, stingy, and point-grubbing, but he wins 1–0 with everyone trailing him and playing horribly. Feo doesn't bat an eyelash, and answers that he's not into adolescent flourishes, he just wants to kick their butts. And the others, as much as they hate to, are forced to admit he's right, because he wins almost every time.

One stormy Thursday, while Castelar floods to the brim, Ruso makes fry bread, Chamaco brings in some salamis he made the previous July, and the five of them get into a long doubleheader round-robin tournament. And it is at that moment, as Feo beats his uncle, 1–0 as always, that Ruso comes from the back room with a new batch of fry bread, sees them, and is waylaid by an emphatic certainty that he has solved the mystery that had been obsessing him ever since he went to Santiago del Estero to see Pittilanga, or since so long before that, he can't say precisely when.

"I'm an idiot!" he declares, and the others pay him no attention because they know their boss is prone to bombastic declarations, and they're more interested in serving themselves up some fry bread before it gets cold.

Ruso places the tray down on the table, goes back behind the counter, opens the register drawer, and tut-tuts because there are only a few small bills, then pats his pants to see if he has a little more money on him. Feo pauses the game because everyone is surprised by his behavior, and Cristo acts as the staff spokesperson and asks what's gotten into him. Ruso looks up at him, his eyes wide with excitement.

"Can't talk now, Cristo. I'll explain when I get back."

"Back from what?"

"I'm going to Santiago del Estero. I just realized."

"To Santiago again? Realized what?" asks Cristo.

But his questions hang in the air, because Ruso is on his way to the door, opening up an old newspaper to keep the rain off his head, and goes out onto the streets, hopping to avoid soaking his sneakers in the puddles.

Reminiscences

D amn my luck, Mauricio said to himself during the ten days following Fernando's giving him the news of Mono's illness. When he heard Fernando, when he saw him devastated, when they fell silent in the office, when Mauricio searched fruitlessly for a comforting word, or a hopeful one, or at least one that gave Fernando the feeling he was there for him, Mauricio had had the terrible idea of offering his assistance. Tell me how I can help you, he had said to him. Damn fool idea. Because Fernando, against all bets—Mauricio's bets, at least— had lifted his head and said yes, there was something he could help him with. Tell Ruso. Please. I don't have the heart. I can't.

That was what Fernando had said, god damn him to hell. And Mauricio hadn't had the quickness of mind or the gall to refuse, half a minute after offering his help. For several days he entertained the fantasy that yes, he could have said no, ask me anything but that. But at that moment, when he could, when he should have done it, he was silent. And the train had passed him by.

He thought about consulting his wife. Women are supposedly better at handling feelings. But it was a ridiculous idea. Mariel received the news of Mono's illness with surprise, perhaps with sad surprise, but that was all. She maintained her aggrieved expression for a while, asked some questions. But then it passed. Like a storm cloud, or a sudden wind. Mariel went on to the next thing. Something about the doctor they had to see together, about the fertility treatment. Well played. Mauricio couldn't say, *Let's keep talking about Mono, don't start with that.* Because that was an important topic. Especially for Mariel. Maybe—Mauricio wanted to think—it was an unconscious reaction on his wife's part: when faced with news related to death, she opposed it with news about life. Corny, but it helped Mauricio to justify Mariel's later silence about Mono's sickness. A silence that wasn't so different, after all, from his own.

On the fifth day he called Ruso up on the phone. He did it without any plan. Almost as if testing to see if their chatting would offer him a chance to fulfill his assignment. But Ruso buried him in an unflagging speech about his imminent new business venture: a car wash. That he'd been thinking it over, that he had the perfect spot picked out, that he was convinced, that he had some money to get it going, that he thought he had the problem over the thing with the place in Morón figured out. Mauricio listened to him, allowing the conversation to go where Ruso was leading it, and he hung up without saying a word.

On the eighth day he tried it again. But once again it was in vain, because Ruso thought he was calling about the credit card trouble, and he started talking about that and some ideas he'd had for the pretrial mediation, and with all that the fifteen minutes of their conversation just flew by. That they flew by was a euphemism, Mauricio knew that. Mauricio let them pass, because once again he didn't know how to start, and deep down he was waiting—anxiously, cowardly—for enough time to pass so that Ruso would hear about what was going on with Mono from some other source.

And that was another thing. Another pending matter. Mauricio knew that sooner or later he would have to call Mono. Go see him. And he didn't want to. Out of sight . . . But he would have to see him. Shit.

Finally, he glimpsed a desperate solution. It wasn't really a solution at all, but in the confusion of wanting to get it all off his shoulders it seemed like it might be a way out. He would call Mono, talk to him about what was going on with him, Mauricio would mention his qualms about facing up to Ruso . . . and maybe Mono would offer to deal with the conversation with his best friend. Or maybe not. Mauricio knew that Fernando had asked him to do it. But in the end, the request came from Fernando, not his brother. And if Mono was the one directly involved, wasn't it better he tell Ruso himself?

Even though he was weighed down with doubts, Mauricio ended up calling. Mono was happy to hear from him. That was lucky, because he was loquacious and confident. He and Fernando had gone to the doctor and they had proposed several things, treatments to try. Mauricio was sincerely glad to hear it and listened to everything he had to say.

Slowly, the subject of Ruso came up. It came up because of the damn car wash. Mono was up on what he was planning, and he was worried it was going to be another fiasco. He was also worried about him getting into another fix without having sorted out the last one. Mauricio reassured him a bit: the proceedings were more or less on the right track. The credit card thing, too. And he had some money to help him out.

"Thank goodness," sighed Mono. "Because I haven't got a red cent. I put it all into this Pittilanga thing, and I don't know how I'm going to get it back, honestly . . ."

Two of a kind, thought Mauricio. Stupid Ruso ruined one business after the other. And Mono hadn't had the best idea when he decided to go a similar route, getting into the soccer business. He felt bad for thinking that. It wasn't the time.

"Hey." Mono's voice pulled him back from his musings. "My brother told me you offered to tell Ruso . . ."

Shit. Holy crap on a cracker. From what he was saying, the way he was saying it, not only hadn't he told Ruso, but he was hoping—just like Fernando—that Mauricio would take care of it.

"Yes, Mono." Mauricio began to frantically push the button on his pen. "The thing is that I don't know how to bring up it, honestly . . . You know how Ruso is . . . And it's so fucked up . . ."

There was a silence on the line. When Mono spoke, his voice sounded affectionate, warm, as if he wanted to protect him.

"Don't get so worked up about it, Mauri. Ruso is no genius but he's not a child. At least not about this. Not like you. Nothing like you."

Mauricio was silent.

"Hello . . . Are you there?" asked Mono.

"Yes. Eh . . . yes."

"Did you hear what I said?"

Of course he had heard him. Son of a bitch. Now he was playing the analyst. It was surprising that he'd remembered that. Especially since he, Mauricio, had forgotten all about it. Or not, but almost.

His sister had gone to pick him up from school. A joy. A surprise. Very rare, because she went to school in the mornings too. She went to Dorrego and was in her fifth year of secondary, but attended in the mornings, just like him. Why was she picking him up? What if it was to take him to the movies?

And what if they were going to have pizza? It was somewhat disconcerting when she said they were going to the parish. But they went because Mauricio would go to the edge of the galaxy, if need be, with his older sister. The best sister in the world. They sat in one of the pews in the front. There weren't many people. Which was normal at lunchtime. It was awesome, this going to church together, but he really would have liked a slice of pizza better. And when Mauricio was about to say that, his sister rested a hand on his leg and told him I have to tell you something about Daddy. You need to know. And Mauricio had stared at the black and white tiles of the church to keep the tears from coming. And while his sister started to say something you need to prepare yourself for, Mauricio had gripped the hems of his school smock because his hands closed uncontrollably, closed uncontrollably into fists, moving toward his sister to shut her up and get her to stop saying that he needed to take advantage of the little time that was left. *Shut up. Shut up already.* And he had thought that it was to get pizza and go to the movies in Morón. What a fool.

"Yes, I heard you, Mono," he finally said.

"Don't get mad, Mauri . . ."

Mono started to apologize, and that was worse. Because he was right. In some twisted way, he was right, god damn it. He had gone back into that church four hundred and fifty times. Sad and happy. Hundreds of times he had gone back. But he always remembered that day. The tiles. The effort to keep from crying. The closed fists. The rage. The parish was always going to bring that back.

"I'm not mad, jerk." It was true. "I'm just surprised. When did you get so perceptive?"

Mono sighed a slight smile.

"It must be the medication they're giving me, asshat. I think it puts a shine on your neurotransmitters."

Mauricio laughed in spite of himself. And he thanked him. Wordlessly, but he thanked him. "You're such a douche, you know that?"

Soon they said goodbye and hung up.

The next day, Mauricio called Ruso again and asked him to come over to his house, taking advantage of the fact that Mariel was going out with her girlfriends. He opened a beer, put some peanuts into a clean ashtray, and told him everything. In ten words, crudely, but he told him.

22.

When the bus enters the hundredth town on its route, Ruso can't take it anymore. He approaches the drivers to ask them when they calculate arriving in Santiago. "Midday," they answer, and Ruso goes back to his seat.

If his goddamned credit card had gone through, he could have traveled in the Sleep Business Bus or Class or Flash or whatever the hell it's called, which made the trip in twelve hours, and not in this spastic junker that had already spent sixteen hours going through every possible town in the provinces of Santa Fe, Córdoba, and Santiago del Estero.

But no. The card was refused. The agent at the little station in Morón gave it back to him after trying to process the sale a couple of times, looking at him with disdain and apprehension, as if both the card and its holder had leprosy. Ruso had to scratch the bottom of his pockets and barely found enough for the Executive Service. *Executive my ass,* he thinks now that it's eleven and the bus is entering town number one hundred and one. Ruso had wanted to get there early, see the whole training session, have a proper breakfast, prepare Pittilanga somehow for telling him what he has come to say.

He doesn't manage any of that, because the bus enters the station at twelve thirty-five. Ruso climbs into a taxi begging the driver to get him as close as possible to the Mitre field, but stop when the fare is ten pesos because that's all he has. That, at least, worked out all right: he hits upon a compassionate cabbie who, when the meter reaches ten pesos, turns it off and takes him the rest of the way for free.

Ruso runs from the club entrance to the field. Luckily, practice hasn't ended; exhausted, he drops onto a concrete bench in the stands. From a distance the grandfather of the fullback waves to him. Ruso returns the greeting, but he is so tired out that he can't say a word. To top it all off he had been running and hadn't taken off his jacket, and now that he's sitting still in the sun he is dripping with sweat. In his annoyance bad thoughts take over: all his capital is the three or four peso coins he has in the smallest pocket of his pants. What lunch could he buy with that? How was he going to fill his time until ten at night, when the goddamned Executive Class leaves to take him back to Morón? Does he have enough credit left on his cell phone to call Mónica?

But just then Bermúdez blows the whistle ending the practice game and Ruso knows that his real problem is about to begin. He walks over to Pittilanga, smiles at him innocently, and proposes they sit down for a talk.

Doctor's Visit

All four of them went to the doctor together just once, an oncologist that Mono had heard great things about. He didn't expressly ask them, but the other three understood that he wanted, and needed, their company. After a month of X-rays, ultrasounds, tomographies, and MRIs, the medical clinic asked him to go see Daniel Liwe, who it seems was a prominent figure in the field. Ruso thought it was a good sign that they shared the same first name. All my namesakes are geniuses, he explained.

They waited a good long while in an empty waiting room, silently, although Ruso tried to start a few conversations. But they were tense, alert, wanting someone to finally give a name to the facts and the possibilities.

When the doctor emerged from his office to summon Mono, he was surprised to see all four of them stand up. Mono was the first to extend his hand. Then Fernando and Ruso. But when Mauricio tried to do so, Liwe raised a hand and said, "No more than three people." They hesitated. "In the examining room," the doctor clarified, "only up to three people. The patient and two companions." Mauricio stepped back and sat down again.

When they took the three chairs that were arranged on one side of the desk, Fernando thought that Mauricio's exclusion wasn't the best way to start the visit. What problem could there be in having four instead of three? He tried to calm himself down: if he was such a "prominent figure," he must have his reasons.

"I was sent by Doctor Casillas," began Mono, "who told me—"

"Let me have a look at your tests," Liwe said, cutting him off.

Behind his brother's back, Fernando exchanged a look of displeasure with Ruso. Meanwhile, the doctor pulled the test results from their envelopes and studied them, one by one.

"Did you fill out the form with your personal information?" he asked, without looking up.

"The—yeah—I left it with the secretary. Why?"

"Did you give her photocopies of the tests?"

"No, no, I didn't know," Mono shifted in his seat.

"They didn't tell us," interjected Ruso.

The doctor lifted the receiver of his telephone.

"Yes, Victoria. They didn't bring me photocopies. Make some. Thank you."

Liwe turned his chair to face his computer. As he started typing, the secretary came in. The oncologist handed her almost all the papers, without looking up from the screen. Mono cleared his throat. His body leaned toward the desk, but he was motionless. Fernando and Ruso looked at each other again. Fernando was increasingly uncomfortable.

"Should we fill you in?" asked Fernando, regretting it almost immediately. That plural, perhaps, put Mono in an inferior, dependent position. As if he couldn't explain and make do for himself. But Fernando couldn't stand the silence anymore, his brother's inert position, the reflection of the screen in Liwe's eyeglasses.

"That's fine," responded the doctor, motioning vaguely toward the papers that his secretary hadn't taken.

He swiveled the chair again to face them. He extended one hand to a prescription pad, pulled out a pen from the upper pocket of his lab coat, and began to write.

"And . . . so?" asked Mono, unable to keep his voice from fading out.

"Here, I'll give you the orders for what you have to do."

"What do you mean, the orders?" asked Mono.

"Orders for what?" let out Ruso.

"Next week . . ." began the doctor, but he stopped, as if talking was distracting him from what he had to write.

He filled out several orders. Fernando counted four. Then he put them in a row on the desk and stamped them with one of those stamps with a built-in pad.

"Where are you going to do the chemo?" asked Liwe.

"No . . . I don't know . . . didn't know I had to start chemotherapy."

"Well, you do," responded the doctor, and Fernando couldn't tell if his expression was one of self-importance, tedium, or annoyance. "That's why I'm asking."

"The thing is, I wanted to know what the treatment was going to be like. What . . . kind, what . . . alternatives," Mono was searching for the words, and Fernando knew that the one he didn't dare use was "probabilities."

"Any questions you have, I want you to talk to Doctor Álvarez about, she's the specialist in palliative care," Liwe said. Then he looked up at Mono for the first time. "With me, we'll look at strictly the oncological. Everything else, with her."

Fernando wondered if his younger brother had caught the expression "palliative care." He looked at him: Mono's face displayed such confusion that he sensed the answer was no.

The doctor stood up. The other three were slow to follow his lead, as if having trouble understanding that they'd reached the end of the consultation. But as Liwe remained standing, impassive, they finally stood up as well. The doctor held out a limp hand. When he shook it, Fernando understood what it was that had bothered him. The doctor kept looking at nothing, at a nothing located slightly above the shoulders of the people he was talking to.

They went out into the waiting room. Ruso, who brought up the rear, closed the door behind him. Mauricio came to meet them, but with a shake of the head they dissuaded him from asking. They went past the reception desk, where the secretary sat. Just then, Ruso told them to wait, that he had to go back.

Fernando looked at Mauricio, who responded with an inquiring expression. Mono was in his own thoughts, his head lowered and his hands filled with all the test results and orders. The secretary looked at them, confused. Then they heard Ruso's shouts. Actually they heard the sound of the examining room door being opened with a shove. And what they heard after that wasn't the crescendo of an argument. Not at all. It was a brutal, monolithic, shouted monologue.

"Are you a doctor or what, you little son of a bitch? Don't you see, don't you realize Mono is sick, asshole? That he's afraid he's gonna die? Or do you just not give a shit? You didn't even look at him, asshole, you didn't even look at him! Don't you realize what he wanted to ask you? Didn't you realize, moron? What? You—you've never been afraid? Are you even alive, you bastard, or what? What are you hiding, what are you hiding, loser? You chickenshit! You see how it sucks to be afraid, asshole? Now you understand, prick? Now you understand? You coldhearted piece of shit! Why do you treat cancer, you little son of a bitch! Why? Why don't you do something else? Become a banker, you fool! An astronaut! But a doctor? You deal with people, you piece of shit! You deal—"

He didn't have a chance to continue because just then the three of them pulled him out, and they got hit a few times in the struggle, because Ruso was beside himself. His face was red from the exertion, from his fury and impotence. In incoherent phrases—as they dragged him back through the waiting room, the reception area, and the hallway—he shouted for them to let him go, to leave him, that he was going to beat the shit out of that son of a bitch. His voice grew more and more choked, because he didn't want to waste time breathing and because his battle cries had chafed his throat. They stuffed him roughly into the elevator and went down the ten floors to the street.

Halfway down, as they watched the floor numbers decrease, Mono spoke.

"We're going to have to switch oncologists. I think we're through with Liwe."

Fernando smiled, because he knew his brother's voice and he knew that, behind his suffering, he was smiling too.

"I think that'd be for the best," agreed Mauricio.

23.

When Ruso asks him to sit down in the shade, Pittilanga accepts but looks at him somewhat warily.

"I didn't expect to see you again for a while . . ."

"I warned you I was planning on coming by regularly."

"Regularly, sure, but you were here two weeks ago."

"No. Yes. It's true."

Ruso, terrified, realizes that he has traveled twelve hundred kilometers and he has no idea how to begin saying what he has to say.

"It's that I was watching you play, last time . . ."

The kid holds his gaze but doesn't say a word. Nothing that helps Ruso continue.

"How'd you do this week?"

Brow furrowed, surprise, slight suspicion from the player. But he responds.

"What do I know? Same as ever, I guess . . ."

Pittilanga looks at his dirty boots, pulls a loose thread on his knee-highs, knocks his cleats against a rough floor beneath the substitutes' bench. Ruso has an idea. It's not a good one, but at least it's an idea. Let the kid talk. Maybe . . .

"Tell me something, Mario. How do you see yourself?"

"How do I see myself what?"

"How do you see yourself. Playing, I mean. With soccer. With your career, I mean. How do you see yourself?"

"Where are you going with this?"

"Nowhere, kid. But I'm interested. I'm interested in you. Who better to ask how you're doing than you?"

The kid shifts his position slightly, turning his head toward the locker room door. He's uncomfortable, thinks Ruso. He's embarrassed to be here with a stranger.

"I don't know . . . what do you want me to say?"

I don't know either, kid, thinks Ruso. *But I need you to give me an opening to talk about it without you getting all worked up and telling me to go to hell.*

"I mean, how do you see your career going, Mario. If you see yourself the same as ever, or if you see yourself making progress, moving to a bigger club, going back to Platense, getting to the premier league . . ."

"Yeah, of course. That's what I'm working toward. I'm here now but players always want to move up."

Worthless answer, thinks Ruso. Pittilanga just answered like a famous player, or some rising star, being interviewed by the press. And he is neither of those things. They're still at square one.

"How do you see me?" counterattacks the boy, and Ruso is surprised by his unexpected initiative.

"Me?"

"Yes. You."

Ruso realizes that he has gotten himself in a sticky situation.

"Psssh . . . what I can say?"

"What you think, go ahead, tell me."

Ruso stammers, moves his hands, finally begins.

"I see that you try hard, you are very professional, you give it your all in practice . . ."

A terrible start. He's stating the obvious too, not saying anything useful.

"But I'm a disaster."

"A disaster! No, why?"

"Then what am I?"

You are a burden, a pigheaded clumsy oaf, a mistake, a jack-ass, a three-hundred-thousand-dollar letdown, thinks Ruso.

"Ehhh . . . you are a kid who's learning, finding his way, seeing how to make the leap into professional soccer . . . that's what you are."

The boy smiles unhappily, kneeling to untie the laces on his boots.

"Why don't you tell me the truth?"

In Pittilanga's voice there is a surrender, a lowering of his guard, a door to possible sincerity, and Ruso decides to take advantage of it before the dumb idea that brought him all the way to Santiago del Estero for the second time reveals itself to be just that: dumb.

"To me, yours isn't a problem of attitude, or technique, or your condition. No, it's not that."

"Then what is it?"

Ruso searches for the words, but he can't find them anywhere.

"I've been watching you, I've been studying you. That other time, when all three of us went to see you at the Nueve de Julio game, last Friday, today . . ."

"And?"

The time is now. No more stalling.

"Did you ever think about playing as a defender?"

Pallor I

You know what I was thinking, Fer?"

"What, Mono?"

". . . Is something wrong?"

"Why?"

"You're pale, Fernando. Do you want me to call the nurse?"

"No. My arm hurts a little, but it's probably nothing."

"Let me call her. What do we have to lose?"

"No, Mono, forget about it. There's no need. It'll pass."

"Has it been a long time since you've given blood, Fer?"

"I think this is the first time. No, let me see . . . We gave blood one time for a classmate. For her father, I mean. But that must have been twenty years ago."

"And how was it that time?"

"Fabulous. I fainted after five minutes and it took twenty dudes to wake me up."

"Ha! So you're that susceptible, blueblood?"

"Weren't you supposed to wait outside, clown? I'm gonna call the nurse now and have her kick you out."

"Are you sure you don't want me to call her? Seriously, I mean it."

"No, Mono, cut it out. Talk to me, that'll distract me."

"You know what I was thinking about recently?"

"You already asked me and I said no. What?"

"It's stupid, really."

"That's to be expected, coming from you, Mono."

"Kiss my ass."

"I can't, I'm donating blood for my dumbass of a brother."

". . ."

"What was it you were thinking about?"

"No, nothing. Forget it."

"Now you're gonna go all chicken on me? Come on. Spill it."

"It's something serious, man. What I mean is, it's half stupid, but at the same time it's serious, and I don't want you taking it lightly."

"But you yourself warned me it was stupid."

"Yeah, because it seems stupid. But deep down I don't think it is."

"Okay, then. Tell me."

24

Pittilanga furrows his brow again, but he isn't mad—*yet*, thinks Ruso—mostly just confused.

"What?" he asks, completely lost.

"Playing as a defender, I mean. Did you ever think of it?"

"What do you mean 'as a defender'?"

"As a defender, kid. Playing defense. A center back, two or six, in the back line. A defender . . ."

"I know what a defender is! Are you pulling my leg? A defender? How am I going to play as a defender? I'm a forward, all my life, since I was little, always a forward." In his voice now there is impatience, pride, growing indignation. "Who do you think you are?"

"Don't get mad, Mario, forget I ever said it." Ruso raises his hands in a gesture of downplaying the importance of what he's just said. But it is only a gesture. He knows there is no going back.

"Oh, sure! How simple! You come, start chatting me up, acting dumb, and finally you say why don't I try playing as a defender. You think I'm a fool. It's the same as telling me that I'm a clod, that I'm not worth a damn, that I'm a total disaster."

"I'll say it again: have you ever tried?"

"I've never tried and I'm not going to, you son of a bitch!"

"Heey . . . You don't have to take it like that, kid."

"And how in the hell do you want me to take it? Are you the owner of my transfer or the enemy? Ah—now I get it . . ."

The sudden pause in his string of insults makes Ruso look at him again. Pittilanga has his eyes narrowed, archly.

"Is it that somebody's asking you for a defender, and you want to pawn me off in the deal?"

"What?" Now it is Ruso who doesn't understand.

"Of course! I'd bet money I don't have that they must have offered you guys some deal, a sale, I don't know what, and you want to stick me in the middle, fill my head with ideas to get out of a jam and make a quick buck. But I'm no fool. Don't take me for a fool, let me make that clear."

Ruso sighs. In the end, the most logical thing is for his dumb idea to end right there.

"Sorry, kid. You misunderstood, or I didn't express myself well . . . Forget I ever said anything."

"Never said anything my ass!"

Ruso thinks that it's the first time he's heard him shout. Far behind them, the sheet-metal door to the locker room opens. Pittilanga's teammates, showered and changed, are heading home. A slight wind blows up some dried leaves.

"Look." Ruso speaks calmly, because he's decided to say the whole truth and that always calms him down. "Maybe I don't know anything about soccer, maybe I'm a dolt, maybe I should shut my fat trap . . ."

"Maybe you should."

Ruso's face contorts but he lets it go.

"But I'm going to tell you two things. Two things that are true. So you know them, or so you can think about them."

"Now you're taking offense?"

"No, that has nothing to do with it," Ruso says firmly. He gets sincere. "The first has to do with us, the owners of your transfer. You know that it was Alejandro Raguzzi who bought you, right?"

"Yes."

"Well, Mono—for us he was always Mono, not Alejandro—wasn't some soccer entrepreneur. He had played, that's true. He was good, very good. A right fullback. He always wore number four. But they released him from his contract in the fourth division and that was it. Then he studied systems analysis. He was a genius at it, the big lug. And he was also my best friend. Well, the thing is that they laid him off from a top job and he got paid, paid big. Salvatierra told him about you, and Mono bought you. That was when you were selected for the Indonesian World Cup. But last year he got a cancer that kicked his ass hard. Six, seven months."

Ruso is silent. We are such little things that our biography fits into five minutes. No matter how much those we left behind love us. Five minutes with time to spare.

"The three of us know even less than Mono did. We got into this to see if we could get back the money, I'm not gonna lie to you. Because Mono put everything he had into your transfer. And he has a young daughter . . . I know it's not your fault. I'm just telling you so you understand."

"It's okay, boss. I'm sorry to hear it. But I can't do anything about that."

"That's the first thing I want to tell you. And yes, you have nothing to do with that. But you can do something about it. And I have nothing to lose, you're not gonna get more pissed off at me than you already are. Listen, Mario: you're in no position to play in the premier league. In the real premier league,

I mean. Here, it's all very well and good. But you know as well as I do that you're not getting anywhere here. When your loan period ends, you'll go back to Platense. And Platense is going to release you from your contract. And you can shove your free transfer where the sun don't shine. And the three hundred grand for your transfer will go up in smoke, I know it already. I know you can think I'm telling you this for my own benefit. But that's how it is. If we weren't involved, even without the dough, I'd tell you the same thing."

"I don't believe you."

"You're right. Maybe I wouldn't tell you, but because I try not to criticize people. It makes me feel bad. But that's why I wouldn't tell you. Not because I really thought you had a shot at the first division. And you know it. Deep down you know it."

The kid looks toward the locker room, as if he was afraid that Ruso's words would reach Bermúdez's ears, like some sort of a premonition. But there is no one around but them.

"I don't think you are understanding me. I don't . . . I don't know how to do anything besides this. For ten years now I've been doing this, day in and day out."

"I understand."

"No. You don't understand shit. I dropped out of school. To train. I've been training since I was eleven. This is a job. It always was. My old man had to take me to practice, my older brother, juggling work, schedules, games. You . . . maybe for you playing soccer is fun, you play because you like it. For me it's work. I have to eat from this. Otherwise, I don't know how to do anything else."

"But that's just wha—"

"Of the kids that started out in the ninth division, you know how many of us are left?"

"I get it . . ."

"Three of us. Three. I'll never stop. I . . . saw so many kids that were better than me, who thought they were stars, end up getting a boot in the rear."

"And who told you that your turn isn't coming up now?"

Ruso intends no harm, and that's how the kid takes it. Pittilanga doesn't shut up because he's bothered, but because he can't find any more reasons to keep talking.

"Playing like this . . . do you see yourself in the first division?"

"Maybe not in first, no, but maybe in second. And from here to there, there's a difference in money."

"I don't think it's likely."

"You don't think it's likely because that would be good for me but not for you guys. If I keep playing in the minors you guys are the ones that get screwed."

"And how much do you think you are going to earn in the minors? You think you're gonna make a fortune?"

"No. But I can go for a few seasons."

"And when you finish those few seasons you are going to end up on skid row, flat broke. Then what are you going to do? Open up a newspaper stand?"

"Maybe I will!" The kid gets his nose out of joint again. "Maybe I will open up a newspaper stand! You have no idea where I come from. No idea. For you opening up a newspaper stand is crap and maybe for me it might be just fabulous. Did you ever think of that?"

He's no fool, thinks Ruso, regretting his thoughtlessness. He didn't mean to offend with his comment about the newspaper stand. But it is true that the kid's goals could be higher.

"What I'm saying," Ruso tries another tack, "is that you have a chance. A real chance. A chance to try something new."

"Yeah. Sure. Play defense and become famous. The next Passarella."

"You never know."

"It's not gonna work."

"Playing forward isn't working either. Or haven't you realized that?"

"Quit fucking with me."

"What do you have to lose?"

"Don't even go there."

"Tell me what you have to lose."

"Time, I lose time. And possibilities."

"Possibilities?!" Now it is Ruso who takes on a sarcastic tone, as he points to his surroundings, the low grandstands, the patchy field, the broken wire fence, and the line of scraggly poplars along the thick wall that encloses the other side. "Playing on this crappy field with this piece-of-shit team? Are you serious?"

The kid grumbles contemptuously, and spits on the floor, a few feet in front of them. For a minute they watch as the earth swallows up the gob of spit.

"Instead of getting all mad, think for a minute. Do you want to end up here? I've been watching you. Not just the other day when I came. My partner, Fernando, has been filming you in a bunch of games."

"I know. I saw him."

"Okay. I swear I watched them all the way through. And I think—don't take this as cocky, but I think I understand what your problem is."

"What? You sniffed it out?" says the kid, gesturing toward Ruso's nose with a sarcastic laugh.

There are few things that ruffle Ruso's feathers, but making fun of the size of his nose is one of them. He feels his annoyance grow, an annoyance he had been keeping down deep inside, an annoyance that had started on the bus's sixteen hours of milk-truck pace and had just kept growing.

"Look here, kid. I didn't need to sniff it out. Because I've been watching soccer for a long time. Since before you even thought about playing soccer. Since before you were born. Since before they made the busted rubber your old man used the day you were conceived."

Ruso takes a breath. He doesn't regret his harsh words. Arrogant asshole.

"You can keep fucking around, trying to score goals all you want. Actually, no you can't. You have less than a year before your loan is up and you go back to Platense one way or the other. And from there, it's all downhill. They're going to kick your ass out so fast you won't know what hit you."

"But—"

"But nothing. And if you don't want to understand it, there isn't a god in the world that can help you. You can't score a goal on anybody, and you know it."

"I scored a goal the other day."

"You score a goal once every ten games. And those goals, I could make them just as well as you, trust me. With this belly, these broken-down knees, and forty-two years under my belt, you can rest assured I can get as many past the goalie as you manage to."

The sheet-metal door to the locker room opens and Bermú-dez comes out, waves from a distance, and leaves. Ruso waves back and looks at Pittilanga, whose eyes are still glued to the ground.

"You lost your touch, as they say. Or I don't know, you grew five centimeters too much, or five centimeters too little. Or you put on a couple of extra kilos and those couple kilos changed the panorama forever. I don't know. This soccer thing is very, very delicate. There aren't many guys who make it. And those that make it have something. Okay, kid: you don't have that something. Up there, fighting to score a goal, it's clear you don't have it. You'll say, 'What does this big-nosed guy know?' Well, I can assure you that I know. About my life I can't say shit because I'm a total screwup. But with others I'm not nearly as dumb as I look. I guarantee it. I know people. I listen. I watch. And that's why I'm telling you what I'm telling you. You are never going to succeed as a forward, not in this lifetime. No matter how much you whine and stamp your feet. You weren't born for it. I'm sorry. Get offended, go ahead. Get mad. Whatever the hell you feel like doing. But you're no forward, and you never will be."

Pittilanga pushes down on his heels with his toes to take off his boots. He still hasn't looked up. Every once in a while he sighs loudly, although Ruso doesn't know if it's out of frustration, anger, or impotence.

"But just like I tell you that, I can tell you that maybe you have a chance farther downfield. You can laugh your ass off. I don't care. Because if you laugh, you're a fool. Or worse, you're clueless. You're not thinking. Not thinking about it calmly, like I'm asking you to. You have to try playing farther downfield. And not as a fullback. You're too big. You're too slow, and they're gonna get past you. As a center. As a number two or a number six. Which do you prefer?"

Pittilanga frowns in an undecipherable expression. He doesn't seem to care.

"I've never played as a center back."

Ruso comes up with the perfect response. He pauses with a passing twinge of prudence, but just for barely a second.

"Are you kidding me? You play every game as a center back. For the opposing team, but as a center back."

That's it. He said it. Get mad all you want. To his surprise, Pittilanga lets out a chuckle. Halfhearted, masked in a snort, but a chuckle just the same.

"Why don't you go fuck your mother?" he says finally, but Ruso understands that he does it without real anger.

"I often get asked that, asswipe, but let's not change the subject. Do you know why I thought you might do well as a center back? Seriously?"

The boy looks at him. And Ruso senses that he's not only looking at him without anger. He's looking at him with interest.

"Because you know what it takes. Even though you always miss, you know what it takes. You know what it is to have to face the goal with a guy on top of you, pushing you, shoving you, bumping into you. You know how the goal area shrinks, fades into the distance, when you are about to kick. How your mouth gets dry when you miss the mark and the crowd grumbles, cursing under their breath. How big the goalies look when they come off their line to close down on you. How you get elbowed when you jump in the area to head a cross. You know all that. Even though you always miss, you know that."

"But I'm a forward . . ."

"You used to be! You were! People change! Besides, that way other players have the responsibility. Not you. The opponents have it. The opposite of how it is now. Right now you have to stick the ball into a square about seven meters by two meters."

"It's not a square. It's a rectangle."

"Fucking great. You dropped out of school, but you're a geometry whiz. Don't get smart, you understand me perfectly.

The forward has to sink the ball into a 'rectangle,' since you insist, of seven meters. That's it. Just seven. And with a goal-keeper standing there in the middle. On the other hand, the defender, the guy who keeps you from scoring every week, has fifty meters on either side to kick it off to. You understand? If you're a forward and you miss the goal the fans boo you like crazy. Right? On the other hand, if you're a defender and to avoid the risk of a goal you send the ball flying into outer space, everybody cheers. You following me?"

That's the gist of his theory. It's the first time he's formulated it out loud, but the idea has been obsessing him since the day before, when he came out of the car wash's kitchen carrying the tray of fry bread only to come up against Feo's infallible strategy for winning PlayStation tournaments, once again.

"I can't." Pittilanga's voice pulls Ruso from his thoughts.

"What can't you do?"

"What you're telling me to. I came here as a striker. I can't just start playing as last man."

"It's a question of giving it a shot."

"No way. Bermúdez would kill me if I suggested something like that."

"Bermúdez? Leave him to me."

"You don't know him. He's fucking crazy."

"Don't you worry. I'll take care of him."

Pittilanga looks at him again. He smiles. And Ruso senses that it must have been a long, long time, since anyone did this kid a favor.

Parallels I

"You know what Independiente means to me, don't you, Fer?"

"Sure, Mono. Why?"

"We've talked about it a thousand times, being a fan, always being on the hook over what happens to your team . . ."

"Uh-huh."

"Well, I was thinking . . . Promise me you're not going to laugh . . ."

"I already said I wouldn't, Mono."

"Well . . . I feel like what's happening to Independiente is what's happening to me."

"What?!"

"It sounds dumb, but let me explain. What was Independiente like when we were kids?"

"What does that have to do with it?"

"You tell me. What was it like? How was it doing?"

"Amazing! It was doing great. We were getting bored with winning championships. But not—"

"Stop! And tell me, now, today, how's it doing?"

"It sucks."

"Big time."

"It sucks ass."

"Exactly."

25.

Unsurprisingly, after the ardent reconciliation brought on by their return from their first and last couple therapy session, things between Mauricio and his wife continue along a more predictable and routine path. But in the subsequent fights Mauricio has a new weapon to use to his advantage: that theory of the individual spheres that Mariel tried, unsuccessfully, to dazzle the therapist with.

They are a team. They complement each other. They have virtues that mutually support each other. They are like a business, a small business that keeps growing. There it is: that's the perfect example. It's a mistake to measure the success of a couple based on such intangible criteria as words or feelings. Why not measure it by more obvious, palpable things? Where were they seven years ago? Newlyweds, in an apartment in Morón the size of an ashtray and with a huge mortgage. And now? There's a reason she can afford not to be working. That counts, that has weight, that exists. And her staying thin, pretty, and healthy also has a price. A cost. Requires an investment. And he doesn't throw it in her face. Quite the contrary. For him it is a pleasure. But sometimes one has to put things like that, white on black, to see them. He loves being able to have her like this. How many of his friends can say the same? And her girlfriends? Has Mariel ever compared herself to them? Most of them look like they are her older sisters. Ten, fifteen years older. They look like they're her aunts.

Really they're a team. Mariel loves sports. She can understand his metaphor perfectly, right? A team in which each one is best in their place. Complementary. Indestructible. No matter who they are facing. A team able to utilize the virtues of each member. That psychologist didn't take the time to understand that. That's their strength, their advantage: the team, the common vision.

She knows his defects perfectly. Mauricio doesn't try to deny them. But they go hand in hand with certain virtues. He is anxious, that's true. A hysteric, she corrects him. Well, okay, a hysteric: but that energy is also boldness, audacity. He is always a leader. And that is priceless in the law office. Isn't it? He's egotistical. Yes. She's right about that. But, what goal scorer isn't? It's in his nature. But that egotism goes hand in hand with discipline, effort, ambition. Ambition in the best sense. The ambition to go further, the ambition to keep improving, progressing. Mauricio tells her to look around. The house. The cars. He even allows himself a mischievous wink, in one of those talks bordering on an argument, and while listing accomplishments and material gains he touches her breasts lightly. They also cost a pretty penny. The best money I ever spent, Mauricio says, interrupting himself. But those titties weren't cheap. And Mariel smiled.

That's how things are going. To top it all off, the fertility treatment is well under way and the doctor tells Mariel that they are ready to try the insemination. Mauricio is happy. Just as things sometimes seem to come together for the worse, sometimes they align to work out well. For example, the day that Mariel comes by to tell him about the treatment, luck would have it that Soledad is out of the office for an exam, and although the affair is over, it's better that way, that they don't even see each other, so that nothing and no one taints their happiness.

Parallels II

"How many championships has Independiente won from when I was born till I turned twenty-five?"

"I don't know, Mono."

"Eighteen, Fernando. I counted. Seven local championships and eleven international cups."

"And?"

"Now tell me, from '95 to now. How many championships?"

"One."

"In 2002."

"In 2002. The only one. And international cups?"

"None."

"None. Exactly."

"I don't know what you're driving at, Mono."

"They released me in 1989. The Red Devils lasted a little longer. Until '95. Then, crying time."

"I still don't get it . . ."

"We both died, Fernando. The Red and I."

". . ."

". . ."

"What you're saying is ridiculous."

"Not at all."

"The Red isn't going to die. And neither are you, Monito."

26.

They arrive early, because Ruso keeps insisting and because there isn't as much traffic as they'd counted on. He is so anxious he almost makes a scene when they stop in Saladillo to fill up on compressed natural gas.

"We're gonna be late, Fer."

"We've got plenty of time, Ruso."

"Seriously. Let's fill up on the way back. It's the third time you've stopped."

"Excuse me, Your Highness. I have a small cylinder that only gives me a hundred kilometers. What are you getting at?"

"Go for a while on regular gas, that's what I'm getting at."

"Look, Ruso. Today's the first of the month and teachers get paid on the fifth working day. Are you paying for the gas?"

Ruso mumbles in protest, but he's lost the battle.

"Besides . . . since when are you so suddenly concerned with punctuality, Ruso?"

"What do you mean?"

He looks at him with such an innocent expression that Fernando immediately knows he's hiding something. He's never been good at keeping secrets. There was a reason why when the four of them played cards nobody would ever partner with him except for Mono. Their entire lives. They enter the town, park near the soccer field, and find a place at the top of the stands so they have a good angle. Ruso notices Fernando's skill in setting up the camera and mentions it.

"What do you expect? After fifteen games, if I didn't learn how to film I'd have to shoot myself. But I still don't understand why you want me to keep filming them. I already told you that idea got trashed, too."

Ruso gestures for him to look at the playing field. The teams are coming out and Pittilanga is in line with his teammates.

"Thank goodness," says Fernando. "Last year I went all the way to Trenque Lauquen and it turns out Pittilanga was injured the week before and I had no idea."

"You told me."

"Well, I'm going to tell you again and you are going to make a face like that's awful, poor Fernandito."

"That's awful, poor Fernandito."

Pittilanga looks toward the stands, where a dozen local fans insult him without enthusiasm. He lifts an arm and waves toward where they are seated. Fernando is surprised because the kid is very rough around the edges and he's never seen him make a gesture like that.

When the players get ready to begin, Pittilanga, who was trying out a few simple shots with his goalie, instead of trotting toward midfield places himself close to his goalkeeper, as a center back.

"What's he doing? Did you see that, Ruso?"

"Uh-huh."

"What's going on? What the hell is he trying to do?"

"Hold on, Fernando."

Fernando notices there is no surprise in his voice, or anxiousness or alarm. So that was the mystery Ruso had up his sleeve.

"I can't believe you, Ruso. You knew about this."

"Uh-huh."

"We're lost. This is a disaster. It can't be . . ." Fernando feels confused, dizzy. "How did you find out? When? Who decided this?" He stands up suddenly. "I'm gonna talk to the coach."

"Stop freaking out, Fernando. Sit down and wait."

The game starts off just like all the ones they've already seen. A playing field filled with craterlike potholes, the ball snaking in unpredictable paths, every shot too long and high, all brawn and no brain, an insult to good taste. What's new, different, disturbing, is seeing Pittilanga standing as the last man, right outside his goal area. After a few minutes of insignificant cluttering up the midfield, the local team sends a ball deep to the center forward. He's short and light, and Fernando knows that Pittilanga would be unable, with his slowness, with his bearlike build, to match the attacker's speed. When the forward gets control of the ball with his back to the goal, Pittilanga deals him a lethal hack that hachets him at calf height.

"Look at the free kick that brute just handed them," comments Fernando in a murmur, because he doesn't want to let their neighbors in the stands know they are rooting for the visiting team.

"Uh-huh," is the only reply.

Fernando looks at Bermúdez, who is observing the game with his arms crossed near the sideline. He hasn't reproached his new defender, and he doesn't seem too alarmed.

"Bermúdez knows about this?"

"Uh-huh."

"Are you going to spend all fucking afternoon saying 'uh-huh,' you little shit?"

"Wait," says Ruso as he chews on a fingernail, absorbed in the game.

Luckily the free kick narrowly goes over the crossbar, and
Pittilanga moves away from his area like all the others. But
since the locals have a slightly better team, or at least more
ambition, they keep attacking. Presidente Mitre gets pressed
closer and closer to their goalie. But unlike the sixteen games
that Fernando has seen before, time passes and they aren't
able to turn them into goals against Mitre. And although he
hates to admit it, the main player responsible for the scoreless
game is none other than Mario Juan Bautista Pittilanga. Because after that childish goof that cost him a yellow card five
minutes into the first half, he has gradually found his place in
the defense and on the field, taking the pulse of their long balls
and forwards' feints, and is very successful at cutting off their
advances.

Of course, he is the same big rudimentary clod Fernando
knows all too well and, therefore, unable to make an accurate
pass to the midfielders. But he doesn't need to, because his
teammates in the rear soon get used to leaving him to his dirty
work of going to ground, cutting off the attacks, and stopping
advances, and to helping him in the later task of getting the
ball far away from the goal area. Astonished, Fernando notices
that the goalie applauds him occasionally, and that his teammates give him words of encouragement as they pass by. Fernando turns toward his friend.

"How did you know about this?"

Ruso makes gestures that say don't distract me and points
to the video camera that Fernando, in his puzzlement, has not
even turned on.

"You shoot, Ruso will take care of the rest."

"Are you going to tell me how this happened?"

Ruso continues watching the game.

"I'll give you the short version," he concedes, as if after long introspection. "I talked to him and it was rough. I told him a thousand things. But . . . do you know what argument I convinced him with?"

"Which one?"

"The one about the hinges on a door."

"What?"

"You don't get it either? That the difference between playing soccer as a defender and as an attacker is like dealing with a door by its hinges."

"I don't understand anything."

"That's why I'm a businessman and you're just a common teacher, you dumbass."

"Seriously."

"Have you ever tried to take a door off its hinges?"

"Yeah, sure."

"Okay. And did you try to put it back?"

"Yes."

"And wasn't it fifty times more work fitting it back onto its three hinges than taking it off those same three hinges?" Ruso pauses. "Okay, it's the same with soccer. As a defender, you are taking off the door. As a forward, you have to put the door back on, again and again."

Fernando makes sure the video camera is in focus and checks the battery level.

"You know something, Ruso?"

"What."

"Sometimes I don't know if you are a genius with long periods of stupidity or a stupid guy with faint sparks of genius."

Ruso turns to look at him.

"And isn't it possible I'm just a genius?"

Fernando smiles. He wants to hug him, to tell him how much he loves him. But he's not about to do that.

"No, Ruso."

"That's a low blow."

Alternative Treatments I

"I don't believe in these things, Mono, but . . . I don't know . . . in the end, what do you have to lose?"

"Let's see if I understand, Rusito. You're telling me that your wife told you that her Aunt Beba went to see a witchdoctor."

"No, stop. I didn't say 'witchdoctor.' Somebody you go to and they cure you . . . they see you, they lay hands on you . . ."

"Yeah. A witchdoctor."

"Witchdoctor sounds like that sketch by Negro Olmedo, Mono."

"Okay, let's see now, excuse my interruption, but this is getting off track. It doesn't matter what he's called. Call him whatever you want."

"Okay, Mauricio. A 'healer.' You like that? A healer who sees people in Florencio Varela and took a tumor out of Beba's ovary."

"Stop, Monito. He didn't just take it out like that, like an operation."

"Well, Ruso, how would you say it? He removed it . . . he . . ."

"He didn't remove it, fool. Not exactly. She had the tumor and had to have an operation, and since she was scared shitless she went to see this guy and a week later she had no more pains."

"You already told me that, Ruso . . ."

"And when they did the tests again, for the preop, the tumor wasn't there."

"Nothing. Zero. She was healthy."

". . ."

". . ."

27.

"Yes, Mauricio, two things: Sabino told me they made the files available for review to the plaintiff in the Muñoz case, and he wants to go over some points with you."

"Okay, Sole, have him come whenever it's convenient."

"Wait, wait. Because the other thing is that I have your friend Fernando in the hallway, he wants to talk to you."

"Ah . . . you didn't have him come in?"

"I was afraid you'd need to tell him you weren't here, like last time. If I had him come in, he would have heard you. Sorry, I didn't—"

"No, no, Sole, don't worry. You did the right thing. Give me a sec . . ."

Mauricio takes a minute to recall. They last saw each other a month ago, at Ruso's birthday. Everything was peaceful, cold but peaceful. He comes up with a solution.

"Let's do this: send Fernando in, and have Sabino come by in half an hour, that way I can cut things off with Fernando."

"Perfect. I'm on it."

As he hangs up, Mauricio thinks how smart it was to keep Soledad on as his assistant. His first impulse, when everything blew up, was to get rid of her. But he thought better of it, and he talked to the girl. They worked well together, they understood each other. She agreed. And in the months that had passed it had been smooth sailing. No complaints or scenes.

The door opens and Fernando enters, dressed like he's on his way to the soccer field: worn jeans, faded sweater, canvas sneakers. He teaches class in a school in that outfit? He remembers his teachers at San José. Sure, it was a different time, but, boy, what a difference. Mauricio stands up, they embrace and pat each other on the back.

"How goes it, Fer?"

"It's all good. And you?"

"All is as it should be. Working. Don't you have school today?"

"On Fridays I have a half day. So I've already started my weekend. Perks of teaching, as they say. Barely dignified poverty, but it comes with extra time off."

"Come on, poverty is an exaggeration. How's everything going?"

Fernando rolls his eyes and makes a vague gesture, without conveying anything specific.

"I don't know if you're up to speed on the news about Pittilanga," begins Fernando.

"Ruso told me something the other day. He was superexcited about some change of position on the field. I didn't pay him much mind, honestly. You know how Ruso is when he gets excited . . ."

"Yeah, that's true. But in this case you have to give him his due. Ruso, I mean."

"Really?"

Fernando summarizes recent events. Ruso's trips to Santiago del Estero, his conversations with the ill-fated rising star and the coach, the results of the experiment.

"I'm not saying he's Beckenbauer but the guy is holding his own," says Fernando finally.

"The truth is you've really surprised me. I'm pleased, but surprised. Honestly, I never even imagined it."

"Me neither, I swear. But it seems like this thing's got legs."

The conversation glides like those flannel slippers they made Mauricio wear as a kid, so he wouldn't leave marks on his grandmother's waxed parquet floor. How to continue? Listening or asking questions?

"You think now he could be sold, maybe . . . ?"

"We hope so. The change of position was six games ago. Ruso and I are taking turns filming them all. The first year I did it alone, but now that Ruso is helping me it's much easier."

"Yeah, I understand. The thing is that with my job, my wife . . ."

"No, no, that's not what I was saying."

Too good to be true? Fernando isn't making him feel guilty and he seems sincere. Mauricio wonders if things are fine or, like in those horror films Mariel likes, everything only seems fine until suddenly vampires attack or some masked lunatic shows up with a chain saw.

"What I'm getting at," continues Fernando, "is that Ruso's enthusiasm has been a godsend. He is so over the moon about his hunch working out that he offers to go all the time. I have to keep him in check or Mónica's going to shoot him."

"That's still complicated . . ."

"And you know how Ruso is. The thing is we have the six games. Well, actually five, because two weeks ago, in General Pico, Pittilanga had an afternoon, man oh man. You either put it behind you or you kill yourself. Let's forget about that one."

Mauricio smiles, as he bites his tongue. The words that come to his mind are: *You went all the way to General Pico, you crazy fools?* He stops himself in time. Why run the risk of putting them in the role of heroes? Anyway, they already put themselves there without any help. Especially Fernando. But he still feels uncomfortable. An anxiousness he can't put a finger on, a kind of sadness. Guilt? Imagining those two dummies traveling halfway across the country to shoot that kid's games. And the worst isn't that they do it. Judging by Fernando's smug expression, it's that they're thrilled to do it.

"Okay. And now?" asks Mauricio, as a way out, to slip off that burden that, come to think of it, he doesn't have to bear.

"Now comes a more complicated matter, Counselor."

Mauricio settles in and cautiously readies himself to follow his strategy for complicated negotiations. He took it from a seminar the firm sent him to once. An American counseling expert, or something like that. You make two circles, two groups, one with the acceptable and the other with the unacceptable. And, in your head, put everything inside one circle or the other.

"Tell me."

"I think it's working. I think we just might be able to sell him as a defender."

"Awesome," concedes Mauricio. That goes into the acceptable circle.

"The problem is I spent all last year visiting entrepreneurs, agents, all that shit. And I gave an awful impression, I think. I think I burned those bridges."

Mauricio's alarm bells go off: what if Fernando is trying to get him to take his place in the negotiations? Because it's true the firm has some dealings with the soccer world. And Mauricio has no intention of mixing the two. Don't shit where you . . . That goes straight to the unacceptable circle.

"Me and Ruso," continues Fernando, "we were racking our brains over it."

A new level of danger. Those two incompetents have resolved it amongst themselves and they've got it all wrapped up. Fernando isn't there to ask him what to do, but to notify him of what they've decided behind his back. And if he's there to notify him, it's because they intend on his taking part. The second circle of his imaginary diagram fills with objections and hazards.

"And what we thought was to give it a shot in the media."

Mauricio is perplexed for a moment. The media?

"Ruso has the radio on all day at the car wash, to that station that only does sports programs."

"Yeah, the Cosmos."

"That's the one. Did you see there's a show, around noon, with that journalist Armando Prieto?"

"Yes." Mauricio is so disoriented that he doesn't know which circle to put this part of the conversation into.

"A radio show and at night on TV. And it's seen all over."

"And you guys want to get him to talk about Pittilanga," throws out Mauricio.

"Exactly! But the thing is, seems this Prieto is a son of a bitch."

"That's what they say."

"Yeah. But maybe, if we offer him a bribe, he might agree to talk Pittilanga up. Salvatierra can give us the contact, looks like."

Mauricio tries to think fast. What do they want from him? Fernando, perhaps sensing his hesitation, explains the plan a little better. What if this Prieto starts saying, casual like, that there is such and such defender, in the Argentine A

Tournament, who's a dark horse, I don't know . . . who seems like a real gem . . .

"Ruso and I are convinced this kind of planted story happens all the time," says Fernando, concluding the idea. "And there must be journalists who charge to make them convincing. It's all a question of casting out the bobber and seeing who bites. And this is where we have a question for you."

Mauricio is barely breathing. He is so alarmed by the turn things are taking that he doesn't even think of correcting Fernando's poorly constructed metaphor: you throw out the bait, not the bobber. But he doesn't think this is the time to look for precision. In all that conjecture there is a main point missing, which is, where are they going to get the cash to bribe the journalist? When he understands that, he feels as if Fernando, with skillful moves, has just placed a grenade on the desk and pulled the pin. It requires composure. Composure and silence.

"As far as the money goes, Ruso and I thought that maybe we could offer him a deal like the one we worked out with Bermúdez, Mitre's head coach."

Slight relief. Maybe this isn't about asking for a loan from the "Bank of Mauricio," an unrecoverable one, just like everything hatched up by those two. Fernando continues.

"But we don't know what figure to throw out. And that's where you might be able to help us, because you're much more of an expert in that type of racket."

Mauricio is so relieved that he doesn't even feel up to getting offended, although the immediate translation of that reference to his erudition would be more or less "you might be able to help us, because you're an expert in bribes of all sorts." They want legal counsel? Great. He's happy to provide some.

"Look, Fer. I think that what we can do"—how great to be able to throw out that first person plural, such a mark of solidarity, bringing the team together—"is start off with ten percent. It's never in your best interests to commit to a fixed amount. Because then later, if the numbers aren't what you were expecting, you've put yourself in a sticky situation. But this way, if the deal comes off well, great, everybody's happy. And if he only sells for two bits, tough titties: he gets his cut and he can go fuck off."

"Then we'd have to be getting something like three hundred and fifty grand, to be able to pay the commissions to Bermúdez and Prieto."

"But didn't you say Pittilanga was doing well as a defender?"

"I guess so . . ."

"Thirty-five big ones, for work that doesn't get your hands dirty, doesn't run risks of any ilk. What more could you ask for?" says Mauricio.

"What a pretty word, 'ilk'!" teases Fernando.

"You see?" he plays along. "And you thought language arts teachers were the only ones who know how to speak."

"There's something else," says Fernando, and Mauricio drops the banter and goes into warning mode again. "We've already made contact with Prieto, through that idiot, Polaco Salvatierra. He's still good for something, after all."

"Great." Great?

"And Prieto wants to meet up in a restaurant in Puerto Madero, not next Saturday, but the one after."

Once again, danger. Mauricio has already lost all notion of the size of the circles in his mental map, but if Fernando is asking him to deal with the meeting with the journalist, he has made up his mind to say no, no way. Not an ice cube's chance in hell. Unacceptable.

"And so . . . ?"

"Well, Ruso and I were thinking that I'm going to have to impress the guy."

I'm going to? So Fernando was going to take care of it. God is good.

"Sure. Impress him."

"If I go dressed like this," Fernando displays his attire, "we're done for. On the other hand, if I go clad in one of those tailor-made Italian-cut suits you use . . ."

"Clad. Now there's a word worthy of a language arts teacher." Mauricio allows himself to return the joke. Everything is okay.

"Most likely. If you could facilitate something of that ilk . . ."

"Ha, very funny." Mauricio wants to close that ellipsis as soon as possible.

"But apart from the suit I need a proper car. My Duna's not exactly going to impress anybody. Or maybe it will, but not in a good way."

"You need mine?"

"Ruso and I thought that showing up at the meeting in a scorching Audi A4 would be an interesting way to get started."

Mauricio reviews the map of circles. He was afraid they were going to ask him for money and that didn't happen. He was afraid they were going to ask him to deal with the negotiating and that didn't happen either. Lending them the Audi is a modest price to pay for getting out of that.

"Done, Fer. Prieto is going to fall flat on his ass when he sees you drive up."

Just then, as if scripted, Soledad peeks in to tell him that Sabino is waiting to go over that thing with the lawsuit. It is just the kind of coincidence that gives Mauricio the feeling, every once in a while, that life is perfect.

Alternative Treatments II

"So what do you think, about me seeing a witchdoctor, Fer?"

"I already told you he's not a witch—"

"Shh, Ruso! Shut up. I want to know what my brother thinks."

"I don't know, maybe it's worth giving what Ruso says a shot."

"That's what I'm saying, Mono! What do you lose? You lose nothing!"

"It's not that simple, Ruso. It's getting the file with the test results again, and getting in the car again, not even that, it's because I can't drive, so it's asking somebody to drive me out to the middle of nowhere again . . ."

"So? He's not going to even ask you for the test results. He didn't even ask Aunt Beba why she'd come."

"It's no problem for me to take you, Mono."

"I know, Mauricio, it's not that. But don't change the subject. What about you, Fer, what do you think I should do?"

"Maybe . . . I know you're fed up, Monito. But as Ruso says, maybe it could be a real chance. I don't know . . . passing it up . . . I'd give it a shot. I mean, I guess."

". . ."

". . ."

". . ."

". . ."

"Exactly, Mono. What do you have to lose?"

"Can I answer, Ruso?"

"Go ahead, Mauricio, you're the lawyer in the group."

"He loses the peace of mind of concluding this once and for all, Ruso. He loses because he has to get his hopes up again. Bah, he mostly loses if that hope is just a fart in the wind, you know what I mean? He'd be grasping at straws. Again speculating on a chance. Doing more tests."

"But he's not going to ask him for tests."

"Okay, whatever. He loses by having to listen to someone again—it doesn't matter who, a doctor, a priest or a faith healer—telling him that yes, he can be cured, that perhaps, you never know . . ."

"You're just a damn pessimist, Mauricio."

"Yup. And I've pretty much hit the nail on the head every time up until now, don't you think?"

". . ."

". . ."

". . ."

28.

He gets to Mauricio's at a quarter to nine, rings the bell, and Mariel answers.

"Hello, I'm the birthday girl. I'm here to pick up my party dress," he says, trying to be funny.

"Hello. How are you, Fernando?" Mariel ignores his joke. "Come in. Mauri's still sleeping."

He follows her through the living room and the dining room to the kitchen. She is wearing a light green tracksuit, and Fernando wonders—without passion, with the cold patience one devotes to purely theoretical speculations—what it would be like to make love to her. It's not the first time he enters into such considerations, because the question had come up several times in conversations with Mono when he was alive, with him and with Ruso, and they never reached full agreement on the subject. Those two—pure primitivism, pure drive, according to Fernando—had declared themselves clearly in favor of the pleasures of getting into her pants. And they had been surprised when he raised objections. It was true—Fernando had conceded—that she is a very, very pretty woman. Beautiful, they had corrected him. Beautiful, he accepted. Did you see her eyes? they asked him. Lovely, he confirmed. Did you see her tits? her waist? her ass? Incredible, he conceded, and the others nodded with lustful eyes. But she was a little—and here it became hard to pinpoint—too much of a "doll" he had once said. A terrible choice of words, because those two clowns had immediately started to slap each other's hands and link the word "doll" with those inflatable sex toys, with which it seemed—judging from the depth of their details—they'd had some experience or at least a hidden longing. Some other time Fernando had described his lack of enthusiasm by saying that he found her flat, like lacking salt and pepper. Another huge mistake: the two monkeys had started making a link between that image and food, condiments and swallowing. At this point in the discussion Fernando had chosen to give up and tell them that yes, she was a real hottie, and leave it at that. One way to leave those two infants happy and satisfied.

"Here's the suit." She gives him an expert once-over. "I put this one aside for you because it has broad shoulders, and you're a little bigger than Mauricio."

"Yeah. I'm breaking my back at the sailing club. Canoeing on the Morón Creek, you know."

"Huh." She looks at him and smiles slightly, a polite way of not leaving him orphaned with his joke again. But she quickly returns to what she was saying. "It's been dry-cleaned recently."

Fine, Mariel, I'll cut out the jokes. He might not be a paragon of humor, but the chick is a rock. She's impenetrable. The word is a perfect fit, although it's lucky he never used it with Monito and Ruso, because they would've had a ball. But he can't find a better label. Always smiling, always attentive, always serene, always well put together. But on the surface, on the outside. She can't just be that. Or maybe she is and he's rummaging around, looking for hidden lives, private secrets where there is nothing more than what's on the face of it. A pretty woman and that's it. Superficial. Or better put, hollow. Pure form and no substance.

"Mauri didn't tell me if you needed shoes. Just in case, I pulled these out for you." She points to a cardboard box, on the floor, which holds a perfectly shined pair.

"You did well," he says, resigned to her monotonous disposition and pragmatic spirit, and points to his faded blue sneakers.

"The shirt, tie, and socks are in the bathroom."

"Wonderful, Mariel. Thank you." He kneels to pick up the shoebox and grabs the hanger with his other hand. "This way, right?"

"Yes. The light is beside the door."

Fernando dresses slowly. It has been such a long time since he's worn a suit and tie that he makes several mistakes with the buttons and the knot. But the final result is satisfactory. Shaved and with his hair combed like that, and with those shoes, he looks like an important executive. Or at least enough like one to calm his anxiety a bit. He puts his own clothes on the hanger and his sneakers in the box. Mariel eats a low-fat yogurt as she waits for him.

"How does it fit?"

"Well. Wonderful."

"Don't you want to leave your clothes there?"

"No. I'll take them with me because I have to coordinate with Mauricio when and where I return the car to him."

They both turn their heads toward the door when they hear footsteps on the stairs. Mauricio comes in with his hair messy, in a robe and flip-flops.

"What's up, Fer? Good morning, my love."

"Is the 'my love' part for me or for her?" asks Fernando, adopting a sorrowful tone.

"Just because she's here, silly billy." While Mauricio is a dumbass about other stuff, at least he knows how to play along with a joke. Fernando opens his arms to show off his outfit. "Aren't you going to say anything?"

"You look lovely, Fer. Prieto is going to fall at your feet," says Mauricio as he serves himself some coffee.

Fernando looks at Mariel. She is scraping up the remaining yogurt with a spoon, her expression distant, vacant. What a dumb broad, he concludes again, and considers the subject closed.

"How should we meet up for the car?" he asks Mauricio. "I can bring it here to your house when I'm finished, that's what I say. I think that'll be around two, or three . . ."

"Aren't you meeting at noon? I doubt you'll be done that early. Let's do this," Mauricio yawns as he sits in front of his cup of coffee. "Bring it to me at the club. I'll go with Mariel in her car."

"But we have tennis from five to six, Mauri."

"That's no problem for me," says Fernando, uncomfortable. "If I get there earlier, I'll wait. Besides, I'll take advantage of the opportunity to walk around your club dressed like this. I'd like to think I'll have some kind of luck." He considers adding something about all the females just farting around in the club all day, but he decides it would seem too obvious that his comment was directed at the beauty dressed in green, so he keeps quiet.

"Okay, I get it." Mauricio points to a shelf. "There are the keys to the Audi."

"It's better if you take it out of the garage. I'm bad with reverse and first. But in first at least I'm going forward . . ." He sees Mauricio's sudden expression of alarm. "It's a joke, you dumbass."

Mauricio smiles. Mariel removes a loose thread from her zip-up sweatshirt. The word "dumbass" must have bugged her, not because he said it to her husband but just because he dared to utter it in her kitchen. Fernando finally understands what makes him most nervous about this woman: that stillness, that distance, that coldness is worse than simple haughtiness. It makes him feel like a bother, like an extraneous object, a bag left in the way. He wonders if she is like that with everything outside of her own world or only with what Mauricio has brought from the world outside to meet her. His past. His friends.

"Come with me to the garage anyway, in case you have some last-minute tips." He makes an effort to make his voice sound neutral, official, businesslike, as he says goodbye to her. "Ciao, Mariel."

"Ciao, Fernando."

Alternative Treatments III

"We're going to do something, ladies."

"What, Mono."

"What are we gonna do?"

"Agree on something, and go through with it. All three. All four: you three and me. Okay? I'm going to go see this 'healer' in Florencio Varela. With the test results, or without them, it doesn't make much difference. We won't say anything about it to my mother. Mauricio's right about that. I think he's right about the rest, too, but whatever. We won't say anything to anyone. You, Fernando, are going to take me to Florencio Varela and we'll see the healer. Whatever happens, whatever goes on, whatever he says, this will be the last of it. It's over. No more doctor's visits, specialists, specially specialized doctor's visits, and we quit fucking around for the rest of the time that's left. Understood?"

"..."

"..."

"Agreed."

"Okay."

29.

An impeccably dressed waiter holds open the swinging door so he doesn't have to bother to push it and Fernando is reminded of a scene in the film *Titanic*: Leonardo DiCaprio, who is poor as a church mouse but wearing a tuxedo, enters the first-class dining hall with princely airs. And the waiters, dazzled by his appearance, treat him like a lord. Here it's the same thing. Fernando does hope that his adventure doesn't have the tragic outcome of Leonardo's story, frozen solid in the icy waters of the North Atlantic. He introduces himself and they show him to the table he has reserved. Naturally, Prieto hasn't shown up yet.

He settles in at a table overlooking the river's inner harbor and realizes he's made an important mistake. The other diners—not many, because it's not yet prime lunchtime—are wearing casual clothes. Elegant, sharp, but casual. It's Saturday. And he is dressed as if it were a workday. He tells himself to calm down. Enough neuroses. What's done is done, as his grandma would say.

Along the paved walkway he sees a group of boys that look like students pass by. Of course. He is very close to Catholic University. He can't help comparing them with his own students and one of those eternal questions with no answer comes to his mind: why are people with money better-looking than people without? That little group, in fact. Two boys and three girls. Why isn't there an ugly one among them? Or is it the opulent atmosphere that makes them look more beautiful?

Fernando has a ton of ugly students, both boys and girls. He considers himself ugly. Ruso is ugly. Mono was passable, but no great shakes either. Mauricio is the best-looking of the four. Was that why he'd made money? Could it be that looks attract money? Or the other way around? Because those kids have money that's come down to them over generations. They haven't earned it. Or if it's not old money, then their parents made it during the Menem years. He detects a twinge of resentment in his thoughts. Long live the revolution, he pokes fun at himself. Is a certain personal frustration creeping into his musings? He likes to think it's not. Not in this case. He shakes his head, refusing to believe it himself. Enough dark thoughts, or he's going to end up hanging himself from a ceiling beam before his meeting with Prieto.

A waiter approaches, and Fernando explains he is waiting for someone else. The waiter leaves him a glass of red wine, a tray of bread, and a couple of appetizing starters. In ten minutes he's made short work of almost all of it. He looks at the other tables and reproaches his own voracity. Those people eat little by little, not with the urgency of a shipwrecked sailor. He shakes off the crumbs as best he can, to erase the traces of his plundering, but the pointy edges stick in the tablecloth and he has trouble getting rid of them. Finally he has it more or less under control. He looks at his watch. Twelve-thirty. Damn. He's been waiting for half an hour. He needs to use the bathroom, but he doesn't want to leave the table for fear the guy will appear, see it empty, and leave the same way he came in.

Finally Prieto shows up forty minutes late. The headwaiter greets him like a regular and points to the table where Fernando is waiting. He gets up to extend his hand. He doesn't even consider reproaching him for his lateness. In this negotiation, he

is the weak party, not the journalist. Besides, lateness is practically a sport in Argentina. Second in importance, perhaps, to
the great national pastime of driving like outlaws and crashing
your car en route.

And anyway, Armando Prieto is there. Not very tall, not
very young, his hair looking grayer than on TV, but with the
same technological tan. He wears a light-colored shirt, with
the neck open and the sleeves rolled up, and pleated pants in
a matching color. Normal attire for a Saturday morning. Fernando again feels like a little wedding cake figure.

"So you're a friend of Polaco's," Prieto breaks the silence, as
he gestures to the waiter.

"Yes. Since we were kids. The neighborhood." There's no
need to correct him, to tell him Polaco's more of an acquaintance than a friend, an acquaintance he detests. At the same
time he is amazed at how nicknames take on a life of their
own. This guy doesn't know, he can't know, that his brother
invented the name "Polaco," thirty years earlier, based on his
erroneous certainty that all blonds came from Poland.

"How 'bout that," adds Prieto, to say something. "You want
wine?"

Fernando nods and indicates that he should choose. Prieto
lifts the menu toward the waiter and orders one that costs
more than a hundred pesos. Then they order their food.

"Well, Armando, I don't know if Salvatierra told you more
or less what the situation is . . ." ventures Fernando, as a way
to get the ball rolling. He doesn't ask him if he can address him
informally. He just does it because he figures, or he wants to
believe, that informality brings them closer.

"Yes, he told me a little. He said that you own a transfer
with some friends . . ."

"Yes. With two others. The guy is named Pittilanga."

"That's right. And he plays in the third division, as a forward."

"Actually, no."

Fernando, somewhat embarrassed, begins to explain. It was predictable that Salvatierra, with his brain as fried as it is, would present Pittilanga as a forward. But having to start off with the change of position is like confessing a weakness, an improvisation. Again he is flooded with the familiar sensation of being a terrible magician, whose tricks are easily seen through. But he bucks up and starts to explain, directly and concisely. In ten minutes, in five, he covers Pittilanga's biography from his training on the farm teams, his appearance in the U-17, his later stagnation, his loan. And he finishes by explaining the change of position. It seems that Prieto appreciates his brevity. He must be a busy guy, thinks Fernando. He doesn't have time for long detours. He congratulates himself on his strategy. His training in auditoriums, with forty teenagers content to remain ignorant, is paying off. If he can capture the attention of such an audience (even if only for brief periods), he can certainly do it with one guy, who on top of it all—if they come to an agreement—will get a cut.

"And what you guys need is . . ." Prieto prompts when Fernando finishes.

"To make him look good."

Just then their food arrives. Prieto refills their wineglasses and they start to eat, although Fernando is so nervous he's not hungry. He eats just so that the other guy isn't self-conscious about his appetite.

"What a fucked-up world this soccer stuff is, huh?" comments Armando Prieto as he cuts his meat.

"Well. You must know more about it than us. From the outside . . ."

The journalist rolls his eyes, as if his experience was too much to express in words.

"It's all about cash. All of it."

Fernando nods. Without wanting to, he remembers his last conversations with Mono. The ones where he talked so much about Independiente. About his love for the team. About his nostalgia for its past glory. About his uncertainties over that ridiculous emotion they shared. How would he have felt about a conversation like this one?

"And even more now. More in recent years, you know. When I started out in all this, a bunch of years back, I don't know, maybe it was different . . ." His cell phone rings and he turns it over to see who's calling. "Excuse me for a second. Yeah, what's up? . . . Here in a lunch, a meeting. What's going on?"

As he speaks, Prieto pulls out a small electronic calendar and brings up on the screen the little boxes for the following week.

"Let's see, hold on. No, on Monday I'm talking about the weekend games. There's no problem there. On Wednesday there's a Cup. If River loses I have my subject for all of Thursday, but if they win . . . Friday?"

Fernando has a particular knack for reading upside down. A good way of detecting the spelling atrocities committed by his students and correcting them on the spot. In the box for Tuesday he reads, "Speculate on the sale of Riquelme to Europe again." Prieto rests his electronic pencil on Wednesday, which is empty.

"No, the Riquelme thing I'm doing on Tuesday, it's a dead day. We need a topic for Wednesday."

With some effort, Fernando manages to hear the loud voice of the person on the other end of the line, but he can't make out his words. He seems to be some kind of prompter, who is suggesting topics for the radio program. Prieto probably prefers to call him the "producer." Producer of asinine shit, thinks Fernando. It's pathetic to think of the thousands of guys who, on Tuesday, will be on the hook wondering where Juan Román Riquelme will be sold to. Wednesday's bullshit is yet to be determined.

"No! We talked about the ball thing recently! You have to write it down, Nacho," Prieto says reproachfully. "Otherwise, you might make me stick my foot in it. Don't you remember we called a couple goalies, to get their opinions on air? . . . Ah, see? You should be keeping this straight, not me."

He pauses, looking at the tablecloth. It's as if Fernando wasn't there. It's for the best. He wouldn't know what expression to make if he looked at him.

"Ah, that's a good one." Prieto straightens up in his chair, as if abruptly excited, and in the calendar he jots down "Goal size." "Yes, I understand that, but . . . Maybe, what do I know? You think so?" Prieto starts to play with a piece of potato on his plate, making it skate over the sauce. "Hey, I like it, I like it."

Fernando sees him add to the calendar: "Make the goals bigger. Debate. Listeners. Players' opinions?"

"Okay, Nacho. Mission accomplished . . . Yes. Yes. See you at the station tomorrow night. Ciao. Yeah, yeah. Ciao."

He faces Fernando again, who is sadly concluding that he's not the only mediocre magician whose tricks are transparent.

Decline I

"I'll argue with you about this from now until the end of time, Fernando. Think about the fans. How many fans does Independiente have?"

"Independiente? A ton, Mono. They still have a ton."

"*Still*. But every day there are fewer Red supporters. They all root for Boca, now. Or at least for River."

"What do you expect? On TV all day they're always going on about Boca and River . . ."

"My point exactly, Fernando."

"They play on Sundays, they get more money from TV, all the shows are going on and on . . ."

"But careful, there are other teams that are getting more fans. San Lorenzo's fan base must be growing."

"San Lorenzo?"

"For sure, man. And Vélez, too."

"Vélez? How many root for Vélez?"

"Doesn't matter. And don't move your arm, you're gonna shake out the needle, and I need your blood. Otherwise, I wouldn't give a shit about your arm, let me make that clear. But I'm talking about trends. They have more and more. We have fewer every day."

"I don't think that's so true, Mono."

"When we were kids, everybody was lining up to root for Independiente. We had fans coming out our ears."

30.

For a while, Armando Prieto keeps the conversation away from the subject of Pittilanga. Fernando remains patient and they talk about soccer, politics, journalists, television shows. Really it's Prieto who talks, and Fernando just gives him enough encouragement so he can construct a smooth monologue. At first he finds it interesting and it feeds the curiosity he's had as a lifelong soccer fan. But then he starts to lose interest, because Prieto has two defects he can't stand: he talks without taking the slightest interest in the person in front of him, and he pontificates about a wide range of subjects as if his mouth were the font of all truth. A born expert. A consummate everythingologist. A real Argentine, damn us, laments Fernando, his mood worsening by the minute. And he weaves together anecdotes and memories so seamlessly that Fernando suspects he must repeat them ad nauseum. Like one of those movies that give off sparks of light and crackly sound in the theater, from having been played so many times.

When they've served the coffee, Prieto pauses and looks at him as if he's just discovered he's there. Well, at least he's realized that he's in front of a human being and not a microphone.

"Well, Fernandito. Let's see." We're off to a bad start, thinks Fernando, who hates when people use familiar, affectionate nicknames when there is no familiarity or affection between them. "You need to tell me what you've been thinking about in regard to this kid Pintalingi . . ."

"Pittilanga."

"That's it, Pittilanga. What a name, huh . . ."

Fernando clears his throat. Here comes the hardest part. He isn't good at business. And he's even worse in this case, when the business is so shady.

"We need to set Pittilanga up"—"set up," he likes his own euphemism—"as a known player. A good player, who is some sort of a dark horse, who's going to move to a big team any minute . . ."

"Aha," is all Prieto says, and Fernando curses him in silence. All of a sudden the bastard's lost his desire to monologue.

"And well, Armando"—what if I call him Armandito, he jokes to himself—"basically we need to give him some good press. And we can't think of anyone better at that than you. I'll tell you the truth. Who has more reach in Argentina than you, in all of Latin America?" *And who is more corrupt, more underhanded, more of a self-serving turd than you, willing to accept an offer like this one?*

"But how were you guys envisioning it?"

What a lovely circumlocution. What an impressive detour to avoid the only valid question at this point in the soiree, which would be: how much are you going to fork out?

"Well, Armando. In our inexperience, the truth is we don't really know how to handle it. What I mean is, we know that advertising has a price, a value. Nobody is going to do it for free. And we have no problem with that, obviously."

"Let's see, Fernando. Let's see. Don't take this the wrong way, because I'm going to tell you this for your own good." Prieto leans on the table and shows his hands. Purity in a state of grace. "This is a very fucked-up environment, very difficult. It's full of vultures, you know? You have to be very sharp to survive, to stay alive. I, yeah, I sometimes laugh at the dumb stuff players say about how hard it is to play soccer, about how difficult it is, about how they struggle to win, get sold well, the preseasons. All that dumb bullshit they use as if they were the pinnacle of sacrifice. And then they fuck with you, you know, when you criticize them, when you put them in their place, they start saying, 'What do you know?'" Prieto imitates a coarse, bullying tone: "'You've never worn the uniform, you never played in your fuckin' life,' they tell you. And, you know what, I laugh my ass off, Fernando. I've been making my living off this for thirty years. Do you know how many players I've seen come and go? Generations!! Generations of boneheads who think they're kings and end up forgotten!"

He pauses because someone is calling him on his cell phone. Either it's not important or he doesn't want to cut short his own fit of indignant inspiration, because he ignores the call and tries to pick up the thread.

"The heroic era of team loyalty is over, the vacant lots, the pickup games, all that shit. Now they're all professionals. All of them. On the field and off. And you must have seen that, by this time. You know I've been looking into this kid too . . . Pintilaga. That you were trying to sell him here, there, and everywhere."

Not again, thinks Fernando. He hears that about "trying to sell him" and it's like being buck naked on a billboard over Avenida Nueve de Julio. Sooner or later, everybody reminds him about it.

"Let's see. What I mean is that it's not easy. You saw that in the flesh, I'm saying. There's no free lunch. Everybody tries to turn things around to make a buck. The days of passion for the colors are over. That's supposing they ever existed. Because I don't even believe things were purer in the old days, cleaner. Bullshit. The thing is they didn't get out. They weren't known. Now, since they've got a microphone and a camera up their asses twenty-four hours a day, everything gets leaked, you know. You're either in or you're out. You understand the rules of the game or you're treated like a joke. And when I say rules I don't mean that bullshit they say on the street, that so-and-so plays by the rules, or what's-his-name doesn't know the rules, that neighborhood thing, that gang stuff, they think they're all loyal, with their rules of allegiance and all that shit. No: I'm talking about understanding the rules of this business. You following me?"

Is he following him? Yes. Reluctantly, without enthusiasm, but he's following him. Again he remembers Mono, loving and suffering for Independiente on his deathbed. What a fool. What fools all four of them are. Even Mauricio, behind his curtain of cynicism.

"Let's see," insists Prieto after a short pause, and Fernando fantasizes about, if he hears him use that pet phrase "let's see" one more time, sticking the dessert fork into one of his exquisitely manicured hands. "Soccer is all about the spectacle. The business of spectacle. The ball is handled by the owners of the spectacle. I'm not sure if I'm being clear."

Clear as a motherfucker, thinks Fernando.

"Now: you realize I have to maintain my prestige. It's the only capital worth anything in the media. Your image. Your—"

He's gonna say it, he's gonna say it, the son of a bitch is gonna say it . . .

"—your credibility."

He said it! The son of a bitch said it!

"And if I recommend this Pintilinga on the air, there has to be a minimum guarantee that the guy can play."

"Yes, Armando. I can give you some videos."

"No, Fernando. I don't have time to watch videos of Presidente Mitre games. I have to trust your guarantee, you follow me?"

"Of course, don't worr—"

"And another thing. Important. There is no way I can be seen to be mixed up in the buying and selling of a player. Ever. Otherwise, my whole shebang is shot to shit."

For the first time in the meeting Fernando feels thrown. Up until that point it had followed a predictable course. Sickening, but predictable.

"The operation with me can't be tied to the kid's sale. I'm sorry, but that's something you'll have to figure out how to handle. I can't be waiting for him to be sold to Polynesia or to the Desamparados de San Juan."

He leans over the table, getting closer.

"Let's see." Again, again with the "let's see, let's see." "You think I can be calling you up every week to see if the deal went through? And another thing: how would you guys do it? Include me in the contract? Ten percent for the journalist who did our radio and television publicity? Let's get serious, kid."

"Kid." Fernando can't help but admire the pertinence of the moniker. Just like that, with three letters, that big jerk just sketched out the real balance of power between them. Enough of the friendly Fernandito or the correct Fernando. No. Now he's "kid." The inexperienced fool who's offering him an interesting deal but with a few weak points. No problem. The big journalist is patient and willing to explain those faults and propose solutions. Don't be a dummy, kid. Listen and learn from those in the know.

"This has to be done under the table, and without delay. Just to start talking."

Prieto turns to his left to attract the waiter's attention and order another coffee. Fernando clears his throat and shifts in his seat, thinking that there is at least one good thing in being called kid: there is no other alternative but to do what the grownups tell you to.

Decline II

"**A**nd what do you want, Mono? Of course kids were gonna become fans of Independiente when we were winning all those championships."

"Exactly, Fernando. The Red Devils were a young team. In their prime. It was . . . I don't know how to explain it. But now we're fucked. Now the only ones who become Red fans are the children of Red fans, if anybody. It's a question of respect, of inheritance."

"And that's a good thing."

"But it's not enough, Fernando! It's not enough! Guadalupe roots Red because I drove her nuts. I drove her nuts. I bought her the jersey before she was even out of the incubator. I made her a member of the club at two months old."

"And that's a good thing . . ."

"Cut it out with that 'it's a good thing'! It sucks! And what about when I'm not around? What are we going to do with Independiente? Don't you realize we're on our last legs? We're going to die."

"Independiente's not going to cease to exist. Look at the messes Racing's been in and they're still around. San Lorenzo lost their field, and until—"

"Don't even talk to me about the field. I'm begging you."

"What's wrong with the field?"

"What do you mean what's wrong? We have no field, Fernando!"

"We don't have one because we're building a new one, Mono. They're almost finished with it."

"Who told you they're almost finished with it? Have you seen it? Everybody's been laughing their asses off at us. It looks like the friggin' Yacyretá Dam, that's what it looks like. They're not finishing it in this lifetime. We're gonna end up playing in San Telmo, Fernando."

"You're exaggerating, Mono."

"Bullshit. I'm not exaggerating. And deep down you know it. You know I'm not exaggerating. You know I'm telling the truth."

31.

Once Prieto leaves the restaurant and Fernando loses sight of him, he looks at his watch: three in the afternoon. Mauricio was right. Between the wait and the meeting it was more than three hours. He calls over the waiter and asks for the check. They bring it to him with a glass of champagne. He's tempted, when he sees the bill, to tell the waiter to please take the champagne back and deduct it from the cost. Three hundred and eighty pesos. What bastards.

He wants to die when he calculates the tip. Ten percent is almost forty bucks. No way is he going to leave them a forty-peso tip. He plucks up his courage and leaves four one-hundred-peso notes on the tray. He keeps the bill, which is actually a kitchen order form that states "not valid as a receipt." A restaurant like that and they're trying to dodge taxes. Piece-of-shit country, he thinks again. But he sticks it in his pocket in case any of his "partners" want to check the expenses at some point. It's a useless precaution because they're not going to skimp on that, but he feels such rage that he has to get mad at someone, and they're closest at hand. Alone again, he says to himself, delving into masochism. Just like those months he spent trying to videotape the goals Pittilanga was unable to make. Just like in those sterile meetings where they pulled his leg, again and again. Where were those two traitors while he was biting the bullet with renowned sports journalist Armando Prieto? Mauricio bumming around in the club. Ruso at the helm of his filthy car wash.

He goes out to the sidewalk. Immediately one of the valets asks him for the stub and runs to bring him his car. You have to tip these guys, too. How much? Should it be a percentage of what you spent? Does it depend on the car you're getting into? He pulls out a ten-peso bill and gives it to the kid who brings him his and holds the door open for him. He doesn't stop to wonder if the employee's "thank you" is grateful or sarcastic. He pulls out onto the avenue at a low speed, more preoccupied with his worries than with the traffic.

He is back where he started. Or worse, because the more alternatives he burns, the fewer options seem accessible. He turns toward the river, crosses one of the swing bridges, and heads toward the southern riverside promenade. Even though it is cloudy and unpleasant there are people running, some sitting in the sun on folding chairs, the occasional small group kicking a ball. He parks and turns off the motor.

He wishes he had a cell phone. He needs to talk to Ruso right away. An idea is taking shape in his head, but he's too unsure about it to go forward without consulting him. He squeezes his nasal bridge with his right thumb and index finger, a way of calming himself down that usually works. But this time he doesn't have a chance because a voice inches from his left ear almost makes him jump out of his seat.

"Hey, sweetheart. You bored?"

With his heart in his throat, he slides his body away from the window and turns to look. His face must be contorted because the person who had leaned into the window withdraws a bit, before speaking again. "Ay, sweetie! I scared you! Forgive me!"

His throat pounding, Fernando is able to make out the full image: the woman has long hair, big black eyes, a lot of makeup, and a pair of prominent tits barely contained by an orange tank top. Without deciding to, Fernando peeks out to see her legs. Long, strong, and definitely masculine. *Bingo,* he says to himself, and leans his head against the Audi's extremely comfortable seat.

"You seem tense, love . . ."

Fernando thinks about how to answer. He doesn't want to offend, but how can he make her understand that his plans for that Saturday don't include hanging out with a transvestite who works the riverside promenade? He lifts a hand and smiles weakly, as he feels around for the ignition.

"You're not going to invite me in?"

"No, thank you."

No, thank you. He suspects that isn't the best answer. But whatever.

"You so busy you can't take a little time?"

Fernando looks at the transvestite again. He tries to put himself in her shoes. Having to work in that place, a Saturday at that time of day, approaching the car window of any asshole who happens to stop by her spot. Poor guy. Or poor gal.

"No, really. Thanks anyway."

"No need to thank me, dollface. Anytime," she responds with a pout and a theatrical shake of her hips.

Fernando starts the engine as he watches her head over to another car that is stopped fifty yards farther ahead. He has an idea. He honks the horn, and the transvestite turns, smiles, and retraces her steps, taking short little steps on her heels. Fernando gets out to avoid any confusion.

"I wanted to ask you a favor."

"Ah, you've got a hankering . . ."

"No, wait. It's an innocent favor. Do you have a cell phone? I'll rent it from you. I need to make an urgent call. Or two."

The transvestite looks at him, furrowing her brow, as if the request was not on her usual menu.

"Don't be like that. What's your name?"

"Celeste. And you?"

"Fernando. Sorry to be hassling you, but I don't have a cell phone."

Celeste turns and seems to be looking at the car. Then she looks at him, her face saying *don't lie to me.*

"The car is borrowed. I swear. And I don't use a cell phone."

"What an old-fashioned guy. I love it. It gives you a retro touch, it works for you."

Fernando smiles.

"I have no idea how much a couple of calls cost. Add something for the favor, and your time, of course."

Celeste looks at him, as if searching to decipher something that just barely escapes her. Soon she digs in the tiny purse she carries and pulls out a flat, golden phone that looks brand-new. She holds it out to him, bending her wrist and shaking her hips, feigning impatience.

"You caught me with my guard down, honey. Go ahead, it's on an unlimited plan."

Fernando looks at the device. Is it just him or is it missing buttons? Celeste notices his hesitation.

"Ay, my love. Were you frozen like Walt Disney? Come here. What number do you want to call?"

Fernando recites the number of the car wash. Celeste presses the buttons and when she hears it ringing she gives it back to him.

"Hi, Cristo. I need you to pass me to Ruso. Yeah . . . No, tell him to quit fucking around with the PlayStation. It's really urgent."

He turns toward Celeste and makes a gesture asking her to check the time, so she can calculate the cost. Celeste downplays the importance with a wave.

"Hey, Ruso. Listen, I don't have a lot of time . . . No. Awful. That's why I'm calling. I need you to talk to your brother. Does he still have that place in Warnes?"

Perhaps so as not to be a bother, Celeste moves aside. She walks around the car a couple of times, admiring its lines, its chrome wheels, spotless interior, while Fernando talks, leaning on the hood.

"Call him and call me back. I can't wait. Ah, hold on a second," he turns toward Celeste. "Can you tell me the number?"

Celeste tells him and Fernando repeats it.

"I know it's a cell phone . . . No, it's not mine. I borrowed it. I'll explain later. I'm waiting. Listen. This is superimportant. Do it right, Ruso. Otherwise, we'll screw this up. Listen. I mean it. If this fails, we're dead. Come on, I'll be waiting."

He hangs up and offers the phone to Celeste.

"No, sweetheart. If they have to call you back, you hold it."

Fernando leans on the Audi's hood and waits. Celeste sits beside him. Fernando wonders what to talk about. He doesn't want to seem impolite, but his experience in this regard is nonexistent. How can he break the ice? Surely not with a question like, Do you always work the streets by the riverside? Celeste throws him a lifeline.

"What a beautiful car, sweetheart."

"Yeah. It's a helluva car. It's my friend's. He lent it to me."

"What a good friend you have. You can introduce us whenever you want."

Fernando makes an expression similar to a smile, but not too similar.

"Dude. You really saved me."

"And you didn't want to go for a ride together. That's where you really saved yourself, Ferchu. What are you laughing at?"

"'Ferchu.' They used to call me that when I was a kid. It's been a long time."

"Your wife doesn't call you that?"

Fernando isn't in the mood to explain his marital status.

"No. She calls me Fernando."

"Ay, how formal!"

Yeah, it is a little. Maybe that's why we got separated so fast, thinks Fernando. A car with a family on board passes. The man who drives stares at them. One of the boys, the one seated behind the father, does too. Fernando concludes that they must be a somewhat unusual sight, the two of them there sprawled out on the side of the Audi, at three-thirty in the afternoon on an autumn Saturday. Celeste speaks as if thinking aloud.

"These weasels act all shocked, and out of every three who look at you like that, one will be back next week, searching for you, drooling."

"Really?"

"Uh . . . you have no idea. You want a lozenge?"

"What kind you got?"

"Mentholated."

"Thanks."

Fernando notices that her long nails are painted a bright red.

"What pretty nails, Celeste. Do you do them often?"

"Ay, what a gentleman." She thanks him for the compliment with a wide smile. "I live with a friend. She works near here.

We do each other. Waxing, nails, everything. Otherwise, you can imagine."

"I can imagine . . ."

Fernando looks at her. He thinks about the daily effort Celeste has to make in order to be Celeste. About the forceful pull of desire. About the unremitting will to be something that we want to be. The phone pulls him from his thoughts. Before making a mistake Fernando holds out the phone to Celeste so she can show him how to answer it.

"Hello," says Fernando. "Yes. Did you talk? Are you sure you explained everything? 'Cause otherwise . . . Who do I need to talk to? . . . No, I don't have anything to write it down with. Lemme see . . ."

"Say it out loud," interjects Celeste, "I have a photographic memory. Ay, what an idiot! What's it called when you remember everything you hear?"

"Terrada 2345!"

"Terrada 2345. Got it."

"I'll call you later, Ruso. I'll explain it later."

This time he dares to press the red button to end the call. Then he hands it to Celeste.

"Tell me how much I owe you, babe."

"Ay, nothing. It was a favor."

"I mean it."

"Do you charge for favors?"

"No."

"Well then, silly. Neither do I."

"But I'm sure I scared off some customers."

"Come on, man. It was a break."

Decline III

"We're playing tonight, right?"

"Yes, Mono. Well, at seven in the evening."

"See, Fernando? How can they make you play at seven p.m. on a Friday? How can the fans that work get to our field at seven on a Friday?"

"It's not our field, Mono. We're playing as locals on Racing's."

"I know, god damn it! It's just an expression. Do they make Boca and River play on Fridays?"

"No."

"You see? They've got Sundays. They play on Sunday afternoon because they are the kings, they rule. Only losers play on any old day at any old time. And we bow our heads like the losers we are!"

"Quit getting bent out of shape, you're gonna hurt yourself. You're all red, Mono."

"I'm perfectly fine. I'm calm. I'm perfectly calm. Okay. We're playing this evening. With who?"

"With Newells."

"Are you going to watch it?"

"Um . . . yeah . . ."

"Why do you say 'yeah' with a face like one of your nuts is in a bench vise?"

"What does your face look like when you've got one of your nuts in a bench vise?"

"Don't start. Did you make a pitiful face or not?"

"Uh . . . let's just say it is highly likely that they'll kick our asses."

"You see? That's what I'm talking about. That's what I'm saying. We're on our last legs. We're dying."

32.

Mariel leaves the tennis court kind of mad but Mauricio decides not to pay any attention to her. If she wants to understand his reasons, she will, and otherwise, she can go to hell. Doesn't matter. That's why he waits for Artuondo and his little girlfriend to put their things away in their bags, compliments the commercial trial judge on his serve, silently admires the legs of his very young companion, and invites them to the club restaurant for a drink after they shower. Luckily, they accept. Mauricio excuses himself and picks up his pace to catch up with his wife. Mariel is walking fast, and he only reaches her when they are at the door to the locker rooms.

"Hey, listen. Do you mind changing your attitude?" He grabs her by the arm to stop her.

"Let go of me. I thought you were with your little friends."

"We're going to have a drink now, that's why I came to talk to you. Don't be a pain in the ass, I've got this in the bag."

"How am I a pain in the ass?"

Did I marry a man? Mauricio wonders. He summons all his patience.

"Don't do this, Mariel. This is business, not pleasure. When you want to win we can sign up for some tournament and we'll kick the shit out of whoever we're up against. But not today."

"I don't understand what letting him win has to do with business."

"You don't understand how guys are, Mariel."

"No, that's true. Explain it to me."

Mauricio tones down his annoyed expression. He calculates that the others must still be on the courts, canoodling. He has a couple of minutes.

"Ay, Mariel. Nobody likes to lose. And even less so in front of their little girlfriend. And I need His Honor in a good mood."

"The little girlfriend seemed to be in a great mood. And you seemed to enjoy looking at her tits, too."

"Don't start, I'm begging you."

"No, of course not. It doesn't look good if the lawyer's crazy wife makes a scene in front of the locker rooms."

"Don't you think you're exaggerating just a little? Think about it. Look at what we're fighting over."

Mariel takes a deep breath. It looks like she's about to drop the subject, but she still has one bullet in the chamber.

"Are you sure you know why we're fighting?"

"Yes. Because you're more competitive than me, which is saying a lot. And you can't stand that I let him win."

Out of the corner of his eye he sees the victors approaching the spot where they are arguing. Mariel, who has also noticed, smiles broadly and straightens to kiss him on the lips. Then she disappears into the locker room. Mauricio asks himself why she can't always act like that, with that clarity, that intelligence. He in turn enters the men's locker room, pretending he hasn't seen the judge and the girl, and he slows his pace so the magistrate will catch up to him. The game Mauricio is interested in winning that afternoon begins there, on the walk to the showers. Of course he doesn't start straight in on it. He chooses a side route, which allows both of them to pretend there is no premeditation. They banter a bit, setting the stage. Some comment about work stress, the hearings, that particular moment in the Las Tunas Shipping Company lawsuit. All set: once the proceedings are named, the rest falls into place. The conversation meanders. It is interrupted each time Mauricio introduces him to a club member he thinks might interest him. When they continue chatting, they sidestep, barely touching on it, so as not to offend or scare anyone. When it comes time to comb their hair and zip up their bags, the basics have been agreed upon. Dates, figures, percentages, and courtesies for the honorable judge and the honorable accounting experts assigned to the case.

From the locker room they head to the restaurant, expecting to wait a while for the women to be ready. Mauricio uses the time to praise his opponent's young tennis partner. He calls her this on purpose, with that false pomposity, so the dirty old man can continue singing her praises to his heart's content and, as he does, boasting about his catch.

But they are barely through the swing door when Mauricio unexpectedly sees Fernando, who is sitting at one of the tables closest to the door, waiting for him. Of course. He had completely forgotten, but this morning they had said they'd meet up at the club so he could return his car and Mauricio would drive him back to the house. A setback, with his guests there. Leaving them with Mariel and making them wait would be bad manners, even though he had the business all wrapped up. And all the way to Fernando's house is a ways. There and back, at least an hour. Impossible. Better to tell Fernando to wait for him. He must not have anything important to do, anyway. That's it. He's going to tell him to wait an hour or so until he's free.

No. It's not that simple, because maybe Artuondo is going to want to have dinner, and it would be rude to say no. It'd be better if Fernando takes a hired car. He'll give him the money.

He can also tell him to take the car and bring it back tomorrow. No. Not the Audi. No way, because Fernando doesn't have a garage and he's not going to leave the Audi sleeping outside. But he can take Mariel's Peugeot. That's a good option. And he'll come off looking good with his friend. He touches the judge's shoulder so he'll stop. The truth is that Fernando, with that loaner suit, looks like a transplant from god knows where. A funeral home or an evening wedding.

"Justice, let me introduce you to my friend Fernando Raguzzi. Fernando, this is the Honorable Aníbal Artuondo, a judge in the commercial jurisdiction."

Fernando holds out his hand and shakes the judge's, but he takes a second to look into Mauricio's eyes, slightly lifting his brow. A fraction of a second. Just enough for him to raise his eyebrows. Sooner or later he's going to ask him about that afternoon of tennis with the judge. And from his tower of superiority, that pedestal of purity that bugs the shit out of Mauricio. Besides Mariel and the girl are about to show up. He has to disarm that imminent quintet as soon as possible.

"Did the car drive well, kid?" The question comes out slightly sharper than he would have liked. Take it easy, he says to himself.

"Perfect. No problem," answers Fernando, who continues as if in suspense.

"I lent my friend the Audi this morning, and he's come to return it."

"You have an Audi, Guzmán? When are you going to lend it to me?"

"Ha! From what I saw out there you aren't exactly walking to work, Justice!" Mauricio does some quick calculations. Artuondo's giant pickup truck must have cost a pretty penny.

About like the Audi, or a little less. Thank goodness. It's not a good time for a virility competition.

"I need to talk to you for a minute," says Fernando.

"Why don't you take Mariel's Peugeot? We don't really have plans with Aníbal, but we might go out for dinner and—"

"I appreciate it, but I have to talk to you about something before I go. Two minutes."

"I'll wait for you at that table, Mauricio," says the judge, excusing himself. "I need to hydrate."

"Yeah, Aníbal, sure." Mauricio realizes that the judge has just addressed him informally for the first time. Something wonderful, at a bad moment. And what a pain in the ass Fernando is being. He has to get rid of him fast. Let him give a quick report. He sounds jocular when he says to the judge, "The barman is a topnotch guy. Tell him to mix you up something to rehydrate after a good tennis match."

The judge swerves toward the bar and Mauricio turns to face Fernando. Now he speaks in barely a murmur.

"Fer, I'm in the middle of something. You won't be mad if we talk tomorrow, right? It's Sunday and we've got plenty of time."

"We need to talk about it today, Mauricio. I'm sorry. I didn't know you were with people."

"It's not that. It's who these people are, and why I'm with them."

He's changing his mind. At first he had thought it'd be best to hide the truth behind the social gathering. Particularly to save himself the sermons and disapproving looks. But now, in up to his eyeballs, maybe it's better to come clean about it, acknowledge the importance of what he's doing so Fernando understands that he has to leave soon. That he has to act like a friend, for fuck's sake.

"I didn't warn you because I thought you would get here earlier, Fer, but it turns out that this guy—"

"Wait. We'd better sit down. I promise I'll make it as short as possible. But there are a couple of things that I have to tell you, now."

"But—"

"It's for your own good."

Mauricio looks at him, increasingly worried. And since Fernando doesn't make the slightest attempt to lighten up the solemnity of what he has just said, his consternation only grows. What does he mean by "It's for your own good"? Fernando sits down and Mauricio follows suit, not taking his eyes off of him, as if he were a bad omen, or a threat. Spit it out. Spit it out already.

"What happened? Did it go all wrong with Prieto?" *Get to the point, stop beating around the bush, get the hell out of here.*

"No. Not all of it. It didn't go great, but not terrible either."

"Let's see, explain, please. Did he get offended about the bribe? Maybe you were too direct, too—"

"Not at all. He loved the idea. That wasn't the problem."

"So? He tried to raise his cut? Look, that can be discussed, you—"

"No, Mauricio. He didn't want a percentage. He wanted the cash money up front."

"What do you mean, the cash money?"

"Yeah, Mauricio. The cash. The money. In hand. Now, up front."

"But that can't be done. That's not how it's done."

"Oh, not how it's done? And how the hell do you know how it's done?"

The conversation has slipped into a whispered argument. Mauricio glances at the judge, who is sitting at his table with an absent, peaceful air, playing with the ice cubes in his whiskey. He turns toward Fernando again and they stare each other down across the table. The girl waiting on that section comes over to Mauricio and holds out a menu.

"No, thank you . . . I'm over there," he says, pointing to the judge's table. How long had they been talking? How long before Mariel finally comes to help him out, even just to keep an eye on Artuondo?

"I'll have a coffee with milk, please," says Fernando to the waitress, and then turns toward Mauricio. "Look, I didn't come here to argue with you about how to negotiate with that asshole. Things are the way he says they are. Otherwise, there's no deal."

"Well, maybe there should be no deal."

Fernando looks at him again, before responding.

"Maybe you'll think up some alternative plan, one of these days."

Mauricio swallows hard and holds his gaze, but doesn't answer. *Now he comes and starts complaining?*

"It's simple: Prieto wants the dough now, in advance. No getting paid when he's sold, no percentage, nothing like that."

"And how much is he asking?"

"Twenty thousand dollars."

"What?"

"Twenty grand."

"How much?"

"Are you gonna keep asking me that? Because it's still gonna be twenty big ones, no matter how many times you ask."

Decline IV

"Isn't that putting it a little dramatically, Mono?"

"No, Fernando! It's true! You know it, I know it, we all know they'll probably wipe the floor with us. And if not today, next time. And the next and the next and the next. We have no hope, you understand. It's not that it's a bad patch. It's not a bad season. That's how it is. We are a disaster, and we are going to continue being a disaster. And we are going to look less and less like what we were, and the moment will come when we won't even recognize ourselves. All we'll have left is the name. Old photos. Don't you understand, Fernando?"

". . ."

"Since '95, one championship. This is 2008, Fernando. One championship in fourteen years, man. And counting."

"Every team goes through—"

"My ass. You know what Independiente was. A sure thing. Or almost. With the local teams we went to town. Boca was our bitch. The only team that consistently beat us was River. The rest, piece a cake."

"Well . . ."

"Now we suck, Fernando. We're Banfield's bitch! Banfield!"

". . ."

"Lánus!"

". . ."

"In the other rematch, Arsenal beat us! When we were kids Arsenal played in third division! And now they destroy us, Fernando."

"What's your point?"

"Nothing. That's it! That it used to be playing against the Red was a challenge for everyone. We used to lose too, I know. I'm not that stupid. I'm not saying we always won. But we always had a chance of winning, of turning games around, of bringing down the best on any field. And playing well. Or trying to play well. Remember? 'The Red mystique'! Do you remember or not? Am I exaggerating or was that how it was?"

". . ."

"Am I exaggerating?"

". . ."

33.

A gain there is silence. Mauricio notices Fernando looking over his back and waving, but not smiling. Mariel and Artuondo's girlfriend have just come through the door. Mauricio glances at his wife, hoping she will understand without his having to explain much. She looks at him for a second and goes straight toward the judge's table. *Good. That's my girl.* When the judge sees them he smiles and settles into his chair. Mauricio can't hear them but he is obviously making some comment about the untimely meeting Mauricio's having, because all three look over at him. Mauricio waves and gestures that he'll be with them soon.

"But how do you plan on getting together twenty thousand dollars?"

Fernando makes a face. Mauricio decides that if he keeps acting important and mysterious he is going to tell him to go to hell.

"Your choice of words worries me, Mauricio." Now the poor soul is getting sarcastic. "I don't think it's how 'I' am going to get the money together, but how 'we' are."

"And do you think I have twenty thousand dollars to invest in this?"

"Do you think I do? Or Ruso?"

"Look, Fernando. This isn't the best time for me to talk about this. I have this guy waiting, I can't think it over right now. I'll call you tomorrow."

"No. We have to find the solution now."

"That's not possible."

"Why?"

"Are you kidding me? You come here, blatantly telling me the guy wants twenty big ones by next week."

"Not by next week. By tomorrow."

"And you agreed?!"

"If you have a better idea, I'm all ears. I have Prieto's cell phone, I'll call him and change plans."

"What do you mean change plans? You weren't dumb enough to say yes to him?"

"Yes. But since you are much cleverer than me, now you are going to give me a more efficient, sure, and cheap way of selling Pittilanga. Saving us twenty grand to boot."

Mariel gives him a look whose meaning is obvious. Mauricio lifts his thumb to indicate that everything is fine. The dopiest gesture in the world.

"I'll say it again, we need to look at this more closely . . ."

"There's nothing to look at, Mauricio. The question I have to ask you is simple: do you have twenty thousand dollars to front us and pay this son of a bitch, so we can pay you back when we sell the kid?"

"Are you fucking kidding me?"

"Not at all. I need to know."

"I repeat. Are you fucking kidding me? Where do you expect me to get twenty grand?"

"I don't know. Maybe you have some invested. I have no idea."

"No, I don't have it."

"Not even ten? Five?"

"Not ten and not five, Fernando, fuck!"

Fernando doesn't bat an eyelash. He keeps looking at him. Staring him down.

"I understand."

"What do you understand?"

"This about you not having the money. It's admissible. It's not your fault."

"My fault? Where are you getting to?"

"To the end of the story. Relax. I'll let you go soon."

"What end?"

"That when I left the meeting with Prieto I was thinking we're screwed. I don't have twenty grand. Ruso, either. You, from what you've told me, don't either."

"Quit being so solemn, if you don't mind."

"I'm not, Mauricio. But I left there having to find some solution. And actually, whether you like it or not, allow me to correct you, Mauricio. You have the twenty grand. Or well, you did."

It is at that moment, perhaps because of the seriousness with which Fernando says those last words, or because the atmosphere has become denser and denser between them, to the point that it is now leaden, or because things come together in Mauricio's head before he can put words to them, that Mauricio sees for the first time the keys that Fernando has been playing with throughout the conversation. He only now looks at them. A key ring with two gold skeleton keys and another silver one, long and cylindrical, the kind used for a deadbolt. The keys to Fernando's house. Not to the Audi.

"I don't know what you're talking about," he manages to say, his voice faint.

"Yes you do. Or you can imagine. Your face looks like you're imagining." Fernando pauses for the last time and continues. "I went to Warnes. They told me about a guy and I went."

"They told you? Who told you?"

"Chamaco. A washer who works with Ruso. The guy, some-body Chamaco knows, has a great spare parts place. All imported cars. But it seems he's also the owner of the biggest chop shop in Buenos Aires."

"Stop, stop." Mauricio feels like the floor has been pulled out from under him.

"Of course the Audi was worth a lot more than twenty grand. But what do you want? He gave me fifteen. I have to figure out how the hell to scratch up the other five."

Mauricio feels his anger grow. He can't make a scene there. Especially not with Artuondo ten meters away, even though he's already on his fourth whiskey. Fernando knows it too, which makes Mauricio even madder. That's why they are talking there.

"I'm asking you not to get all up in arms, Mauricio. Until now you've been getting off easy."

"Fuck you."

Fernando pauses and looks at him. There is no anger in his expression. Just concentration, as if he were jotting the insult down on a longer list. Or an older one.

"I didn't come here to fight. Later you can curse me all you want. But there was no other alternative. That's why I started by asking you if you had the money. You don't. Or you did, with the Audi. Don't play the victim, because you have insurance, Mauricio. For sure. You have to wait three days to report it."

"You're crazy. Or much dumber than I thought."

Again Fernando is slow to respond.

"It's possible. Both things are possible. But don't change the subject. The guy in the chop shop needs three days. To either take it completely apart or get it to Paraguay."

"Are you telling me that my car is at that criminal's place, and that in the next few days it's going to Paraguay, under my name, and my liability?"

"I suggest you don't raise your voice. For your own sake. I don't care, but these people might mind a scene. I swear I wasn't planning this, Mauricio. Not because we owe you anything. In fact, you are still pretty far in the red."

"What are you talking about?"

"Let's leave it at that."

"You, your brother, and your friend have me at the end of my rope."

Fernando clears his throat. He adjusts the empty cup on the saucer. He seems to be thinking.

"I thought that I, my brother, and my friend were also your friends. But maybe you are in a phase where you're rethinking things."

He pauses, as if giving Mauricio the opportunity to retort. But since there is no response, he continues.

"What I will tell you is that it was high time for you to chip in. It's three days. On Tuesday you file the report. I'm sure your insurance company will give you a loaner car until you are reimbursed."

"Do you have any idea of the jam you're putting me in? Do you know what can happen to me if those guys use the Audi for a robbery, a kidnapping, something like that, and I haven't reported it stolen? Do you have any idea or are you too stupid to realize?"

"You already asked me that. And yes, I'm too stupid. But that's another subject. What I can assure you is that if you file the report now you are going to find yourself in a much bigger jam. Me too, but you won't get off scot-free. Three days. If they strip it here, once they throw out the satellite tracker they can breathe easy. But the three days is in case they send it to the border."

"And who gave you the right to get me involved in a deal with those piece-of-shit criminals?"

He's not shouting, but close. Close enough that the people at the next table turn to look at them. Fernando remains undaunted.

"It's true. I've just gotten you mixed up with some piece-of-shit criminals. But don't tell me you're not used to that." He looks at the judge for a long moment, and then back at Mauricio. "In any case the difference is that, this time, you're not the one choosing the criminals."

Fernando stands up, takes ten pesos out of his pocket, and leaves them to pay for his coffee. He points to the clothes he's wearing.

"I'll have Ruso return the suit this week. Like a fool I left my clothes in the trunk. My whole outfit. So I lost something of mine too, can you believe it?" The last part he says from the door, pointing to his legs. "You don't know how much I loved those jeans."

Pallor II

"Is your arm still hurting, Fer?"

"No, not now."

"You've got better color."

"Yeah, Mono?"

"Yeah. Before you were white as chalk. Now you are a little bit green. Maybe green is the color of hope."

"Thank goodness, man."

". . ."

". . ."

"It must be that with everything I told you about Independiente your heart started hurting and it made you forget about your arm. That's why you don't realize."

". . ."

"That's the way it is, Fernando. The Red is dying. It's been dying for a while, but it's only recently that it's really noticeable."

". . ."

"And what's wrong with you now?"

"Nothing."

"Nothing? What's that face then?"

"What do you want me to say? That you're right?"

"If I am, yes. I'd like that."

". . ."

". . ."

"Okay. You're right, Mono. Everything you said about Independiente is right."

". . ."

". . ."

34.

Fernando plans to meet her in a bar on the corner of Ituzaingó Plaza, on a Friday in the late afternoon, because Lourdes explained that any earlier would be difficult for her because of work.

Anyway, she arrives almost a half an hour late. Fernando tries not to get mad about her tardiness even though it's a defect that drives him nuts, because he needs for their conversation to be as calm as possible. When Lourdes finally sits down in front of him, and while they wait for their coffee, Fernando wonders what Mono would think now, ten years later, of the woman he had Guadalupe with.

It would be unfair to say she'd aged. She's . . . how old? Thirty-five? Thirty-six? She's still young. She's still pretty. She's kept a good figure, considering her two pregnancies. Fernando calculates how old Guadalupe's little brother must be, the one Lourdes had with the Swiss guy. Six. Matías is six years old.

"How are the kids?" asks Fernando, as a way to start off on the right foot.

When she hears that, Lourdes loosens up.

"Good, great. They're with Claudio now."

Claudio is Lourdes's new man. She got together with him after separating from the Swiss guy. They've been together for a couple of years. Fernando would like to ask how it's going, but they're not that close. He hopes things are going well. Not for Lourdes's sake. He still holds on to deep bitterness for all the damage she did to his brother. But for Guadalupe, so that she lives in a home that is as close to a family as possible. Fernando has pretty traditional guidelines for such things.

"Things good with you?" asks Lourdes, as if conceding to the demands of civility.

"Good, yeah, good," nods Fernando, thinking of how to broach the subject.

"Your mom?"

"Good, hanging in there," answers Fernando, who doesn't feel like getting too specific.

What would be more specific? My mom? Bitter, stubborn, angry, scatterbrained about everything except hating the world and venerating Mono's memory. Better to abbreviate that as "Good, hanging in there."

"I had you come because I wanted to talk about something that has to do with Guadalupe." Better to cut to the chase, Fernando says to himself.

"Look, I already talked to the lawyer about the visits and—"

"Wait. Give me a second."

Fernando stops short. Being polite is one thing, but having to tolerate being taken for a fool, or her trying to scare him, is quite another.

"I know that you and Mono went over this a million times."

Went over this a million times. A nice euphemism for the back-and-forth, the anguish, the suffering, the threats, the accusations that bitch threw at his brother.

"Exactly, that's why—"

"I asked you to let me speak. If you agree, I think it's best we be honest. As honest as we can."

"Okay," responds Lourdes as her cell phone rings.

She has the good sense to turn it off, but as she pushes the button it slips and falls to the floor. Fernando can't help checking out her cleavage as she kneels to pick it up, even though he looks away fast. Was it a male reflex or is he a pervert? Nice tits. She always did have those. Poor Mono. They were always his weakness. Better get back to the subject at hand.

"Now that Mono is dead the whole visitation schedule is a hassle. You know full well there should be visitation rights for my mom, and for Guadalupe's aunts and uncles."

"I'm not saying there shouldn't be, but I prefer that you speak to my lawyer about it."

"Your lawyer is a pain in my left nut, Lourdes, and you know it because that's why you hired him and that's why you pay him the big bucks. Big bucks that, I should mention, you got from Mono."

That was a mistake, thinks Fernando, as he sees Lourdes firmly putting her cell phone, dark glasses, and car keys into her purse in the manner of someone about to leave.

"Sorry. It just slipped out."

Lourdes looks at him with daggers in her eyes, but stops her show of leaving. Killer eyes, really, thinks Fernando, who holds her gaze anyway. Poor Mono, he thinks again.

"It doesn't make sense to go over ancient history. Let's think of the future."

"I don't think you and I can understand each other."

"I think that we can, if we're practical. Practical and honest, Lourdes."

She adjusts her hair. She looks around, as if searching for something.

"You can't smoke here. Sorry. We can go outside if you want, but it's cold."

"Doesn't matter," says Lourdes, dropping her cigarettes and lighter back into her purse.

"Let's start by making one thing clear. You can't stand me and I can't stand you. And it doesn't make sense for us to look for reasons or try to explain why. Deep down, there's no way we're going to understand each other."

Lourdes looks at him, her eyes wide.

"Brutal honesty, as they say."

"As they say. But there is one thing we do agree on," he replies.

"Oh yeah? What's that?"

Fernando is about to get enraged again with Lourdes's sarcastic little tone of voice, but he makes the effort not to lose his temper. If he can do it with his students, he has to be able to do it with this bitch. He breathes two, three times. Okay.

"Look, Lourdes. I always thought that you were a cold, calculating, manipulative, hysterical, frigid, neurotic, egotistical, lying bitch . . ."

Contrary to what Fernando was expecting, Lourdes lets him continue his list until he runs out of epithets, or inclination.

"And I'm sure you think worse things about me. But that's not the point. What is important to me is that I know that there's something in you that is good. Very good."

"Is that so?"

"Yes. I think you love Guadalupe very much."

Lourdes stares at him. Fernando returns her gaze. Her eyes fill with tears. Fernando now looks down. Other people's tears always affect him, and he can't afford to crack now.

"Isn't that right?"

"Yes. Of course it is."

"Good. Me too. All of us. When I say us I mean me, Ruso, and Mauricio."

"The three musketeers," says Lourdes, sarcasm again replacing emotion in her voice.

"We love her so much that we want to make you an offer. You, not your lawyer. What's more, if you take part in this, make like we never spoke. Any agreement we might come to today, if that guy sticks his nose in it, forget about it."

"Sounds like you're about to propose something illegal."

"Not at all. A gentlemen's agreement. Or a lady and gentleman's."

"I'm listening."

"Mauricio and Ruso and I are dealing with an investment, some serious money."

"Don't mention words like 'investment,' because it reminds me that I haven't seen a dime of the indemnity they gave Alejandro when he got fired by the Swiss."

Can't you stop being so hardheaded and call him Mono just once in your life, thinks Fernando, as he takes a sip of the water that comes with his cup of coffee. Everybody called him that. Even the Swiss guys. Everybody except Lourdes. As if from the very beginning she had wanted to make clear that nothing that Mono was—beyond her, above, below, or outside of her— was of any importance or good for anything.

"The Swiss guys didn't fire him. Mono left of his own accord."

"My lawyer said that when it ends like that there is always money involved. Serious money."

Yup, thinks Fernando. *Two hundred thousand dollars is serious money.*

"Your lawyer was wrong."

"I don't think so."

"Are you calling me a liar?"

The tone has gotten tense again, but Fernando doesn't care. That tension works in his favor. Because, of course, he is lying, and lying makes him nervous. It makes him feel uneasily guilty. Guilty with this broad who did everything possible to make visits between Guadalupe and his brother difficult? Guilty with this train wreck who, when she lived with Mono—Fernando is convinced—was still sneaking around with that friggin' Swiss guy? Guilty with this bitch?

"I'm not calling you anything."

"Ah."

Good, thinks Fernando. His noble, offended tone came out well.

"The money I'm talking about doesn't have anything to do with Mono. And I don't have to tell you where it comes from. Suffice to say that it is completely legal. Completely."

"Okay." And Lourdes lets out an unexpected, sudden laugh. "The truth is I can't imagine you guys having the balls to get involved in something shady."

Fernando again thinks what he often thinks with his students. *He who gets mad, loses. He who gets mad, loses.* Like a mantra. *So you take us for three fools? Even better, Lourdes. Even better. Because you are never going to see a dime of that money for as long as you live.*

"Indeed. It's legal money, that we hope will come in handy for Guadalupe."

"And how much money is it?"

"I'm not authorized to say."

Lourdes makes a derisive face, as if surprised by the solemnity of his response.

"I'm not authorized and I don't want to, because I know you're an opportunist, and materialistic, and I'm afraid you're going to do something dumb and fuck things up. I don't know how, but I need to make it very clear that you are never going to see a red cent of that money. And deep down we don't know, not Ruso, not Mauricio, and not me, if you're going to be with this Claudio you're with now for two months or for forty years. Or if next week you're gonna fall in love with some Norwegian and want to go fuck off somewhere with the Norwegian, you know. Or if the Swiss guys at the lab offer you a promotion in the Republic of Fuckoffanddie and all of a sudden you're moving to Fuckoffanddie and you're taking Guadalupe with you, you follow me?"

"Who do you think you're talking to?"

"To you, Lourdes, but let's not get off the subject. Let's stick with what works, which is what I told you before. You adore Guadalupe, and we do too."

Fernando pauses and waits to see if Lourdes has some retort. Silence. Perfect. He knows he is in charge. He knows he is in control.

"Which is why, from now on, and starting in a few months, you are going to receive a monthly sum. Apart from the pension, I mean. You are going to receive a monthly sum from us."

"On account of?"

"On account of nothing. Some money that we're going to give you so you can pay for a good school for Guadalupe. Really good, not one of those fancy piece-of-shit ones. Good and where they treat her right. There are schools like that that aren't so expensive."

"Are you trying to tell me what school I have to send her to?"

"You are going to have the right to an opinion and we are going to listen to you, Lourdes. Think—think of us as

Guadalupe's father. Instead of one she has three, what can you do. But the advantage is that this father is going to contribute a thousand dollars every month."

"A thousand dollars?"

"A thousand. In one lump sum every month. From now until Guadalupe turns twenty-one."

There is silence. Lourdes, not caring about the rules, pulls out a cigarette, lights it, and takes a long drag.

"So how much money do you guys have?"

At the moment, we have zero, so fuck off. But we will have a bundle soon, thinks Fernando. *I hope.*

"I told you that's our business. And when she turns twenty-one, we'll work out the rest with her."

"But, what? You guys robbed a bank?"

No, you shrew, we have the registration rights of a player who sucks so hard he can't score a goal.

"Not even close. All above board. From now until twenty-one, Guadalupe will get a hundred and ten thousand dollars, through you. But let me make one thing clear: if you fuck up, you go your own way, you hook up with some asshole who treats the girl badly, whatever, forget about it. We stash the dough and we give it all to her later."

"And why don't you just wait, then?" she challenges.

"We thought about it, because we don't trust you. But we want Guada to grow up well. To get a good education, a few special treats. Not for her to get carried away, let me be clear. But it seems fair that she start enjoying it now. And that's what Mono would have wanted."

"I don't know," says Lourdes, but it is an I don't know that sounds like yes to Fernando, that sounds like she has no objections.

"Another thing. Not only will you take our opinions into account with how the money is used, for the girl's education, but we will also work out a good visitation schedule and you'll respect it. And when I say visits I mean with my mom and with the three of us. And I mean vacations, trips, that kind of thing."

The waiter approaches and reminds Lourdes that smoking isn't allowed. Reluctantly, she puts the cigarette out in an empty cup.

"And the same thing goes for rules. She's a kid now, but pretty soon she's gonna start going out, the clubs, the dances, and the parties and the boyfriends."

"But what do you guys think? That I can't take care of her myself?"

"Not at all, Lourdes. But we're not interested. I mean, we are interested. And we know that you take care of her. But we want to take care of her too. If you want that money, you are going to have to tolerate this kind of shared custody, very, very shared, with the three of us. Are you following me?"

Lourdes lifts up her purse from the chair beside her and places it on the table. She opens it. She pulls out her cigarettes and lighter in an automatic gesture, but when she realizes she puts them back. She leaves the purse on another chair again.

"One thing. The first month the money doesn't show up, forget about it." Again the sparkling eyes. Again the hatred, the bitterness."If there's one month when you and your friends don't send the money, the deal is off. It's off. You understand me?"

"I understand you. You are going to have to wait two or three months, until the cash comes through."

"I'll wait as long as you want. But until then don't even think about seeing the girl."

"You do remember my mom has a right to see her?"

Lourdes picks up her purse and crosses it in her arms, like a shield.

"Yes, your mom does. But not you and not your friends."

Fernando lifts his hand to ask the waiter to bring the check. As he waits, he stares at her. How long was Mono in love with this woman? Until they got together and his life turned into a shitstorm? Until they separated? What if he always loved her? What if up until he got sick and died of cancer he was still in love with this shrew? What made him fall in love with her? What did he see in her? What virtues could he have imagined she had? Is loving a woman always that, imagining virtues in some broad just because we're attracted to her and we want her?

"Fine," says Fernando, as he pays. "Until we have the money, things stay the way they are now. When we start making the payments, things change. Sound good to you?"

"Sounds good," answers Lourdes, as she gets up and leaves.

Remaining Time

"Do you know what bugs me the most, Fer?"

"What, Mono?"

"..."

"..."

"That there's nothing more I can do. That I ran out of time to try anything."

"And what were you going to try?"

"I don't know. Get involved in club politics. Participate. Run for president, or member of the board, something. Now it's like I have nothing left to do."

"I guess not, Mono. All you can do is suffer."

"..."

"..."

"Hey, Fer."

"What?"

"Did you see how before, when I was saying that Independiente was on its last legs, dying just like me, you didn't say anything?"

"..."

"..."

"I didn't say you were going to die, Mono."

"Don't play dumb."

"I'm not."

"..."

"..."

"Yes, you are, Fernando. But thanks anyway."

"Thanks for what?"

"Because if I say something like that to anybody else they interrupt me with all that bullshit about hope and miracles, because nobody can stand that it is what it is and that's that. Those people really piss me off. For me it's like they can't stand to face up to the fact that I'm dying."

"I don't know, Mono. First of all, you don't know. If you are dying, I mean. And then . . . what do I know . . . everybody does what they can. Maybe they think it's a way of giving you strength to carry on, to not give up."

"And you?"

"What about me?"

"You don't want to give me strength?"

"I do what you asked me to. I don't take pity on you and I don't say stupid shit. That's what you asked me to do, isn't it?"

"It's true."

". . ."

". . ."

"But do you do it because I asked you or because you really think I'm done for?"

". . ."

". . ."

35.

"**D**on't you think it was a little risky confronting Lourdes with the monthly payment idea?"

Ruso asks without wanting to offend, as he runs a rag over the headlights of a caramel-colored Fiat Idea. Fernando is standing beside him. He jumps at the sudden sound of the high-pressure hose Chamaco turned on to loosen the grime on the next car. Feo is doing his part by shooting foamy streams onto the wet exterior.

"No."

His response is so curt and definitive that Ruso stops working to look at him face-to-face.

"You know why I did it?" continues Fernando. "Because I was more afraid of talking and coming to an agreement with that bitch than negotiating Pittilanga's sale to whomever the fuck. Now I'm more calm. I know I have an uphill climb ahead of me. We have one. But at least I got that out of the way."

Ruso returns to drying the headlights. Fernando adds something more.

"And it felt good, Ruso. It was like knowing the last chapter of a book that's rough going, but the last chapter shows me that it turns out fine, you understand? If all this mess brings us to the conversation with Lourdes, and to that agreement, then it's all okay. It'll be worth it. I want to get to there, to what was already agreed on, you understand."

Ruso stands up with a groan, because his back's hurting a little.

"I understand you perfectly."

He puts the rag on his shoulder.

"You're gonna soak your T-shirt," points out Fernando.

Ruso looks down and sees that he's right, but he leaves the wet rag where it is.

"It's true, Mama. But I'm hot and I thank God for the drenching."

"You're crazy."

"And you're obsessive."

Ruso starts toward the office.

"Come on, I'll put the kettle on," he says from the doorway.

Resignation

"Hey, Fer . . ."

　　"What, Mono."

"I asked you a question."

". . ."

". . ."

". . ."

"I asked you if you don't console me because I asked you not to, or because you think I'm done for."

"I heard you, Mono."

"And?"

"The truth?"

"Of course."

"Both."

". . ."

". . ."

". . ."

". . ."

". . ."

"Are you crying, Mono? With this tube in I can't turn around and I can't see you. Come closer."

"I'm not crying, you jerk, I'm laughing."

"What are you laughing for?"

"I was thinking about resignation."

"What were you thinking?"

"That being a Red fan helps us, man. We're already used to expecting the worst."

"True."

". . ."

". . ."

". . ."

". . ."

"Are we gonna beat Newells, Fer? What do you say?"

". . ."

". . ."

". . ."

"Snowball's chance in hell, right?"

"Snowball's chance in hell, Mono."

". . ."

". . ."

"Motherfuck it all."

36.

They are sitting in the car wash office. Cristo is brewing maté halfheartedly and the flavor has already been boiled out of the leaves. The other two, absorbed, don't complain and drink it without a peep, when the shared gourd makes its way to them. Outside, Chamaco, Molina, and Feo are finishing off a wash.

"How we doing today?" asks Ruso all of a sudden, coming out of his distraction.

"Good, especially since it's the end of the month. The cars aren't backed up because all three," says Cristo, pointing to the washers, "are superexperienced. They almost never need me now. Even though we're getting more and more cars. But they keep working faster."

"Just like that?"

"Just like that."

"So I can kick your ass to the curb, no problem, Cristo?"

"You'd lose the best automatic car wash manager in the west, Ruso."

"It's true."

Fernando lifts a hand to shut them up, because even though the radio is turned up to a good volume, sometimes the noise from the street and the washing machines drowns it out.

"Are you sure Prieto's gonna do it today, Fer?"

"No. I'm not sure. The day before yesterday I brought him the dough. But I'm not sure."

"Did he sign something when you paid him?" Cristo asks, stirring the metal straw in the wet yerba maté, as if trying to extract its final remains. "Because that's some real cash."

"Yeah, Cristo. He signed a receipt that says 'For payoff/bribe for saying good stuff about Mario Juan Bautista Pittilanga.'"

"No, of course not, what a stupid . . ."

They keep listening. Prieto is talking about River Plate's problems. He's been going on about it for almost half an hour.

"Does this guy really have a big audience?" Cristo stretches his legs, without standing, trying to pull the garbage can resting in the corner toward him. "He sounds pretty damn boring to me."

"Yeah. People listen to him. Even though it's hard to believe," concurs Fernando.

"Stop, stop: he knows about soccer," interjects Ruso.

"What does he know . . ."

"Seriously, Fer. He may be as disgusting as a spoonful of snot, but the guy knows . . ."

Fernando dismisses the comment, and tries to concentrate again, but Cristo makes a horrific noise dragging the can along the floor.

"Don't you want to bring over some cellophane and stick it in my ears, too? I mean, that way we make sure there's no chance of my hearing anything at all."

"What's eating you, Fernandito?"

"Nothing, you idiot. But I'm trying to listen and you two won't stop talking shit."

Ruso and Cristo look at each other and, like almost always, understand each other perfectly. Better to leave it at that. After all, Fernando did pull the shortest straw. Dealing with bribing the journalist, dealing with the chop shop to sell the Audi, dealing with Mauricio to explain it to him.

And in that order of increasing difficulty. And to top it all off, bringing the money to that swindler Prieto, who accepted it with a princely flourish and put it away without even counting it. That was on Tuesday. And he still hasn't said a single word.

"Have you listened to him every day, Ruso?"

"Yup. On Monday he talked about the weekend's games. On Tuesday he talked a lot about Boca."

"And yesterday he must have talked about the size of the goal areas, right?"

"Yes— How'd you know?"

Fernando wonders if it's worth the bother opening up his friend's eyes to Prieto's professional virtues. He decides it isn't. He hears the beep marking 1:00 p.m. and the program switches to the news. Fernando rocks in his chair, annoyed.

"Well, there's still an hour left in the program." Ruso is trying to cheer him up.

"Yeah. But I don't know why I think he's not gonna say a word, that Judas."

"There's also the TV show at night," adds Cristo. "Maybe he'll say it there."

"Did you offer to bring him some videos, for the TV show? We've certainly got plenty . . ."

"No, Ruso. Stop," Cristo intervenes again. "If he starts showing videos, it's gonna be clear as day. That'd be the same as going on air saying he's mixed up in the sale."

Ruso thinks for a second.

"Yeah. You're right."

"The only thing I can think of is that he got greedy and he wants more money," says Fernando gloomily.

"No, Fer. How's he gonna want more dough without saying

a single word? He's probably just trying to keep us in suspense, make us want it more."

They look at each other, their expressions reflecting their lack of answers to all these questions.

"Have you talked to Mauricio?" asks Ruso, mostly just to get the conversation flowing again, pull them from their doubts.

"No. Not since Saturday, when I saw him at the club. Did he say anything to you?"

Ruso remembers the rage, the mute bewilderment in Mauricio's eyes when he went by his office on Monday. They had spoken standing, Ruso leaning on the desk and Mauricio tightly gripping a bookshelf. He hadn't accused him, at least not directly. There was no evidence against Ruso, because Fernando had been careful to leave him out of it, to lead Mauricio to believe that he'd consulted Chamaco directly, and Mauricio might have his suspicions and want to murder him as a result, but he couldn't be sure, and his inner pettifogger kept him—frustrated, but restrained—from acting. He'd had to make do with insulting Fernando with such bitterness and such patience that Ruso understood, as the envoy that he was after all, that he was to repeat all the reproaches and threats to the absent party. However, and uncharacteristically, Ruso had kept almost all of it to himself.

"Yesterday I talked to him again on the phone and he told me he had filed the police report."

Mauricio had added, "And I hope they find the car half stripped and you all end up in jail, starting with that son of a bitch friend of yours." But Ruso kept that to himself too.

"I guess they've already gotten it to Paraguay."

"Or stripped it . . ."

"Yeah. Or stripped it. But I bet they sent it over the border. It was brand-new."

Dubbing

"What's that noise in the background, Mono?"

"What noise?"

"That yelling."

"Ah . . . a cartoon Guadalupe is watching."

"How long is she staying with you?"

"Until tomorrow, Ruso. Tomorrow Fernando's taking her back."

"Do you think it was a good idea to have her today? I mean, with the way you've been feeling . . ."

"What do you want, Ruso? Fucking Lourdes does everything in her power to keep her from coming. When I manage to force her to I can't back out."

"Besides, she wants to come, Ruso."

"Yeah, Fer?"

"Of course. She's always happy to come. Tomorrow I'll take her home."

"My girls are bigger, otherwise I'd bring them over to play."

"When Guadalupe's bigger, Ruso. Then they'll get along great."

". . ."

". . ."

". . ."

"Dude, is it me or is the dubbing on that cartoon unbearable?"

"See what those voices are like, Ruso?"

"What cartoon is it?"

"I don't remember the name. One with some little bug-ger . . . Do you remember, Fer?"

"Hold on, yeah . . . *The Fairly Odd Parents.*"

"That's the one! Excruciating."

37.

Ruso stares at him. He knows even his tiniest signs of worry by heart. Biting the tip of his thumb. Tapping on the table as if it were a piano keyboard, but with the childish rule of never using adjacent fingers: thumb, ring, index, pinky, middle finger. Faster and faster. But there is something more in Fernando's face. A different anxiety, a different confusion. His friend is an organized, tidy guy who thinks ahead. Ruso admires him for that. Not just that, but it's definitely one of the reasons. His ability to anticipate things, be ready for possibilities. Sometimes it surprises him that Fernando, being as he is, accepts him as a friend since everything with him is off the cuff, improvised. And on top of that, he makes a lot of mistakes in his improvising. But Fernando's face, his face today, reveals him to be overwhelmed by events. A guy used to playing chess who, all of a sudden, finds a pair of dice in his hands. Maybe that's a bad image, but it's the only one that comes to him.

"What are you looking at?" asks Fernando suddenly, stopping his tapping just as he rests his ring finger on the table.

Ruso shakes his head and looks at the clock on the wall. He turns toward Cristo.

"Can you turn it up, Cristo?"

He nods and turns the dial.

Let's take a look at River's training, Prieto is saying, over the end of the musical divider he always uses.

"How long is this asshole gonna go on about River?" asks Fernando as if he's talking to himself.

Cristo sits down again after fulfilling his mission.

The journalist's voice is loud and clear. *I have Ventura on the line,* says Prieto.

"Who's Ventura?" asks Cristo.

"He's the field reporter who covers River's practices," explains Ruso.

Any news over there, Ventura? There is a silence occasionally interrupted by a voice that goes in and out. *Let's see if we can improve our connection,* Prieto's voice has quickly veered into annoyance. *While the brains in production deal with this screwup, I'll tell you . . .* He leaves the sentence unfinished, and Ruso can't help but feel compassion toward the poor radio producer on the receiving end of Prieto's rage.

I want to ask Ventura, if they can ever get him back on air, about . . . now they tell me they have him on the line. Let's see. Okay, Ventura. Can you hear me? "Perfectly, Armando. How am I coming in?" *Perfectly, Ventura,* imitates Prieto, who seems to still have plenty of venom in him. *I was asking if there was anything new going on at River's training.* "Well, as usually happens on Thursdays the team is practicing behind closed doors, but we have the probable lineup to face—" *Wait, wait,* Prieto interrupts him. *We have time for the lineup. I was asking if there was any more important news, about the future . . .*

Poor Ventura is silent, as if he didn't know how to process his boss's attack. Suddenly Ruso realizes that Fernando has stood up, as he does when he's listening to an Independiente game on the radio and they are ahead in a risky play. Prieto continues: *Keep in mind that the championship is ending. And luckily for River. But I got some info, dear sir, that River is preparing an acquisition . . . and what an acquisition . . .*

Now Ruso stands up too.

"Well, I'm not sure what you're thinking of, Armando, but I heard that a forward who plays in Europe, a former River player . . ." Cold, Ventura, cold. Not even close. Or should I say, the player they were telling me about plays much closer to here. Although not that close, now that I think about it . . . *"You mean here in Argentina?"* Ay, Ventura. The idea is that you, a man steeped in all things River, in their day-to-day, informs me, not that I inform you. Some exclamations celebrating Prieto's sarcasm are heard from those in the studio with him. *"Well . . . they told me about a midfielder from Banfield who . . ."* Cold, cold, Ventura. You are about to freeze, and you're awfully close to the shore. Are you wearing a good coat? I'm asking because I'm sincerely concerned about your health, Ventura . . .

More laughter in the studio. Ruso wonders if this Prieto is being particularly prickish today, or if he's always like that and he'd just never noticed. *"Well, if you toss me a line . . ."* The poor guy's voice is at the edge of resignation and annoyance. *Relax, Ventura, I'm gonna help you so then you can go back through the hallways and confirm this rumor for me. It turns out that recently River's been having a lot of defensive problems. And I mean a lot. And somebody close to the club, and I mean very, very close to the club, mentioned to me, this Saturday . . . He mentioned to me this Saturday . . . you sure you haven't heard about this, Ventura?* More laughter in the studio. *Well, as I was saying, they told me . . . they told me that he's in their sights, and that they've been watching him very, very closely, a kid who plays as a center back for a team in the Argentine A Tournament. Do*

you need more clues, Ventura, or is that enough? "In the Argentine A? It's strange for a club like River to have someone in their
sights . . ." I know, I know, my dear sir. That's why I say it's a
strange case. Actually it's a kid who's owned by a National B club,
who plays in the Greater Buenos Aires . . . "Almagro?" No, my
young friend—more laughter—It's not Almagro, my friend . . . I
think if I give you the detail I have on the tip of my tongue, you'll
get it. But I don't know if I should, what can I say. I'm thinking about it, but I don't want to stick my nose in your business,
Ventura. "Honestly, this comes as a surprise to me, Armando."
I know that, Ventura, I know. That's why I'm the host of this
program and you are freezing to death out there covering practices, my son. But I have it from a very, and I mean very, good
source. That's the only reason I'm mentioning it. I've given you
the pieces of the puzzle. And let's see if you can put it together.
The player I'm talking about is now twenty, twenty-one years
old. No more. And he played in a U-17 juvenile selection in the
Indonesian World Cup. Ruso and Fernando look at each other.
Cristo lifts his arms. "Could it be Felipe Castaño, Armando?"
Let me finish, Ventura. It's not Felipe Castaño. Castaño's outlook
is unclear, Ventura. But that's not the player's name. The player
is named . . . the player is named . . . Maybe we'll leave you in
suspense for a while. Go ahead, finish your report, Ventura.
"But Armando, now you've got me wondering." Don't worry,
my young friend. Your ignorance, if you'll allow me the word,
is understandable. I know this because of a meeting I had this
past weekend. And the truth is it surprised me. Obviously when
I left that lunch I checked it out immediately, you know what I
mean? And it seems that what this person close to River told me
was completely, completely true. "A defender, you say." A center.
It's an original story, Ventura. This kid played, in that juvenile

selection, as a striker. But they switched him to a center back a while ago and it looks like he's really bearing fruit . . . "Tell me what team he's on at least, Armando . . ." You're right, Ventura. Watch out, all this hard work is gonna give you a hernia. A team in the Northeast . . . "San Martín de Mendoza?" Ay, Ventura. I'm gonna send you back to high school, to Argentine geography class, my boy. Mendoza's in Cuyo, not in the Northeast. From the home province of General Taboada, Ventura. "Um . . ." Ay, Ventura. Ay, Ventura. I see I'm not going to send you back just to study geography. You could use some Argentine history classes too, my boy. "Gimnasia y Tiro de Salta?" Ay, Ventura. Ay, Ventura. "Presidente Mitre? Does he play in Santiago del Estero?" About time, Ventura. In Presidente Mitre. But while I'm at it, I'll give it to you in full. "If you want, I can guess the rest . . ." No, my dear. The horse is out of the barn. He's on loan to Presidente Mitre. Platense's got his registration rights. And the player's named—the player's named—you still don't have it? "Honestly, Armando, no . . ." That's not surprising, because River is handling this with the utmost discretion because they don't want somebody else to get him. "But I haven't heard a thing about this here, Armando, I swear . . ." Top secret, Ventura. They are handling this with utter secrecy. But you know that it's important for us to give this information. We aren't interested in the club executives' well-being. That's not our job. So I'm sorry if this is putting a crimp in their negotiations, but we're not gonna hold back the scoop just for them. Don't you agree? "Sure, Armando, you're the boss." Management is gonna say there's nothing. No interest. They're gonna tell you that it's an unfounded rumor. Just going around the grapevine. But you should trust what I tell you. You can trust my source. I'll tell you what you should do. "Yes, Armando?" You go and tell it to their faces. Ask them straight out, use his name. Then you tell me how they react. They are gonna want to kill you. So I'm thinking maybe I should send one of the boys with you, one of the boys here from the office, for backup . . . More laughter. Somebody makes a joke. *No, here I've been worried about you getting too cold and catching something and now they might just beat you to a pulp, Ventura. Honestly, I wouldn't want that to happen. Can I trust them not to knock you out?* "Don't worry about that, Armando." Okay. Well, *don't come later saying I didn't warn you, my young friend. You go . . . find some exec . . . and ask him what's up with the rights to Mario Juan Bautista Pittilanga. Should I repeat that? Pittilanga. Go. Go and then tell me what their reaction is.*

Hitmen

"I already got used to it, but it's true. You listen to *The Fairly Odd Parents* for fifteen minutes and you start having hallucinations, I swear."

"Were cartoons like that in our day?"

"No way, Ruso. They were nothing like this."

"The twins drove me nuts with *Dexter's Laboratory*."

"That's nothing compared to this. I'd take Dexter over the fairly odd parents any day. You know what I'd do if I had a lot of money, I'm talking a lot of money, Ruso?"

"What, Mono?"

"I'd open up an account in Banco Nación, you know how they do, to help out when somebody needs a transplant, some fucked-up surgery, some treatment out in bumblefuck, that kind of thing? Well, I'd be collecting money to hire a hitman."

"A what?"

"A hitman, stupid. A hired killer to shoot them down."

"The fairly odd parents?"

"The fairly odd parents . . . Timmy . . ."

"Who's Timmy?"

"The kid, the main character. He's the one who has the fairly odd parents."

"Aha, I see you don't miss an episode . . ."

"What do you expect, when they're bursting my eardrums?"

"I'll chip in, Mono. I'm not talking a fortune now, but I'll kick in a few pesos."

"Me too. If it will shut those sons of bitches up, I'm in."

"That's the way. Friends have to stick together, right?"

38.

There is no other sound in the classroom than Fernando's footsteps, going up and down the aisles that separate the desks, until he stops at the front and turns to look at his students as they take their tests. He takes a few steps back while keeping his eyes on them, leans against the wall beside the chalkboard, and immediately regrets it: he's convinced that his back is covered in chalk. He again wonders, for the nth time, which of his stupid colleagues cleans erasers by banging them against the wall, instead of doing it in a ventilated spot outside the classroom.

"Can you see well or do you need me to turn on the light?" he asks out loud.

Several students, in chorus, respond no, it's better like this, this is fine. But Fernando feels the weight of his grandmother's old warnings, when she would sanctimoniously turn on the light in the room because that boy spends all his time reading and he's going to go blind. So he walks toward the switch and turns the light on. Of the twelve fluorescent tubes only four go on. Two of them immediately begin to flicker nonstop because their starters are damaged.

"It's better off, teach, because that's irritating," says Castillo without looking up from his exam.

Fernando does as he says, although he promises himself he'll bring up the subject of the light tubes at the next full staff meeting. He will entitle his intervention "The Great Teaching

Quandary: Dark Classroom or the Adventure of Psychedelic Visual Perception." It's possible that his position won't yield many supporters, and that it will only serve to confirm the opinion almost all of his colleagues have of him, namely that he is a curmudgeon and a hairsplitter.

Cáceres's hand in the air pulls him from his musings.

"Come over, teach," says the boy.

"Let's see now, Cáceres. Give it a try: 'Please, sir. Can you come over?'"

"Please, teach. Come."

Fernando figures it could be worse and he goes over.

"What does 'discern' mean?"

"It means to glimpse, see something hidden. Do you understand?"

"No."

"Uh . . . it means something that you don't see, that gradually, bit by bit, you begin to see it. Discern is when you realize something, or you start to realize. Something that you didn't understand, and that suddenly you begin to grasp. Now is it more or less clear?"

Cáceres nods and goes back to what he was doing. Which is, suspects Fernando, perpetrating an exam worthy of a grade of somewhere between one and three points out of ten.

Maybe both things are true. He is a hairsplitter and a curmudgeon and the principal and the vice principal are fools, and most of his colleagues serious cretins, starting with the cretin who clapped the eraser against the wall, filling it with chalk dust and paving the way for his wrecking one of the few presentable sweaters he has. Another raised hand.

"What do you need, Mendoza?"

"Dis—"

"Discern."

"Yeah, teach, that's it. What is that?"

"Okay, kids," he raises his voice, so they all pay attention. "Let me explain it for everyone." Twenty-five heads lift to face him. "Discern means seeing something . . . starting to see it, realizing something, a solution to a problem you were having, or something you don't yet know. That is discern. Is that clear? Do you understand it, Mendoza?"

"Yes, teach. Thanks."

As he tries to remember in what part of the test he used that verb, he is startled by the vibration, at his waist, of his cell phone. He is slightly thrown off by the phone number, and Fernando attributes that to the fact that he's only recently started using a cell phone, and isn't very adept at it. It's a really long number, much longer than usual. Suddenly he realizes that the first few numbers are the area code for Santiago del Estero.

"Kids. Listen up for a second. I have an important call on my cell. Do you mind if I answer it?"

Several heads shake indicating they don't.

"Go ahead and answer it, teach. But it might be better if you go out into the hall, there's better reception there," suggests Sierra, and several kids laugh.

"Thanks, Sierra. But if I leave you might be tempted to cheat. And since I'm sure you don't know how to cheat, or who to cheat off of, you would get confused and upset. I'd better stay."

He goes to one side of the room and speaks in a murmur. Perhaps one of them is actually thinking and he wouldn't want to interrupt that.

"Hello."

"Hello . . . I'd like to speak with Fernando, please. Fernando Raguzzi."

"Yes, speaking."

"Ah, how goes it. This is Bermúdez, head coach of Mitre."

"What a surprise, Bermúdez. How are things going? Is there some problem?"

"Fine, fine, no problem: but there's news."

"News? Cáceres, please keep your eyes on your paper. Excuse me, Bermúdez, what were you saying?"

"If you're busy I can call some other time."

"No, no, there's no problem. You were saying—"

"The president just told me that they called from Europe. From Ukraine. Seems they wanted to inquire about conditions for the kid, for Pittilanga."

"What?"

"From Ukraine, they called. About the kid. I didn't catch the name of the club. But they wanted to ask about conditions . . ."

Fernando swallows hard. He leans against the wall beside the chalkboard again. This time he doesn't mind getting covered in chalk.

"Hello? Can you hear me?"

"Yeah, yeah, Bermúdez. It's, it's good." For the first time he's hearing what he has been waiting a year and a half to hear, and now he doesn't know how to feel. "I guess they'll talk again."

"Yeah, of course. I gave them your phone number. Yours and your friend Daniel's. But I wanted to warn you. Bah, I mean, because I guess you might be interested."

"Yes, yes. In theory, yeah. Of course it depends on what they're offering." He has the strength to keep up appearances. "But yes. Of course we're interested."

"Good, good. I don't want to take up any more of your time."

"No, please. Thank you. We'll be in touch."

"We'll be in touch."

"Ciao, Bermúdez. Thanks."

"Ciao, take care."

Fernando puts his cell phone away in its case.

"Pardon the interruption, kids, but it was important," he says aloud.

"No problem, teach," respond a few of them.

Now he notices that he has gotten chalk on himself again. He turns to slap his sweater vigorously a few times.

"Teach, come over."

Fernando looks up. It's Yanacón.

"Please, can you come over, teach?" the girl corrects herself, without his having to remind her. Good. Manners are still alive and well in Argentina.

He approaches her desk.

"What does 'discern' mean?"

"Tell me, Yanina. Didn't you listen when Cáceres asked that, or when Mendoza asked that, and I explained it to everyone?"

Yanina Yésica Yanacón (what witty parents, combining names like that) looks up at him, as innocent as can be. Fernando sighs and explains, again, the meaning of the verb "discern."

Promise

"Dad . . . what did he leave us, Fer?"

"I don't understand, Mono."

"You and me. Papá left us Independiente. The cups, the mystique, the success . . ."

". . ."

"Is it true or not?"

"I guess so, Mono."

"Well. And me?"

"You what?"

"To Guadalupe . . . what am I leaving her?"

"Let's not start, Mono."

"Stop fucking with me and answer, Fernando."

"A ton of stuff, you're leaving her."

"In the future, I mean."

"What do you mean 'in the future'?"

"Sure. In the past I understand what you're saying. I'll leave her memories, photos, what we did together. And in the future?"

". . ."

"You see? That's what I'm getting it. I have nothing to leave her. From now on, I mean."

". . ."

". . ."

"And what would you want to leave her?"

"I want to leave her Independiente, Fer. But an Independiente that's a real gift, you understand. Like saying, 'Here, I leave you the love for this team, this really great team. Have it, forever.'"

"..."

"..."

"You don't have to worry, Mono."

"About what?"

"She's going to be an Independiente fan. The rest of it I don't know. I mean, about the cups and the mystique, I can't say that for sure. Maybe it comes back, maybe it doesn't. But we'll get her to root for the Red."

"..."

"..."

"You promise me?"

"..."

"Hey! You promise me?"

"..."

"..."

"I promise, Mono. I promise."

39.

Mauricio explains the situation with the help of some notes he pulls from his briefcase. He uses a clear tone and precise vocabulary and summarizes the possible scenarios for the near future. Ruso finds his coldness, his caution, a bit strange, although he definitely prefers it to the outbursts of rage and the recriminations that he'd feared in his darkest predictions. After all, it's the first time that Mauricio and Fernando have seen each other since the Audi incident, two months earlier. Two months? Have two months passed already? What a strange thing time is. Sometimes it's like chewing gum and sometimes it just evaporates, like now.

Maybe it seemed like it had flown by because they'd had him acting as the go-between, running back and forth like a chicken with its head cut off, relaying all the messages, sarcastic quips, and digs that Fernando and Mauricio had been dishing out all that time. He had let them do it, because he had no choice and because he was holding on to the hope that they would reconcile. To protect them from each other he had held back the most hurtful reproaches and the most cutting insults. For example, he had kept from Mauricio that Fernando never missed a chance to make fun of his concern over the insurance money, or to condemn him for all his betrayals and every single time he'd left them in the lurch. And he had saved Fernando from all of Mauricio's indignant complaints over having to put up with the insurance company's investigating—with a fine-tooth comb and a furrowed brow—every detail of his theft claim, because they didn't understand how the satellite tracker—which they themselves had provided—had failed.

Ruso had said yes to everything they'd each said, and now he was satisfied. If his sinuous maneuvers and his dancing around the issue and his numerous lies of omission had served to calm tempers and heal wounds of the distant and recent past, then it had been well worth it. At least the three of them were there. At the same table, like civilized people, listening to the information that Mauricio had compiled.

"From what I can tell, these guys from Chernomorets are serious. They've already bought several players, and they always go about it in the same way."

"What's that?" asks Fernando.

"First they get in touch with the club and then the agent. In this case, where there is no clear agent, even though Salvatierra is in the mix, they go to the owners of the transfer."

"There's something we haven't talked about, something I want to throw out there," interjects Ruso. "I wanna be the one who goes to the Ukraine with the kid to sign the papers."

The other two men look at him without smiling. It's clear they're in no mood for jokes. Mauricio continues.

"The negotiations are done here, in Buenos Aires. They have some kind of agent, an intermediary, who handles all the earlier conversations for them. If they settle on something, then they send two or three from the head office, to wrap things up, initial things, and close the deal."

"We have to get in touch with that guy," asserts Fernando.

"I already did," answers Mauricio, with such ice-cold politeness that it feels almost like an insult. "Karmasov is his last name. He called me the other day."

Ruso is surprised, because he didn't think things were that far along. Fernando remains impassive, but Ruso is sure he's only doing it to avoid giving Mauricio the pleasure of seeing his reaction.

"He offered two hundred and twenty thousand," informs Mauricio.

"And what did you say?" asks Ruso anxiously.

"That there was no way we were selling him for less than four hundred thousand."

"How could you ask for that much? He's worth three hundred at most!" Ruso spits out.

"Cut it out, Ruso," Fernando says to curb him. "Let him finish."

"We don't know what he's worth," says Mauricio.

"There's no way in hell he's worth four hundred."

"It's a negotiation." Mauricio says it like that, flatly, with a tone so very patient it raises hackles. "He offers, I say it's too little, he makes a counteroffer, we act tough, we end up working it out. But if the first number was two hundred and twenty, there's no way I can't get him up to three hundred."

"And now what happens?" asks Fernando, and to Ruso it seems that his friend is trying to speed up the process and, collaterally, take the initiative away from Mauricio, wipe that little smug know-it-all expression off his face.

"When we meet with the Ukrainians they'll offer us a little more. Two hundred and fifty, probably. We'll say no again, that we won't let him go for less than three hundred and fifty. That way we definitely end up working it out."

"But . . . what if they back out?" asks Ruso, who is much more concerned with his own anxiety than with these virility competitions the other two seem intent on.

"Why would they back out?"

"I mean, maybe in the meantime they see some other kid they like . . ."

"Of course they're going to see others, and they're going to buy them up, too. Or you think they're coming from Ukraine just to sign this contract? These guys come here with a pile of money and they buy up a bunch of kids. It's not like they're coming just to buy Pittilanga and then they head home. They do it like this," Mauricio gestures with his hand, lifting it and bringing it down like a cutter, "in a series. Pittilanga is just one of the bunch. To play in Chernomorets, to loan him out some-where, whatever. He's part of a package. And thank god for that, because nobody would come just for him, no way in hell. You understand, Ruso?"

From the tone of the question, Ruso understands he has to say yes, but deep down he feels an absurd disappointment. What Mauricio is saying makes sense. He's nothing more than a dime-a-dozen kid that the Ukrainians have heard a bigtime journalist talking about. Since they're here, they'll buy him. Nothing more than that. They make the most of their trip and include him in the next package. But the whole situation seems tarnished. He doesn't know why, but it diminishes it for him.

"Another important subject is the fifteen percent that sup-posedly goes to the kid."

"What fifteen?" asks Ruso.

"Why 'supposedly'?" asks Fernando.

Mauricio makes an annoyed expression—slight, but it's there.

"You have to give fifteen percent of the total sale to the player. That's how it works." That part he directs at Ruso. He then immediately turns to Fernando. "And I say 'supposedly' because if we have to subtract fifteen percent, there's less money for Guadalupe. If we get three hundred thousand, fifteen percent is forty-five thousand. And the girl gets, instead of three hundred, two hundred and fifty-five. And there's still the matter of the taxes, which will surely be another cut."

There is silence, and Ruso can sense Fernando's discomfort. He doesn't want to let Guadalupe down. But he also doesn't want to wrong Pittilanga.

"I don't see it," Fernando finally murmurs.

"You don't see what?"

"I don't see leaving the kid without his fifteen percent."

A new silence. Mauricio looks at Ruso, perhaps expecting some solidarity, but Ruso remains quiet.

"Happens all the time," argues Mauricio. "If the kid wants to go play in Europe, he can do his part. Don't you think? After all, he's gonna be getting paid in euros."

"They use euros in Ukraine?" asks Ruso.

"Whatever." Mauricio doesn't want to get further off topic.

"Well." Notwithstanding his dubious tone, Ruso wants to side with Mauricio. They've come so far. They are so close to accomplishing what they set out to . . . "If that's the case . . ."

But just then Fernando speaks.

"The kid has always been good to us."

"So?" Mauricio seems to be struggling to control himself. "Wasn't Mono good to him? Weren't we? Can't he make an effort?"

"You think it was easy for him to accept the crazy idea of changing the position he's played all his life? Listen to Ruso and start playing defense? Swallow his pride? Start from scratch?"

What Fernando says is true, and Ruso is ashamed not to have thought the same thing. It's that sometimes Fernando can be insufferable: that honesty, that integrity, so quick to call an infraction. Without meaning to, he can make you feel contemptible. In that, Ruso sometimes feels tempted to share Mauricio's tedium at that rank-and-file rectitude, as he calls it. But only sometimes.

Mauricio makes another disgusted face.

"We'll do it your way," he concludes, and looks at Ruso, as if to let him know that now is the moment to support him in his suggestion. "But giving the kid fifteen percent lowers the margin or makes the operation more expensive and puts it at risk."

Before Ruso can speak Fernando adds, "There's also Bermúdez."

"What about Bermúdez?" asks Mauricio, almost losing his patience.

"We offered him ten percent to accept the change of position."

"What? Are you kidding me?"

Ruso decides to intervene. Better that he take the brunt, instead of Fer.

"I had to offer him something, Mauri. Otherwise . . . how could I convince him?"

"But what do you think? That this is a joke? That we can just give away the money?"

"No, bu—but . . ."

"Ruso is right," Fernando again sounds unyielding, but now Ruso appreciates it. "If it weren't for his idea we could have shoved the transfer up our asses. A while back."

Mauricio mutters something, low enough so the others can't tell if he is thinking or simply insulting them. He scribbles something onto one of his pages of notes.

"Make up your minds. Pittilanga's fifteen or Bermúdez's ten. But there's no way we can do both. Or we're talking seventy-five grand less."

He's right. Ruso knows he's right. He looks at Fernando, who looks back at him. Please let something, someone, persuade him to stop being a stickler with his ethics straight out of the Buenos Aires Student Handbook.

"Well, Fer, . . . maybe," Ruso fumbles along.

"Whatever," says Fernando finally, and there is a note of surrender in his voice. Slight, but it's there. "I guess we'll have to sit down with the guys and see what comes out of it."

"Sure." Ruso gets excited, because he always needs something to believe in. "That's what I say. Once we're there, in the meeting, we'll see how we handle it."

Mauricio looks at them. It looks like he has something to say, but he ends up not saying anything.

The Same Thing I

"Is it okay or is the water too hot, Fer?"

"It's perfect, Ruso."

"You want some, Mono?"

"No. I can't. The shots they're giving me are turning my stomach upside down like you can't believe. Shit is killing me."

". . ."

". . ."

"Your loss. Mauricio?"

"Yeah, thanks."

"Hey, Mono. Mamá told me the other day that the doctor told you to try a new medication . . ."

"This remote control works like shit . . ."

"Are you trying to crush it, man?"

"No, freak, but it's not working. Must be the batteries. Here, Mauricio. You try, you're closer."

"What do you want to watch?"

"Isn't there a National B game on today?"

"I think so."

"Put that on."

"Is it on 17 or 18?"

"18, I think."

"No. It's on 17. Did you hear what I asked you, Mono?"

"Yes, Fer. I heard you."

"Well, what do you think? Are you gonna try it or not?"

"Can we talk about it some other time, Fer? Here's the game. Rafaela's playing, but I don't know who with."

"Aldosivi?"

"No. Aldosivi played on Thursday."

"Unión?"

"No."

"Mono . . ."

"What . . ."

"I asked you something."

"I don't know, Fer. I'll think about it later. I don't know. Now I don't want to even hear about it."

"You can't answer us like that, Mono."

"I'm answering my older brother, Ruso. Not you."

"It's the same thing."

"Besides, why can't I? Why?"

"Why do you think? Because you're sick and you have to . . ."

"Yeah, Ruso. I'm sick. It's true. I've been sick for six months. But you know how it is. I don't know if you guys are going to understand. That's not all I am."

". . ."

". . ."

". . ."

"You guys don't understand because you love me, and you worry, and you know that I'm fucked up, and you'd like to be able to help me, and, and, and in the end we've been talking about this shit for six months. Do you understand?"

". . ."

". . ."

". . ."

"I know I'm sick. But it's not the only thing I am. You don't go around thinking about it all the time. At least I don't. I don't know about the other guys. But not me. I can't be going over it in my head twenty-four hours a day. Or do you guys spend all day thinking about the same thing? Not me, no way. I can't spend all day obsessing over this cancer, man. Over whether they told me this, or told me that, whether this treatment sits well with me, whether I should try another one, or if the tests look better or really suck, if I should listen to the oncologist or the hospital, or heed the guy who gave me the latest tomography scan and recommended whatever. Can't you see? I can't be thinking about that all day. Six months ago they told me I had cancer and my goose was cooked. Okay. But here I am, still alive."

"Luckily, Monito . . . "

"No, Ruso, you don't get it. When I say I'm still alive I'm not talking that stupid bullshit about keeping up the fight, betting on life and all that shit. I mean that things keep happening to me. Sometimes I'm hungry, sometimes I'm horny, sometimes I'm angry, sometimes I want to call Lourdes and tell her she's a bitch. But not angry about being sick. I mean angry about whatever, you understand? It's not like I got sick and I changed into a different person, man. I'm still me."

". . ."

". . ."

40.

"Hello, Elena. Humberto needed to see me, I believe."

"Yes, Counselor. Go right ahead."

Mauricio heads in thinking about how he and his boss don't share criteria for choosing staff. Elena is sixty years old, with a bulky frame more appropriate to a center back than the secretary of the firm's main partner.

In his office, Williams is talking on the phone. Surprise, surprise. Mauricio never comes in to find him doing anything else. He is never studying a file or preparing a document. He doesn't even waste time with the computer. He's of another generation, that must be the reason. The younger partners slack off just as much as he does, but they do it in front of a screen and with circumspect expressions. Williams—he's said it himself—doesn't even know which is the enter key. With the phone, on the other hand, he's an ace. It's almost an extension of his arm.

Anyway, Mauricio hasn't lost respect for him over that. He imposes an aura of dignity, of serene superiority that has a deep impact on the younger man. From his scattered gray hairs to his perfect cuticles and the knot in his tie and his dignified wrinkles. Mauricio wants to age like that. Ignacio and Gonzalo, the other partners, aren't even fit to tie Williams's shoelaces. They are just as much partners as the old man, but they lack his charm, his luster. They can line their pockets and drive around in slick shiny cars. But Williams plays in another division. The one Mauricio wants to play in. Someday.

Williams invites him to sit down with a gesture. He is talking on the phone and he laughs. He listens more than he speaks. He intervenes every once in a while, but he lets the other person speak without interrupting. Finally he says goodbye affectionately and turns to face the new arrival.

"How are you, Mauricio?"

"Fine, Humberto. They said you needed to speak with me."

"Yes, yes. Would you like something to drink?"

"Thank you, but I just had a coffee."

"Fine, fine," says Williams and he grows quiet, looking at him.

It's something important, Mauricio says to himself. That "fine, fine" is an introduction, a prologue.

"Mind if I give you a piece of advice?" Williams asks him with a stare.

"Yes—I mean no, I don't mind," stammers Mauricio. "Yes, please, I'd love you to . . ."

"The thing is . . . how old are you?"

"Forty."

"Forty. Okay. Imagine that what I'm about to tell you comes from a guy thirty years older than you. Which is to say, an old has-been."

If he were more calm, more focused, Mauricio would say something to butter him up. Like "you're no old has-been," or something just as ridiculous. But he can't. Where is he going with this age stuff?

"A good lawyer always has to keep a cool head. Always. He who gets hot under the collar, loses. Are you following me?"

"Yes."

"Good. Really I'm telling you this and you already know it. I've seen you work a thousand times and I know that's the case. And that's why we've been considering improving your situation in the firm. Otherwise, we wouldn't even think of keeping you in mind . . ."

"We've been," "we wouldn't even think." There's nothing bad in those expressions, but Mauricio finds them strangely distant, or vaguely threatening, although he doesn't understand why.

"But there are things that you handle a bit . . . green. I don't know how to explain it to you. You move a bit . . ." Williams seems to be searching for the most painless description. "A bit wet behind the ears. This thing with the player you are trying to sell at all costs, with your childhood buddies . . ."

Mauricio's heart sinks. Problem number one: how did Williams find out about the Pittilanga deal? Problem number two: again his words, those damn words: "at all costs" and above all "buddies," which sounds like a gang of uncouth boys, like awkward teenagers weighed down by their barrio roots. He clears his throat, but he can't keep his voice from coming out choked.

"The thing is that . . ."

"You are wondering how this little old guy knows that you have a meeting planned for the day after tomorrow in the Hotel Miranda around five . . ."

Of course. The funny thing is that he is racking his brains trying to figure out how he knows. If he were less nervous, Mauricio would have to admit that, yeah, it is impressive.

"But . . ." stutters Mauricio, and he stops himself. But why? What does the word "but" have to do with what Williams has been saying to him? Nothing. Imbecile.

"Karmasov, the Russian who is their liaison, is a friend of Fernando Vidal. You know him."

"Yes, of course." If Mauricio's met him, he doesn't remember, but it doesn't matter. Williams doesn't need him to know him, just for him to say yes and not interrupt his story.

"Vidal is close with Boca, and this Russian is usually very involved in the European markets. Especially in the weaker markets. The thing is I ran into Fernando at the club, and he brought you up and he mentioned this operation you're trying to pull off."

Williams smiles as he pauses and observes him: the hamster running around in his little wheel for a while.

"What I'm going to give you is a tip. Nothing more. You can take it or leave it. This isn't part of your job."

Yeah, right, you old liar, thinks Mauricio. This is not only part of the job. It's the crux of the job, although he doesn't say it. Or especially because he doesn't say it. Williams leans back in his armchair and puts his elbows on the desk.

"I don't know if you are aware of the opportunity you have on your hands, with that player . . ."

"Actually the player isn't mine. The transfer was bought by—"

"Yes, yes, I know all that. The player is owned by some Margarita Núñez de Raguzzi."

Mauricio nods and holds himself back from saying that Margarita is Mono's mother.

"What do you have to do with this?"

"Me?" Stupid question, which only serves to show his nervousness, his insecurity. "Nothing, Humberto. It's just some people I know from the neighborhood. From Castelar, where I grew up. An acquaintance of mine was the owner of the transfer. He died a while ago and his mother . . ."

"Yeah, some guy called Alejandro Raguzzi. Friend of yours?"

"No." Mauricio's answer comes out almost before he can finish the question. "An acquaintance from the neighborhood, I told you."

"Okay. Great, then."

Williams flips a few pages back in his notepad and brandishes his fountain pen. The only tools of his trade.

"I have the info here," he says, and Mauricio sees, upside down, a series of words and figures surrounded by scribbles, the kind Williams makes as he talks and listens on the phone. "Pittilanga, born in 1986, minors in Platense, U-17 World Cup in Indonesia, on loan to Mitre in Santiago del Estero. Did I get it right?"

Mauricio clears his throat for the nth time.

"Yes, Humberto. From what I understand, yes."

"And when the loan ends he goes back to Platense."

"I guess . . . the truth is I'm not really that up on it . . ."

"Don't worry. I am. Another friend of mine is an executive in Platense and I have it from a good source that they don't have the slightest intention of taking this kid back. They're going to release him. Are you following me?"

It's crazy. Suddenly Williams is an expert in the Pittilanga case. Some sort of Fernando, thirty years older and well dressed.

"And when they release him, this good woman is going to be the owner of a player worth nothing to her, am I right?"

"Yes, I think so. Anyway I barely took part . . ."

"Well. Here's where we have the opportunity to make an interesting profit."

Mauricio is perplexed by the sudden appearance of the first person plural. *We* have?

"We let him get released. Then the value of Pittilanga's transfer is zero pesos. A couple of months pass. This woman (or whoever it is, because it looks to me like they're using the old lady as a front) is left holding the bag. We let, I don't know, four months pass, and we offer twenty thousand dollars for the kid's transfer. Are you following me?"

Williams's cell phone rings but he turns it off so it doesn't interrupt. Behind his surprise, Mauricio can see the perfect logic of things. As Williams himself always says, it's not about the merchandise, it's about the revenue.

"And once we have the transfer, we shake things up a little. Don't forget I have people to hit up, people to interest, people to involve, so we can get a number that really makes it worth our bother. Maybe three hundred thousand, maybe four hundred. Four hundred thousand, half for you and half for me. Or half a million, who knows? Depends on how we negotiate it. Vidal told me that the player changed positions and he's getting much better results now."

"Yeah? No, I had no idea . . ."

"I don't know anything about soccer. Nor do I care, honestly. I never played. That must be it. But what I'm getting at is that we invest twenty thousand and we make ten times that, or fifteen or twenty. Am I being clear?"

"Yes, yes, it's that—"

"Let's see, Mauricio, my dear friend. Now the important thing is that you do nothing from now until Platense releases him. Above all, that these acquaintances of yours don't think of coming up with any other clever ideas, because then we've blown it. We go from three hundred or four hundred thousand dollars to zero. Do you understand me now?"

"Yes, yes, Humberto. I think I understand."

"I need your commitment on this, Guzmán," concludes Williams, and his smile is placid, frank.

A master. It's been three years since he's called him by his last name. Ever since he began to stand out from the mediocrity of the average new lawyer, Williams has favored him by using his first name. He's been bringing him into the fold, praising him, making him feel like part of the family. Not only with that, but with much more concrete and eloquent things, such as his office, his assistant, and especially his salary, and by calling him Mauricio as well. This fleeting return to his last name is not casual. It's a way of hammering home the pecking order, an efficient way of pointing out his place and circumstances. Mauricio holds his gaze as long as he can, which isn't very long. In that lies the secret to the old man's power, in some recess very far behind or above the suits and the Rolex and the angelic manicured hands.

He returns to his office, trying to process what Williams has said and ordered him to do. As if he had just fallen down a staircase and was patting himself down to see if he had any injuries. To begin with, there is nothing irreparable. Williams didn't accuse him of anything. He wouldn't have been able to, because Mauricio didn't even know he was interested. Now it's different, but he can't complain about anything that happened before. Good. It was perfect that he'd defined them as acquaintances from his childhood. Perfect. Quick reflexes. The only thing he has to do is take care of himself from here on out. Williams played his hand well, because he didn't threaten him. He spurred him on, which isn't the same thing. And, he offered him the chance to do business together. Those are the loyalties that are valuable. The guy who pays your salary, and not the boys who throw old photos in your face to make you feel sorry for them, who want to trap you with three or four childhood memories that they can't even remember right.

The Same Thing II

"The other day, for example."

"What happened, Mono?"

"When we lost to the team from Jujuy."

"Yeah, what about it?"

"I wanted to kill them all, man! That's what about it. How can they manage to play so bad, those bastards! They couldn't put two passes together!"

"It was horrible, it's true."

"They're disgusting."

"And I was kinda like, at first, because Mamá came in, she had come to cook something for me and she heard me cursing and she thought something was hurting me and that I was calling her. And when I saw her frightened face I said to myself, no, stop the train. With what's going on with you . . . because, hey, even I fall into getting all obsessed."

"It's not getting obsessed, Mono. It's taking care of yourself."

"No, Fernando. It's getting obsessed. I take care of myself. I take all the shit they give me. I do all the tests they tell me to. But I can't leave everything on hold, you understand? I can't stop living my life until I get cured or until I die. Is it that hard?"

". . ."

". . ."

". . ."

"And I know you guys are doing it for me. But there comes a point where it drives me nuts, what can I say. We can't talk about anything, we can't just watch a game. You guys don't even fight anymore, and you live for fighting with each other."

"Who?"

"You and Mauricio, Ruso. Don't play dumb. Or you think I don't realize? Have some respect, douchebags. You've been treating each other like shit for thirty years and now you're like two English ladies at teatime."

"And couldn't we be in a new phase of our friendship?"

"My ass, Mauricio. Quit fucking around. Let's watch games, let's talk about the same dumb shit we always talk about, let's fight over the same dumb stuff, tell me about the stupid shit you do out there, those of you who can go to work . . . well, that doesn't include Ruso, since what he does isn't work."

"I'm not gonna let you—"

"And quit busting my balls, for the love of god."

41.

One year, seven months, and twenty-seven days after Mono's death, Fernando Raguzzi, Daniel Gutnisky, and Mauricio Guzmán take the elevator of the Hotel Miranda to the twentieth floor, where executives of the Chernomorets of Ukraine are waiting for them to sign the transfer contract for Argentine player Mario Juan Bautista Pittilanga.

They are silent, until Ruso points into the full-length mirror at the image of the three of them, and smiles.

"A good day to die," he says, paraphrasing the hero of some movie he doesn't remember, not managing to get the other two to loosen up.

When the doors open he can't help but gasp. Before them is an immense window from which they can see the Wildlife Reserve, the dikes of Puerto Madero, the cargo ships being towed through the buoys. Fernando lightly touches his shoulder to silence his gasping, because it's not like they want to reveal their cards to the Ukrainians so early in the game.

Fernando suddenly thinks of the school in Moreno where he teaches language arts. The broken windows, the missing lights, the wobbly tables. *Piece-of-shit country*, he thinks, which is his classic phrase for these occasions. Anyway, his indignation isn't entirely legitimate. He's using it as a distraction to shake off his nervousness. A sandbag he can punch to vent.

Mauricio crosses through the door of the conference room and they follow him. Fernando quickly counts the seven people who are waiting for them. Behind them they hear Ruso's voice, in a murmur: "At least they didn't pull out the machine guns."

Fernando can't help but smile. For a week Ruso has been entertaining himself by saying that these guys are actually Russian mafia and are laundering money from their illicit businesses. And when they realize that Pittilanga is a clumsy clod, they are going to send hitmen to shoot them down. He turns ever so slightly and answers in a low voice.

"They don't use machine guns, Ruso. They strangle you with a steel string."

Mauricio is already shaking hands. There are three Ukrainians, or four, if they count the intermediary, this Karmasov who lives in Buenos Aires. Or is he Russian? Fernando thinks he remembers Mauricio saying Russian. He is the one who now makes the introductions and does the translating.

Mario Pittilanga waits a bit farther back, standing beside a guy as tall and dark as him, but fat and in his fifties, whom the kid evasively introduces as his father. Fernando, somewhat perplexed, shakes the pillowy hand the other man extends without smiling. It makes sense that he's here, Fernando tells himself, but it's hard for him to place him in this scene he has been replaying over and over again for two weeks, every sleepless night. The father and son are the only ones not wearing ties. The kid has on a jersey with the insignias of Presidente Mitre. The man wears a long-sleeved shirt with a single open button at the neck, stuffed into the waist of a pair of jeans that are tight and draw attention to the belly spilling over their top.

They sit down. To one side of the rectangular table, the Ukrainians from Chernomorets. On the other side, the three of them. At one head, Pittilanga and his father, and at the other, the liaison and translator. There is a brief silence as they settle in. Mauricio takes the initiative.

"Okay. First I wanted to thank you for graciously coming so far to wrap up this operation, as well as for the confidence you've put in Mario, to whom we wish the best of luck in this new stage of his career . . ."

Karmasov leans forward and translates as he listens to Mauricio's introduction. He has the Ukrainians' ears, but they look at Mauricio and nod occasionally. Ruso signals to Fernando and he leans toward him behind Mauricio, who continues reciting his introduction. Fernando comes closer, intrigued.

"Did you see how the Russians talk?" whispers Ruso with a mischievous smile.

"What?"

"They remind me of the Uruguayans from *Hupumorpo*. Remember?"

Fernando is confused for a moment. Ruso is a child. The son of a bitch has the attention span of a larva. They are closing a three-hundred-thousand-dollar deal that has taken them almost two years and tons of bad blood, and the half-wit is reminiscing about comic TV shows from the seventies.

"What were they called?" continues Ruso.

"Who?" He immediately regrets his own question. Who knows what the Ukrainians must be thinking about this whispering behind the back of the main negotiator.

"The Uruguayans, man. They did a sketch where they were pretending to be Russians. They were talking all kinds of shit, making out like they were KGB agents. Don't you remember?"

Yes, he remembers. But he doesn't want to play along with Ruso. Maybe he'll get tired and quit fucking around.

"One was Espalter. And the other one?"

No such luck.

"Cut it out, Ruso."

"Come on. Espalter and—"

Fernando weighs his alternatives. Answering to appease him or leaving him with his question, in which case he'll keep going on about it.

"Almada."

"Almada!" agrees Ruso, pleased.

Fernando sits up straight in his seat with the idea that Ruso should do the same. Mauricio has opened up a file and lays out several copies of the contracts he's prepared. Fernando feels a tap on his shoulder. Again Ruso is crouching down behind Mauricio's back.

"Cut it out, Ruso," he whispers, with daggers in his eyes.

"Just one thing. Which one was which?"

Fernando looks at him, somewhere between incredulous and confused.

"Which one was which what?"

"Dude, the one who played the Russian. Espalter or Almada? Or was it both of them?"

Exasperated, Fernando is about to answer very rudely, when he is stopped by a voice coming from beside him.

"One moment." Pittilanga's father is suddenly speaking.

Fernando turns his head toward him. Everyone else does the same. The contracts are open like a deck of cards on the polished table.

"I'm not going to just sit here and let you rip my son off," he adds, leaning forward with his elbows on the table, pointing an accusing finger. At them. At the three of them.

A new pause in the translation. This time Ruso forgets to compare it with the sketch from *Hupumorpo*. Fernando feels like the floor is being taken out from under him. In his successive sleepless nights he had given free rein to all his anxieties. The Ukrainians changing their minds, Mauricio being overconfident, even Pittilanga's sudden death on his way to or from a game. But this he hadn't foreseen. He turns toward Mauricio. He is mute. Why isn't he saying anything?

"What is he talking about?" asks Fernando finally, when he sees that Mauricio still hasn't said a word.

"I'm talking about the scam you three are running. That's what I'm talking about," responds Pittilanga Senior, and Fernando sees that his son's eyes are lowered.

The interpreter translates. The Ukrainians look at each other, and then at Pittilanga Senior. Ruso looks alternately at everybody, with a contorted expression. Fernando senses that if he lets this guy keep talking, all is lost. Why doesn't Mauricio speak? He decides to intervene.

"Look, sir. If you'd like we can sit down and discuss this all you want, at some other time. But here we are determining very important things and from what I understand Mario is old enough to decide what he wants to do with his career. So if you will please excuse us . . ."

"No. I won't excuse you, blondie."

Fernando feels the skin on his face reddening. But he is determined not to lose his cool. He turns to face Mauricio.

"I suppose that a good measure would be to have the meeting only between the interested parties, I don't know what you think."

Mauricio takes his time before answering.

"Actually," he says finally, "the father is an interested party."

He is silent again and, like a distorted echo, the murmur of the Russian translation is heard. Fernando can't even find the voice to ask why.

"Mario is twenty years old and seven months," informs Mauricio, as if that were a key piece of information, or worse, as if just with that Fernando and the others should understand.

"So? Didn't you say that at at least eighteen he could sign the contract?"

"Yes. He can. But to leave the country he needs his parents' permission. Until he is of legal age, twenty-one."

Fernando does the math. That will be in five months. In five months' time—in Ukraine, in Acapulco, and on Mars—they will be well into the season. These guys aren't going to wait that long. *The goddamned son of a bitch,* thinks Fernando. *It can't be. It can't be that this all fails.* He faces Pittilanga's father. He is desperate, and Mauricio's silence heightens his anxiousness.

"Forgive me, but don't you think that—"

"I don't forgive you anything," the man cuts him off, and spitefully holds his gaze. "You think I was born yesterday? That I don't realize when I'm getting screwed?"

This time there is no translation. The Ukrainians don't complain because even though the words escape them, the gestures and expressions are plenty eloquent. Fernando looks at Mauricio, who looks at Pittilanga Senior blankly. The son's eyes are still lowered, fixed on the table.

"Tell them," now the father faces the interpreter, "tell these men that I am sorry, and that I don't doubt that they may be honest people. But these three, these three are bad news, they can't be trusted."

"I won't allow you to—"

"You don't allow me or not allow me, baldie," he says, standing up. Fernando also rises, and Ruso imitates him. Mauricio makes a vague gesture with his hand, but quickly desists. "Why don't you tell these men what you have up your sleeve? Why don't you tell them?" He faces the Ukrainians. "I don't know if you know, but my son played in the U-17 World Cup in Indonesia. He was one of the twenty kids," he shakes his neck, as if his shirt were bothering him, "of the twenty kids from all Argentina who went to the World Cup. When he came back, these so-and-sos bought his transfer—"

"His transfer was bought by Alejandro Raguzzi."

"I couldn't care less. The thing is that you three ended up with the transfer. And now not only do you want to sell him off like closeout for two bits—"

"Sell him off like closeout?" Fernando feels he is reaching his limit. Ruso tries to grab his arm, but he shakes him off.

"Like closeout, you idiot. Like closeout, I said. Or you think I'll believe anything? That I don't know what players are worth? Huh? Just because I don't have an education you can just dupe me like a stooge? Is that what you think?"

Fernando faces the interpreter. He is livid, but speaks calmly.

"Please convey my apologies to them for this scene, it's just crazy."

"Crazy! I'll give you crazy, you cut-rate crook!" And he bangs both hands on the table. The Ukrainians also stand up. The only ones still sitting are Mauricio and Mario Pittilanga. "And what is that bullshit of making him play as a defender? Eh? What kind of shit is that, would you mind telling me?"

This time the interpreter rushes to translate, and the effect on the faces of the Ukrainians is immediate. Even the father, as beside himself as he is, notices it, and he redoubles his efforts, knowing that he's hit the nail on the head. He continues to address the executives from Chernomorets.

"Because I'm sure these jerks didn't tell you that. No. No, sir. They kept it nice and quiet. Because my kid is a forward. I—" He interrupts himself, as if for the first time he has to search for words. "I trained him there, for the goal area, since he was a little boy. Since he was little. And not so these sons of bitches could come and fill his head with garbage!"

"I don't think the conditions are such that—" Mauricio speaks without emotion.

"I'm gonna shove the conditions up your ass!"

Pittilanga Senior charges toward them, knocking over the chair and moving the desk to one side. Fernando prepares himself for the onslaught. After all, now that it's come to this, maybe he'll get a chance to sock him a good one. But it doesn't get serious because the kid, emerging from his inaction, stands up and stops his father's charge with a hand on his chest, as if stopping a train or a wall that's collapsing. The father lets him, but he keeps shouting, more and more enraged.

"I don't know what kind of scam they're running! Or how they're planning to get their hands on the big money!"

"Big money? What are you, drunk, you gutter trash?"

It is the first time Fernando uses that insult. And even though later he regrets it and tells himself he didn't mean it, he still feels horrible and spends several days feeling mortified for what he has just said. The father charges again when he hears the insult; the son, still without saying a word, vigorously holds him back.

"We're trying to find a future for the kid!" Fernando stumbles over his words in his rush to get them out. Anything to get him past the insult he just said. "Didn't you see where he was playing when we found him?"

"That's just for now . . ."

"For now because his loan isn't up for a few more months! After that they're cutting him loose! Or what do you think's gonna happen?"

"Cutting him loose my ass!"

"Cutting his ass loose and all the rest of him! Or do you think he's going to get a spot in Platense?"

"If not in Platense, then somewhere else!"

"Another team, at his age and—" Fernando stops himself just in time, before adding, *and as lead-footed as he is?*

More silence. Now the translator's words are nervous and interspersed with comments and questions. They are no longer just listening. They are making decisions. Fernando wants to die, because he knows what those decisions are. In fifteen minutes everything has gone to shit.

"Mr. Guzmán," says the interpreter finally, facing Mauricio. "As you can imagine, under these conditions, it's not possible . . ." The Russian's pronunciation is somewhat metallic, but his grammar is perfect. "If in the future . . ."

They are polite guys, and so they take the time to make that little speech before clearing out. But all is lost, and the eight people in the room know that perfectly. Fernando drops into his chair and rubs his face with his hands, as if this was something he could wake up from.

"Yeah, cover your face in shame," he hears the father say in the background, still threatening.

He hears footsteps around the table and behind his back. When he lowers his hands and looks around, Fernando sees that the Ukrainians, the interpreter, and the Pittilangas have gone. Only the three of them are left at the table covered in scattered contracts.

Shaman Carlos

"**M**onito, the thing is that—"

"The thing is bullshit, Fernando! My life has already changed enough with this fucking cancer, I don't need you guys changing on me too. And I'm not saying we act like nothing's going on. I'm not that stupid. But we don't always have to act like the wake's already started."

"It's not the wake."

"You're right. That came out wrong. But you guys are always talking, about the medications, the treatments, the new chemo, the oncologist, some other so-called expert, about what we told Mamá, what we didn't tell her . . . And don't even remind me about the last kook we went to see!"

"Uh—not that again . . ."

"Don't start, Mono . . ."

"Motherfucking Shaman Carlos! Cut it out already! Just because he made Aunt Beba's ovarian tumor disappear we go there, all four of us go all the way to Lomas de Zamora, so that quack can touch my stomach and make two hundred bucks disappear. Quit busting my balls!"

"Stop, 'cause it was Mónica's aunt, not my aunt."

"Doesn't matter, Ruso. God knows what he did to her in that little room in the back . . ."

"Didn't he take you to the back room?"

"Again with the back room! He only saw me up front, that's

it. He had me there with my shirt pulled up for ten minutes while he made a wise expression. He hugged me and told me I was cured."

"Okay, man. What did I know. Her aunt—"

"I told you, Ruso. Her aunt liked him because he must have rearranged the plants on her patio."

"That's just crude, poor auntie . . ."

"Seriously, Ruso."

"Now, I wonder . . . Mono, did he . . ."

"What, Fernando?"

"He didn't rearrange your patio . . . ?"

"Fuck off."

"Maybe that's why the treatment didn't work, Mono."

"Ditto for you, Ruso."

"Sure. You either do these things all the way, or you don't do 'em at all."

"When even Mauricio is making fun of me, I know I'm lost . . . "

"Were you clear that you wanted the same treatment Aunt Beba got?"

"Why don't you just go—"

"Oh, it's very easy to criticize, isn't it? Listen, Mauricio, will you take us there again?"

"Sure, Rusito. My pleasure. We'll just grab the car and head to Lomas de Zamora."

"Don't worry about the two hundred bucks. We'll all chip in."

"That's it. We'll ask the shaman to give him the full treatment, nice and slow."

"Why don't all three of you go fuck off?"

"We can go to the healer this Saturday. Or are you busy?"

"Count me in, Mauricio."

"You three are impossible, you bunch of boneheads."

"It's true."

"You're right."

42.

Fernando approaches the large window and looks down. Ruso gets up too, but he goes toward the corner where the hotel staff have set up a table with coffee, soft drinks, and cookies, and he asks the other two if they'd like something. They don't answer, absorbed, but Ruso serves himself a large cup of coffee and a plate loaded with cookies: he's not going to miss out on free treats like this. As he returns to the main table he hears Mauricio's phone ring.

"Hello?" The caller is shouting. "Yes. In a meeting, Humberto . . . Yes, everything's under control. I'm on my way there."

Mauricio's tone is jovial, energetic, kind. Daniel guesses that he's talking with his boss at the firm.

"Sure. If you want to save some time go ahead and ask Soledad, but there won't be any problem . . . Of course . . . What? Ha, ha! Sure, Counselor. See you soon."

He hangs up, closes the phone and places it on the table.

"It's a good thing you recover quickly from bad news," says Fernando, his eyes glued on the street and the opposite sidewalk.

"What?"

Fernando is slow to reply.

"That you bounce back, I mean. Just five minutes ago we lost almost two years of work and you're already laughing with your boss like it was nothing. It's a lucky thing, in my opinion."

Ruso, in other circumstances, would intervene, apply cold compresses. A joke. A dumb question. Anything to shift focus. But he's not up for it. He's fed up too. Doesn't he have that right?

Mauricio forces an unenthusiastic smile: "You looking for a fight, Fer? Take it easy."

"Looking for a fight? No, not at all. Lucky for you. The truth is I envy you. You always fucking land on your feet."

"And what do you want me to do? Tell my boss about all our innermost pains?"

Now it is Fernando's turn to smile reluctantly. "Innermost? Good, Counselor. Good adjective. Not bad at all for a lawyer."

"Go to hell."

"You go to hell. And don't come telling me that you're holding back your feelings, because nobody's gonna buy that."

"Of course, it was only a matter of time. Here comes the pure of heart, the clean of spirit."

"No, just the moron."

Mauricio shakes his head and turns to Ruso.

"Hey, Ruso, if you want to say something hurry up because he's about to start in on his victim monologue, and you won't be able to get a word in edgewise."

Ruso doesn't have the slightest intention of saying a word, although, if they forced him to intervene, he thinks he'd do so in favor of Mauricio. Fernando's anger seems excessive, or at least ambiguous. Old grudges coming out in the wrong place.

"Are you really trying to make me believe that you care, even though you don't show it?"

"I'm not trying anything, Fernando. Do what you want. Believe it or don't. It doesn't matter."

Ruso leaves his coffee half-drunk, and some cookies on the plate. Suddenly he's not hungry. But he isn't going to say anything. He's sick of them. Both of them.

"Does picking a fight with me calm your nerves, Fernando?"

"Picking a fight?"

"Yes, picking a fight. Because honestly I don't understand why you're starting with me. My boss called, I answered the phone. Does that really bother you that much?"

"Oh, man. My dear friend. The phone is the least of it. Although it doesn't take much to see."

"To see what?"

"To see that you couldn't give two shits. You leave here, go to your office, grope your secretary's ass, and go have a coffee with that son of a bitch Williams, like the good brownnoser you are. Anyway, your stupid friends can always pick up the pieces after your screwups."

"What pieces? What screwups are you talking about?"

"What do you mean what? What about what just happened?"

Mauricio continues without losing his cool: "You're blaming me for this? Are you even hearing yourself?"

"Oh, no? And whose fault is it? Ruso's? Mine, is it my fault?"

"No, fool, but it's not mine either. Who could have imagined that Pittilanga's father was going to fly off the handle like that?"

"Who? Who? Who was in charge of the legal part?"

"Of the legal part, Fernando!? I did the contracts! I did the paperwork for the transfer! How could I know that the 'gutter trash' was going to make a scene?"

"So now the problem is that I called him gutter trash—"

"Look. I'm sure calling him gutter trash didn't help."

"Oh, fine! And if I hadn't said that we would have made the sale? Are you a nitwit or just acting like one?"

"Ay, Fernandito. Some day you are going to have to realize that life isn't your kitchen at home."

"What does my kitchen have to do with it?"

Mauricio now addresses Ruso.

"Have you seen the matches, Ruso?"

Ruso just blinks.

"What the hell kind of problem could you have with my kitchen matches, Mauricio?"

"Haven't you noticed?" Mauricio continues talking to Ruso, as if he knows that that would make Fernando even madder, which he would enjoy. "This guy saves his used matches. He saves them! In one of the box's little drawers. On one side he has the new ones, and on the other he keeps the used ones."

"Why don't you just shut your mouth?"

"He saves the used ones for when the time comes, oh, yes, for when the time comes that he needs to light another burner, and he already has one lit."

"I don't understand . . ."

"It describes you to a tee, Fernando!" Only now does Mauricio face him again. "Foresight, control, everything is like that. And all for nothing! Because nobody ever remembers to reuse a match. For the fucking time that you fucking happen to have to light a second burner, everybody strikes a new match. And you do, too, Fernando!"

Fernando looks at him, furious, but doesn't respond.

"Well, life isn't like your kitchen, Fernando. It's a mess. It's disorganized. You don't understand. You aren't in control. You aren't in charge."

"And you are, bonehead?"

"You think that insulting me makes you right?"

Mauricio stands up and starts to gather the contracts strewn across the table. Fernando addresses Ruso.

"And now he's gonna get offended?" Fernando is speaking to Ruso, who is sick of being used as a mute witness.

"No, but you blame me as if I could see the future."

"No. But I had to drag you along all this time to get you to do something, and when it's your turn to handle things you fuck it up."

"And you? All this time, how'd you handle things?"

"I fucked them up, but at least I handled them. As far as I know, you spent all this time playing the fool."

"Playing the fool? You want me to remind you where the money to bribe Prieto came from?"

"Yeah, it came from the company that insured the Audi. Or did it come from your pocket?"

"And you think that covered it? I had to put in extra money on top."

"Really? What a pity. What a shame. You don't know how deeply that moves me. I bet you spent two months eating polenta to make up the difference. You probably got a newer model. Am I right?"

"Ten big ones I had to put in!"

"And what do you want? A standing ovation? Consider it your quota of sacrifice in all this. At least you didn't go all over the humid pampas filming a leadfoot, like Ruso and I did. You got off cheap, if you think about it."

"They still haven't made mass cards with your image on them, douchebag? Seriously. They'd sell like hotcakes! Saint Fernando the Martyr. Why don't you give it a shot?"

Fernando is silent, with his head turned toward the picture window. Red as a tomato, but with his eyes fixed on the street.

And Mauricio, who has finished gathering the papers, works the lock on his briefcase. He exchanges a glance with Ruso, who can't help making a very slight expression of support. This time, he thinks, it's Fernando who is screwing up.

"Ciao, Ruso," says Mauricio, who leaves and closes the door.

Fernando waits just long enough not to have to share an elevator with him on the way down.

"Ciao," he says, and also leaves.

Ruso drops into one of the chairs that a little while earlier the Ukrainians had been sitting in. He's there for a while until a bellhop opens the door slightly and peers in. Seeing him sitting there he is about to close it and leave him alone, but Ruso stops him.

"Don't go, kid. Stay," he says, and his voice sounds dismal. "We're done here."

Oversized Ambitions I

"You know what I sometimes think, Mauri? You're gonna laugh your ass off."

"I doubt it."

"You doubt what, Mauricio? That I think?"

"No. I doubt I'm going to laugh my ass off."

". . ."

". . ."

". . ."

". . ."

"I think . . . I know it sounds stupid, but I think . . . I wonder, bah . . . if what's happening to Independiente . . . if it isn't my fault. You see? I told you you were going to laugh your ass off."

"Dude, the chemo is seriously burning up your noggin. I didn't think it was that bad."

"It's not something I thought of just now. I'm telling you now, but I've been thinking it for a long time."

"You're a great guy, Mono. Why are you wasting your time with this nonsense?"

"I'm serious. Are you going to let me explain or are you just gonna keep making fun?"

"I'm serious."

"No, you are totally laughing your ass off, bonehead."

"Okay, okay. Go ahead. I'm listening."

"You remember when we were champions in '83?"

"Of course I remember."

"Well, do you remember that time . . . what happened before . . . ?"

"I already told you I remember. We were losers, Mono. We lived for that shit."

"Well. There you have it. We lived for that shit. Independiente had just lost two championships in a row."

"Metropolitan '82 and National '83."

"Exactly, Mauricio."

"Exactly. And?"

"They lost both championships to Estudiantes de La Plata."

"Uh-huh."

"One by two points, the other by a difference of one goal in the final."

"You remember, I remember. What I don't know, Mono, is where you're going with all this."

43.

R uso opens the refrigerator and stands there, engrossed. He looks at the shelves, the food, the bottles. Why did he go to the fridge? He can't come up with the answer.

"Come on, Dad."

Ruso heads back to the table. Mónica and the girls are watching TV. Lucrecia has an arm raised and an empty glass in her hand. Juice. They asked him for some juice and that's why he went to the refrigerator. He comes back with the bottle and fills everyone's glass.

"Didn't they kill that guy in the last episode?"

"No, Papá. That was his twin brother," informs Ana.

"He looked just like him. You have no idea," adds Lucrecia.

"And if they're twins . . ."

"Shh." Mónica lifts a hand without taking her eyes off of the screen. "Let me listen, Dano."

Ruso obeys. He doesn't mind her reprimand. Actually he likes it, because Mónica just called him Dano and that means that the universe is aligned as it should be. Immediately he admonishes himself: he shouldn't surrender so meekly to happiness. Ruso is a total optimist, except when it comes to his daughters' health and his wife's attitude about their marriage. Because he loves them too much. When the twins catch a cold, Ruso thinks pneumonia. When they have a fever, Ruso prays and bewails the fact that his religion, half inherited and half personal, has no sacrament like Catholic extreme unction. It's been like that since they were born. He can't help it. And with his wife it's something similar. He always fears the worst. It doesn't matter how good things are now. Pain and distance can always come back.

The telephone rings. Ruso moves the chair back but Mónica puts a hand on his arm and stops him.

"Wait and see who it is."

Ruso looks at Mónica's fingers. He loves when she touches him. The phone stops ringing when the answering machine switches on. Almost immediately a man's voice, a young man's voice, is heard.

"Hello. I wanted to speak with Daniel. This is Pittilanga. Mario. I wan—"

"Hello!" Ruso had crossed the two yards between him and the telephone in a flash. "It's Ruso, what's up, kid?"

"Shh, Papi! We can't hear!"

Ruso takes the telephone into the girls' bedroom and closes the door.

"Tell me, kid. How are you, what's up?"

"Ehh . . . okay. Pretty pissed off, actually."

Ruso doesn't know what to say. He's pissed off, too. Frustrated, disappointed. In the two nights that have passed since the fateful meeting with the Ukrainians from Chernomorets, Ruso has had trouble sleeping. A lot of trouble. And that, in him, is a symptom of anxiety.

"Don't get discouraged, Mario. I think that sooner or later we're going to find something."

"Okay, but listen, the next time, how are you gonna do it, how are you gonna handle it? Because like this it's just a mess."

"Well, Mario, I already explained to you that we're not businessmen, that—"

"I know, Ruso, but I'm talking about your friend, the lawyer."

Ruso furrows his brow. Distractedly, he rearranges some teddy bears on Lucrecia's pillow. She likes them that way. Why is this kid talking to him about Mauricio?

"I don't understand . . ."

"I talked to one of the guys who played with me in Platense, and he told me that the rule about being of age doesn't count anymore."

"What do you mean, doesn't count?"

"Well, it counts, but it's eighteen, not twenty-one. So I say, if this friend of yours is a lawyer, he should know that, right?"

Ruso tries to think quickly but he can't.

"And another thing." The kid sounds really angry. "What's the point of calling up my old man the night before the meeting and to talk about that?"

"When did he call him?" Ruso sits the last of the bears against the pillow, but it's off-kilter and falls to the floor. He doesn't pick it up.

"Tuesday night."

"But he called to talk to you or to your old man?"

"No, to my old man. I happened to have the day off and I answered. But he asked for him."

Daniel tries to think fast. To understand. But he's having trouble. Although he's having more trouble accepting than understanding. Or both.

"I'll tell you the truth." The kid decides to express his annoyance again. "The way I see it, that, basically, was what screwed it all up."

"What?"

"Telling my old man like that. Preparing him."

"Preparing him with what?"

"What do you mean with what? Didn't you guys make the decision? To call my old man and let him know he had to authorize my leaving the country. That. Besides the other thing: is the legal age twenty-one, or is it eighteen?"

Ruso is still trying to sort things out. But how? He feels that he has to retrace the steps and conclusions. What he had interpreted as bad luck, as Mario's father's bullheaded pride, is now something else. It is Mauricio inventing a problem. And Mauricio spreading the venom. Why?

"Hello?" asks the kid.

"Yeah, hello, hello." Daniel keeps hesitating. With his last traces of lucidness he tells himself that the kid doesn't need to know. "It's nothing. I was just thinking about what you said." He clears his throat. "Mauricio called . . . he called him to avoid problems at the meeting itself . . ."

"I guess so," affirms Pittilanga. "That's why I mention it. In my opinion it would have been better not to say anything to him. And also to find out the law. About the age. If I can sign the contracts myself. I say if we did everything, signed everything, and then, with everything ready, with the passport ready, with everything done, then we told my old man, and if we needed authorization, we'd deal with it then. My old man wouldn't have tried to undo it all at that point. Don't you think?"

Ruso leaves the girls' bedroom and enters his. He sits down on the bed. He wonders if it's worth telling Fernando what he just found out. He guesses it's not.

"That . . . yeah . . . it wasn't a good idea. We didn't imagine . . ."

"Sure, of course." Pittilanga's tone is less belligerent, as if expressing his complaint has calmed him down. "That's why I said it. But, well, there it is. Now, well, fuck it. What can we do."

"Yeah. We just gotta suck it up. But don't worry, Mario. I promise that something's gonna work out, you'll see. When do you go back to Santiago?"

"Tonight."

"Ah, I was thinking we could have a coffee."

"Next time."

"Definitely, next time. You let me know when you're coming and we'll find a good moment."

"Okeydoke. Take care."

"You too, Mario. Have a good trip."

He hears the twins calling him from the dining room.

"I'm coming!" he says, so they stop shouting, but he doesn't feel capable of ever getting up again.

"Come on, Dano! Get over here, this is the best part!"

Should he tell Mónica or not? He thinks about Fernando again. He doesn't want to tell him about it, but Fer is a bit of a mind reader and he senses things. Or Ruso is just a simpleton and his face is an open book. He goes back to the dining room and puts the phone on its base. He sits down.

"Come here, Pa," Ana says, clinging to his arm with her gaze on the television.

Ruso looks at the three of them. He thinks about Fernando. He thinks about Mauricio. Mónica looks at him and furrows her brow. He must look worried. He smiles, to melt away that wrinkle on her forehead.

"Is that the live twin or the dead twin?" he wonders.

"The live one, Pa. Can't you see he's talking and moving?"

"That's true," he concedes. His family watches the screen. Ruso fills their glasses again, as he thinks love means, sometimes, keeping secrets.

Oversized Ambitions II

"Do you know, Mauricio, do you have any idea how much I cried over those championships we almost won and didn't? In '82 and '83?"

"I can imagine, Mono."

"Okay. The thing is that the Metropolitan '83 starts and the Red is in the running again. Am I right?"

"You're right."

"And, to top it all off, Racing was shit that year."

"Exactly, they ended up getting demoted on our field."

"Yeah, there you go! That's what I was getting at! Do you remember the date?"

"December 23, 1983."

"You see how you remember it as if it were a national holiday, Mauri?"

"Well, Mono. Let's just say it doesn't happen everyday that you win a championship playing your crosstown rivals, on your home field, and that Racing ends up demoted to B that day. Well, actually the week before, because they had already gotten demoted."

"Yeah, okay, but it was the last game they played in the top division, before going down. That's what I was getting at. You remember what I was like at thirteen . . ."

"In what way . . ."

"That I was a huge numbskull."

"Well, Mono. At fifteen, at twenty, at thirty . . ."

"I'm serious now! When I got older I learned how to follow soccer. But at that time I was the typical numbskull who repeats what he hears in the stands, who wanted Racing to go down to B, leave them reeling . . ."

"It's true. You are more civilized now."

"Because now I can see the other side, you know. I couldn't put myself in their shoes, their pain. For me, everything was a joke. One long party."

"We were kids."

"We were. But except for two or three games in that '83 Metropolitan, I had a feeling that they were going to cream us. That it was all going to hell, you know what I mean?"

"No."

44.

Mauricio checks his calendar and clicks his tongue: he scheduled a lunch with Judge Benavente forgetting he had a hearing in Commercial Court 23. He pushes the button on his intercom.

"Yes?" The voice of his new assistant comes through a bit distorted.

"I have a problem, Natalia. It turns out that—"

"You set up a lunch with Judge Benavente and you didn't realize you had a hearing set, right?"

Mauricio smiles. These chicks are like a curse. They sent him this one when Soledad went to work with Ignacio. A solution, a sigh of relief, after the mess with Mariel. And they end up sending him this chick who is not only as efficient as Soledad but even more tempting. If that's possible, Mauricio shakes his head, because Soledad truly had a stunning ass.

"Tell me you are going to save me, Nati."

"I guess we can reschedule Benavente . . ."

There is a smile in the young woman's voice. Mauricio sent her that "Nati" as an encrypted message, or better put, as an advance guard. That smile, the possible blush in the office next door, are proof that the troop has come back alive. No minefields or sharpshooters. Life is a beautiful thing.

"Perfect. I leave it in your saintly hands to find the perfect excuse."

Another smile. And the hope that those hands, if they are saintly, will soon cease to be. Since the intercom line is still open, he hears Natalia speaking to someone else.

"Mauricio? A friend of yours is here who needs to speak with you."

Mauricio has a moment of concern.

"Daniel Gutnisky."

Mauricio sighs and relaxes.

"Yes, send him in."

He stands up, goes around the desk, and opens the door wide, ready to receive Ruso with a hug. Yet, to his surprise, when he opens the door Ruso is already in the threshold and coming through it. He doesn't have his usual sunny expression, actually he looks furious. And, instead of drawing his face close to greet him with a kiss on the cheek, what leads are his arms, which grab Mauricio by the lapels of his suitcoat (and his shirt and tie) and lift him up in the air. And Mauricio tries to grab onto those arms in turn, because he senses (a mix of the furious expression in those eyes, the energy with which he lifts him off the ground, the momentum in Ruso's body) and he senses correctly that Ruso is going to throw him backward, with a shout that is half a result of the effort and half an insult, and Mauricio is going to go almost clean over the desk that he just went around sociably to greet his friend at his office door, and his feet will hit the polished floor, but it is his feet that will hit because the rest of his body has already made a terrified flight, and his arms will try unsuccessfully to establish balance and brake, unsuccessful because Mauricio will hit his back, head, and neck against the bookcase packed with volumes of case law wrapped in burgundy; Mauricio will fall dumbfounded on an arm of his chair which, in turn, will fall onto him, and in the midst of his shock, Mauricio will hear Natalia's screams of fright and disbelief, and shortly afterward he will see Ruso's feet approaching and kicking away the armchair that half squashes him but also covers him, and again Mauricio will feel himself being lifted up but this time from behind, by his back, and again the brutal shove and the useless waving of his arms and the final bang, this time not against the bookcase but the bathroom door, and more screams from Natalia, and Ruso will approach him again and block the light that comes in from the window, and Mauricio will cover his face thinking he is going to punch him hard but no, because what Ruso will do will be to bring his furious, red, vociferous face over to shout son of a bitch, traitor, son of a bitch, there's no excuse.

And afterward the air would clear because Mauricio is no longer covered by Ruso's shadow, because Ruso is going to stand up and turn toward the door, in whose threshold Natalia will continue screaming, but she will have the clarity of mind and the lightness of feet to move to one side when Ruso passes briskly toward the elevators, and then she will approach the place where Mauricio has been thrown and tell him she's going to call a doctor, or call the police, or call both, and Mauricio, who can barely move his right arm (because it was his shoulder that took the brunt of the impact with the bookcase), will lift his hand with incredible pain and tell her no, wait, don't say anything, just leave it.

Oversized Ambitions III

"It's simple, Mauricio. The year 1983 goes on, Independiente is again battling for the Metropolitan championship, and I can't get the idea out of my head that we are going to come in second again. That Racing is going to win on our field in the last match, that they are going to save themselves from the demotion, and that San Lorenzo or Ferro, who are second and third, are going to pass us and win the championship. Do you understand?"

"Yeah, more or less. And?"

"And they'll be making fun of us for the rest of our lives."

"And then what, Mono?"

"And I made a thousand promises to God to keep that from happening. That he let us win, and send Racing down to B. And this is the delicate part: I promised, I swore to God, that if he gave me what I asked for, that then I would do whatever he wanted. Do you understand?"

"No. Well, yes, I understand, but I don't understand why you're bringing it up now."

"Because in the end it turned out well. It was like a dream. We won. We did the lap of honor. The next year we won the Copa Libertadores, the World Cup in Tokyo."

"Yeah, the last one."

"There you've got it! You said it, not me. The *last* one."

45.

Fernando pushes the gate door up slightly to be able to work the lock. It's very damp and the wood is swollen. In the dusk he sees that the plants by the walkway are brown. It hasn't rained for weeks and he forgot to water them. He can't help but feel a little guilty. His grandmother, when she lived in that house, maintained the plants with the same great care she put into everything. Fernando remembers seeing her kneeling beside the pots, turning over the earth, pulling out weeds, putting out poison for the snails. An indestructible Italian. In the backyard she had a vegetable patch. Garden in the front, veggies out back. *"In avanti, decorare, in fondo, mangiare."* Nana said it in Italian, but Fernando can't remember the exact words. He does remember his grandmother's smile when she said it, just as he remembers the summer evenings when she would send him out to water the rows of plantings while she prepared him an afternoon snack worthy of a sultan as a reward.

Mono didn't get to enjoy her as much as he did. By the time his brother grew up, she had started to get stiffened up with arthritis and was never the same. Or maybe it wasn't just a question of health and illness, and the bond between Fernando and the old woman came from a deeper place, more tied to temperament and a way of doing things.

Well, if it was about a way of doing things, poor grandma for the grandson she got, reflects Fernando, thinking of the brown plants along the walkway. He'll have to replace them. Remember to go to the nursery and buy some. But there it is: for him taking care of the plants is an obligation, a tribute he pays to the memory of that old woman he loved so much. It's not something he does with pleasure. Actually, if he wants to get analytical, he could ask himself what he does for pleasure and not out of obligation. But it's best not to get analytical because it's almost nighttime, his throat hurts from teaching, and he's feeling lonely.

At the door to his house, at the end of the walkway, he does a maneuver similar to the one he did at the door to the street. He enters, leaves his coat and backpack on the table, and heads to the bathroom. On the way he notices the blinking light on the answering machine and pushes it. In the silence of the house, and while he is in the bathroom, he hears the message from Alicia, the math teacher who was flirting with him at the school's last general staff meeting. He wonders if it's worth it to call her back. He decides he will, but not tonight. Tomorrow.

He goes back to the kitchen, opens the refrigerator, and reflects for a long while over what to make for dinner. He decides that it's still early and he's not very hungry. He takes off his sneakers using his heels as levers, heads to the bedroom, and lies down. He turns on the television and goes straight to the sports channels. On one they are showing tennis. On the next, a car race. He wonders why he never learned anything about car racing. On the third they are showing a football game. He decides to watch it to try to understand the rules and find something exciting in it, but after four minutes he's totally bored. Between that and baseball, God help them . . . Obviously a country can be a great superpower despite its national sports' being horribly boring. On the fourth channel he finds a soccer game. Finally. It's a European game, but he can't figure out the initials on the sign superimposed on the screen, so he doesn't know what teams are playing. The jerseys don't help him either. A close-up catches his eye: it's an Argentine player. What's his name? He's seen him a bunch of times. From Central or Newells, the kid. But what the hell was his name. Now his hair is longer, pulled back into a ponytail. The game is tied 0–0.

Fernando stands up, heads to the fridge, pulls out a beer, and goes back to the bed. As he lies down again he stops to look at the nightstand. Beside the lamp are three framed photographs. He has always had them, ever since he left his bachelor pad. When he was married, he had the three of them there, beside the lamp. And now that he lives in the house that was his grandmother's, they are still right there. The two smaller frames are identical, and they each hold a black-and-white photograph. His mamá and his papá, who seem to gaze at him in silence. Fernando gives them an equally silent look. The other one is a little bigger and the photograph is in color. He reaches out a hand to it. He rests it on his chest to see it better. Four boys, eleven and twelve years old, and a soccer player a little more than twenty. One of the boys is him. He is on the far left, from the perspective of those posing. Next to him is Ruso. On the other end, Mauricio, and beside him is Mono. In the middle is Ricardo Enrique Bochini, the four boys' biggest idol. Bochini in the Independiente colors. Red jersey. Cotton, as they used to be. Red shorts. Red socks. Black soccer cleats. He smiles with just half of his face. It isn't a bad smile, but it has nothing in common with the full, absolute smiles of the four boys. They pulled it off. A photographer from *El Gráfico* did the deed for them.

It was Ruso's idea. Like almost always. And Mono agreed. He, on the other hand, had made every possible objection. The barbed-wire fence, the police dogs, that Bochini wasn't going to want to, that they didn't even have a camera. And between Ruso and Mono, they shot down those and all qualms, with pure optimism. And Mauricio? What had Mauricio done? Wait without interfering, maybe. Or think about a photo with just him and his idol. Maybe he's not being fair in his memory, thinks Fernando. Maybe he is judging the Mauricio of thirty years ago through the lens of today's Mauricio. Did he change or was he always the same?

As Ruso was still trying to convince him, Mono started climbing up the fence, and before they realized it he was on the other side. As his older brother, he had no choice but to follow him, to take care of him or to punch him for his disobedience. But he had to jump over the fence. When they landed on the grass, Independiente was coming out onto the field. Ruso took care of talking to the photographer. And Mono, of convincing Bochini, who looked at them with some shyness and nodded.

Fernando lingers on their facial expressions. The photographer captured the moment. Of course—he says to himself—to be a photojournalist you have to have quick fingers. The four of them smiling. The five, counting Bochini. Fernando searches, in the faces of those boys, for the adults they are now. He wonders what remains the same. What got lost along the way. Well, looking at it like that, at least one of them was lost. Mono is no longer here. And life sucks, letting a kid be that happy, with his hand on Ricardo Enrique Bochini's shoulder, and then snuffing out that happiness and killing it.

Fernando extends his arm and puts the frame back on the nightstand. The game on TV is still 0–0.

Oversized Ambitions IV

"You still don't understand? I asked for too much, Mauricio. I went too far. I was cruel. I went overboard."

"And . . ."

"And God punished me. We were never the same again."

"Stop the train, Monito. 'Eighty-three wasn't the last time we were champions."

"No, Mauricio, but almost. We got a couple more out of pure inertia. A couple of championships more, a couple of cups. And then we went to shit. Never again, you understand."

"But, Mono . . . every fan asks for stuff like that. Winning a championship . . ."

"Yeah, but not all of it at the same time."

"Sure, the fans ask for all of it, all at the same time."

"Fine. But God doesn't give it to them."

"Again with this idea about what God gives you or doesn't give you. Weren't you arguing with Ruso and your brother the other day, saying that God doesn't give you what you ask for?"

". . ."

". . ."

". . ."

"It's just that, that time, he gave me everything."

"Well, using that logic, he gave every single fan of Indep—"

"No. I asked for that. And I knew that I was going too far. But I asked for it anyway. And now I'm paying for it. Bah, Independiente is paying for it."

"..."

"It's not right to ask for so much. You can't. You shouldn't. You have to be less selfish. No, selfish isn't the word."

"Ambitious, Mono?"

"That's it. Too ambitious. That's what I was."

46.

"But . . . didn't you tell me that the one who was fucking up was Fernando? I don't understand. Now you tell me it was Mauricio."

Ruso holds his gaze. That's the problem with only saying half of stuff. Nobody understands. But he doesn't want to divulge any more either. He decided not to tell Mónica or Fernando, and so he's not going to tell Cristo either. Much less in a situation where he himself doesn't even understand everything. He gets that Mauricio betrayed them, but he doesn't understand why. It doesn't make sense.

"What do I know, Cristo. I don't know what to tell you. The whole thing sucks."

They are quiet for a little while. Outside the washers hustle and bustle. A car arrives and Cristo goes out to receive it. When he returns he comments that, with that one, they just set a new record for washes in a month.

"It's the twenty-fifth and we've already topped the total number of cars last month, which was the best ever. This car wash is a success, Ruso."

Ruso smiles, but his lack of enthusiasm is clear.

"And what are you going to do?" asks Cristo, returning to the previous subject.

"Do? Nothing. What the hell can I do?"

Cristo sits down again. He has known Ruso for almost four years, and he's never seen him like this. He tells him that.

"What do you mean like this?"

"Like this, down in the dumps. Broken."

Ruso laughs in spite of himself.

"Don't people get down?"

"Sure they do. But you? I've only ever seen you happy. Even when things are going like shit for you. And at first this shitty car wash was looking really bad. Right?"

"Eh. That's because you didn't know me before the car wash. These have been the best times of my life, Cristo. You should have seen me when I had the chicken joint."

"You had a chicken joint?"

"I had a ton of businesses . . . Didn't I tell you?"

"You told me some stuff. But you never mentioned the chicken joint."

"Today's not the day for it. If I start talking about the chicken joint I'll say goodbye with a kiss on your forehead and shoot myself in the temple with the high-pressure washer."

"It's still strange, seeing you like this. You're the only guy I know who's always happy."

Ruso stretches, a bit uncomfortable talking so much about himself.

"Maybe I'm bipolar. Have you seen those guys who are totally down and then are all of a sudden racing around, euphoric?"

"Yeah, fool, but in the four years I've known you I've never seen you depressed."

"Now you've jinxed me, Cristo. To four sucky years."

Cristo stands up because Chamaco is signaling that he needs him, but he waits another second, as if searching for some word of consolation. Either he doesn't find it or he's afraid to make Ruso uncomfortable. In the doorway he passes a tall, dark guy dressed in sports clothes. Since Cristo doesn't know he's Mario Juan Bautista Pittilanga, he greets him with a nod of the head and goes about his business. Pittilanga murmurs a good morning as he knocks twice on the door frame.

"What's up, kid? What a surprise!" Ruso approaches and shakes his hand, hesitates, and then finally hugs him. "How did you know the address?"

"Internet. I got the address off the Internet."

"I didn't know we were on the Internet."

"Yeah. On the Internet you can find even the stupidest things."

"I know you're not referring to this lovely car wash . . ."

Ruso is joking, and the kid gets it, because he smiles broadly.

"Can I tempt you with a PlayStation tournament? We're closing up for an hour now and we really get into it. You could partner up with Feo."

"Feo?"

"Yes, that handsome guy over there, with the vacuum cleaner. What do you say?"

"Eh . . . okay. Or I don't know, maybe it's better for us to have a cup of coffee. Is there a cafe around here? I mean, so we can talk with a little more quiet."

Ruso is surprised a bit by the invitation, but he quickly accepts it. He doesn't want the kid to feel uncomfortable. It's not his fault his father's a son of a bitch. If we're gonna start blaming people for having sons of bitches among their nearest and dearest . . .

"Yeah, good idea. Two blocks from here there's a service station that has one of those little stores with tables and all that."

They leave the car wash and Ruso asks Cristo to take over. They cross the street and walk the entire block in silence. They don't say anything until they turn the corner, as if neither of them can find a way to broach the subject. Whatever the subject is.

Finally Ruso asks, "And how are you doing, Mario?"

"I'm good. Good. Tonight I take the bus back. Bermúdez let me stay for these last few days. To be with my family, and all that."

"Bermúdez is a good guy, isn't he?

"Yeah. A good guy. Can't complain. He didn't give me any problems about coming here for the Ukrainian thing."

Ruso thinks that his kindly disposition could perhaps have something to do with his ten percent commission. Ten percent of zero, in this case. In the service station they buy some coffees that a girl with a little red hat serves them on a plastic tray. They sit against the window, watching the activity on the beach. The table wobbles a bit, and they have to be careful not to spill their cups.

"The coffee here is like unrefined petroleum," says Ruso, after tasting his.

Pittilanga takes a sip. "True. I hope their bathroom's not out of order."

"Don't worry. I take you to the best places. Don't forget that you are an investment. The Golden Kid." Ruso takes another sip. "What are you laughing at?"

"The Golden Kid."

"I just remembered all of a sudden. That's what they called a midfielder for Boca in the thirties, forties. I like the nickname. It's nice, right? Innocent, I don't know. I read it in a short story by Soriano."

"What's the name?"

"Soriano? Osvaldo. You never read anything by him?"

"No, the player. The Golden Kid."

"Ay. You got me there. I don't remember. But it'll come to me. An Italian last name. Yours is too, right?"

"What?"

"Pittilanga, I mean. It's Italian?"

"I guess, I don't know."

"You should ask your old man."

The kid makes an annoyed face.

"Don't bring him up," he says, but Ruso realizes that that is precisely what he has come to talk about.

"You look alike." Ruso raises his hands, to convey that both of them are tall and wide as doors. They also have a similar dark skin tone and hair like bristle brushes, but he can't come up with a translation into gestures for those features.

"Yeah. Everybody tells me that," the kid concedes, although his tone doesn't suggest he thinks of the resemblance as a compliment.

They finish their coffees in silence.

"I—my old man—" He stops, then starts again. "I didn't know my old man was going to make such a scene. I didn't think . . . even though every time we talked about it he would get crazy."

"Crazy about what?"

"Everything. You guys, Bermúdez, the change of position on the field, the transfer . . ."

"Well. Truth is the whole thing was never too well thought out."

"No. But . . . you don't know my old man."

Luckily, thinks Ruso, but he stays silent.

"He thinks . . . I don't know. He thinks he's the father of Maradona, or Messi. I don't what the hell he thinks."

Pittilanga speaks with his eyes lowered. Out of shyness, Ruso thinks at first. No, he corrects himself. Out of shame.

"Well," Ruso tries to help him. "All parents are a little bit like that. They think their kids are perfect, different . . ."

"No, I don't mean it that way. That's not why I say it. Or maybe that too, but it's not just that."

Again they are silent. Ruso feels sorry for him, but he realizes that the kid needs to make his own way out, without help. Or not find his way out.

"My old man is kind of thick. Like me, maybe. Or worse, because he only did up to fourth grade. At least I finished seventh. Not him. I'm one of six kids, and the first three are girls. After me, another boy, and the last one is a girl, too. I'm the oldest male."

"Does the other one play soccer, too?"

"Jonatan? Nah, no way . . . My mom has him . . . I don't know . . . like tied to her apron strings. He's terrific at school. He's a brainiac, that kid. He's talking about studying nursing or something when he finishes high school. But my parents are always fighting because my papá says that her keeping him so close is turning him into a faggot."

"And what do you think? Is he?"

The kid looks unsure.

"The thing is my old man always had me, I don't know, like . . . like . . ."

"Like a model."

"Model? No, not a model. What—what do you call it when someone has you in their sights so you do everything they want? They keep after you, they keep after you, to make some-thing of youself, whatever it is."

"I don't know if there's a word for it. But I understand."

"Well. My dad's been taking me to practice since pre–ninth division. At thirteen he took me to tryouts for Platense and I stayed. And from then on, he's always been on me."

"Well. You could also think that he has faith in you."

"Yeah, but that's not it. It's not like that. It's not some-thing . . . it's not something good. I don't know how to explain it. It's . . . like an obligation, you understand?"

"No. His obligation?"

"If only! No! My obligation! First he changed his shift at the factory to be able to take me to soccer in the afternoons. He went into work at four in the morning, every day, so he could be free by midday. You understand? And then, when they fired him, it was worse . . . Because he could have gotten some other gig. I'm not saying like at the factory, but something. And there were things he wouldn't take because they interfered with my training schedule, you know?"

The girl from the minimart passes by their table to clean and organize some shelves, and they are distracted for a mo-ment looking at her ass.

"And your mom couldn't do it?"

"Couldn't do what?"

"Take you, I mean."

"No. My mom was the one who kept the family afloat. Her cleaning other people's houses always paid our bills. And that killed my old man, that she would clean by the hour. I don't know, for him, he'd rather have her at home. That she didn't work outside the home. But she couldn't. He bet all his chips on me, you understand? One return game—it's

just an example—one return game we had to go play against
Boca. All the minors the same day. I was still in ninth division. No, I was already in eighth. Must have been fifteen.
I still didn't travel alone because we lived super far from
Platense. And even farther from the stadium. The thing is
that we were playing there, in Casa Amarilla, in Boca. We
were scheduled to play at noon on a Friday. You realize? As if
nobody had anything else to do. Well, nobody does. Because
all the families are doing the same thing. Somebody takes
the kids. A father, a grandfather, somebody. A neighbor. In
my house there was nobody to take turns with. Anyway, so
my dad takes me and they do roll call at noon. I found out
later, but two weeks before he had gotten hooked up with a
lottery agency, from six in the evening on, till ten, because
he was in front of the station and people passed by on their
way home from work, you know? It wasn't much money, but
better than nothing . . . The thing is, that day I'm telling you
about, we got there on time, the coach took attendance and
had us sit to one side because the fifth division was playing.
Okay. Then came the sixth. Okay. Then the seventh, and then
us. My dad wanted to die because he realized there was no
way he was going to get to work on time. And he couldn't
miss work his second week. What was he going to say? So
he spent the afternoon in a cold sweat. Until at one point,
when he realizes he's not going to make it, he goes to speak
with the coach. I don't even remember his name. An old son
of a bitch. And he explains it to him, you know. He asks him.
He says could I, just this once, leave without playing. That I
really wanted to play. That he could rest easy on that count.
And the old bastard, do you know what he told him? That if I
left I shouldn't come back. That's what he told him. Can you

believe it? Old son of a bitch. Later he died. Being such an old bitter prick must have killed him. There are some real dicks, coaching the minors . . . Well, the thing is we had to stay. We headed back around seven. In those days my dad didn't even have a cell phone. So he dropped me at home and went to the agency. Super late, but he wanted to show up. But they sent him right back home. They never used him again. And I could tell you thousands of stories like that one."

"And so in the games . . ." Ruso feels he can ask. That Pittilanga wants to talk. "Did he meddle a lot, in the games?"

"He drove me nuts. Nobody could stand him. Sometimes he would follow me along the sideline, he looked like a linesman. Luckily, in seventh, I got a coach who knew how to handle him. Otherwise, you have no idea. I think I would have killed him. And also, luckily, I had grown up enough to get around by myself. So I got to practice on my own, on the bus. I was on my own for the games. But after what the head coach in seventh told him, he calmed down a lot, you know . . ."

"And then did he get more work?"

"Some . . . odd jobs. In my neighborhood, most people are in the same position . . . It wasn't like this before, they say. But now, work is feast or famine. But yeah. He knuckled down with that and stopped fucking with me so much. My mom still kept cleaning. They fought so much over that. My dad told her no, that now that he wasn't tied to taking me around they didn't need her money. But she wouldn't hear of it. She had lost faith in him, I think. She didn't believe him. She doesn't believe him, because it's still the same now. The good thing about going to Santiago was not having to put up with their fighting every day."

"They fight a lot . . ."

"Stupid shit. Never more than a little yelling. Luckily. But there comes a point when you're just sick of it. But still you have the feeling—you have . . ."

"You have what feeling?"

"With my old man, I mean. You have the feeling that he's still waiting . . . to cash in, you know. Cash in on all that sacrifice, those years of feeding you, of not making you look for work, of making sure you ate well . . . I don't know. You, with your old man, was your old man like that with you?"

Now it is Ruso's turn to open his eyes wide and think.

"My old man?" He smiles. "Poor guy. No. The old guy had me like on a pedestal . . . Maybe he should have been tougher on me. I don't know. Maybe I would have turned out a little less stupid."

"Do you know what he did? Do you know what he did when they selected me for the U-17 team?" Pittilanga interrupts without meaning to, suddenly worked up, as if he really needed to get this memory off his chest. "My old man always sat at the head of the table. We have a long table, in my house. The TV on one end, always blaring. And my old man on the other. And the rest of us, on the sides. My mom, my brother and sisters, and me. Like normal, I figure." He pauses, mired in his memory. "Do you know what he did when they called me up? He made me sit at the head of the table! At home they were shocked. Just imagine. I was sixteen. And I didn't want to hear it. I didn't like it. Give me a hug, if you want. Or I don't know, congratulate me. Laugh. But don't make me sit there. I'm not the father. Quit fucking around. I remember that I looked at my mom, but she didn't say anything. Neither did my older sisters. Sure, what were they going to say, when my mom was dumbstruck. And I was too. On top of it all, my dad was happy as a pig in shit. He kept talking, saying that he was imagining that, I don't know, I'd be playing in Europe within six months, maybe. From then on he stuck to me like glue again. Practice, games, everything. He even came to the World Cup, with money Salvatierra had given him when we signed with him as my agent."

He pauses. Ruso realizes he's never heard him talk so much.

"You want another coffee?"

Theology I

"Praying is a waste of time, Fernando. A total waste of time."

"Not for me. For me, praying works. Maybe it's not enough, but it works."

"And what God do you pray to, Ruso?"

"What do you mean what God?"

" You know. Yahweh, God, Jesus . . ."

"You're so complicated, Mono. I pray to God, with whatever name."

"It doesn't make sense, guys."

"What doesn't make sense, Mono?"

"Asking God for things. It doesn't make sense. Asking him to give you something, and then supposedly God gives it to you, and everybody's happy."

"Because you don't believe in God, Mono. I do. And I pray because I believe."

"No, don't get me wrong, Ruso. I do believe in God. What I'm saying is that praying is pointless."

"I don't understand. You believe in God but you think praying is pointless?"

"Exactly."

"You're nuts."

"You're more nuts, for praying to God and asking him for stuff."

"And what's the problem if I pray to him asking for stuff?"

"There's no way that God is going to pay attention to you. Don't you get it?"

"No."

"Uff, Ruso. Imagine you pray asking him for something and he doesn't grant it."

"Yeah, so what?"

"So that. You ask God for something and he doesn't give it to you. What does that mean?"

"I don't know, Mono. I go and ask him. Now, whether he gives it to me or not . . ."

"You see what I'm talking about? Your praying has no effect on whether what you want to happen happens or stops happening. I'll give you a concrete example, Ruso. You are on the field. You are tied at zero, in a deciding game that you have to win."

"Oy, Mono. If it's about that, it's been years since Independiente's played any kind of deciding game."

47.

"L et's see . . ." Ruso checks the time. He's just had an idea.
They are still sitting at the cafe in the service station.
"You want to come over to my house for lunch? Look what
time it is. Or do you have to be somewhere?"

"No," responds Pittilanga. "Yes. I mean, no, but I don't want
to be a burden."

"A burden? I'm inviting you, aren't I? Quit fucking around
or you're gonna start looking like Fernando."

"Looking like him in what?"

"Oh, because Fernando is all . . . all formal, all serious, all
business. Didn't you notice?"

"Yeah. But he seems like a good guy."

They are leaving the minimart. Ruso points in the direction
they need to walk.

"It's seven blocks. Good guy? He's great. Amazing."

"And why do you say it like that?"

"Like what?"

"Like unsure. If he's amazing, he's amazing. Right?"

Ruso looks at him carefully. He is increasingly convinced
that this kid is nobody's fool.

"The thing is that sometimes he's, like, . . . too much."

Pittilanga looks at him with a perplexed expression. They
cross the street.

"Sure. Too responsible. Too supportive. Too upstanding."

"Too too."

"Exactly! The guy forces you to admire him. You have no other choice."

They walk two entire blocks in silence, until Ruso points to the opposite sidewalk.

"Here, around the corner. That two-story house."

"Ah. Nice house."

"It's the upper part. My dad built the bottom. Well, the top too. When I got married, he built the upstairs for me. He did it intending for me to keep it all when my parents were gone."

They reach the gate.

"And?"

Ruso turns the key in the lock, has him enter, and closes the door behind them. He indicates that he should go up the staircase on one side.

"His idea was partly right. My parents were old, he had other properties he could leave my brothers and sisters. A hardworking Jew, the kind that toiled from dawn to dusk. My grandfather, same thing. But it worked out for him, poor old guy."

Ruso stops as they go up the stairs and picks up the thread on the landing: "So when they died, I got the house. But I couldn't keep it up."

"Sure . . . it's some house . . ."

Ruso pauses for a second before opening the door, to be sure Pittilanga isn't pulling his leg. No. He's not making fun.

"No, not because of that. If I made you a list of all the businesses I ran into the ground . . ."

They go inside the house.

"My wife went to pick up the girls from school. They must be about to arrive. Make yourself at home."

Pittilanga settles into one of the chairs. Ruso, used to the petite dimensions of Mónica and the girls, is surprised to see such a beefy figure seated at his table. He opens the refrigerator and kneels to look inside. As he feared, there is nothing to offer as an appetizer. He tries to cover by pulling out a bottle of soda but Pittilanga declines. Ruso serves himself a tall glass and sits down.

"And then what happened?"

"With what?" Pittilanga asks with surprise.

"After you were placed at the head of the Pittilanga family." Ruso motions toward the head of his own table.

"Uh . . . then the shit hit the fan."

"Because?"

"I'm not sure. I don't know. I came back from the World Cup. In Indonesia I was a reserve, I barely entered the game. But in Platense I played all the time. I was playing in sixth. When I went to fifth everything was good: that was when your friend Alejandro bought my transfer. My old man had rainbows coming out of his ass, you don't even know."

"I can imagine."

"No, you can't imagine. You saw him once. Well, he's always like that. A total prick, all the time. He never laughs. Do you know what it was like when I got the fifteen percent of the transfer? Well, it wasn't even fifteen, because the club kept five."

"They screwed you out of part of the commission?"

"What do you think? They're fast as lightning. They could catch a fly by the wing."

"That's nice, the fly. Never heard that one before."

"You never heard that?"

"No."

"I say it all the time."

"I'm going to start using it. And then what happened?"

"He used the money well. I can't fault him for that. He's a straight-up guy. He bought materials, added two rooms we could divide up. So the boys took one room and the girls the other. The oldest had already gone to live with her boyfriend. We had to help her out because she was pregnant. But he stretched it for the additions, and a bunch of other stuff."

Ruso feels bad. When the kid said "nice house," he thought he was being sarcastic. Now he realizes it was sincere.

"It was later when everything started to go to shit."

"At home . . . ?"

"No. With me. Playing. I don't know what the fuck happened. In fifth I lost the top spot. I was playing alternate, bah. But I started spending more time on the bench than a judge. And then they brought in a kid from Colegiales, or some place like that. Albani, maybe you've heard of him."

"Isn't that the one who was playing for Estudiantes recently?"

"That's the one. Now they sold him to Portugal. Well. They brought him in in fifth and he started kicking everybody's ass. I got bummed out, I argued with the head coach. It sucked."

"What a mess."

"And in fourth everything went to shit. I did a year. No, I did half a year. 'Did' is a way of saying it, because I didn't play once. I got fat. I lost it a couple of times. Right when I could have played, because they sold that other kid. There was a lot of bad blood. And, to top it all off, Salvatierra was in the clink. Maybe I should have looked for somebody else, what do I know. Or my old man should have. But we're not very hands-on, in those things, I think."

Ruso nods.

"But I saw it coming, that they were going to release me at any moment and it'd all be over. What could I do with the transfer then? Shove it where the sun don't shine . . . That was when I grabbed Salvatierra and I told him that he had to find me something, find me somewhere to play, one way or another. And there was this with Mitre, in Santiago del Estero, which wasn't much but at least I could be a regular first-team player again. I don't know. You know the rest."

Ruso couldn't help laughing a little.

"What?" asks Pittilanga, smiling too.

"And then these two crazy guys show up out of nowhere."

"And yeah . . . Well, no. I wanted to know what was going on, because I had heard about what happened to Alejandro. Through Salvatierra, I found out. And I didn't know what the hell to do. So thank goodness you guys showed up after a few months, otherwise . . ."

"And the best I could come up with was to go to Santiago and tell you that you were playing the wrong position."

"Shut up, 'cuz when I met you I wanted to beat the shit out of you."

"Yeah, I noticed."

"Well, it wasn't that bad. I would have just fucked with you a little, that's all."

"Yeah, it's true. You weren't a big fan of the idea."

"What'd you expect? I played number nine my whole life and you come and tell me to play defense. Who would have liked that?"

"Only a soccer genius like me, Mario." Ruso leans back in his chair, as if he's about to say something important. "But tell me the truth. Aren't you better off?"

"Better off with what?"

"Quit screwing around. With the ball, with the game, what else?"

Pittilanga makes a vague gesture, which Ruso can't quite decipher.

"Hand on your heart. Don't you think you have more chances to sell better as a defender than as a striker?"

From the expression on his face, Ruso thinks the kid agrees, but a faint trace of pride keeps him from admitting it out loud.

"Well," the kid seems to find a tangent. "Soon I'll turn twenty-one. And then my old man won't be able to butt in."

Ruso looks away. If he didn't tell him the truth before, there's no point in telling it now. "Right."

"Thing is that something needs to show up before the loan ends and I go back to Platense. Those jerks will set me loose for sure."

"I think something will turn up."

The kid looks at him for a long moment.

"What are you looking at?"

"You're not a very good liar."

"Give me some time. You're not getting me on my best day. But give me some time. Tomorrow, you'll see, I'll be firing on all four cylinders."

A ton of footsteps are heard on the staircase, as well as a string of requests for carefulness in a mother's voice. Then the lock is heard and the door opens. Ruso stands up and Mario follows suit. Ruso makes the introductions. He knows Mónica won't mind this unexpected guest for lunch. If he had brought Fernando, Mauricio, or Cristo, she definitely would have thrown him a couple of death stares. But so much back-and-forth with the story of Pittilanga has gotten her so curious that she's dying to meet him, and Ruso knows it. The girls greet both the young man and their father with a kiss.

"Are they twins?"

"Uh-huh. I'm a powerful lay."

"Pig!" scolds Mónica, and turns toward Pittilanga as if apologizing. "He always makes the same tasteless comment."

Ruso ignores her with regal dignity and heads to the bathroom to wash his hands. It doesn't take too deep of an introspective effort to know that his sadness is fading, and that he is this close to his old self. The same old fool, but himself. And he likes that better than the alternative. From the bathroom he hears Pittilanga offering to set the table. Out of the blue he remembers, and his joy is so sudden that he leaves the bathroom without drying his hands.

"I remembered, Mario! Lazatti! The Golden Kid was named Lazatti!"

Theology II

"The 'deciding game' part was just an expression, Ruso. Quit fucking around. You go and you pray to God for Independiente to win."

"Okay, Mono, and?"

"On the other side, in the other stands, or at home, there are a ton of guys asking for the opposite, you understand? What you are asking God for is exactly the opposite of what all those guys need and are asking for. God can't listen to every request. Or what do you think? That he does a survey and the majority rules? 'I got forty percent for Banfield and sixty percent for Independiente, so Independiente wins.'"

"I don't see what you're getting at."

"That there is no way everybody's gonna be happy. When somebody wins, somebody else loses. And for every person who asks something from God and gets it, there is another person who asks and gets left holding the bag."

"Okay, Mono. That's in soccer, but—"

"In soccer and with bigger stuff. Or what do you think happens in wars? The other day I was watching a documentary about World War I. And there were the French, in the trenches, praying. And the Germans, in theirs, also praying. Don't you realize it doesn't add up? That somebody's gonna get screwed?"

"But now that's not the case. If I ask God to cure you, nobody loses out if he listens to me."

"And you think I'm going to live or die based on how much you pray?"

"Cut it out, Mono. I have enough problems without you starting in with this. Shut up. Please."

". . ."

". . ."

48.

Fernando studies the puddle in front of him carefully, trying to remember. On the way to school he passed it on the right. He's almost positive. He puts the car into first and turns the wheel. It veers left and swerves a little as it goes around the pit filled with water. Once he can tell he's past it he returns to the middle of the road, which had been filled in a few months earlier and isn't as weak as the sides. When he passes the first of the two flooded blocks he stops, surprised, because he sees Ruso approaching on foot along the asphalt, making feints and pirouettes to avoid getting muddy. Fernando smiles. He moves the car a bit to one side and turns off the engine. Ruso doesn't notice him because he has his eyes down, focused on all the mud. He has just found a concrete sidewalk in the middle of the bog. But when he's walked the length of it, he finds there is no way to go on without stepping in the mud. Fernando just watches him. Ruso still doesn't notice he's there, having a laugh at his expense. He stretches out a foot trying to create a long enough stride to save himself from a soaking that, from where he is, Fernando can't foresee. Finally he goes for it. From his skid, it's clear that he's failed. Fernando laughs as he watches Ruso's arms flail like windmill blades, trying to recover his balance. He is about to fall on his ass but just manages to stay vertical. In the middle of his fancy footwork he lifts his head enough to see Fernando, thirty yards away, cracking up inside his car. He frenetically gestures for him to come over. Fernando obeys, although he takes care to continue in the middle of the street, so he doesn't get stuck. When he gets close he lowers his window to greet him.

"Hello, Rusito."

"Hello my ass. Come here."

"Where do you want me to go? You come."

"I'm gonna get stuck in the mud up to my balls, Fer. Bring the car over here."

"I can't. How do you want me to do it? Headfirst? That's ridiculous. You can't get in over the hood. Turn around carefully."

"I'm gonna get all fucking muddy."

"And what do you want me to do about it? Who told you to do a tour of the Santa Marta district anyway?"

"I needed to talk to you. I thought you got off later."

Fernando nods and stares at him, amused.

"Come on, man, come closer!"

"You come! Hurry up or we're gonna spend the day here."

Ruso thinks it over another moment, as if making sure Fernando is serious. Then he starts heading over.

"Watch out for the ditch," warns Fernando.

"I already saw it." Ruso moves, trying to rest his feet on the pieces of rubble that stick out of the mud. Some are big and steady, but others slip under his weight.

"I'm gonna fall into this shit . . ."

"Uh-huh."

On one slip, worse than the others, it looks like he really is going to fall. He opens his arms and closes them in a vise grip on one side of the car. Finally he gets around the car and finds the door Fernando has left ajar. He opens it completely and falls inside.

"Hold on, Ruso. Before you get all the way in, let me see your feet."

"What about my feet?"

"Lemme see. No way! Take off your shoes."

"Why?" Ruso follows Fernando's gaze toward his lower extremities. "Damn, shit! Look at me!"

The shiny, sticky mud is above the soles and stuck to the leather of his loafers. The cuffs of his jeans are also blackened and wet.

"Ay. *Look at me*," Fernando mimics him in a shrill voice. He puts the car into first and starts off, taking the same precautions as before. "Santa Marta is for machos. Not for little pussies from Castelar."

"When are they going to pave around here, anyway?"

Fernando looks at him mockingly.

"Any day now, Ruso. One of these days we're going to build a country club."

Ruso mumbles something unintelligible and settles into the seat. He leaves his dirty shoes on the plastic mat to one side.

"Now you understand what I meant when I told you that before I bought the Duna, I would get muddy up to my balls coming here."

"And wouldn't it make sense to work in a school closer to home? Just saying."

"Here they pay me extra because it's rural, Ruso."

"A lot extra?"

"A fortune."

"Stop fucking around. I'm serious."

Fernando turns at the streetlight. As he speeds up, you can hear the mud from the wheels hitting the splash guards.

"Can't you go to a better school? I mean, like one of the other ones you teach at?"

"No. I have to wait to have more seniority," he lies. "Why did you come? Or did you just feel like sliding around in Santa Marta?"

"No, I need to talk to you."

"Mónica is pregnant!?"

"Nah. Unless it's the Holy Spirit."

"Why?"

"She's not that inclined toward amorous encounters with me lately."

"I never said it was your kid, Ruso."

"So clever. No, I'm here about our Pittilanga matter."

"You still have energy for that?"

"No. I have no energy for it. But something has to be done."

It's true. A few days have passed and Fernando has reacted the way he always does, getting bitter and depressed. Now, in addition to getting bitter and depressed, he'll have to do something. Luckily Ruso is coming with some idea. If it's not total nonsense, he's going to go along with it. Let him do the thinking. Let him make the decisions.

"Cristo and I were talking about it a lot."

"The nation is saved."

"I'm being serious."

"Me too. What do you guys think?"

"We went over it a million times. I say, and Cristo agrees with me, that we have to make another push. Something new. Something to spur the kid on."

"If you were thinking about bribing that journalist again, forget about it. I don't have a dime. And I don't think Mauricio wants us to pinch his car again."

"No. I already know that. Besides, it has to be something new. Something different."

"Different like what?"

"You don't know how many times we went over it."

"Over what?"

"Over and over debating with Cristo . . ."

"Over and over what!?" Fernando's getting impatient, even though he knows it's useless. For Ruso, when he's telling something, the form is more important than the content.

"A while ago I found out that there are statistics companies that sell information to foreign entrepreneurs, clubs, all that. Remember I told you about it?"

"No."

"One time I told you guys about it. You and Mauricio."

"No."

"One time when we went to see Pittilanga. The first time, I think. You don't remember? They collect data on the players. The balls they touched, the defenders they shook, the times they tried for a goal . . . Don't you remember? I told you."

"I don't remember, fool."

"I did. They put everything down, every tiny thing about each player. I told you."

"But I'm telling you I don't remember. I must not have been paying attention."

"Sure! That's what makes me mad! I talk and it's as if . . . I don't know, as if nobody was talking!"

"You're breaking my heart, Ruso."

"Nah, man, seriously. Since it seems like I'm always just talking shit, when in the end I say something for real, nobody is paying me any mind."

"Hey, slow it down."

"Yeah, you and that asshole Mauricio, same thing. Seems like the only ones allowed to be serious are you two. The geniuses. The brains. Look where we ended up with your plans."

Fernando doesn't answer. His friend has a point. But he doesn't have to be so sensitive. He drives a few blocks in silence. After all, Ruso gets over things quickly. And Fernando isn't good at apologies.

"Okay. Are you going to tell me?" he says, when he figures enough time has passed for Ruso's tantrum to blow over.

"You get the kind of database I'm talking about?"

"Yes. I understand."

"I guess they don't do it for all the players. But they exist. That's for sure."

"And?"

"And yesterday Cristo and I were screwing around, in the car wash, because it's been raining and it was still cloudy so there's little or no work, sitting around scratching our balls, and the subject of what to do came up."

"Yes."

"And I mention this about coming up with something to get a new start. An initiative. Something new. And I mentioned this thing about the companies to Cristo, and how it's too bad we have no way of getting Pittilanga's stats into a company like that, to see if someone bites."

"What do you mean, get his stats in?"

"Sure, man. It's a database. You put in the name of the player and the information comes up. Well. If we could get Pittilanga in there, just imagine."

"But they're not going to do that for players in the third division, Ruso."

"I know, fool. I'm just saying. But if he were a crack player, maybe we could get him in."

"They aren't going to give you the time of day."

"I know, genius. I'm not saying we go to one of those companies and ask them to put Pittilanga in. They'd kick us out on our asses."

"So?"

"Cristo was talking about sneaking the stats in. Get it? Fake stats, like the kid is a star . . ."

Fernando looks at him, to make sure he's serious. Yup. He's serious. He imagines Cristo, hunched down under a trench coat with raised lapels, going through the offices of one of those companies, with a briefcase and the latest microprocessor, as in those computer suspense thrillers they show on cable every so often. It's ridiculous.

"You guys watch too many movies."

"I know we can't do it like that. First of all, we have no idea how."

"Thank God."

"Oh, sure. Let's see, wise guy. What better plan do you have?"

"None."

"So?"

"But at least I'm not fantasizing about computer espionage, Ruso. Quit fucking around."

"I already told you that's not the idea. We thought about it, but we ruled it out." Ruso moves his hand from one side to the other, like someone wiping away harebrained hypotheses. "The plan is something else."

Fernando can't help but smile at Ruso's conspiratorial tone, but he turns his head toward the window so he doesn't get offended again.

"I'm listening."

"Cristo and I went over it a billion times. Until yours truly came to a brilliant conclusion, if I may."

"You may."

"Thank you. We have a problem of information."

"Fake information."

"Whatever. Of fake information. We need to introduce fake information into a database that we don't manage. And we have no way to do it."

"Great. And how were you thinking about getting in?"

"That's it. You can't get in. There's no way."

Fernando stops at a red light. He looks at Ruso with an expression that says, *And—?* Ruso remains silent. Fernando loses his patience: "Do you take me for a fool?"

"Not at all. I'm waiting for you to have a full understanding of the real dimensions of the problem. There is no way to enter the databases of those companies. There's no way. We don't have a way and we're not going to. Which is the same thing."

"And so?"

"Since we can't get into the database to plant the information, the solution is simple: we are going to create our own database. Perfect solution. We run it ourselves, and we fill it with whatever floats our boat."

"I don't understand."

"I don't expect you to understand. What's more, it seems reasonable that you don't. Even better. It means that our project surpasses your mediocre intellect."

Theology III

"And what about you guys?"

"You guys what, Ruso?"

"You and Mauricio, Fer. What do you think? You've been quiet this whole time. Who do you think is right about this God thing? Me or Mono?"

"What do you want me to say, Ruso?"

"What you think, Fernando? If praying is worth it, for you, or if it's useless."

"Forget it, Ruso. I don't want to get involved in a theological and existential debate like that. You guys can continue."

"You're a coward, afraid to take the plunge. And you, Mauricio?"

"Can I abstain, like Fernando?"

"No, tell me what you think. Don't laugh, fool."

"I'm not laughing, but look at what you're asking, Ruso. It's as stupid to think that God answers prayers as to think that God exists and is looking down on us from above. Quit screwing around. Mono's just as big a dumbass as you, Ruso."

"..."

"..."

"But what . . . for you God doesn't exist?"

"He does for you?"

"I asked you, Mauricio."

"Of course he doesn't exist, Ruso! Or you think that God loves us and takes care of us and protects us?! If God existed, do you think life would be as shitty as it is?"

"No—yes—"

"Well, you don't need to get like that, Maur—"

"Stop fucking around, Mono. And don't start with the whole eternal life story. I'd like to see you, in eternal life . . . I, for the time being, haven't seen the slightest proof that heaven exists. And from what we can see down here . . . I wouldn't bet on it."

"Oh, so, according to you—"

"Not according to you, not according to me, not according to any damn one, Ruso. God doesn't exist, death sucks, and Mono is going to get cured or not, no matter what we do, no matter who we pray to, and let's stop this bullshit."

". . ."

". . ."

"Let's see, Mauricio, and if God doesn't exist, who created everything, according to you?"

"I don't give a flying fuck, Ruso."

"You're being evasive, Mauricio."

"Ugh, Mono, weren't you the one who was just arguing with Ruso about how useless it was to pray?"

"Yes, but that doesn't mean God doesn't exist, Mauri."

"Oh, no? And what does it mean, Mono?"

". . ."

". . ."

"It means that God exists, he just doesn't pay attention."

49.

Fernando closes his umbrella when he reaches the awning that protects the sidewalk in front of the car wash. He pushes the door and finds the staff in full. Feo and Molina are playing a soccer game on the PlayStation. Barcelona against Manchester. Feo, with Barcelona, is winning 1–0. Chamaco is brewing maté, with his eyes glued to the screen. On the other side, Ruso and Cristo are hunched over a tiny table where they've set up a computer.

Fernando greets everyone and they respond.

"Now that he's here, ask him, Ruso," says Feo, his eyes on the game.

Ruso peeks over Cristo's shoulder.

"Ah, I wanted to ask you something. Do you know anybody who brings in cheap electronics, the kind that don't go through customs?"

"What?" Since they were kids, Ruso has always had the habit of starting conversations right where his thoughts are, without prologues or explanations, which tends to confuse Fernando.

"Yeah, man. Those guys that bring things in and out. I don't know, laptops, GPSs, phones . . ."

"What do you need?"

"Not me. These guys," he points to his employees. "They won't quit about how they need a PlayStation 3."

"And this one?" Fernando points to the console they're using.

"This one is a PS2," says Chamaco, with a tone of *I can't believe I have to explain something that obvious to you.* Fernando thinks he sees Feo and Molina also shaking their heads, pitying and snickering.

"Apparently the PS3 is much better," clarifies Ruso. "Right, Feo?"

"Much much . . . Ha!" Feo is pleased because he's just gotten the ball away from Molina, using that gigantic defender he created according to his strategy.

"You can't win against this kid," Molina surrenders, philosophical. "I'd be better off cleaning the washing floor."

"Great," agrees Ruso. "It's clearing up and we might get some cars in."

The employees put the joysticks down and leave the office.

"But how much does a PS3 cost, Ruso?" asks Fernando, worried for his friend's constantly shaky finances.

"Cristo says they cost seven hundred, eight hundred dollars around here."

"Yeah, but they can bring you one in for six hundred, maybe," says Cristo, still working on the computer.

"But that's still like two thousand five hundred pesos."

There is a silence, but Fernando notices that it's not due to their realizing the inappropriateness of spending that much money on a toy, but because they are very focused on the computer screen.

"And where'd you get the computer? It looks new . . ."

"Uh-huh," concedes Cristo. "Your friend Ruso here got it, in a swap."

"He swapped a computer for car washes?"

"If you let him, the bastard can get you enriched uranium. It's amazing. I can't even believe it, I swear. Every day I learn something new with this guy."

Fernando turns toward Ruso, who can't help a modest shrug.

"Yes, but they're bad things, Cristo. When you came here you were a good kid. Ruso is going to ruin you, remember what I'm telling you."

"Maybe."

"Stop talking trash, we've got things to do," says Ruso. "Bring over that chair, Fer. Did you open the page yet, Cristo?"

"No. You told me to wait."

"Good, good. Just asking." He looks at Fernando over Cristo's shoulder. "Are you ready, man?"

"Ready when you are."

"There it goes. It's loading."

The screen takes on a greenish-blue background color. In the foreground the main logos start to appear. MARCA PEGA-JOSA is the first. Cristo and Ruso burst into applause.

"What's this Marca Pegajosa?" asks Fernando.

The other two look at him but don't respond. Beneath the main logo comes a small subtitle. "A project by Ruscris Communications." Fernando starts to understand. On the screen several photographs open up of players on different teams. Immediately various icons are drawn, corresponding to different categories of professional soccer, and a search bar.

"Give me the name of any player, more or less known. Not a superfamous one. They're not worth rating," says Cristo.

"From now?"

"Yeah. Someone who plays here, too."

"Morel."

"Morel Rodríguez, from Boca?"

"No, Morel from Tigre."

Cristo types in the info and hits enter. Another page opens with the player's photo and a statistics chart. Fernando glances at the downward columns: games played, won, tied, and lost. Goals. Assists. Streaks.

On the sides there are other entries with special icons. One reads "game by game."

"Can you go in there?" asks Fernando, excited.

"Well, yeah, but—" Cristo hits enter, but a message comes up in English saying the page is under construction. "There's still a lot of info to put in."

"You need to shake a leg, Cristo. We need a critical mass," says Ruso.

Cristo considers him with hushed patience.

"Keep in mind that I have to run this piece-of-shit car wash for you fourteen hours a day, Ruso. And I have a wife. And a son."

"Ah, yeah. As if the time you spend here is so busy." Ruso turns toward Fernando. "Cristo's sister set up the page for us. But we have to input all the information."

"And where do you get it from?"

"The stats? If we can, from other pages. And if not, we just make it up."

"But aren't people going to get mad?"

"Ay, Fer. This is the Internet. Who takes responsibility for anything, in all this shit?"

"Okay. I see you're now Ruscris Communications . . ."

"You saw?" Ruso is obviously proud. "And what do you think of the name?"

"Marca Pegajosa?"

"Yeah."

Fernando takes a minute to think or, rather, to pretend he's thinking. The domain name is a play on words that can mean a persistent defender in soccer or a catchy brand.

"Honestly, it's great."

Cristo and Ruso look at each other, pleased.

"And Pittilanga's stats?"

Ruso moves in his chair, a little uneasy, like a chef who has just been asked for his specialty. Cristo types the name into the search engine. A photo appears of the kid in the jersey of the national team, from his days in the U-17.

"He gave us the photo himself," Ruso says, anticipating Fernando's question.

"He already saw the page?"

"Heh. Did he see it? He goes on there twice a day. He's nuts, the dumbass."

Fernando moves closer to the screen to read.

"Forty-two goals? Nobody's gonna believe that, Ruso."

"We counted all the ones from the minors, Fer."

"But now that he's a defender . . . Is Pittilanga's game-by-game up?"

"Of course. What do you think, we're just making it all up as we go along?"

Fernando reads the graph that's just opened up.

"Who's going to believe that in a game against Boca Unidos de Corrientes he cut off forty-three rival advances?"

"Is your friend always this negative?" asks Cristo.

"You have no idea. It's a nightmare."

"I'm being serious."

"And you haven't even seen the link for Best Game."

"What?"

"Every player has it. Show him Pittilanga's."

Another screen opens, with stats on a supposed game between Bartolomé Mitre and Santamarina de Tandil, two months earlier.

"Is the date of the game correct?"

They look at each other as though the question almost offended them.

"Of course it's correct. The only thing we retouch is the individual performance of Mario Juan Bautista. Nothing else."

"Well. Sometimes we also touch up the results."

"Sometimes, yeah."

Fernando reads. For that game Pittilanga's statistics show fifty-five stolen balls: on forty of them he passed to a teammate, on two he headed upfield on his own, and the rest he kicked out on the sidelines. For the same games, these insane guys had given him an assist and a free kick into the crossbar.

"Do you guys really think anybody is going to believe this?"

"Faith moves mountains."

"You don't say."

"I told you he was a skeptic. Show him the contest."

"What contest?" Fernando's interest is piqued.

"It was your friend's idea," informs Cristo. "Because we couldn't keep up with the input of data."

"Yeah, because for it to be realistic we can't just put up stuff about Pittilanga."

"So we thought up using collaborators."

"Outsourcing the fieldwork."

"You're fucking with me."

"Show him."

As they talk Cristo returns to the main page. He clicks on a box entitled "Future Stars of Sport Statistics 2010." On that screen they invite young people from all over the country to take part in the contest of the same name, each volunteer sending in the stats form for the lower-division games they are able to cover.

"You guys are fucking with me. And did anybody send you anything?"

"Man of little faith. How many collaborations do we have so far, Cristo?"

"I'll tell you. Six hundred and forty-four, captain."

"Thank you."

"They're pulling your leg."

"Not at all. They are boys who trust in the seriousness of Ruscris Communications and have faith in being worthy of the prize. We aren't going to stand in the way of that dream."

"And what's the prize?"

"Becoming part of the staff of marcapegajosa.com.ar. No more, no less."

"You guys are crazy."

"Okay." Ruso swivels in his chair to face Fernando. "Tell us what you think."

Fernando looks at the page again. He doesn't believe it will do any good. But seeing Pittilanga surrounded by those authoritative numbers is still some sort of amends, a consolation.

"The truth is it's impressive. I don't know if anybody from abroad is going to visit . . ."

"Stop! Stop!" Ruso cuts him off as if he had suddenly remembered something crucial. "Show him the stars of the page! Let him see the crack players!"

"Ah!" Cristo rushes to obey.

He returns to the page's main search engine, types in three words, and hits enter. On the screen a photo unfolds that is a bit bigger than the others, of a player with a Deportivo Morón jersey and number five on his shorts. The strange thing isn't the photo itself, a typical photo of a player in midgame, his body slightly turned on its axis after kicking the ball, his leg muscles tense, arms open. It's the face. Because crowning that figure of a player in his prime is Ruso's face. And the page's headline reads "Daniel Hugo Gutnisky."

"Ha!" Ruso lays a brutal smack on Fernando's shoulder. "Did you see me? Ha! What a player!"

"You are insane, Ruso."

"Check out the bio. Read."

Fernando obeys. The imaginary star is thirty-two, plays as number five for the Deportivo Morón Club, is nicknamed "The Rooster," and with them has risen two divisions. Fernando doesn't need to look at the detailed stats to know that his record must be even more stunning than Pittilanga's.

"You have no shame, Ruso. And what if somebody goes in and sees this shit? All the credibility of the page is shot."

"Too bad. I wasn't going to miss this chance. Show him yours, Cristo."

He doesn't have to ask Cristo twice. Another image loads: equally athletic, also in a Morón uniform, although playing as number seven.

"I'm a winger. I made this guy a midfielder."

"Cristo is a goal leader in two successive seasons. Show him."

"Aren't you embarrassed?"

"With all the work we're putting into this, it's the least we could do. Hey, Cristo! Since yesterday you added like fifteen goals."

"No, that's a lie."

"Yeah you did, I went in yesterday from home and you had a hundred and twenty. Now I see you have a hundred and thirty-five."

"Far from it, Ruso!"

"How can he have a hundred and thirty-five goals?" Fernando is wasting his breath.

"You're a dick, Cristo. If you're gonna give yourself a hundred and thirty-five, give me at least eighty."

"I can't give you eighty, Ruso. You're a midfielder."

"Come on, don't be a jerk."

"Give me a raise."

"Quit fucking around, Cristo. Come on, give me eighty goals."

"You guys are both disasters." Fernando shakes his head. Chamaco comes in looking for some rags.

"No, Ruso. Okay, if you won't give me a raise, invite me over for a barbecue."

"How's Sunday?"

"With offal."

"Classic offal."

"Sweetbreads."

"You must be dreaming, Cristo."

"With sweetbreads or all you get is sixty goals, Ruso."

"Do you know how long it's been since I've had sweetbreads? You want to take the food right out of my daughters' mouths?"

"Do you want more goals or not?"

Fernando looks at them. Suddenly he remembers Ruso, collapsed over a flowerbed in the cemetery, his eyes violet from crying. It's nice to see him like this now. Ruso turns toward him to say something and he catches something strange in Fernando's expression.

"What's wrong with you?"

"Nothing, why?"

"Don't play dumb. Something's wrong."

"Nothing's wrong, fool. I'm weighing the possibility of you guys putting me up on the page too, but as a center back."

Theology IV

"And you, Fernando?"

"What about me?"

"Have you all got your heads in the clouds or what? What we're discussing about God, man."

". . ."

". . ."

"Fernando!"

"I'm thinking. Don't rush me, if you want me to answer, let me think."

"Okay."

". . ."

". . ."

". . ."

". . ."

"Up to a certain point I agree with my brother."

"About what?"

"That it seems ridiculous to ask for stuff. The example of the game was a good one. You are asking, the other side's asking. God can't answer both."

"I'm a genius."

"Stop, Mono, he said he agreed with you 'up to a certain point.' And what do you think about what I said?"

"I don't know, Ruso . . . I like to think that God is on our side. I'm with you on that. But it's hard."

"What's hard about it?"

"Because we are people, Ruso. And we can only understand God's ways up to a point."

"Uy, man. I can't believe it."

"What can't you believe, Mauri?"

"That I'm stuck in a hospital room filled with gullible dupes."

"Dupes? Who votes for Mauricio being right that God doesn't exist?"

"Cut it out, Mono."

"Shut up. Let's vote."

"…"

"…"

"One vote for Mauricio. Who votes that he's an idiot who's totally wrong?"

"…"

"…"

"…"

"Three to one. You lose, Mauricio."

"And he's going to hell."

"Uh-huh. For being an atheist, the fool."

"Don't get too big for your britches, Mono, with all your theological doubts I think you're coming with me."

"Poor Mauri."

"Yeah, Mauricio, it sucks to be you. The three of us will be looking down at you from paradise."

"And you'll be sweating like a stuck pig down in hell."

50.

As the three pages of his document are printing out, Mauricio gathers each of the previous drafts and starts balling them all up together. Then he has an idea: he squeezes each page into a more or less spherical ball, lines them up in a row on the desk and prepares to practice his aim into the basket in the corner of his office. The first one lands a little to the right. Before shooting the second one he makes sure to squeeze the paper more, to make it uniform and heavier. This one bounces off the wall and then falls into the basket. He allows himself a tiny celebration and prepares his third shot. Which is what he's doing when Natalia knocks on the door.

"Come in," he says.

As she sticks her upper half through the door, Mauricio can't help comparing her to Soledad. How can she be even hotter?

"You have a visitor . . . or something like that," says the girl, as if struggling to categorize the situation.

"What?"

"A guy who's asking for you. Salvatierra's his name. I asked him if he had an appointment, because he hadn't made one with me but maybe he made it directly with you, but he said no. That it was a personal matter, not work-related."

Mauricio nods. Sooner or later it had to happen. Better sooner than later. Get rid of the problem and that's it. Why put it off?

"Send him in, Nati. Wait. Here's the document for the To-losa file."

"Ah, wonderful. I'll add it and send it off."

Almost immediately Salvatierra enters, and Mauricio understands his assistant's strangeness when announcing him. He is wearing white pants, a plaid jacket, and an aquamarine shirt. Suburban pimp mixed with Rocky Balboa's brother-in-law, thinks Mauricio as he shakes his hand and invites him to sit down.

"How's it going, Mauri?"

Mauri. All of a sudden they're close buddies. Nobody calls him that, except for his friends. And it's better if he doesn't think about his damn friends. He hasn't heard anything from Fernando since their fight in the Ukrainians' hotel. And he still has a faint pain in his shoulder from his last meeting with Ruso, and the secret indignation of not having paid him back in kind. Worse, Ruso didn't even beat him up. He pushed him, tossed him through the air, like he was a bag, a thing. Payments on the money Mauricio lent him to open the car wash have arrived punctually. Three months, three payments. But he sends one of his employees. And he asks for a signed receipt. Idiot.

"I'm well, Polaco. And you?"

"Good, good. I was trying to get you on your cell but I couldn't."

"Really? Well, maybe because they stole my phone and I changed the number," he lies. "I'll have my assistant give you a card. But tell me what brings you here."

Salvatierra rolls up the sleeves of his jacket before speaking.

"I have news. Very important news."

Mauricio has a moment of uneasiness. Could it be true that this grotesque creature comes bearing news? He doubts it, unless his mother promised him homemade noodles or he's thinking of checking into a new rehab.

"They got in touch with me the other day about Pittilanga," he lets fly, and he waits, radiant, to see the effect his words have. "From Saudi Arabia. From the Al-Shabab. One of the most important clubs there, I swear. Several Argentines have played there."

Mauricio swallows hard.

"Wait, wait, Polaco. Where?"

"Saudia Arabia, man. I couldn't believe it, at first. I thought it was a joke. But it's true. They sent me a fax and everything. Well, actually a few."

He extends some folded papers—faxes, photocopies of e-mails written in English and dated in Riyadh. The faxes have, in the upper left, a logo, some kind of a crest. The thing's for real.

"Tell me more . . ." Mauricio murmurs as he reads them.

"They've had him on file since October. Apparently they first got interested because of Armando Prieto's show. You re-member that he was giving him a real boost?"

Mauricio stops reading for a moment and looks at him. This fool's naïveté is poignant and distressing. Didn't he have any idea that Prieto's praise was bought? He remembers his black Audi and feels sorry for himself again.

"And then?"

"Well. Turns out that, at that time, their coach said they had a full roster of defenders and they didn't need any more. But the guys remembered him. I don't know how they found out that some Ukrainians were interested. Thing is, now one of their center backs left, some black guy who was really good but got bought by the French, looks like. And well," he stops to laugh with pleasure. "They sent me those faxes you have there. The first one, of course. Then the others. I kept answering them because they were making inquiries. Looks like they also were checking Pittilanga's statistics. Those they got off some website. Did you know about this?"

The question is left hanging because Mauricio has gone back to reading the faxes. His English is slow and hard-going, but what he grasps coincides with what this imbecile has been saying. One of the e-mails talks about a website, www.marcapegajosa.com.ar, and Mauricio wonders where all that could have come from. "Amazing numbers." What did "amazing" mean again? It's something good, praise. He doesn't remember exactly, but that doesn't really matter in this case.

"I'll give you the short version: in the last fax they ask for conditions, and they reference an Argentine businessman who handles the preliminaries for them."

Mauricio clears his throat and adjusts the knot in his tie, involuntary rituals he falls into when trying to buy time. He calls Natalia and when she peeks in he holds out the bunch of papers.

"Can you make copies of these documents?" And turning to Polaco, "You don't mind, do you?"

"Not at all, not at all," he replies solicitously. "That's why I brought them."

When Natalia leaves, Mauricio rubs his face. He tries to think. God damn it all to hell. What timing.

"Is there something that—something that doesn't look right?"

"Eh? No, no. You say that this comes from the club, directly . . ."

"Yeah, sure. The e-mails come from their official website, the faxes have letterhead. All aboveboard. I didn't answer the last one because I wanted to talk to you guys first."

"Did you already get in touch with Fernando?"

"No, not yet. I preferred starting off with you. I don't know. Since you're a lawyer it seemed . . ."

"You did well. I'd leave it like this for the moment. You know, too many cooks . . ."

"Yeah, they spoil the soup," finishes Salvatierra, and he seems pleased with his intervention. It's hard to believe that this guy ever represented players. Well. As hard to believe as Mono, Fernando, and Ruso ever being owners, or Pittilanga being a player.

"The kid's situation, as far as the club is concerned . . . what's it looking like, Polaco?"

"Yeah, that's what I'm getting at!" Salvatierra gets excited again. "His loan from Platense to Presidente Mitre is about to end. Now. It's up. It ends with the season. The coach in Mitre wants him, but it's already the second year and they can't renew. He'd have to go back to Platense. But Platense has no plans for him. They're going to release him. But if we can get another club to take him on loan, we should go for it. They don't want him."

"Did you talk to the guys at Platense about this offer?"

It's the million-dollar question. If they know in Platense, Vidal knows. If Vidal knows, Williams knows. And if Williams knows, he'll have to swear to God and the Holy Virgin that he had nothing to do with it. Nothing at all.

"No! The only one who knows is me. Well, now you and me."

Mauricio tries not to show his relief. Things aren't that bad, then. Time to get to work.

"About that," he adopts an intimate tone, more cordial than he's been using. "You, Polaco . . . what's your situation with Pittilanga? I mean, you're not his agent anymore, are you?"

"Well . . . actually . . . if we stick to what it says in the paperwork . . . just the papers . . . not anymore. Because the representation contract had a deadline. It's passed."

"And you didn't renew it, I mean."

"Renew, no. But . . . you understand me, Mauri. This shows that I'm still his agent, contract or no contract. There's a reason those guys contacted me, you understand."

"Sure, sure," nods Mauricio, but his face says that things are not sure at all. He adds a sigh, a strange expression.

"You . . . why do you ask?"

Mauricio leans on the desk. He can't match Williams, but with this dimwit he doesn't need to.

"Do you want me to be honest with you?"

"Yeah, sure. Of course."

"You're in an irregular situation, Polaco. I understand what you're telling me. But reality is one thing and contracts are another. And in the contracts it says you're out of this. Am I explaining myself?"

Polaco is sweating. He looks to either side, as if making sure that there is no witness to such a conclusion.

"Yes, but I think that can be discussed."

"It can be. But it's a real mess. At this point, you're not likely to win."

"Maybe so, Mauricio. But I need to fight for it."

"If you fight for it now you'll lose it, Polaco. Remember that you're not exactly in your best moment."

Mauricio is silent and observes him: the bags under his bloodshot eyes, the slight tremble of his upper lip. How much

longer can he last before having to go to the bathroom for a
fix?

"Will you allow me to suggest an alternative?"

Salvatierra nods his head.

"Here at the firm there's some interest in getting into the
world of soccer. My boss, in fact, the main partner, has friends
on River's board, and he was mentioning to me that they're
interested. I told him a little bit about you. To get into a new
field, you need people with experience in that world. You following me?"

Another nod.

"And maybe, I'm not saying tomorrow or the day after, but
in the short term we might be able to do something together."

"You think so?"

"Sure. But we have a problem . . ."

He stops because Natalia returns with the papers. He
thanks her for them and the girl leaves. He hands the originals
to Salvatierra and leaves the copies on his desk.

"I was saying we have a problem. If we do it now, you're
out. I'm not the one saying it, Polaco. It's in the contracts. Or
it isn't: you don't figure as his agent. And so we're screwed."

"But isn't there any way . . . ?"

"Trying to find an easy solution is the worst thing we can
do. If it's not working out, the best thing to do is let it go. There
must be a reason. It means it's not the right moment. Your moment, I mean. Ours. Now I ask you, what's the rush?"

"Well, the thing is that the Arabs are making the offer now.
Later, if the kid is released . . ."

"If the Arabs are seriously interested, maybe we can keep
them on ice for a couple of months and then do the deal.
Maybe we can raise the price."

Salvatierra makes a long face.

"Mmm, I don't know, Mauricio. What if the Arabs get annoyed and disappear forever? I think it's best to strike while the iron is hot."

"Of course. You could be right . . ." concedes Mauricio. It's useless. It's not the moment to burst his bubble. "You said you didn't tell Fernando and Ruso."

"No, I didn't tell them."

"Good. Don't worry, I'll do the talking. Right now Ruso is closing on a big deal with a house, he told me. You know how that is."

"Uh, yeah. Buying a house is a big mess."

"Right. Leave it to me, I'll explain it to him when I can. Let's stay in touch for anything you need. We'll ask Natalia for a card now, I forgot to do that. You call me whenever you want, anytime, for whatever you need. And we'll take care of it."

He stands up and Salvatierra follows suit. Instead of shaking hands, as he did when Polaco came in, Mauricio goes around the desk to give him a kiss and a pat on the shoulder.

"Ciao, Mauri. I'll ask the girl then."

"Yes. On the card is my cell and the direct line here in the office. Put them in your phone. And call me on the cell so I have yours."

"I can just give it to you now, if you want."

"No, don't worry about it. I'm a scatterbrain and I lose everything I jot down. Call me, that way I have it in my phone."

They say goodbye in the doorway and Mauricio closes the door. He waits a prudent amount of time. Then he goes back to his desk, picks up the stack of photocopies, leaves his office, and heads to Williams's.

Nostalgia

"What I'm saying is that it's very difficult to put up with a present like this, after the past we had. That's what's happening."

"I don't understand, Mono."

"Sure. Maybe for other fans it's easier to put up with the bad. Like they're more used to it, more prepared for losing. You understand me, Ruso?"

"Well, yeah . . . I guess."

"What Mono's saying is that it's harder to put up with a present like this, because of the past we had."

"Yeah, yeah. I got it, Fernando."

"But you don't seem very convinced."

"Look, maybe it's easier for the kids today than for us. They don't have anything to compare it to. For a kid who's fifteen, twenty years old, Independiente is just what it is now, you know? They can't imagine another era. You can tell them about it, but it's not the same. It's like Racing fans clinging to the memory of Chango Cárdenas's historic goal against the Celtic Glasgow in that Intercontinental Cup. We're the same."

"I don't know, Fer. I don't think we're *that* bad."

"Yes, Ruso. Think. Compare. Compare your teenage years with a kid who's a Red fan now, some kid who's twelve, thirteen, fifteen years old."

"Uh . . ."

"There you go! Remember us? Championships, cups, der-bies. We had our pick."

"And at that age, everything has more impact, Fer. Right, Ruso?"

"Maybe, Mono."

"For sure! Everything affects you double. That period: you're growing up, the dances, the girls, the Red. I don't know, it was like everything was one big party. Right, Fer?"

"Like losing wasn't a possibility. Don't you remember it like that?"

"Exactly. It was winning . . . it was seeing how many points you'd win by. In everything. With Independiente and with everything."

". . ."

". . ."

51.

Mauricio turns in bed too violently for Mariel's light sleeping, and she complains in her dreams and settles in facedown. He looks at the time. Three twenty-five. He picks up the television remote control from the nightstand, trying not to make noise, but when he is about to press the button to turn it on, he stops. The sudden light of the screen will wake her up, and so he puts the remote back down in its place.

He turns to look at her. He has been awake for so long that his eyes have grown used to the dark and he can make her out perfectly. Her face turned toward him, her tangled hair curling over her neck and chin, the sheets a little bit above her waist.

He likes to look at his wife while she sleeps. Taking the time to really look at her. Looking freely, without being watched. *Without being discovered*, he thinks Fernando would think if he were there, with him. It's ridiculous to waste time thinking about Fernando, but he can't help it. About him and the others. He thought it was going to be different. Easier. His shoulder doesn't hurt anymore. It's been almost five months since he's had news of them. And yet he can't get them out of his head.

Mauricio sighs and looks at the clock again. Three twenty-seven. He gets up on tiptoe, picks up his slippers, and carries them down the stairs, putting them on when he reaches the bottom. When he turns on the kitchen light the sudden brilliance makes him furrow his brow. He closes the door and turns on the television. He passes through the news channels, the movie channels. On one of the sports channels he comes across the Temperley–Platense game, a night game for the Metropolitan B championship. It's not live, obviously. For a moment he thinks of turning on the computer and checking the results online. If there were goals, he'll keep watching it, and if it ended 0–0, he'll turn it off. He decides not to. He'll watch it as if it were live.

The game is terrible. He puts up with the rest of the first half and all of the second. It ends 0–0. He wanders through the channels again, sports, news, movies. He goes out into the yard. It's cold. He feels the damp grass beneath his slippers. He amuses himself watching the steam of his own breath. The wind must be blowing from the south, because he hears a train from Sarmiento passing in the distance. The cold makes him shiver and he decides to go inside. He doesn't want to get sick.

What if he tries a glass of warm milk? He's heard that's good for getting to sleep. No. He hates milk. Especially warm. He looks at the wall clock. Quarter to six in the morning. He turns off the television and the light, opens the door, and heads toward the staircase. Before going up he takes off his slippers, so Mariel doesn't hear him coming back to bed.

Counternostalgia

"What are you thinking, Ruso?"

"Nothing, Mono."

"Come on, prick. Don't do that. What are you thinking?"

". . ."

"Come on Ruso, don't shake your head. What are you thinking?"

"Nothing, man. You guys are weird . . ."

"Which guys?"

"You two, man. Fernando and you, the ole Raguzzi brothers."

"Why?"

"Because sometimes it seems you're out of touch with reality, man."

"Out of touch? Why?"

"No reason, fool, no reason."

"Come on, Ruso! Out of touch why?"

"All those explanations of your golden teenage years . . ."

"Yeah?"

"Bullshit, Fernando. Bullshit. That's what *your* teenage years were like. And this guy's. But it wasn't the same for all of us, eh? Rest assured it wasn't."

". . ."

"For you guys it was 'seeing how many points you'd win by.' Cut the crap, okay? For those of us who saw the world from behind this nose, or above the craters of zits, the dances were a drag, and the girls a mystery, trust me . . ."

"No, but—"

"For you guys it was easy. Same with school. You, Fernando, studied some. But you know this son of a bitch wouldn't touch a book even if it had tits. And in the end, he passed every class. He didn't have to repeat a single one."

"No. Third-year history, Ruso."

"Don't jerk my chain, Mono. One class in five years. While training with the club and everything. I didn't lift my ass from the chair, I studied like a saint, and I would repeat three or four. All summer indoors, studying . . ."

"It wasn't that bad."

"Yes, Fernando. It was. And just admit it. It's not your fault. But at least don't make me feel like a jerk. Ask Mauricio. You'll see. It wasn't easy, eh? I can guarantee you that period was really fucked up. Independiente had the Midas touch. But everything wasn't like it was for the Red. Maybe that was why we loved it so much. Us, I mean. Not you guys. I was a real meathead, but the Red tied up the score for me. But I learned to lose real young, I didn't need to grow up for that."

". . ."

". . ."

52.

Cristo presses the directional buttons on the joystick to make his number eight take the ball from Molina's forward. He gets it and begins an advance. He presses it again for a deep pass. He turns the movement key and his forward cuts the ball back in the other direction. Molina's avatar passes him by. He hears the onlookers exclaim, rooting him on. He presses the circle button to send the cross—Cristo has a tendency to press that button a lot, and the crosses end up too high to the far post. The power bar indicates his precision; this time the ball will land near the penalty spot. A rapid brush to the R1 key allows him to choose who receives the pass. The tallest of his forwards connects with the ball but the shot goes high and wide.

"You did everything right, Cristo. Everything right," rallies Feo.

Cristo shakes his head. He doesn't have enough time to tie the score. Molina also plays with Cristo's desperation, circling the ball among his players to let the last few seconds slip away.

"Don't be a chicken, Molina," says Cristo, but he knows he's not going to shake him.

"Uh . . . look at the ride that just showed up," says Feo, behind his back.

Just then the ref on-screen ends the game, so Cristo lets go of the joystick and turns to look. It's a brand-spanking-new Audi, navy blue. The driver is a young guy who looks like a fast talker. Light brown suit, sky blue tie, white shirt, briefcase. When Chamaco goes out to meet him and take his keys, the guy refuses. Following Chamaco, he walks toward the office. Cristo approaches the counter. Was he a federal government inspector? Municipal? If so, they're screwed. Goddamned Ruso. He told him. He warned him that sooner or later they had to get things in order. When does his friggin' boss plan on showing up?

"Good morning."

"Good morning. How can I help you?"

"Is Ruso here?"

Cristo feels the relief travel down his body. If he asks for his boss that way he's no inspector. Or if he is, he's already been neutralized. Nobody who calls Ruso Ruso wishes him any harm.

"He must be about to arrive. Can I help you?"

"I'm Mauricio. A friend of his."

Cristo gets alarmed again. Here is someone who calls Ruso Ruso and could very well wish him harm. Uneasy, he glances at the computer screen, where he sees the blue home page of Marca Pegajosa. Mauricio looks too. And even though Cristo rushes over to the machine and turns off the monitor, he knows perfectly well that the visitor has seen it.

"Maybe he'll get in later. Do you want me to tell him something?"

Cristo tells himself that he is an imbecile. The more natural he wants to seem, the more artificial he acts. And the visitor's little eyes show that he saw the screen, that he got an eyeful. Just as he saw the car wash employees—all of them—huddled over a PlayStation tournament. Cristo isn't afraid he will tell Ruso. In fact Ruso will play his games when he gets there. But because sooner or later this Mauricio will rub it in his face. When Ruso needs money, or something.

"Yes. Or I can wait for him for a while."

Cristo takes his time to think. On one hand, having him there hanging around the office makes him nervous. On the other, it's better that they see each other directly and that Ruso decides what he wants to do with this guy. When he is about to say yes, no problem, wait, he sees through the glass that Ruso has just crossed the street with a newspaper under his arm.

Bad Attitude

"Hey, Mono."

"What, Ruso?"

"Now you guys are gonna play the victim?"

"Why victim?"

"You say that because you haven't seen their faces, Fernando."

"No, Ruso. I was just thinking."

"About what, Fer?"

"About learning to lose. That the truth is it's just bull."

". . ."

". . ."

"Why bull?"

". . ."

"Can you ever really learn to lose?"

". . ."

". . ."

"What bull? It happens all the time."

"What?"

"Losing, dummy. You lose more than you win. Or no? And you never learn."

". . ."

". . ."

"I think I'm gonna kick you two out on your asses. You're supposed to be visiting to lift my spirits, assholes. No, don't laugh! Stupid Fernando starts off with Independiente and its glorious past that we'll never see again. You, Ruso, with your autobiography about what a pathetic big-nosed teenager you were. Cut this shit out. Now you're leaving and I'm gonna have to commit suicide, hang myself from the IV stand, damn it!"

"Ah, you're sensitive . . ."

"Quit it, Ruso. Pay him no mind. Seems we got very philosophical and he got lost, poor pinhead."

"It's true, Fer. Listen, Mono: you want me to translate it into the language of a systems engineer, so you can understand?"

"Why don't you guys just both fuck off?"

"What an attitude, Mono."

"Really."

53.

Ernesto Salvatierra moves through the supermarket pushing the cart with his elbows. He is reading the list his mother made, and mentally checking off what he's already gotten and what he still needs to search for. He grumbles when he realizes that he's passed the condiment display rack. How urgent is the mustard? He returns to the central aisle. He checks the signs. He'll have to go back four aisles.

Then he sees him. Ruso has just turned toward him, coming out from behind the bread section. He sees his expression: first indifferent, then surprised, finally smiling. Ruso approaches with his hand out.

"How's it going, Polaco?"

"Good, Ruso. Shopping. You?"

"Same," says Ruso, displaying the two loaves and the package of noodles he's carrying.

"You're not gonna get a cart?"

"No. This is it. My wife did the shopping the other day, but there's always a couple things to pick up."

Polaco nods, with resignation. His mother sends him shopping every day, and she always complains that there's something missing.

"Any news, Polaco?"

"Did Mauricio tell you?"

Ruso looks at him questioningly.

"Tell me what?"

A sudden disconnect opens up in Polaco's thoughts. On one hand, he is stringing together the story of the news: the Arabs, their e-mails and faxes, his talk with Mauricio. On the other, the lawyer's recommendations: stealth, waiting, silence. Polaco feels, murkily, that he has just screwed up. But how can he get out of it?

"Tell me what?" insists Ruso.

What to do? Polaco knows that he doesn't have very fast reflexes, but he realizes that "Did Mauricio tell you?" has to be followed by an important announcement. In other words, that he can't make up some innocent little lie. Besides, his nerves aren't up to it. Best to tell the truth. But then he remembers Mauricio's insistence. How did he get himself into such a mess? And all for the fucking mustard his mother asked him to pick up.

Side Effects I

"The truth is it hurts. Bah, I don't know if it's pain. But I'm uncomfortable."

"I don't know what to say, Mono."

"And are you sure it's from the shots they're giving you?"

"I don't know. They give me fifty million things. But I haven't felt like this until the other day."

"It's a pretty big coincidence . . ."

"Of course, Mauri."

"Did you tell Mamá?"

"No, Fer. I don't want to worry her. Worry her more, I should say."

"Yeah, it's probably better."

"Let's see . . . maybe Ruso . . ."

"Hello, Mauricio! I didn't see you come in. I was in the nurses' break room."

"Yeah, they told me."

"Did you get it, Ruso?"

"Who do you think you're talking to, Mono?"

"He's talking to Ruso the idiot. That's why he asked."

"Ay, God. Such ingratitude in the pastures of the lord. Why didn't you go, Fernandito?"

"Because I'm a shy boy, that's why."

"I didn't go because I get dizzy. I get up to go to the bathroom and I fall on my ass. That's why I sent you. What did you find out?"

"Hold on, Mono. Wait, I have the information sheet for the medication here. Let's have a look."

". . ."

". . ."

". . ."

54.

They ring the bell and La Gallega opens the door. She looks exactly the same. Just like thirty years earlier, the few times Polaco's mother was seen around the neighborhood, when her children were young. Either she doesn't recognize them as old neighborhood kids or she prefers not to mix false nostalgia into what her son has surely presented as a business meeting. She has them go into Polaco's "office," where Pittilanga and Mauricio are also waiting.

Polaco greets them as if they were old friends, but since they aren't, his gestures and words are clumsy. Mauricio just nods his head, without getting up from his seat. A shame, thinks Fernando, that when Mono died he thought that the three of them could make a nice group of uncles for the girl. Well, it won't be a trio. It'll be a duo. A shame. One of many.

The only honest and affectionate greetings are those they exchange with Pittilanga. He is wearing his usual sports outfit with the club's colors and crest, and he seems happy and enthusiastic.

Polaco invites them to sit on the white Italian leather armchairs he bought when they were in style some years back, when a dollar was worth the same as a peso and guys like Salvatierra could afford these and other eccentricities. Fernando notices that, unlike the entryway and the living room, this room still has a ton of furniture and decorations. Not only the armchairs but also the lacquered credenza, the photographs, the autographed jerseys. But the other parts of the house are much more bare. Salvatierra must be liquidating the furnishings gradually, and he is trying to preserve his sanctuary for as long as he can. Now perhaps he can stop that bleeding, although Fernando doesn't know what the nature of his involvement in the negotiation could be. Nor how much of a chunk he'll get.

Before sitting down Pittilanga goes over to a bunch of photos of national teams that decorate one wall, and he looks for himself in the Indonesian World Cup. Fernando also goes over to do the same thing.

"Which one is you?" asks Mauricio.

Pittilanga just points to one of the silhouettes kneeling in the bottom row. He looks at himself for a long moment and goes back to his armchair. Fernando stays there looking at the photo for a little longer. Several of those kids have been playing in Europe for a while now. Two or three are in Argentine clubs. The others he doesn't recognize at all. The earth just swallowed them up. He thinks that Pittilanga, since that photograph was taken, has been swimming in the turbulent waters that separate those two groups: the unknowns and the winners, the drowned and the saved. And he's still floating.

La Gallega comes in without knocking, holding a tray with a coffeepot, mugs, and cookies. She leaves it on a side table and retreats with that weary swaying walk that old people sometimes have.

"I'll serve the coffees and you can pass them down," says Salvatierra. "I've already confirmed that the Arabs are traveling the day after tomorrow, through Madrid. They arrive on Thursday evening. I think it's best to set something up for Friday morning, to avoid getting nervous about the flight schedules and all that."

"Fine, good idea," agrees Ruso. "Before we start I wanted to ask you something on a whole other topic." He addresses Fernando and Mauricio. "Did you see the movie *The Sting*?"

"What?!"

"I ask because of something I remembered you told me the other day."

"Do you think this is the moment for this, Ruso?"

"Paul Newman and Robert Redford," interjects Mauricio.

"Ah, you saw it?" asks Ruso.

"Uh-huh. It's good. I saw it in the theater, when we were kids. In the Ocean, in Morón, I think."

"Excuse me, but if you could leave movies for another time . . ." Fernando isn't about to give Mauricio a chance to look good.

"Okay, sorry," Ruso apologizes.

Ruso's apology is followed by a long silence, which Salvatierra ends by bringing up the business at hand.

"I kind of called you all to this meeting so we could come to an agreement on the details."

"You called us kind of or you actually called us?" asks Fernando, who can't stand the loser being the one in charge. Four pairs of eyes turn to look at him. He shrugs vaguely. "Doesn't matter. Go ahead."

"No . . . I didn't understand you, Fernando," Salvatierra displays the tenacious attention of a fawn sniffing the morning air of the forest in search of danger.

Fernando looks at him without affection. He feels Ruso's reproachful gaze on his temple. He knows what he's thinking. Avoid problems. Sidestep fights. Get it all on safe ground. He's right. But Fernando can't stand this meddler. Besides, seeing Mauricio with his shark's uniform and his smart briefcase doesn't help improve his mood. He turns his head and comes up against Ruso's face, which tacitly reproaches and implores him. Fernando frowns, scornful, and looks the other way.

"Doesn't matter, Polaco. Forget I said anything."

"What—whatever. There will be three representatives of the Al-Shabab Club at the meeting: president, treasurer, and another whose job I didn't catch. You three as proxies for your mother, Fernando. And us two. I mean Mario and me. Is that right?"

"Cristo's gonna be there too," adds Ruso shyly.

"Cristo?" Salvatierra is confused.

"He's a friend who works with me. I want him to be there because he did his part to make this happen."

"We can't stick him in the meeting as your friend, Ruso," interjects Mauricio.

"Stick him in as secretary, as assistant, as whatever you want, Mauricio." All of a sudden Fernando is Cristo's guardian angel. "If it's for merit, some of the people present have no right even eavesdropping on this meeting on Friday."

Mauricio blushes, but keeps his lips sealed.

"Eh . . . if it's a problem, I won't bring him." Ruso doesn't want to create even the slightest conflict.

"Cristo's coming and that's final," concludes Fernando, who is sorry that Mauricio hasn't reacted, because he would have liked to continue arguing.

A long silence falls over them.

"Wellll . . . there's no problem with this friend coming. There's plenty of room."

Fernando settles into his seat. As the conversation goes on, his anger grows. He doesn't know why this is happening to him. But he doesn't want to delve into it, or stop.

"One thing to make clear from the very start," Fernando adds. "Now that Mario is twenty-one we would have to be total shitheads to miss this transfer opportunity. I guess we have everything under control." He turns toward Polaco. "Mario's father doesn't have to come this time, does he?"

As he speaks, he has the feeling that Ruso and Mauricio are exchanging a glance whose meaning escapes him. He is about to ask about it, but Mauricio speaks first: "You know what? I don't think I can even stand the sight of you anymore."

"Really? The feeling is mutual."

"Boys, please don't star—"

"Mutual means that I feel the same way," explains Fernando with a weary expression. "I'm clarifying that because I know that, poor thing, you might not have learned that word in law school."

"At least I went through six years of university."

"That's true. In the most difficult department at UBA. Studying to be a lawyer is one of the most complicated majors in the world. That's why there are so few of them."

"No, there are a lot. Little language arts teachers, on the other hand, are a rare species."

"Cut it out, boys, what are Mario and Polaco going to think?"

Fernando emerges for a second from the volcano he is treading on and looks at the others. Salvatierra looks at them in horror, something Fernando couldn't care less about. But Pittilanga also seems nervous. He tries to put himself in the kid's shoes. In three days his professional future is going to be decided and the guys who have the legal authority to set him up for it are arguing like unreliable assholes. Fernando lifts a hand apologetically.

"Okay. Forget I said anything. Unresolved issues, as they say. But you guys have nothing to do with it. Let's continue, please."

"Fine. That's probably better." Salvatierra checks his papers and lifts up a fax. "These guys are going to make us an offer of two hundred and fifty thousand dollars, net."

"It's not enough. We need three hundred and fifty thousand," interrupts Fernando.

"Yeeeaah . . . I know," Salvatierra tries to placate him. "That's why I thought we should start our bid at four hundred. We go down and they go up. It seems possible."

"Sounds good to me," confirms Ruso.

"For me, no problem," says Fernando, calmer. "As long as that's the floor, I'm on board."

"One thing," says Salvatierra. "We have to see about the question of Mario's fifteen percent and my commission."

Fernando turns decidedly in his chair to face Pittilanga.

"Look, Mario." His voice has a friendliness to it, which he hadn't used until then. "I understand that you deserve your percentage, no doubt about that. But then we have to squeeze the buyers a little more, because we need the three hundred grand net for the girl."

"As long as it's all for the girl," Mauricio mutters softly toward the wall, but Fernando hears him. He hears him and he hates him.

"Okay, boys. But it could be," insists Polaco, "that when we get to that point of the fine print we have to—"

"I don't give a rat's ass about the fine print or the big print." Now that he is speaking to Polaco, Fernando's tone has lost all trace of affection. "The three hundred grand has to be net. The

Arabs will put in Mario's fifteen on top. And your commission, honestly, can suck my balls."

There is an uncomfortable silence. The fourth or fifth since their gathering started. Fernando looks at Ruso.

"Cat got your tongue? Or do you agree with what I said?"

"Me? No, yeah, yeah. We already talked about it with Mario. That dough we need in full. He understands."

"Anything else?" Fernando's question is for Salvatierra.

"Eh . . . I don't think so, I think that that's . . . I don't know if Mauricio wants to say something . . ."

Mauricio takes his time. He finishes his coffee and leaves the cup on the plate. He adjusts the knot in his tie.

"I think everything's been said."

"Well, okay, I think we've reached an agreement." Salvatierra looks at each of them, one by one, but nobody meets his eyes. The other three look at Mauricio, who looks at his shoes. "But if there is any rough spot that needs to be sanded down maybe it's better to talk about it now and . . ."

And not fuck up in front of the Arabs, Fernando finishes the thought in his head, and smiles ironically.

"And what are you laughing at?" Mauricio asks him insolently.

Fernando thinks it over. He is no longer smiling.

"Don't get nervous. I know you put a lot into making this negotiation a success. I understand your nervousness. But we're about to reward your efforts."

"Are you always the yardstick, measuring what others do?"

"Me, the yardstick? No, not at all."

"That's what it seems like."

Fernando nods, but remains silent.

"Boys, why don't we just leave it . . . ?" Ruso seems like a signalman trying to keep two locomotives from crashing at a crossroads.

"If you have something to say, why don't you just say it?"

"No. I'd just like to know . . ."

"What, Fernando? What would you like to say?"

"Why did you wait three weeks to tell us about Al-Shabab wanting to buy Mario's transfer? I'm just wondering." He brings a hand to his head as if curling something around his finger near his temple. "You know . . . sometimes my brain doesn't work that well . . ."

Mauricio looks at his shoes again.

"I mean . . . because it seems like if Ruso hadn't bumped into Polaco in the supermarket last time, we wouldn't have even found out about the offer. I don't know. Maybe it's just that I have an evil mind. Maybe you were handling it . . . I don't know . . ."

"Fernando," intervenes Salvatierra. "I wasn't trying to hide anything from you guys, why would I do that?"

"This isn't about you . . ." Fernando cuts him off, without taking his eyes off Mauricio.

"No." Mauricio shifts in his chair, smiling halfheartedly. "It's about me. This is about me."

"But maybe there is some reason that I don't understand, why you kept us in the dark for a month."

"Maybe I thought it wasn't worth getting too excited about."

"You thought? You thought that all on your own? And since when did we agree that you could think for yourself?"

"Ah, I didn't know I needed your agreement to think. Your guidance, I should say."

"I'm not saying you should ask my permission. But let me know."

"I'm not asking your permission and I never will. I don't know who put you in charge. I don't know who let you out of your cage, but I'm fed up. You've got a degree as an expert in selling players and I didn't even know, so let's just do this, okay? I'll be leaving, since I have things to do. You stay, or go to one of those crappy schools where you teach the difference between the subject and the predicate."

"Stop, Mauricio!" Ruso wants to hold him back. "Don't leave like this."

"Don't you think I'm a little too old for this moron to be telling me off? To tell me what to do like he's my dad? See you on Friday."

"But we need you. We need to be together, all of us."

Ruso has stood up, but when Mauricio strides past he doesn't dare stop him. Mauricio turns when his hand is already on the doorknob.

"Me? Me? No, you guys don't need me, Ruso. Ask him. He's more than enough. He doesn't need anyone. He doesn't need you either. The thing is that you say yes to everything, so it's all fine between you guys. See you on Friday."

He leaves and slams the door behind him.

Side Effects II

"And?"

"I'm reading. Wait."

"Come on!"

"What was it you had?"

"Quit fooling around, Ruso! Let me read!"

"Hands off, Mono! You're in no condition. Let's see . . ."

"Ooh, Ruso's mad."

"You guys should have gone to chat with the nurse."

". . ."

". . ."

". . ."

"Vertigo, did you have that, Mono?"

"Yes . . . vertigo . . . dizziness . . ."

"Well, according to the Adverse Effects, it's normal, man."

"It says it like that? 'Adverse Effects'?"

"No, fool. It says 'Cooking Directions.'"

"Don't be a jerk."

"Don't you be jerk, Mono. It's in Adverse Effects and it says, it says . . . vertigo . . . migraines, ha!"

"What are you laughing at?"

"Vertigo, migraines, psychiatric disorders. That last one you can't blame on the injections, Mono."

"Really, Ruso? Show me."

"Look, Fer. You read it too, Mauricio."

". . ."

". . ."

"It's true, man."

"What's going on? What are you reading?"

"Nothing, Mono."

"Nothing my ass! What does it say?"

". . ."

"Mmmmm . . . this has more Adverse Effects than a mother-fucker. How many of these did they give you?"

"What do I know, like five, six . . . why?"

"Lemme see, Mono. This could be terrible . . . in your case, I mean."

"Why?! What's wrong?!"

"You said something about increased perspiration, Fer?"

"No, Mauricio. Well, that too. This son of a bitch usually stinks like a barn, imagine what he's like on this medication."

"Why don't you guys go fuck yourselves?"

"But that's not what I'm talking about. I'm talking about the other thing."

"Let me see . . . Ha! Look, Ruso, read this!"

"Aren't you guys embarrassed to be cracking up like this in front of me?"

"Let's see . . . Noooooo! 'Increase in intracranial pressure.' Holy shit! His head's gonna explode and fuck us all up!"

"Stay still, Mono! Stay still! Don't move! If you blow up we'll all die from the shock wave."

"Don't shake, you're going to make the needle come out! The nurse already told you off because she had to start the IV again."

"No! I said no! No pillow fights for you, Mono! Listen to this! Listen! They gave this to Independiente's entire defense! 'Nausea, general discomfort, ataxia, hiccups, rare cases of blindness . . .'"

55.

"I hate these elevators. They're like aluminum coffins. They give me . . . what's it called?"

"Claustrophobia," suggests Fernando.

"That's it. Claustrophobia."

They don't speak for a few minutes, watching the floor numbers pass on the illuminated display.

"Hey, Fer . . ."

"What, Ruso?"

"I was thinking about this thing with the Arabs."

"What about it?" Fernando runs a finger inside his shirt collar. It's not too tight, but he repeats this same gesture of discomfort every time he wears a tie.

"Are we gonna have problems?"

"Problems? Why?"

"I—I don't know. It's just that they're Muslims . . ."

"So what if they're Muslims? Why does that bother you?"

"No, it doesn't really bother me. But maybe . . . I don't know . . . What if they're into that terrorism stuff? Bin Laden and all that."

Fernando turns to look at him. He notices he's serious, and that his fuchsia tie shines beneath the elevator's white ceiling lights.

"Don't worry about that, meathead. What does that have to do with our deal? There are millions of Muslims that have nothing to do with all that."

"Are you sure? Imagine we escaped the Russian mafia only to end up kicking the bucket at the hands of Islamic fundamentalists, man."

Fernando takes a second.

"Well. With that schnoz of yours I can't make any promises."

Ruso touches his nose.

"What's wrong with my nose?" he asks, tense.

"Are your family Sephardic or Ashkenazic Jews?"

"Eh . . . I don't know . . . Ashkenazis." Now Ruso looks at himself in one of the mirrors. "Why, man? What's the problem?"

Fernando wonders how far to torment him. A little more.

"Thank goodness."

"Why? If I'm Sephardic there's a beef? Why?"

Fernando makes a face as if he's filled with doubt. But when he sees Ruso's anguish he takes pity on him.

"I don't know, man."

"I'm seriously asking."

"I'm seriously answering. I have no idea."

"Then why are you talking?" Behind the mortification, he can make out the relief in Ruso's tone.

"Just to fuck with you a little, I guess."

They hear the chime that the elevator gives off before it stops. Fernando feels the nauseating density of his innards, which are slower to stop their ascent than the elevator and pile up at the height of his diaphragm. The doors open. The carpeted hallway, the pictures on the walls, the bronze polished to a high shine, the elegant silence. Let it all be over soon, for God's sake.

"How should we greet them?" asks Ruso, as they advance along the hallway looking for the number they were given.

"You bow your head. Does that schnoz show up less in profile?"

Fernando is joking, but at the same time he feels like he needs more air, more space. A growing oppression, a gradual cornering that he can't put a name to. As they turn a bend in the hall an image comes to his mind, of those white lab rats running through a maze beneath a scientist's attentive gaze. Then he has a much more primal feeling, more concrete: the feeling that comes over him at the stadium, in the stands, when an unfailing intuition whispers in his ear that Independiente is dead meat. That no matter what they do the other team is about to score.

"Hey, dummy. I asked you a question," says Ruso.

"What?"

"Whether there could really be a problem with me being Jewish."

Fernando stops walking for a second.

"No, fool. Relax."

"Why are you messing with me? Don't you see this is serious?"

"You see how wrong it is to mess with somebody in moments like this?"

It's that feeling. That one from the stadium. Something Fernando senses, in the air, that announces defeat. At the stadium he can appeal to a whole string of superstitious rituals for luck to get him through the emergency. Taking off his hat (or putting it on, depending on the situation), moving two rows down, or one up, carefully watching the next train that passes behind the visiting stands, reciting some childhood incantation, like *if I see the train pass right now, they won't make the goal*. But in this spongy, silent place those spells have no power. He thinks—and not by chance—of Mauricio.

"And your stupid friend? Is he coming?"

"*My* friend? Isn't he your friend too?" Fernando doesn't answer, and Ruso adds, "Yeah, he should have already arrived. I told him we should all come together but he said he'd rather come on his own."

Fernando nods.

"Why is that, you think?"

Ruso lifts his hand and knocks on the door.

Side Effects III

"Really, Mono. Now I get it."

"What?"

"Ha! Ha! What a bastard! Now I understand everything! Now I get it! They gave you this shot when you were a kid, Mono! They gave you the shot when you were a kid and you didn't realize!"

"Can I see, Ruso?"

"See?"

"Look. You, stay right there, Mono. Don't come over."

"I'm going to call the nurse and have her kick you guys out on your asses . . ."

"You're right, Ruso! Poor Monito! You should have told us . . ."

"Told you what? Give me the paper so I can read it! Give it to me!"

"Shhh! Hands off."

"I'll read it to him."

"No. I'll read it to him, I'm the one who found it. Okay: 'Menstrual irregularities,' that's always been—"

"He always had that—"

"That's nothing new—"

"I'm talking about this—ha!"

"Come on, fool! Read it already!"

"'Stunted growth in children.' Should have known, Mono, that's why you're so short."

"Why don't you go fuck yourselves?"

"Poor little Mono. Forgive us. It seems it was from the medication."

"They shot him full of injections, as a kid, and that's why he's like this."

"You guys are assholes. All three of you."

"Tiny."

"Squat."

"Yeah, runty."

56.

A giant, six feet five with the face of a serial killer, lets them in. They enter a room with six people seated around a long table. They all stand at almost the same time.

In a quick glance Fernando locates Pittilanga, dressed in his perpetual sports attire; Salvatierra, wearing the same suit as last time, which must be one of the last vestiges of his decade of glory; and Cristo, in a meticulous tapered black suit and narrow tie of the same color. Ruso had wanted him to be there as a secretary, partly in case some reference to marcapegajosa .com.ar comes up in the conversation and partly because he doesn't want to leave him out of the conclusion to this soap opera he has been following so diligently.

After greeting them, Fernando faces the Arabs. There are three, not counting the bodyguard at the door, and they look more friendly than the Ukrainians. Well, he thinks, remembering the surly expression and ice-cold looks of their previous potential buyers, it doesn't take much to be more sympathetic than they were. Salvatierra takes care of the introductions. One of the Arabs answers in shaky Spanish. The other two just smile during the handshakes. They take their seats. Soon Ruso touches Fernando's arm and leans over to whisper in his ear.

"Man, they have the same nose as I do."

Fernando has no more ammunition to torment him with. The guard at the door comes over pushing a rolling table with coffee, cookies, and sandwiches. He serves in silence, without asking who wants what, but no one dares to object. When he finishes putting a cup of coffee in front of everyone present and the trays onto the table, he retires to his place at the entrance, pushing the little table back with him.

"Well," says Salvatierra, after clearing his throat. "First of all, and in Mario's name and my own, as his representative, as well as Daniel and Fernando, two of the proxies of Margarita Núñez de Raguzzi, owner of the economic rights, I would like to welcome you to Argentina, and thank you for your interest in acquiring Mario's services for the Al-Shabab Football Club."

One of the Arabs begins to translate Polaco's speech into their language, and the other two answer with serious nods of the head.

Something in the air, thinks Fernando, and although he knows that the image is pathetically obvious, he can't find a better one, and he repeats it to himself: *something in the air.* Something bad, something tense, something threatening, something crouching behind the thick curtains or the comfy stuffed chairs they are sitting in. Something that is everywhere and nowhere, and when it shows itself, it'll be too late, fuck. Independiente could seem safe. It could even, apparently, have the game under control. And yet . . . *there is something*. Perhaps it's nothing more than a tremble in the air. In these circumstances things take on an inscrutable symbolism. A throw-in at midfield, a sugared-almond vendor whose elastic gives out on his tray and his pyramid of packets collapses, an old guy in a beret who snorts, undecipherable, three seats over. And all of a sudden, the throw-in leads to a scramble in midfield, and the scramble into a deep, penetrating pass over the defense, followed by a cross into the penalty area met with a header and suddenly tragedy. And the something takes shape and becomes everything.

There is something here too, thinks Fernando, as Salvatierra explains, convinces, smiles, flatters, suggests, disagrees, summarizes, insists. What a character Polaco is. Fernando can't help but acknowledge his respectability, even considering his obvious decline. The nicely cut suit, a little out of fashion, a little big in the shoulders (too 1990s, too boom days of Menem), his hair taut with gel, his shave perfect except for two or three nicks, perhaps due to anxiety or tension. A shipwrecked man lighting the last bonfire as the last ship passes.

Just then Salvatierra waits (they all wait: Ruso, Pittilanga, Cristo, all of them except Fernando, who is struggling to emerge from the thicket of his intuitions and doubts) for the president of Al-Shabab to finish speaking in his language and the Arab to his right to translate what he's said.

"Mr. Zalhmed says that four hundred thousand seems a bit high. That he understands the fine qualities of Mr. Pittilanga, and that is why we have come here."

As the translator pauses, Fernando sneaks a glance at Ruso and confirms his suspicion: he is looking at Cristo with gleaming eyes, as he struggles to hold back his desire to laugh out loud and shout out how hilarious it is that he calls him "Mr. Pittilanga," and Cristo looks back with an ecstatic gleam in his eye too. Obviously his grandmother was right, birds of a feather flock together. And Fernando wonders why God didn't give him Ruso's disposition, incapable of worrying for more than ten minutes without happiness distracting him and pulling him out into calmer waters with the flimsiest excuse, like, for example, an Arab who barely speaks broken Spanish calling Mario Juan Bautista Pittilanga mister.

"And so Al-Shabab suggests an amount of two hundred and fifty thousand dollars for the player's transfer."

Fernando plays with his empty cup, because he doesn't want to look at the others. Luckily it's Polaco who has to make a face saying *that's not enough* and struggle to get the figure up as best he can. Let him earn his commission, the big nitwit. Fernando wants to run away.

And just then Ruso's cell phone starts to make little hops on the enormous table they sit around. And then to the vibrating hops is added the music of "Bombón asesino," which to top it all off increases in volume by the second. Salvatierra gets distracted and loses his train of thought, while the Arabs watch the cell phone as if it's an intolerable insect and Ruso swipes at the table, captures it, and brings it up to his eyes so he can see who's calling. Fernando wants to kill him, for ineptitude, for improvising, for being scatterbrained, for not realizing that he should turn it off instead of answering. But to his surprise Ruso looks at him with dismay, perhaps trying to send him a message that Fernando doesn't understand anyway, and he gets up and walks to a corner as he answers the call. And Fernando is again overcome with a sense of unease, that things are about to go south and nose-dive. And from that point on he experiences the disturbing sensation that reality is split in two, like the television screen when they are simultaneously playing two games that could decide a championship, and again the old soccer metaphor but it doesn't matter, because on one side he has Salvatierra picking up where he left off and repeating his arguments, to defend the principle that Mario Juan Bautista Pittilanga's transfer cannot be worth less than four hundred thousand dollars, or three hundred and eighty thousand minimum, and on the other side it has

Ruso standing like a punished child (a child from fifty years earlier, since those kinds of punishments are no longer used) with his face against the angle of the wall, talking in a whisper. And just as happens to him with the television's split screen, now again he doesn't understand a thing, not what's on his right nor what's on his left, not Salvatierra on his final sprint toward twisting the Arabs' arms nor Ruso the wallflower in the corner.

Luckily, Ruso finishes talking (luckily is just an expression, because the face with which he turns back toward the meeting, the face with which he folds up his cell phone, the face with which he looks at Fernando as he comes over, declares everything but good news, but at least the schizophrenia of the two halves of the screen has ended) and sits back down. He sits and scratches his head, not like someone who has an itch but like someone who wants to tear out his hair but doesn't because there are witnesses, and through his fingers Fernando sees his eyes filled with tears and he feels like the floor is being pulled out from under him, and when he is about to stand up and go over to Ruso, he sees him extract a pen and rip out a sheet from a notebook and write a few quick words and slide it along the table, and since he does it with a certain vehemence the page lifts up at one end until Fernando places his hand on top and the paper again rests on the table.

Fernando reads: "Williams called me, Mauricio is on his way here, and he said we should stop the meeting because he has to be here." There are some other words, but Fernando looks up at Ruso before he reads it all because he doesn't understand what Williams is doing giving that order over the phone but it scares him anyway and he does understand the fear. Suddenly he notices the silence that surrounds him. He looks up and meets the eyes of Polaco, who looks as if he is waiting for a response from him. And on another of the table's sides are the three Arabs with the same questioning expression, also waiting for Fernando to respond with who knows what to the representative of Mr. Pittilanga. Luckily that's the entire head count of those who are staring at Fernando, because Cristo and Pittilanga are turned toward Ruso trying to understand what the hell is wrong with him, which was the same thing that Fernando was doing until he realized that they are talking to him and he's there with his head in the clouds. Fortunately, Polaco speaks, in the tone of someone reiterating what he has just said.

"Isn't it true, Fernando, that our bottom line is three hundred thousand dollars and we can't go any lower?"

Fernando swallows hard.

"Yes, yes. Any less, impossible."

He says it mostly out of solidarity with Polaco. He doesn't owe him any particular loyalty, but it seems wrong to leave him in the lurch. After all, he's doing his part, and he doesn't have the slightest idea that the something that was in the air is now on the table, in Ruso's bugging-out eyes, in his pulling on his hair: the throw-in that leads to a scramble and the deep pass, god damn it to hell. Luckily this is the cue Polaco was waiting for to start in again with his arguments, so he turns toward the Arabs and starts to speak in short, deliberate sentences to give the translator time to do his job. And Fernando can turn toward Ruso and touch his arm to ask for an explanation, even though Ruso just looks at the table with his eyes full of tears.

Fernando loses all composure and, completely washing his hands of the negotiation with the Arabs, he makes his way over to Ruso's ear and asks him what the hell is going on because he doesn't understand a thing. And Ruso, elbows on the table, hands tangled in his hair, turns slightly toward him to say that Williams knows about everything because Mauricio told him, and he called me to threaten me, the son of a bitch. Threaten you with what? asks Fernando. Threaten me that we'd better get out of here because they are the ones in charge of this negotiation and because we don't have anything to do with it and if we don't stop fucking around we are going to end up behind bars. Why behind bars? asks Fernando. How the hell do I know, says Ruso, losing his patience even though he keeps his voice at a whisper, exasperated but still a whisper.

Fernando settles in his seat, not to play it cool in front of the Arabs but because he is so disoriented that he needs a corner in which to organize his ideas, even though deep down it is precisely ideas that he lacks and, since he has no corner, he uses the black leather back of his extremely comfortable chair. The deep pass that transforms into a cross into the penalty area met with a header, and him there not knowing where the shots are coming from, and in that moment three short knocks are heard at the door, three knocks that freeze his blood because that is the knock that Mauricio always uses.

Papers in the Wind I

"Do you know what image, what thing leaves me at peace with the world?"

"Let me think, Mono . . . Ruso in briefs and white ankle socks?"

"I'm being serious, Mauricio."

"What's wrong with me in briefs and white ankle socks? Huh?"

"Nothing wrong with it, sweetheart, but I think Mono is talking about another type of peace and beauty."

"Ah. That makes me feel better, Fer."

"Are you making fun of me?"

"No. It's okay, Mono. Go ahead."

"Because if you guys are going to tease me I'll shut my mouth right now and not say a damn word."

"Come on, Mono, talk!"

"Lately we've been talking a lot about Independiente. Of how bad we're doing, how much we're suffering."

"Again?"

"Let me finish. Haven't you guys been telling me all the time to talk, to not hold stuff in, to tell you what's going on with me? Well, here you go. Now you have to put up with it."

"Okay."

"Go on."

"I know that with all this soccer stuff we act like idiots."

"Speak for yourself. I'm a ninja."

"I'm being serious, Ruso! Quit fucking around!"

"Okay, okay. Okay."

". . ."

". . ."

"Besides, what the hell does a ninja have to do with anything?"

"I meant one of those guys that does meditation, everything slides off his back, nothing stresses him."

"And according to you, that's a ninja?"

"No, but I can't remember what they're called."

57.

The giant at the door moves to one side and Mauricio enters, taking them all in with a quick glance. He approaches Salvatierra, who stumbles a bit as he moves his chair back to stand up. They shake hands and Polaco introduces him to the Arabs. He greets Pittilanga, who is on the far side of the table, with a nod of the head, and he doesn't even look at Fernando and Ruso, even though they are very close by on his left.

There is such an uncomfortable silence that even the Arabs seem upset. Salvatierra comes out to meet him and sums up what has been said. "Aha," says Mauricio every once in a while, and his expression remains severe and inscrutable. When Polaco finishes, Mauricio nods and thanks him. "Thank you, Ernesto," he says, and Fernando thinks that it's the first time he hears Mauricio calling him by his given name. The detail unsettles him, as if it were a way of marking allies and enemies, as if there were increasingly fewer doubts as to who falls into which camp.

"Now I need to ask you something," says Mauricio, addressing both Polaco and the Arabs. "I need to ask you to forgive the sloppiness of this meeting and—"

"Sloppiness?" shouts Ruso, and Fernando jumps from his reaction.

Mauricio considers him for a second and then returns to face the others.

"It seems important that from now on the negotiations should be conducted exclusively between the parties involved in the negotiation."

Polaco makes a motion with the palms of his hands facing upward, as if to say that is exactly what is happening. Mauricio frowns and shakes his head slightly.

"I firmly believe, Ernesto, that in order for this meeting to succeed it is essential that each person confirm his role in this matter." He pauses dramatically and takes his seat in the only free chair as he searches through his briefcase. "I mean: the player, his representative"—as he lists them he points with an outstretched hand to each of them—"the hypothetical buyers, and the proxy for the seller." And at this last one he points to himself.

"What? What are you saying?" Fernando hears Ruso, to his left, confusing himself with his own questions, but he doesn't pay attention to him because he begins to understand and a frozen pain and fierce disenchantment begin to overtake him. From where he is, he can see a document that Mauricio has just pulled out of his briefcase. And the signatures on its pages. And one of those signatures Fernando knows all too well.

"There's more. It seems essential to me that we avoid, from this point on, the presence of relatives and close friends, who for all their goodwill are only going to drag out the negotiations. To begin with," and as he says this he turns to Salvatierra, "the price they are discussing is completely beyond our expectations."

"Our? Who's our?" Ruso sits up in his chair. "Who, god damn it . . . ?"

Mauricio's face hardens, as if he were clenching his jaw tightly.

"Let's be clear," he says, and he holds out the papers to Salvatierra, inviting him with a hand that he then extends to include the Arabs. "Mrs. Margarita Núñez de Raguzzi is, for all intents and purposes regarding the economic rights of the player Mario Juan Bautista Pittilanga, the sole proprietor. Which is to say, my principal."

"Yes," accepts Polaco, "but the power of attorney that Margarita signed accredits all three jointly and equally and—"

"That is no longer the case," Mauricio cuts him off. "The previous power of attorney, yes."

He makes a pause more dramatic than the previous ones, and places his index finger on the document he left in front of Salvatierra, the one whose signature warned Fernando, so he no longer has any questions or doubts. He merely hates.

"But this other power of attorney," continues Mauricio, "which I invite you to review, designates me, representing the firm Williams and Associates, as the exclusive proxy of my principal. And this power," he adds, punctuating rhythmically with his index finger on the first page, "revokes all previously bestowed powers of attorney."

For a minute the last phrases of this bizarre scene can be heard, echoed in Arabic by the translator. Then, silence. Polaco picks up the contract and reads it.

"It's true. Here it designates you alone . . ."

"And the clause revoking the previous power is here, clearly visible."

Salvatierra reads the part Mauricio is pointing to. He puts the contract down on the table.

"Yes," he concludes.

"What is the date of the new power of attorney?" asks Ruso, his face red.

Salvatierra looks on the last page.

"It's dated yesterday."

"I don't understand anything, Polaco," says Pittilanga, who until that moment had remained silent.

"Neither do I," says Ruso soon after, "and honestly it's making me nervous that I don't understand the—"

"There's nothing to understand," Fernando cuts him off, and as he says it he feels strangely cold, distant, numb, as if he had known that things were going to end like this. "Mauricio convinced my mom to give him a new power of attorney, revoking the previous one. But this time the only one who can negotiate is him. Not us."

"What? Why? What are you saying? How?" Ruso asks, looking at everyone and no one, his face growing redder and redder.

"I suggest you calm down . . . " begins Mauricio, but he can't go on.

"I suggest you shut your fucking trap," Fernando stops him. "Don't talk to him. Don't ever speak to him again."

Mauricio clenches his jaw again and looks away. Fernando speaks with his eyes on the table.

"Somehow your friend Mauricio convinced my mom that a bad deal was about to be made. And that she had to revoke the power of attorney that included the three of us and leave him in charge. Him and his boss, that son of a bitch."

"What do you mean his boss?"

"You didn't hear him mention the Williams firm?"

"But what does that have to do with it? All three of us can't sell him and he thinks he can do it alone?"

"Not exactly," says Fernando, shocked because as he explains it he understands it himself. "Mario's loan is ending.

Now he'll go back to Platense and they'll release him. So then Mauricio will give my mom his regrets, saying he's terribly sorry and offering to minimize her losses. Minimize them very little, actually. He offers her thirty grand, forty grand. He comes out smelling like roses by buying Pittilanga off her. Then they sell him for the kind of money we're asking."

"But that's the same thing—"

"No, Rusito. Now the money is for us. Or rather, for Guadalupe. Later the money will be for them."

"Is that true?" Ruso asks him in a faint voice, but Mauricio doesn't acknowledge him. "I'm asking you if it's true . . ."

"Look, Ruso," he seems to finally make up his mind. "I suggest you go home and some other time when you're more calm you call me and—"

"I asked you if it was true!" Ruso stands up and closes his fists. From that point on everything he says is shrieked. "I asked you if it's true! Answer, motherfucker! Answer!"

Fernando puts both hands on his chest to keep him from charging toward Mauricio.

"Calm down, Ruso—"

"How can I calm down? How can I calm down? He won't even answer me! Answer, damn it! Answer!"

Mauricio doesn't stand up. He speaks without getting ruffled, addressing Salvatierra and the translator.

"It seems the most advisable thing would be to take an intermission and resume this negotiation once the condition I mentioned earlier is complied with."

"Answer me, god damn it! Tell me if you screwed us, motherfucker! Tell me if you screwed us!"

Ruso's voice ends up choked with rage. Fernando can barely keep holding him back. Cristo helps. The security mastodon has opened the door to the suite and lets in two others who have a similar look. Meanwhile, Mario Juan Bautista Pitti-langa, without any fuss, gets up, goes around the table, behind the Arabs, grabs Mauricio by the nape of the neck, lifts him up so he's well in his reach, and gives him a punch in the face that knocks him flat on his back. Then he approaches his fallen body and begins to kick him again and again, until one of the security guards leaps onto him.

Papers in the Wind II

"..."

"..."

"..."

"It's hard to believe, dude. Do I have to slam you just so you'll let me talk?"

"..."

"..."

"Okay, Mono. Talk. Go ahead."

"What I'm saying . . . what I'm saying is that when your team is losing, you see things clearer. Am I right?"

"What do you mean by clearer?"

"Clearer in that soccer is a lie. That it's all a farce. That it's all business. The players, the managers, the journalists. Even the hooligans are on the books. All about the benjamins. They all do it for the money."

"Well, yeah."

"It's true."

"Because when everything's going well you get kinda naive, kind of reckless. You get happy, partying, getting excited. You think everything's great. But when things aren't going so well, on the other hand, you see things clearer. Am I right or am I right?"

"Yeah, maybe so, Mono."

"Yeah, I guess."

"And in all this time, all these years that Independiente's been shit, from bad to worse, all my innocence is gone, all my delusions, my pride . . ."

"Oof. When we were so famous for our 'pedigreed play.'"

"Exactly, Fer! The pedigreed play and all that bullshit. You see how you guys understand? And yet . . . somehow . . . there's still a 'but' . . . There's still something that pulls me in. Something I just love."

58.

Fernando touches his chin, barely brushes it, and winces.

"Did they hit you?" Ruso asks.

"No. One of the bodyguards roughed me up a little, but just to get me out of the room. When he stuck in his arm to grab me he hit me by mistake."

"No way was that a mistake."

"It was by mistake. If one of those guys punches you, you're out cold, man."

"Maybe so," accepts Ruso. And he turns to Cristo. "And you?"

"I'm fine. They didn't actually throw me out physically."

Fernando gestures with his chin toward Ruso. In the scuffle with the security guards they ripped several buttons off his shirt, and now, sitting at the cafe table, his fuchsia tie rests on the hair of his abdomen. He notices his disarray and tries to stuff his shirttails into his pants, for lack of a better idea, and he takes off the tie. For a while they are silent, watching people and cars pass.

"And the kid?" remembers Cristo.

"Polaco took him," says Ruso. "I think they went down in another elevator."

"Before or after us?"

"I don't know. I guess after. When they took me out I saw that he was still beating the shit out of Mauricio."

"Man, did he hit him a lot?" Cristo asks with a giggle.

"From what I saw, he kicked him like there was no tomorrow."

"Ha! And that kid can kick hard."

"Fuck him," says Fernando. Now he feels a cold hatred, as if it went way back.

Ruso scans the sidewalk across the street, toward the corner, toward the hotel entrance.

"What's wrong? Is something going on?" asks Fernando.

Ruso shakes his head no.

"Mauricio didn't come out yet?"

"No. Not yet."

"It's a waste of time, Ruso."

"What's a waste of time?"

"Waiting for him."

"Why?"

"Because that's it. It's over. We lost." Fernando plays with his empty cup.

The waiter comes by and without meaning to—but without bothering to avoid it or apologize—shoves Fernando's shoulder slightly. Fernando usually gets mad over people's rudeness and complains as if it's going to do any good. But this time he remains silent. When you're down everybody takes advantage.

"And now?" asks Ruso.

"Now? Nothing, Ruso. He'll have to talk to Lourdes."

"To Lourdes? Why?"

"Because I made a pact with her, that we'd pass Guadalupe money every month. And that she was going to quit fucking around with cheating us out of visits. And the moon on a string. And now all that's gone to shit."

"And what are you going to do about seeing the girl?" interjects Cristo.

Fernando winces.

"It's all a mess, again. We'll have to go to court to review the visitation rights. But it's a real mess."

"Why?"

"Because it's one thing with my mom, because she's the grandmother. But I'm the uncle. It's not the same. And this guy . . ."

Fernando points to Ruso, as if to say that his not being related made the panorama even bleaker.

"And getting a lawyer?" insists Cristo, as though he has trouble accepting that the justice system is so out of line with common sense.

"Let's not even mention lawyers," concludes Fernando, feeling dirty, fed up.

They pause again. The waiter comes over to ask if they want anything else. His attentiveness is somewhat surprising. Could it be that their appearance, like riffraff down on their luck, is making him edgy? They tell him no, not at the moment. The guy goes back to the bar.

Fernando distracts himself watching an old woman stop at the flower stand and buy some freesias. She is wearing a straight, black, old-fashioned coat and high heels. She has on too much makeup. Is it because of her age? He also wonders whom those flowers are for. A friend, herself, a grave. The old lady must really like freesias, because they aren't in season yet and they probably charged her an arm and a leg for that pathetic little bouquet.

"You didn't talk to Pittilanga, did you?" Cristo asks Ruso.

"When did you want me to talk to him?"

"I don't know . . . when they tossed us out."

"I was very busy being carried around by my shirt collar by an orangutan who was going to bust my ass while cursing me

out in Arabic. I didn't stop to talk to the kid, dearest Cristo."
Ruso pulls out a crumb that had gotten stuck in his teeth.
"We'll have to see what happens now."

"Have to see what?"

"Nothing. We have to see. That's all."

"Now you're acting all mysterious?"

"Me, mysterious?" Ruso directs the question at Cristo, as if
he wants him to corroborate his blamelessness.

"Well—a little," affirms Cristo.

Ruso shrugs it off and they fall into silence again. Until
Cristo points to the sidewalk across the street.

"They're coming out," he says, and the other two follow his
index finger with their eyes to the hotel door.

On the sidewalk, Polaco Salvatierra and Mauricio are shaking hands. Then Salvatierra again disappears into the building and Mauricio looks both ways, and then at the opposite
sidewalk. He starts across the street, in the finest Argentine
style, without waiting for the light to change, dodging cars.
Fernando thinks he notices a slight limp, and remembers how
Pittilanga kicked him when he had him on the floor.

"Is he coming over here?" Fernando asks, puzzled.

"Looks like it," says Ruso.

"Imagine he comes right into this bar . . ."

"He could," adds Ruso.

Cristo glues his face to the window to get a better view,
then gets up and rests his hand on Ruso's arm.

"He is coming this way, but please, don't do anything, for
heaven's sake, Ruso."

Fernando, seeing Cristo's alarm, thinks that he should intervene, too. It's one thing to pound on that bastard Mauricio

in the privacy of a closed room, and a whole other thing to start a row in the middle of a cafe. They'll all end up behind bars. Ruso can't get out of Cristo's grip, but he looks at him. Their eyes meet. And Fernando is surprised to see a strange expression on Ruso's face. Or strange considering the situation. Because he looks calm, almost placid, even—content.

"What's up with you?" Fernando asks him, looking up at Cristo to see if he has any answers. But the kid looks back at him with identical confusion.

At that moment, Mauricio Guzmán enters the bar and heads straight toward their table. Either Ruso is strong enough to get away or Cristo, in his distraction, lets up the pressure on his friend's arm, because Ruso leaps up and walks over to Mauricio. Fernando remains seated. Cristo gets halfway up, his legs hampered by the table and the chair that Ruso just left behind.

"Stop, Ruso! Calm down!" Cristo manages to say.

When Ruso and Mauricio are ten feet from each other, they stop. Fernando doesn't realize it, but he feels something he hasn't felt since he was eleven years old. The desire, the deep, archaic, animal desire for his friend to bash the school bully's face in. To see Mauricio bleed, cry, pay somehow for all the humiliation, all the selfishness. Fernando also doesn't realize that he is tightening his fists, as if in anticipation of the first blows. Ruso doesn't have Pittilanga's height and weight, but he was always a good fighter. Mauricio is already the worse for wear. He has a scrape on his forehead, another on his chin. And his wrinkled suit must be hiding a few bruises. *Fuck his shit up good, Ruso,* thinks Fernando, *wipe that unforgivable, smug (happy?) look off the bastard's face.*

But things go another way. Because Ruso and Mauricio study each other from the ten feet separating them. Mauricio with his arms lax at his sides. Ruso with his hands on his hips. And, strangely, they smile. They open their arms. They let out a laugh. They embrace in a long, long hug.

Papers in the Wind III

"We already know. Everything's money in soccer. All bullshit. All lies. But—but—but there's something . . ."

"What, Mono?"

"The image I'm talking about, that's worth all the bitterness, all the crap you put up with, is this. You know the end of the game? Any game. Any game that Independiente won, that is. Because otherwise, it's not the same."

"It's never the same."

"No."

"Well, so imagine they won. It doesn't matter who they beat. It doesn't matter how much they won by. It doesn't matter where they are in the classification. They won and night is falling . . ."

". . ."

". . ."

". . ."

"You won. You suffered but you won. Good. The game ends, the police make the visiting fans leave, and you, who's local, they let you stay half an hour, forty-five minutes, not doing anything, waiting for the visitors to leave the Avellaneda."

"Boring."

"Endless."

"Wrong! Wrong! If you lost or tied, it's horrible, so boring you want to kill yourself. But if you won . . ."

"..."

"..."

"..."

"Think about it."

59.

Mauricio and Ruso disentangle themselves a little and speak in shouts. The other people in the bar look at them, disturbed, embarrassed for them, but they don't seem to care. Cristo drops into his chair. He looks at Fernando, who is pale and has his mouth hanging open. Cristo laughs happily. Still standing, the other two shout so much that you can understand everything they're saying.

"What happened?" Ruso is asking.

"It's done."

"What's done?"

"Done deal."

"Really?"

"Of course, fool."

"No! You're shitting me."

"Not at all. I'm telling you it's done."

They hug again. Cristo looks at Fernando, who is still motionless.

"Tell me, what did they say?"

"At first it was a mess, I thought that—"

"What'd they say when we left—"

"I'm telling you! At first they weren't even paying attention because they started to talk amongst themselves and—"

"Did Mario hit you bad?"

"Bad? What a motherfucker! He fucked my shit up! I hurt all over. I think he cracked one of my ribs."

"Naah."

"Yeah, I'm serious."

"You've always been such a chickenshit. Do you know how much a cracked rib hurts?"

"Yeah, man. You want me to show you? It's all black and blue."

"I'm not even interested. Tell me what happened."

"Fine. You guys left and—"

"We didn't leave. They kicked us out on our asses."

"Well, same thing."

"No, it's not the same thing, idiot. We got the shit kicked out of us."

"What do you want? A contest over who got more fucked up? Stop busting my balls."

Fernando turns to Cristo to ask him, "Do you mind telling me why the hell Ruso is cracking up laughing over there with that fucking asshole?"

Cristo smiles again. He feels like he's in heaven. When he started working with Ruso he never even imagined something like this was going to happen. He wonders if he should explain it to Fernando or not. He decides not to. He's just a witness here.

"You'll see. Just wait."

"Wait my ass."

Cristo doesn't have to respond because Fernando turns again toward the other two. Ruso has just rested a hand on Mauricio's shoulder and is leading him toward the table. Cristo wonders if Fernando is going to start shit up again. Doesn't look like it. He is too shocked. Ruso points Mauricio to the empty chair.

"Sit there, you'll be blocked by the wall. We don't want the Arabs to come out of the hotel and see us together."

"They're not coming out, Ruso."

"Just in case. Let's not fuck it up now."

Mauricio obeys. Fernando keeps staring at them, shaken. Cristo is happy because Ruso gives him a glance of mutual understanding.

"Are you going to explain?" asks Fernando. His voice is trembling slightly, as if he were at his limit.

"Did you see the movie *The Sting*?"

Fernando furrows his brow, totally confused. He tries to pull himself together.

"*The Sting* can suck my left testicle, Ruso. Explain to me what the hell he is doing here, and what you are doing laughing with the bastard who ruined everything for us."

"Wait," Ruso tries to calm him down. Cristo understands that Ruso wants to tell the story right, with all the bells and whistles, but of course it's hard for him to control Fernando's anxiety. He turns to Mauricio. "How many times did we watch the movie *The Sting*, Counselor?"

"Oof. Fifty times."

"This guy"—he points to Fernando, but addresses the others—"saw it too. He saw it with us at the Ocean in Morón. It was hard to get in because it was rated fourteen and over. But he doesn't remember."

"We watched it three times in a row," adds Mauricio.

"Exactly," confirms Ruso. "But talking to this guy about movies is like talking to you about minor league soccer, Cristo. No offense."

"None taken," concedes Cristo, who has no problem admitting his weak points.

"I don't understand what the hell I'm supposed to remember."

"Paul Newman," says Ruso.

"Robert Redford," adds Mauricio.

"The bad guy . . ."

"The gangster?"

"Yes. The gangster . . ."

"Wait, wait. I got it—Robert Shaw!"

"Robert Shaw, what a son of a bitch, what a memory you have, Mauricio!"

"I'm still waiting for an explanation!" says Fernando.

"It's coming, Fer. Do you remember how lately I've been asking you about that movie?" says Ruso.

"What? No—you asked me about it?"

"See how you don't listen when I talk?"

"I do."

"Yeah, I can see how much. I asked you."

"You're drunk. You didn't ask me."

"Did I ask him or not, Cristo?"

Cristo nods his head. Ruso settles into his chair to enjoy his own story more. Cristo does too. Even though he's already heard it twenty times, he loves the way Ruso tells it.

"Robert Redford is a con man. The thirties. Chicago. A con man who works with a partner. A friend. Black guy, bigger. Older. Who's the actor, Mauricio?"

"Uh, you got me," says Mauricio, as he touches the bruise on his chin.

"Doesn't matter. A mob boss kills his friend. The black guy. And then Robert Redford goes looking for Paul Newman."

"To kill him?" Fernando is confused.

"How's he gonna kill him, you big dummy! To partner up with him! Paul Newman is a con man too, but with more class, he plays in a different league. And they join up to get revenge on the mob boss. The one who killed the black guy."

"You don't remember the music?" asks Mauricio, and from the look Fernando gives him, Cristo suspects that it might not be the best moment to talk about movies. Better to clear things up. But good luck convincing Ruso to stop.

"The counselor mentions it," intervenes Ruso, who, sure enough, is hell bent on continuing, "because the music is really famous. Ta, ta, ta, ta . . . ta, ta . . . ta, ta . . . Ta, ta, ta, ta, ta, ta, ta . . . ta, ta, ta. I used to play it on the recorder."

"Fuck the recorder, Ruso, and its mother!"

"Calm down, you're going to explode, fool. Relax."

"How can I relax if I don't understand a goddamned thing?"

"Relax. Let Mauricio tell you. Counselor: is it all worked out or not?"

"Yes."

"And you want me to believe this fucking asshole?"

Ruso jumps and looks at Cristo, as if asking for help. Cristo debates between advising him to get to the point and just letting him say what he's going to say. That's just the way Ruso is, there's no stopping him when he starts telling a story.

"No, Fer. Wait. Don't call him names. Trust me. You'll see, it's fine. Wait for me to tell you. It was like in the movie, you understand?"

"Will you quit busting my balls with the movie? Don't you get that I'm not following you?"

"Why don't you just explain it to him, Ruso. Maybe then he'll calm down," intervenes Cristo, who fears things will get out of hand again.

Ruso hesitates and seems to resign himself.

"Things got—I don't know how to explain it to you. Everything that was a mess suddenly fell into place."

"Oh, yeah?" Fernando sounds skeptical.

"That's what happened. First this guy came to see me."

"Who?"

"Mauricio. At the car wash. When was it you came?"

"Uh . . . I don't remember."

"Three weeks ago," affirms Cristo, who still remembers how impressed he was with Mauricio's Audi.

"Okay. The thing is he came to see me."

"And why did you go see him?" Fernando's voice is still dripping with resentment.

"To see what we could do." Mauricio sounds cautious, as if he still feared a sudden rain of insults or blows.

"And why?" Fernando continues to be hostile.

"We talked for a long time, that day," Ruso picks it up again. "I had seen the movie again recently."

"Again with the damn movie."

"And how do you want me not to mention the movie when I thought it up while I was watching it? I meant that the guys are two amazing con men, they trick that guy with a fight and—" Ruso stops, rethinking.

"And what?" Fernando grows impatient.

"I want you to see it, man. And if I tell you what I was going to tell you I'll ruin the ending."

"Are you kidding me, Ruso? Don't you realize that I couldn't give two shits about the movie?"

"You say that because you haven't seen it. If I tell you and then you watch it, you're gonna want to kill yourself. What you need to know now is that the guys, the main characters, it looks like they're going to rip each other to pieces. It looks like they're fighting, that one has betrayed the other, and they start shooting at each other. They kill each other, but not for

real, you get it?" He turns toward Cristo, a little upset. "I think
I spoiled the ending for him after all, man."

"Too bad, Ruso. You do the best you can," Cristo consoles
him, knowing how much his storytelling means to him.

"Should I give you the short version?" Ruso faces Fernando.
"I lied to you."

"What?"

"I lied to you, man. I lied to you. We lied to you. He did too."

"What do you mean, you lied to me?"

"First of all, I didn't just bump into Salvatierra in the supermarket and then he told me about the Arabs."

"What do you mean?"

"Well, actually I did. I bumped into Polaco in the supermarket, but because I went there to find him. Mauricio and I had
set it up that way. We set it up ahead of time, knowing that
Polaco wouldn't be able to keep a secret. And that way it was
more believable."

"So you guys set this up?" says Fernando, and Cristo thinks
he can make out a hint of . . . jealousy?

"Us and this guy," confirms Ruso, pointing right at Cristo,
who shrugs his shoulders innocently.

"Then you knew all about it? About the power of attorney
my mom signed?"

"Of course I knew about it. The important thing was that
you didn't know. So your anger would be real. Yours and Pittilanga's, of course."

"You didn't tell Pittilanga?"

"No, because we needed a balance." Ruso moves his hands,
imitating a scale. "Some knowing, others not. Some acting,
others being spontaneous."

"Salvatierra?"

"No, you can't count on that dimwit. When I saw him in the supermarket he told me everything in two minutes. And Mauricio had made him swear silence."

"What? So it was your plan?" For the first time, Fernando speaks to Mauricio.

"No. When I told Salvatierra not to say anything I hadn't come up with it yet."

"Let me explain it to you," Ruso cuts in, and Cristo realizes that he is going to do things his way. "I went to see your mom the day before yesterday and she signed everything without asking a single question."

"And she couldn't have asked me first?" Fernando sounds offended.

"Supposedly you were the one who sent me."

"She could have called me."

"Impossible."

Ruso gestures to Cristo, who feels entitled to put in his two cents: "To avoid complications we cut her phone line, Fernando. Sorry. I was following orders."

"What do you mean you cut it?"

Cristo mimes cutting a cable with a pair of scissors.

"We already got it fixed, anyway, don't worry."

"And what if my mom had an emergency and needed to call?"

Ruso and Cristo look at each other without knowing what to say, until Cristo comes up with a solution.

"I saw her the day before yesterday and she looked fabulous, Fernando. Your mom is as healthy as a horse."

"Okay, but stop interrupting," Ruso picks up the thread. "You came to the meeting convinced that Mauricio was going to try to screw us. When he pulls out the signed power of attorney—"

"Stop, stop. But Williams called you in the middle of the meeting—"

"Ay, chump, it wasn't Williams. It was this guy, who was calling from the hotel lobby."

"Why?"

"Oh my God! To act like he was coming to ruin the negotiation, when we had the deal all ready to sign. So the hate in your eyes was real. Did you see how he looked at you, Mauricio?"

"I think if he had a knife he would have skewered me . . ."

Ruso makes a rectangle with his fingers, imitating a film director.

"I needed that look of hate, Fer."

"You could have told me."

"No. You're too good."

"Too dumb, you mean."

"Well, yeah. Dumb, too. But you aren't a good actor. It would have shown."

"Hold on a second." Fernando rests his palms on the table. "I saw you get red as a tomato when you got that call."

Ruso looks at Cristo and lifts his eyebrows. Cristo smiles in agreement.

"Holding my breath, dude. And a bit of intestinal strain. A master," Ruso congratulates himself.

"But when you hung up your eyes were filled with tears."

Here Ruso widens his gaze to include Mauricio, so more eyes can witness the magical moment of his recognition.

"Emotional recall. Shostakovich—"

"Stanislavsky," corrects Cristo.

"Exactly. Stanislavsky . . ."

"You could have told me," insists Fernando. "You told Cristo."

"I had to tell Cristo because if things went wrong I had to have an ally! But Pittilanga didn't know. And the Arabs didn't either."

"Great. So I was as ignorant as an illiterate loser who only knows how to kick a ball and three Arabs who didn't even know where the hell they were."

"What do you mean they didn't know where they were! Those three are so fast they can catch a fly on the wing." He turns toward Mauricio. "Are you sure you got it all wrapped up?"

"Sure, Ruso. Everything is signed. Salvatierra took Pittilanga outside, and when I finished everything, he explained it to Pittilanga while I worked out the details."

"And they didn't give you a hard time?"

Mauricio looks at him with some irony, as if he had asked him something obvious.

"Of course they gave me a hard time. They got mad, they threatened me, they said they were leaving—"

"You see what I mean? They're tough. And then?"

"And that's when things got really rough. Even a little out of hand."

"Really? How'd you handle it?"

"Nothing special. I'm used to people fucking with me lately."

Although he says it without looking at anyone it is obvious he is dropping a hint to Fernando, who chooses to look out the window.

"Well," Ruso hurries to push the conversation in another direction. "And then?"

"And when they saw I wasn't going any lower, they thought that it was true what Fernando had said: that in the firm we wanted the deal to fall through so that Pittilanga would be released and the firm would buy him in a few months for next to nothing—their translator understood perfectly that part of what Fernando had said, it seems, because later they brought it up, right when they were calling me a supreme son of a bitch in perfect Argentine slang. Then they did a little whispering and they started to come up with numbers."

"And you?"

"Nothing. Biting my nails on the inside. But nothing. And in the end they went for it. I called Polaco on his cell phone, who talked to Pittilanga and then brought him in to sign. Luckily he had calmed down by that point and didn't start kicking me again."

"Did he really hurt you?"

Mauricio just lifts up his shirt and shows the side of his chest, beneath his armpit, which is scraped and red.

"Ah . . . he hit you pretty bad . . ." concedes Ruso, perhaps somewhat regretting his earlier lightness. Fernando keeps looking out at the street.

"And then we signed everything and that was it. There are still a few details to be cleared up. And the payment, of course. But the deal is done."

There is a silence. The waiter brings over the coffee Mauricio had ordered. Cristo, seeing that the others are quiet, gets up the courage to ask. Before speaking, he clears his throat.

"And how much did you close with?"

Mauricio waits another second. He looks them in the eyes. Now Fernando returns his gaze. Mauricio's eyes are gleaming. Pride, thinks Cristo, or something very similar.

"Four hundred and twenty thousand dollars." He puts a packet of sugar into his cup. "Net."

The others hesitate for an instant, as they put the figure into the empty graph that has been worrying them for the last two years. As always, Ruso is the first to react.

"It's a miracle! And the kid's commission?"

"Them. They pay it. The four hundred and twenty is net. I already told you."

"I can't believe it. Finally something worked out right. Shit!"

"I got Polaco to accept thirty grand. Forty for Bermúdez. So we have three hundred and fifty grand clear, if I'm calculating correctly," adds Mauricio.

There is a silence. Cristo sees Fernando pull out a napkin from the napkin holder and make a calculation. The others watch him do it. He multiplies a thousand by twelve by eleven. He jots down the result: one hundred and thirty-two thousand. He draws a box around it. That is what they will give Lourdes for Guadalupe until she turns twenty-one. Then he does another calculation. Three hundred and fifty minus one hundred and thirty-two. He puts a box around the result again: two hundred and eighteen thousand dollars, which they'll give Guadalupe when she comes of age. Mauricio lets out a little laugh and Ruso joins in. The contrasting seriousness of Fernando is almost shocking, and Ruso notices.

"What's wrong with you?"

Fernando doesn't look up.

"Me? Nothing. I'm shocked, I guess."

"You look like you're at a wake, man."

"Nah. I'm happy. Really, I'm happy. I came out looking a little bad, I guess. That's all."

"Looking bad? Why?"

"Are you seriously asking me that? You can paint it any way you want. But I dogged him bad."

He speaks without looking at Mauricio, barely pointing at him, but Cristo understands that it's not because he's still angry, but because he is overcome with shame. Ruso doesn't know what to say. After a long silence, it is Mauricio who speaks.

"Don't worry. Almost every time you guys dogged me, you were right. You had a reason, bah. Just because once you made a mistake . . ."

He leaves the sentence unfinished. Cristo thinks about saying something, but again he thinks that today his role is as a witness. Nothing more. Some time passes.

Suddenly, Fernando speaks to Mauricio. "Can I ask you something?"

"What?"

"Why?"

"Why what?"

"Why did you do it? You said that you could be in hot water with your boss."

Mauricio shrugs. He looks out the window.

"Luckily he's not in Buenos Aires. Supposedly he went to a conference in San Pablo, but I know that he went to Recife to screw some chick. I guess he'll come back happy. Happy and relaxed, I hope."

"Hope so," adds Ruso.

They are quiet again for a while. Mauricio checks the time, calls over the waiter, and pays the check. He stands up and says goodbye with a kiss.

"You didn't answer me," Fernando says, when he has already taken a few steps away from the table. Mauricio hears him, stops, and turns his head.

"Didn't answer what?"

"Why'd you do it? What made you want to help us out like this?"

Mauricio is slow to answer. So slow that it looks like he's going to leave first. When he speaks his voice sounds choked, as if it had trouble getting out.

"Look," he begins, and then he clears his throat, perhaps in an attempt to eliminate the falsetto in his tone. "A few weeks ago something really good happened to me. Something of mine. Something good."

"You got promoted?" asks Ruso.

Mauricio shakes his head.

"And I realized that without you guys . . . without you guys I didn't have anybody to tell it to."

Without adding another word he walks toward the door. He is stopped by Fernando's voice.

"And what was it?"

"What was what?"

"What you had to tell us. What happened to you."

Mauricio smiles.

"Some other day. I'll tell you the next time we get together."

He waves, turns, and leaves. Cristo follows him with his gaze as long as he can and then looks back at the other two. Fernando's face is turned toward the inside of the bar, as if he didn't want the others to see him. Not Ruso. Ruso is crying openly, without trying to hide it in the least.

Papers in the Wind IV

"The sun's going down."

"..."

"..."

"..."

"The cops with their dogs stand near the fence, on the field, looking at the stands. I don't know why, but they stand there."

"..."

"..."

"..."

"People comment on the game . . . buy a burger, a chorizo sandwich. Kids pick up the plastic soda cups and throw them into the ditch, to watch them float in the dirty water . . ."

"..."

"..."

"..."

"If you're up high you look over the balconies behind the stands, the ones you can see down from, and you spit to see what you can hit . . ."

"..."

"..."

"..."

"And imagine there's a little bit of wind. You know the pieces of newspaper that people throw at the beginning, to greet the team? If there's a little bit of wind the papers lift up, move a little, spin in the air, float down again . . ."

"..."

"..."

"..."

"Guys with radios listening to the final commentary, the players' remarks, the press conference . . ."

"..."

"..."

"..."

"They take down the advertisements, the nets, they turn off the lights gradually . . . you're still there, leaning on the railing. And the papers are still there. The marks left on the grass by flying bottle caps. A streamer . . ."

"..."

"..."

"..."

"That's all I'm asking . . . forget about everything else. The cups, the championships, all the rest. Just that. Forget about the business, that everyone is after the money, that you're the only asshat doing it out of love. Just that. Isn't it worth all the shit you have to deal with the rest of the time? Isn't it worth it?"

"..."

"..."

"Maybe."

"Well, yeah."

"..."

"..."

"Yeah, Monito. It really is."

60.

When he hears the car horn, Fernando pats down the pockets of his jeans to make sure he hasn't forgotten anything. ID cards, some money, some coins. He turns the key in the front door and opens it wide. Mauricio's car shines in the afternoon sun. From the backseat, Guadalupe waves at him and smiles. Ruso does the same.

As he walks around the front of the navy blue Audi he notices that they have saved him his usual seat, and he likes that. A while back they had argued with Mauricio over the traditions. He doesn't remember what was said, but today Fernando concludes that that's what traditions are for. So the world is a more welcoming, more predictable, more reliable place. They have to go to the field like that. Mauricio at the wheel, he riding shotgun, Ruso behind. And instead of Mono, Guadalupe. Not bad.

"Hi, Uncle."

"Hello, gorgeous."

"Is it true we are going to go out together every Sunday?"

"Is that what your mom told you?"

"Yes."

"It's true. Every Sunday, and a lot of Saturdays, and a lot of Wednesdays. With me and with your grandma. These two will come every once in a while. They'll always come when we go to the stadium."

"Is it true that Uncle Ruso has a PlayStation 3?"

"Why don't you call me Uncle Daniel, Guada? 'Uncle Ruso' sounds kinda . . ."

"But they call you Ruso."

"Yes, but that's 'cause they're anti-Semites."

"But I like 'Uncle Ruso.' What's an anti-Semite?"

"You gonna ask questions all the way from Castelar to Avellaneda?"

"Yeah, why? Do you have a PS3 or not?"

"He has one, Guada. He has a PS3," confirms Mauricio.

"And where'd you guys get it from?" questions Fernando.

"The board of directors of the Guadalupe Foundation felt it was appropriate to give it to the brains behind Marca Pegajosa for services rendered."

"That seems fair," agrees Fernando.

"Very fair," adds Ruso, although his voice is muffled by his wide-open window.

"And can I come over to play, Uncle Ruso? What Guadalupe Foundation, Uncle?"

"Yes. But just so you know, we are always playing soccer games."

"I know. I don't mind."

"That's my girl."

"What are you thinking about when you've got that expression on your face?" Mauricio asks Fernando.

Fernando is surprised by the question. He wasn't thinking about anything special. He was enjoying the others' chatting and letting his thoughts wander and his eyes roam over the rapidly passing landscape of the highway.

Before he can answer, Ruso beats him to it: "Ah! I forgot to tell you guys! Pittilanga called me yesterday!"

"What does the kid have to say?"

"Oh, man. Looks like things are going great for him."

"Who's Pittilanga, Uncle?" asks Guadalupe.

"A soccer player, friend of ours."

"You guys have a friend who plays?"

"Yes, he plays in Saudi Arabia. He's Argentinian, but he went there to play."

"And how did you meet him?"

"We'll tell you all about it. Your papá knew him too."

"Really?"

"Yeah. Pittilanga is his name. Your papá discovered him when he was younger and he realized he was going to be big."

"Seriously?!"

"And what does Pittilanga have to say?" asks Mauricio.

"He's doing great. They've played four games, and he's been a starter in every one."

"Wow."

"He was in the newspaper. He said he'd send me the clipping in an e-mail."

"And how does he like living there?"

"Fine, he says it's fine. He doesn't understand a word of the language."

"And his teammates?"

"There's a Colombian who translates. And since the coach is Dutch there is a general translator, because nobody understands a thing."

"What a mess."

"But it looks like he's a total wall, the kid, there on the back four. What an eye I've got for football, *mamma mia*."

"Get over yourself, Ruso."

"Why are they telling you to get over yourself, Uncle?" asks Guadalupe, and Fernando thinks that from now on that male universe of theirs is going to have to get used to incorporating that squeaky voice and its questions, and he also thinks that that makes him happy.

"Where are you going to leave the car, Mauri?" asks Ruso.

"Over there, close by, I guess. Why?"

"No, thinking of the thieves, that's all."

"Why, Uncle?"

"Because the area around Independiente's stadium isn't exactly . . . it's not the safest, you know."

"It's not?" Guadalupe's voice sounds slightly intimidated.

"It's nothing to worry about," intervenes Fernando, who fears Guadalupe's fear, but especially Lourdes's fear, or Lourdes's new husband's. "This is the most beautiful stadium in the world."

"That's true," agrees Mauricio.

"I know, I know," Guadalupe hastens to agree, as if she were afraid they would confuse her hesitation for a lack of enthusiasm.

"Should I go down Belgrano or Pavón?" asks Mauricio, when they get to the end of the highway.

"Go down Belgrano," recommends Ruso. "Since there's no game I'm sure you can park easily there."

"It's better to take Pavón," suggests Fernando. "So Guada can see how we always come. Today there's no game. But when there is we go that way."

"He's right," agrees Mauricio, as he puts on his turn signal.

Fernando stares at him.

"And what's wrong with you?" inquires Mauricio.

"Nothing. For a while now, lately, it's almost like you're a good person, man."

"What a thing to say!" Guadalupe is startled, half amused and half shocked.

"You see how they treat me, little one?"

"I'll defend you!"

"Make no mistake, girl," says Ruso. "Of the three men in this car, two of us are good people. Two good people and the driver."

"But what a car he has, eh?" boasts Mauricio.

"What's that?" asks Guadalupe, pointing to the dirt slope on their right.

"The train overpass. You can't see it, but above that are the tracks."

Fernando turns to the backseat, to look the girl in the face.

"You have to remember that the stadium is new . . . but unfinished."

"Yeah, I know that, Uncle."

"I mean, in case you don't like it. In a few months it's going to look a lot better."

Mauricio murmurs out of the side of his mouth, close to Fernando so only he can hear: "In a few months, a few years, a few centuries . . ."

"Sure," says Ruso. "You're gonna see one part that's not done, another that has some iron rods still sticking out . . ."

". . . that needs some painting, some finishing touches," continues Mauricio.

The girl nods and keeps looking out the window, toward the monoblock buildings of the General Belgrano District.

"But—are they going to finish it?"

Ruso curses, to himself, that keenness a kid and a woman have for hitting you where it hurts the most. And this little person is both.

"Of course. It's almost ready."

Mauricio parks when he gets to Alsina Street. They are still a block away, but they agree to walk it. The neighborhood is deserted.

"They're gonna steal it from you here," says Ruso, just trying to make Mauricio nervous. "Do you have good insurance, man?"

"The best," jokes Fernando.

Mauricio holds back the insult that comes into his head and looks around. Some kids are drinking beer at the stand across the street. He approaches them and talks to them, pointing to the car.

"Done," he announces, satisfied, when he returns.

"You're nuts," continues Ruso. "They're gonna fuck it up for you themselves."

"For twenty bucks I can assure you they'll watch it for me."

"Twenty bucks! If you'd told me that I'd stay and watch it for you myself, man."

"You have a rich uncle, Guada. You're saved," says Fernando.

"Do you seriously have a lot of money, Uncle?"

"He's got plenty of money. It's morals he lacks," says Ruso, beating him to it.

Guadalupe looks at them unsure and Fernando is about to explain that it's a joke, but he resists. It's better for her to learn on her own. Kids learn fast. If his niece can handle a computer at the speed of light, learning the rudimentary sarcastic code of three old uncles should be easy.

They walk in silence down Alsina. When they are twenty yards from the next corner, Ruso trots ahead to be the first to get to the signpost and point to the name.

"Look what the street's called, Guada," interjects Fernando.

The girl obeys.

"Bochini? Like the Independiente player?"

"The greatest soccer player of all time," Mauricio informs her solemnly, as they approach the corner.

"Better than Maradona, Uncle?"

Fernando and Mauricio look at each other.

"Hey! Better than Maradona?" insists Guadalupe.

"No, not better than Maradona. Similar," decides Fernando. "And do you know what team Maradona was a fan of when he was your age?"

The girl opens her eyes even wider.

"Independiente?"

Fernando feels like a ranch owner displaying his vast lands to the frozen contemplation of a group of relatives from the city.

"Of course."

The girl takes a second to think.

"Okay. I'll do the same thing. When I'm little I'll root for Independiente and then I'll switch to Boca."

Mauricio laughs, while Fernando thinks that they are going to have to stay on top of things to keep up with this kid.

"Stop, stay right there," says Ruso, to keep Guadalupe from getting to the corner, because from there you can already see the stadium, and he wants to make the moment more spectacular. "Don't look."

Just in case, he puts his open hand over her eyes, like a blindfold, and leads her along Bochini, slowly, as the girl takes short steps to feel her way. When she is afraid of tripping, she grips Ruso's enormous hand, which covers half of her face like a mask.

"Don't worry. Don't worry, I got you. Now stand still. And—"

"Wait," says Fernando.

"Wait for what?" asks Ruso.

Fernando doesn't answer, but he points to the girl.

"Okay, little one. You are about to see the greatest stadium in the world."

"Come on, Uncle."

"The first concrete stadium in all of South America."

"All right! Come on!"

"Now it's new, but not finished," adds Mauricio.

"Come on, I wanna see!"

"Since it got a little old, the Red Devils are having it redone," adds Fernando.

"Come on, Uncle!!"

"But it's gonna be a lot better, a lot, lot better—"

"Lemme see!!!!!"

"Ta ta, ta taaaannn . . ."

The girl squeezes the hand that covers her eyes, to get away. Before letting her, Ruso takes a second, lifting his head toward the other two men. They exchange quick glances, they blink rapidly, they look at the girl.

"Are you ready?"

"Come on, Uncle, I can't stand it anymore!!!!!"

Ruso feels the girl's eyelashes tickling his palm. He looks at his friends again. And then, with a matador's flourish, Ruso takes away his hand and moves to one side, so that Guadalupe can see.

Ituzaingó, December 2010

ACKNOWLEDGMENTS

To Gaby, for being my companion, also, through the ups and downs of this story's slow construction, and for accepting its losses.

To Clarita, for lending me the name of one of her best friends for the character of Guadalupe.

To Fran, for his pure love of Independiente.

To Jessie and Valeria, for their kind reading of the drafts of this novel.

To Pablo, for sharing the exacting art of unrelenting irony.

To Facundo Sava, for his generosity in offering me his knowledge.

To my Saturday soccer friends, for that world filled with simple and untransferable privileges offered by the friendship of men.

To my editor Julia Saltzmann, for her patience and perseverance.

To my agent Irene Barki, for her tireless dedication.

The translator would like to thank Tomás Nochteff, María Nochteff Avendaño, Ignacio Lois, Graciela Pérez de Lois, Aaron Milberg, and Doug Fielding.

EDUARDO SACHERI is a professor of history as well as a writer of fiction. His first collection of short stories was published in Spain in 2000, and three later collections have become best sellers in his native Argentina. The film adaptation of his novel *The Secret in Their Eyes* won the 2009 Academy Award for Best Foreign Language Film, and the book was published in English the following year by Other Press. Most recently Sacheri has lent his scriptwriting talents to Juan José Campanella's animated film *Foosball*.

MARA FAYE LETHEM has translated novels by David Trueba, Albert Sánchez Piñol, Javier Calvo, Patricio Pron, Marc Pastor, and Pablo De Santis, among others. She is currently translating Jaume Cabré's most recent work.